BERTRICE SMALL

the
Twilight
Lord

Book Three of the World of Hetar

HQN™

HQN™

ISBN-13: 978-0-373-77203-2
ISBN-10:   0-373-77203-3

THE TWILIGHT LORD

Copyright © 2007 by Bertrice Small

www.HQNBooks.com

Printed in U.S.A.

To all those people who, like me,
know that the Light will forever prevail

From the darkness came a maiden
From the golden light came a warrior.
From a distant tomorrow will come
Hetar's true destiny.

Prologue

HE HAD NOT THOUGHT it possible to be vanquished by a creature half-human, half-faerie. But as the stones concealing the tower window exploded outward with her incantation and the bright light poured into the chamber, Usi knew that he would not survive. He howled a moment in frustration and with his last vestige of strength tried to tempt Lara into the darkness, but her powers and her resolve were too strong for him now. The light scorched him cruelly with its fierce cleansing burn.

In that single instant before he was finally hurled into the realm of the Lord of Oblivion, he thought of how long ago he had prepared for just this moment, though he had not truly believed it would ever come. The faerie woman had defeated him. But his essence would survive in his descendants. His enemies never knew that he had deliberately fathered children on two of the women he had brought to his tower. He had sent the women away before their condition could be known, not just for their safety but for the safety of the progeny they would bear him.

Aye! His black blood ran in the veins of others to this day. And as he called out to that blood with his last dying breath he heard it answer him, and rejoiced. The final battle was yet to be fought.

THE GREAT WINGED HORSE galloped across the skies above the Emerald Mountains, a single rider on his back. Strapped to the animal's side was a woven basket in which a sleeping child lay. Lara glanced now and again at her daughter Zagiri to make certain she remained asleep. She was a beautiful little child with her father's dark gold hair; her golden eyelashes fanned out over her pale-pink cheeks. She looks like him, Lara thought. The only bit of me in her are her green eyes.

"We're almost there," Dasras said as they left the mountains behind them. "I can see the fields of the Blathma below us, and just beyond and to my left are the meadows of the Aghy. I wonder if Roan has any pretty new mares."

Lara chuckled. "You are as lusty as a Shadow Prince," she told him.

Dasras chortled. "Well, I was born and raised among them," he said drolly. Then he asked, "Is the princess still sleeping?"

"Aye," Lara responded. "She'll be delighted to see Dillon again—and he her. I hope Anoush has gotten over her jealousy by now. She doesn't even understand that I am her mother and her invidiousness toward Zagiri is hurtful."

"She is too young to have developed that attitude without help," Dasras remarked.

"Who can have planted the seed of envy in Anoush? Certainly not your good Noss. She has always been a fine foster mother to your children."

"Vartan's mother," Lara said sadly and with certainty. "She grows madder with each passing day. I have asked Noss to limit my children's visits to Bera but she is their grandmother. Of course there is Cam, as well. Adon's son is Anoush's cousin. And Bera is raising him. I have never found him to be a pleasant child."

"You should investigate the situation and see that it is corrected," Dasras advised. "It does not matter that your children are blood kin to Bera and Cam. If they pose a danger to Dillon and Anoush, you must do what you must to keep Vartan's younglings safe. Bera's feelings cannot matter to you, and Cam has no sensibilities at all to consider that I can see. The safety of your children must come first and foremost."

"I am fortunate to have such wise advisers as you, Verica and Andraste," Lara told the great stallion.

"And the Dominus?" Dasras teased her.

"Villain!" Lara laughed. "My husband is a good man and a wonderful lover, but he does not understand humanity as well as he thinks he does. However, we shall not tell him that, shall we, Dasras?"

The horse shook his head, then began his descent to the lands below him, which were possessed by the Fiacre Clan. He preferred galloping the last few miles into the main village, New Camdene, rather than just descending into its midst. The cattle in his path scattered as his hooves touched the ground. There was no one this bright summer morning to see their arrival until they drew close to the dwellings. To Lara's delight it was her son, Dillon, who first saw them coming and ran toward Dasras to welcome his mother. The horse came to a stop.

"Mother! Welcome!" Dillon said. "Have you brought Zagiri?" Standing on his toes he peeped into the basket. "Ahh, Zigi, wake up now," he cooed.

The little girl slowly opened her eyes and, seeing Dillon, smiled and held out her arms to him. "D," she said excitedly. "Uppy, D!"

Dillon lifted her from the basket and set her on her feet. Zagiri slipped her hand into his and together they began to walk. Lara slid down from her saddle to join them as Dasras followed. Lara smiled as she watched Zagiri toddle along beside Dillon on her fat little legs. Her son carefully matched his steps to his younger sibling.

"Where is Anoush?" Lara asked the boy.

He stopped and turned a serious face to her. "We must speak on Anoush, Mother," he said quietly.

"Did you know I would come today?" she asked, nodding.

He smiled at her now. "Aye, I awoke and felt you drawing near. That is why I came out to meet you. I know Dasras's habit of landing several miles outside the village and then taking a leisurely gallop. My instincts are growing stronger."

"You will go to your grandmother and Prince Kaliq one day for training," Lara said. "Not yet, but one day, my son."

"When?" he asked eagerly.

"When you are twelve," she answered.

"I should go sooner," he protested. "That is almost three years away."

"The fact that you cannot accept my decision in the matter but proves to me that you are not yet mature enough," Lara told him.

"Ah, you are too clever, mother," he said with a chuckle.

"Aye, I am clever but I am also wise, Dillon. Anoush has no magic in her I can yet see and I cannot yet tell if Zagiri will have magic. But you, my son, from the beginning I could see the magic in you, but I said nothing and let you discover it for yourself. With the proper training you will be a great sorcerer one day. But you also need time to be the little boy you are now. You need long summer days feeling the sun on your back, picking berries and eating them until your tongue is blue, swimming in the lake, riding your horse and lying on a hillside at night looking up at the stars. Your summers must feel as if they would go on forever and ever. For now, you must be taken unawares by the summer's end and your return to lessons," Lara told him. "When you feel the summers going quickly, then I will know you are growing up and we will begin to discover how much magic is in you. Then and only then will you go to study with Prince Kaliq and your grandmother. You will be old for far more years than you are young, Dillon. Enjoy these years."

"Mother, you are wise and I know your words are truth," he told her.

Lara smiled. "Tell me of your sister now," she said. They began to walk again.

"Our grandmother infects her with discontent," Dillon said.

"And your cousin?"

"Cam is cunning and sly," Dillon replied. "He panders to Anoush's every whim, and he does it, I believe, to bind her close to him."

Lara nodded. "That is unlikely to change even if I forbid them contact," she said. "I have left you and your sister with the Fiacre because you are Vartan's children, as well as mine. Perhaps it is now time for you both to come and live with me. You could come this year after the Gathering, and then return each summer staying until after the Gathering. This would allow you to remain close to the Fiacre, too. Once, I thought you would follow in your father's footsteps, Dillon, and lead the clan one day. But I see now that your fate will not be among your father's people. You have a different path to follow."

"I am glad that you finally see that, Mother," he said.

"You are so old for one so young," Lara remarked as her attention was drawn to her little daughter. "No, Zagiri, do not eat that." She pulled the flower from her daughter's mouth and picked her up. "Noss will have a treat for you, I am certain."

And Noss, Lara's old friend, did indeed have a nibble for little Zagiri. She sat the child at a wooden table outside of her kitchen, beneath a pergola thick with grape vines, and gave her a cup of fresh-squeezed juice and a slice of newly baked bread with butter and honey. Then she hugged Lara, and brought them two cups of frine. They sat beneath the pergola sipping the fruit and wine mixture while Noss told Lara what had transpired with the Fiacre over the last months since they had seen each other.

Lara listened and then she asked after her elder daughter.

"She has probably gone to Bera's house," Noss said. "Of late she has been spending too much time there. With three rambunctious boys and another child in my belly, I sometimes lose track of her these days. She has become most disobedient, Lara, and I do not know what to do about it. Of late she does not call me Mama."

"What does she call you?" Lara asked, curious.

"She calls me *lady*," Noss said sadly. "I do not understand it or even who might tell her such a thing."

Lara nodded. "I would not hurt you, dearest Noss, but with three sons and another child on the way, perhaps it is time that Anoush and Dillon came home with me to the Dominus's castle. You and Liam have been so good to my children, but now I have a home and husband once again. Even if I must leave Magnus for a time, the children will be safe with him. Would you mind if I took Dillon and Anoush with me when I return?"

Noss sighed. "No," she said candidly. "Dillon is no trouble at all. He is always willing to help me even without my asking and he is a wonderful influence on Tearlach, Alroy and Val. But Anoush has become difficult. I love her dearly, as you know. I have always thought of her as a daughter and we were close with one another. But suddenly she is secretive and rude. I am afraid for her and I don't even know why," Noss said. Then she lowered her voice. "I never believed I should have a daughter of my own, but Dillon says this child I carry is a female. Given how Anoush has behaved toward Zagiri, I am afraid now for this child I carry, Lara. I think Bera has told Anoush who you are. She will not have spoken favorably of you, I fear. Anoush needs to be with you now. She needs to know her mother and not take the slanders Bera spews as truth."

Lara sipped her frine thoughtfully as Noss spoke. "Aye," she said. "Anoush is six now, and very impressionable like all little girls her age. The only way I can expunge Bera's venom is to take her back to the castle with Dillon."

"How long will you be with us? Your rooms are ready, for Dillon told us this morning that you were coming," Noss said with a smile.

"A few weeks," Lara replied. "Magnus is now more concerned with the trading season than anything else. The emperor's representative, Jonah, has gone home to Hetar—he does not like to leave Gaius Prospero alone too long, for he prefers to be the emperor's only influence. I convinced Kaliq to allow Jonah the use of magical transport instead of having to sail across the Sea of Sagitta each time he needed to confer with his master. I send him when he desires to return to The City and one of the princes returns him to us."

"Why does Gaius Prospero insist on keeping him in Terah?" Noss wondered. "It should be obvious to him that the Dominus is not interested in furthering ties with Hetar."

"The emperor thinks that in time Magnus will change his mind. What he really wants is to conquer Terah so he may add it to his little empire," Lara replied. "I understand he is attempting to duplicate some of the goods we make for Hetar in an effort to get our attention through economics. Unfortunately, Hetar has not the proper materials, and we will not trade with them for those materials. Their efforts so far have produced an array of shoddy goods that despite their cheap prices sit in the market stalls unsold. It is an interesting standoff between us."

"But what do you think of all of this?" Noss probed, curious.

Lara laughed. "Terah and Hetar must eventually come to an understanding," she said. "I think we may have a more dangerous enemy in the Dark Lands."

"Well, whoever they are they have caused no troubles so far," Noss noted.

"I would be happier if I knew who they were and what they want," Lara responded. "I do not like mystery, as you know. My destiny has been calling to me for some months now, but for the first time I do not know exactly what it wants or where I am to go. Nor has my spirit protector Ethne had anything to say on the matter though I have asked her. All she will say is 'you will know in time.' 'Tis most annoying. Kaliq says I must wait for my path to be made clearer to me before I act."

"Well," Noss said in her practical way, "I suppose you must wait then. Now let me send Dillon to fetch Anoush for you."

"Thank you," Lara replied. "I am not in the mood to face Bera right now. She grows no better, Noss? Can no one help her? Vartan and Adon have been dead now for over five years."

"Sholeh and her sister, my own mother-in-law, have tried. After you left, Sholeh would come from her village every few weeks to be with Bera, but when we moved from the Outlands to the New Outlands she stopped because the distance from New Rivalen to New Camdene is greater. And it did no good anyway. It is as if something evil has gotten a hold of Bera's heart and spirit," Noss said.

"And Cam?" Lara wanted to know.

"He makes my skin crawl," Noss admitted frankly. "He is as beautiful as his parents and is all kindness where his grandmother is concerned. At least publicly. But even I can sense the wickedness in him, Lara. And of late he has devoted himself to Anoush. Whatever she wants, he gives her. If she is angry at Dillon or me, he encourages her anger. He is working very hard to draw her away from us and he is close to succeeding. Such deviousness in so young a boy is frightening."

Lara nodded. "Dillon," she called to her son who was amusing Zagiri. "Go and fetch your sister to me, please."

Dillon arose, kissing Zagiri's little fingers as he did to make her giggle. "At once, Mother," he said and hurried off. Reaching his grandmother's house he entered and greeted Bera who sat at her loom weaving. "Good morning, Grandmother. I have come to fetch my sister. She is needed at home."

"This should be her home," Bera said. "And yours. You are my grandchildren. You do not belong to Liam and Noss and their ilk. You are the children of my beloved son, Vartan. Tell them you would come and be with your old grandmother."

"You are kind to want us, Grandmother," Dillon said quietly, "but we are where our mother would have us be. And we are content there."

"The faerie witch! She who murdered in cold blood the son of my heart," Bera muttered darkly. "She will regret it! She will regret it! Send her back to Hetar where she belongs. She should be among her own kind, not here among us."

Dillon ignored the old woman's outburst. He had heard it all before. He left Bera and went out to the garden where he found his sister with their cousin. They were seated in the grass, and Cam had his hand on Anoush's own. He quickly pulled it away when he saw Dillon. Dillon's eyes narrowed speculatively, then he spoke quietly to his little sister. "You are needed at home."

"No," Anoush said. "I don't want to go. Cam and I are having fun. He is teaching me a new game." She did not look directly at her brother.

Dillon did not argue. He reached down and pulled his sister up roughly. "I am sure it is not a game that a maid of six should learn," he told her harshly. "Now come, Anoush, we are needed at home." He began to pull her away.

"I should rather live with Grandmother and Cam than with the usurper and his alien wife," Anoush said rudely.

"Say farewell to our cousin," Dillon told her through gritted teeth. His dark, threatening look met Cam's, but their cousin merely smiled at him. Dillon did not wait any longer. He dragged his sister from their grandmother's garden, back through her house and out into the town's square as he made their way home. "You ought to be ashamed of yourself," he scolded Anoush as they went. "What has come over you, Little Sister? You have always loved Noss and your recent coldness has hurt her greatly."

"She is Hetarian like the bitch who bore us," Anoush said coldly.

Dillon stopped dead in his tracks. "Look at me!" he said fiercely. His tone was so dire that Anoush turned startled eyes up to him. "So you understand that Noss is our foster mother, do you? It is true. The mother who gave us life and who loves us beyond measure is Lara, the Domina of Terah. She was born in Hetar of a mortal father and a faerie mother. She was our father's wife. She is a great lady and she has a destiny to follow. She did not choose to have a destiny. She would have been content to remain our father's widow and our mother, but such is not her fate, Anoush. Our mother knows she has no choice but to follow until she meets and claims her destiny. She saw to our comfort and our safety before she left us. She saved the clan families from Hetar when she and the Shadow Princes transported us from the Outlands here to the New Outlands. You will speak of her with respect, Sister." Then, taking Anoush's hand again, Dillon half dragged her to the lord's hall where their mother was awaiting them.

Noss saw them first. "Anoush, come! We have a visitor," she said.

Seeing Lara, Anoush stopped. Then she said, "Good morrow, *Mother*."

Noss paled.

"Good morrow, Anoush," Lara replied quietly.

Tread carefully. She heard Ethne murmur silently.

"You grow prettier each time I see you," Lara said.

"And how often is that, *Mother?*" Anoush asked sarcastically.

Lara was surprised, although she did not show it, at the bitterness in the little girl's question. Noss was right. Someone—Bera? Cam?—was working hard to separate Anoush from her family and her heritage. And it was going to stop as of today, she decided. "I have not seen you often enough in the past few years," Lara answered, "but that is all going to change now, my daughter."

"What?" Anoush responded. "Has your latest lover thrown

you out, and you are returning to the Outlands once again to cause trouble?"

"Anoush!" Noss gasped, almost faint with shock at the girl's words.

But Lara remained calm with the child. "Did your grandmother tell you that? Or was it your cousin, Cam?" she asked pleasantly. "No matter. Nothing they have told you is true, I suspect. And Anoush, you are no longer in the Outlands. These are the New Outlands. The clan families were brought here several years ago."

"That is a lie!" Anoush said. "Grandmother says you told us that to confuse us and make us vulnerable to Hetar's conquest. Nothing has changed. Nothing!"

"Oh, dear," Lara sighed patiently. "I can see there is much you must learn and unlearn before I take you and your brother home with me." She smiled at Anoush and then said, "Come and greet your baby sister, Zagiri."

"Your bastard, you mean," Anoush answered her mother.

Noss clutched at the table's edge, her fingers digging into the wood.

"Zagiri is a princess of Terah as you are a noblewoman of the Fiacre Clan, although I must say your language is more that of a peasant child than the daughter of Vartan," Lara remarked. "Come here to me, Anoush."

Reluctantly Anoush moved to stand before Lara. "What?" she said.

"Noss, would you take Zagiri and Dillon? I think I must speak with Anoush alone."

"I think I should stay," Dillon said.

"Thank you, my son, but no. Anoush and I must speak alone. If she becomes too difficult I shall simply turn her into a warty toad until she learns reason." Lara could not conceal the twinkle in her eye for she saw Anoush's eyes dart about nervously at her words.

Dillon grinned at his mother, picked up Zagiri and followed after Noss.

"Sit down, Anoush," Lara said.

"I wish to stand," Anoush replied.

"But I prefer that you sit," Lara answered quietly, pointing a finger at the little girl who suddenly sat down, a surprised look on her face. "There," Lara said, "that's much better, isn't it? Now, you will ask your questions and I will answer them. What is it you wish to know of me, Anoush?"

Anoush looked defiantly at her mother and then burst out, "Why did you kill our father? Grandmother says you wanted his power and that you killed Cam's father and mother when they came to my father's defense."

The shock on Lara's face was evident. Then drawing a long deep breath she said, "I did not kill your father, Anoush. His brother Adon, Cam's father, killed Vartan with a poisoned dagger that Cam's mother had obtained from Hetar. Adon's wife, Elin, had been suborned by the Hetarians and was convinced that if your father were dead, her husband would be made lord of the Fiacre. Even if Vartan had died of natural causes, Adon would have never been selected to lead the Fiacre. He was a weak, foolish and vain man who wasted his life and his energies in envy of your father. Whoever told you that I killed your father lied to you, Anoush, and a wicked lie it is."

Anoush looked confused. She was a child, and the only people who ever spoke of her father were her grandmother and her cousin, Cam. Liam and Noss did not speak of him. And until recently she hadn't even known that the beautiful woman who appeared now and again in the hall was her mother. Her brother had known and he had confirmed what Cam had told her of their parentage. Why had she not been told? But then recovering somewhat, she said, "Do you deny killing Cam's parents?"

"No," Lara said, "I do not. When your uncle murdered your father before our eyes, I had no choice but to revenge him. Fiacre law gave me that right. Adon murdered Vartan in front of their own mother and me. And Elin stood smiling at his side as he did the deed. I silently called to my sword, Andraste, who hung over the hearth, and slew them immediately before either of them might even enjoy the fruits of their treachery, Anoush. You were in the hall that day. You slept in your cradle as Vartan was slain. Now what else have you been told by that sad old woman? You know that she is totally mad, don't you?"

Anoush said nothing.

"Surely you have more questions for me?" Lara demanded.

Finally Anoush spoke. "Grandmother says you are a faerie witch," she said.

"I was born in Hetar of a mortal father and a faerie mother. You have met your grandmother, Ilona, queen of the Forest Faeries. Your grandfather is John Swiftsword, a Crusader Knight commander. My instincts are more faerie than mortal, Anoush, and my powers have grown stronger in the last few years. I was born to a destiny I have yet to find or fulfill, but I grow closer to it with each change in my life and I will meet that destiny one day. It is my fate to do so. I cannot escape it.

"I remained in the Outlands the summer your father died and I saw to his cremation and did him honor. I saw that much honor was done to him by the others who had admired and loved Vartan. Dillon will tell you of that time. You have only to ask him. But my destiny called and I had no choice but to follow."

"Would you have done so if my father were alive?" Anoush asked.

"Aye, I would have and your father understood that. We both knew that one day I would go, but he would be there for you and Dillon. And then he wasn't. Liam is your father's blood kin. He is yours and Dillon's, too. Noss is my best friend. I asked them to take you and your brother—for where I go you cannot always follow. My destiny is not yours. They have been good foster parents to you, Anoush. I journeyed to Terah, where I met Magnus Hauk. We fell in love and married. Much else has happened in the years since your father's death, but I suspect I have already told you more than enough. You need only know that I love you and your brother. When I return to the castle in a few weeks, you both will return with me. It is time now for you to know your mother and your little sister. Magnus will be a good stepfather to you."

"Is this place really the New Outlands?" Anoush asked. "Cam says it is not and that you have told us it is so when the Hetarians want us they can enslave us easily, for you are lulling us into a false sense of security."

"This is a new place," Lara reassured her daughter. "You are very, very far from Hetar now. Across a wide sea, in fact. The lords of the clan families know it is truth. They will tell you that the land, while similar, is not the same. The Fiacre never had a nearby lake in the Outlands, but you have one here in the New Outlands. When we go to the Dominus's castle, you will see that Terah sits between two great oceans."

"How can I see such a thing?" Anoush wanted to know.

"You will sit before me on my saddle as Dasras gallops across the sky," Lara told her older daughter.

"I don't want to leave here," Anoush said. "I want to stay with Cam and Grandmother. Cam says Noss and Liam don't want Dillon and me any longer because Noss is fat with another baby. Cam says they don't want to be bothered with your children when they will have four of their own."

"Noss loves you, and would keep you forever if I would let her, but I will not," Lara replied. "You are Fiacre, but you are also my children."

"If Zagiri is a princess why can I not be a princess?" Anoush wanted to know.

"Zagiri is the daughter of the Dominus of Terah," Lara said. "She was born royal. You and Dillon are of noble birth, but not royal. You will have to wed a prince one day, Anoush, if you desire to be a princess."

"Could you really turn me into a warty toad?" Anoush asked her mother.

"I could. My magic is very strong, my daughter."

"I don't have any magic, do I?"

"It would seem not. You are like your father. The only magic he possessed was his ability to shape-shift. Perhaps when you grow up a bit more we shall see if you, too, have his talents," Lara told her daughter. "Or perhaps even some of your own."

"Dillon has magic," Anoush remarked. "Grandmother says he is a wicked boy."

"Aye, your brother does indeed have magic, but he is not wicked," Lara said.

"Does Zagiri have magic?" Anoush wanted to know.

"She is too little for me to know if she does," Lara replied.

"Mother?"

"Yes, Anoush?"

"Why did Grandmother lie to me about you?"

"Your grandmother went mad when your father was killed and I was forced to slay her younger son in retaliation. She has never recovered but instead rewove the event so she would not have to face the truth of Adon's treachery. It cannot be easy to accept that your youngest son has brutally murdered your eldest. And then I took my revenge on Adon and Elin so poor Bera has made me her villain. Before your father's death, she and I were great friends and I loved her like a mother."

"Do you still love her?" Anoush asked.

Lara shook her head. "Nay, but I feel no animosity toward her. I feel pity."

Then Lara reached out and took her daughter's little hand. "Have you understood all I have told you? Is there more you would ask me or tell me?"

"I understand, I think," Anoush replied. "My faerie grandmother frightens me, Mother. When she comes to visit she is more interested in Dillon than she is in me, and she shoos me away. Dillon says it is her way and I must not be offended."

"How typical of Ilona," Lara murmured, almost to herself. Then she said, "Faeries can have cold hearts, my daughter. She means you no ill, but Dillon's talents intrigue her. Did you know that I did not know her until I was grown? But that is a story for another time, I think. You will be relieved to know that your stepfather is all mortal. He will love you because he loves me, Anoush. Be kind to him, please."

"What will I do at the castle?" Anoush was clearly fascinated now.

"You will have lessons as you do here. You will ride your own horse by the sea, and I will teach you to care for your very own garden. At night I will tell you stories before you sleep and then I will kiss you so you may have sweet dreams," Lara said.

"I am still angry at you, and I have many more questions," Anoush said frankly.

"I do not expect to win your heart back in an afternoon," Lara told her child. "Just know that I love you and that all I have done is for you and Dillon and for your safety."

Anoush nodded. "May I go back to Grandmother's now?" she said.

"Nay," Lara told her daughter. "I will not allow you to ever enter Bera's house again, Anoush. You must be freed from her poisonous ravings."

Anoush's eyes grew dark with her annoyance, but then she said, "What am I to do if I must remain here?"

"Perhaps you might go to Noss, and give her your apologies

for being so unkind to her these past weeks. She really does love you and she has taken such great care of you and your brother when I could not," Lara said.

"Will I get to play with Cam again?" she asked.

"I don't think so," Lara responded. "He is not a good influence on you, Anoush. He has embroidered on his grandmother's fantasies, I suspect, which was very cruel. Do you understand what they were doing? Bera and Cam were trying to lure you from those who love you. Why would they do that?"

Anoush swung her legs back and forth as she thought. "I don't know," she finally said.

"Nor do I," Lara replied. "But it was wicked nonetheless, Anoush." *Of course she knew,* Lara thought. While Adon had killed his brother and somewhere deep in her mind Bera knew it, she could nevertheless forgive him. But she could never forgive Lara for slaying her surviving son. Elin had meant naught to her, but Adon had been her baby and Lara had killed him. Deep within, Bera sought to have her revenge—what better way than to destroy Lara's daughter who was young and impressionable? Dillon was safe from his grandmother for Bera could not reach into his heart and soul and twist them as she had twisted Anoush's trusting little heart. *If she knew the power I have gained these last years, the old woman would be truly afraid,* Lara thought.

"May I go now and tell Noss that I am sorry, Mother?" Anoush said.

"Give me a kiss first, my daughter," Lara said, wrapping her arms about the child and hugging her. "I will try not to leave you again, Anoush, but know wherever I am that I love you with all of my heart." She kissed her daughter's cheek as Anoush rose from her seat and then, giving her a little push, sent her off to find Noss.

Dillon appeared from out of the afternoon shadows and came to sit at Lara's feet.

"How much did you hear?" Lara asked her son.

"Only the end," he said. "Do not be lulled by her acquiescence, Mother. Anoush is a very willful girl. It is not Grandmother you need worry about—it is Cam. He will not like it that she is no longer available to him. When I found them today, they were in the grass and my cousin had his hand on my sister's in a most proprietary manner."

"I think Cam must be sent to our Sholeh in New Rivalen," Lara answered her son calmly. "He is old enough to work in the fields until it is time for the Gathering. I had intended to remain in the New Outlands until after it concluded, but I think now I must take you both home sooner. Bera may protest the loss of Cam at first but then she will be silent. I shall ask this of Liam when he comes home today. You will tell him what you saw and he will do this for me. Where is Zagiri?"

"She fell asleep and so Noss laid her down for a nap," the boy answered.

"Have you released Dasras into the meadows?"

"Aye, and he immediately found Sakiri and their latest foal," Dillon said.

"After he has sated himself with her company he will fly off to the Aghy," Lara chuckled. "He is of a mind to visit Roan's new young mares."

"His offspring have increased the stamina and beauty of the Horse Lord's herds," Dillon remarked. "Will I like Terah, Mother?"

"It will be different for you," Lara said, "but aye, I believe you will like it. And there is so much that you can learn. You will need to know everything that you can absorb, Dillon, before you go Prince Kaliq to study the magical arts. I am frankly surprised by your talents, my son, for you are but a quarter faerie."

"I don't know if what I possess is so much magic as it is intuitiveness. I see things that others do not, Mother. And I sense things, too—like I knew you were coming today. You had sent no faerie post, but I knew."

"This is a great gift, Dillon," his mother said. "And Kaliq will help you to refine your gift and use it for the good."

"Anoush has a gift, too, Mother," Dillon told her.

"Does she?" Lara was surprised. "And what is it, my son?"

"She is clever with plants and herbs. It is not magic of course, but I believe if her interest continues she might become an excellent healer," the boy said.

"I offered her a garden," Lara replied thoughtfully. "She seemed pleased by the notion she might have one of her own. Thank you, Dillon. This will be the means by which I win her back and bind her to the light."

"I am so glad that you have come, Mother," he told her.

Liam, lord of the Fiacre, came now from the kitchen. "Welcome, Domina," he greeted her with a smile. He was holding a pitcher in one hand and refilled her cup with frine as he sat down to join her, sipping from his own cup. "Noss tells me you would take your children with you when you return home. We will miss them."

"I will return them to the Fiacre each summer, and if they choose they may remain through the Gathering time," Lara responded. "But it is now time for them to be with Magnus and me. They both know their parentage and their history."

He nodded in understanding. "The children of Vartan will always be welcome here among their Fiacre kinsmen and women."

Reaching down, Lara drew her son to his feet. "Go and stay with your sisters, for I must speak with Liam privately," she told him and Dillon immediately left them.

"What is it?" Liam asked her. "Is there trouble coming of some sort?"

Lara laughed. "Nay, not any of which I am aware. I need a favor from you, lord of the Fiacre. I want to send Cam away while I am here with my children. Both he and Bera have been filling Anoush's little head with all manner of lies. Had I not come when I did today they might very well have stolen my daughter and dragged her into their dark world. Once the children are in Terah, neither Bera nor Cam can harm them. We will not be able to keep Anoush from running off to find Cam if he is here. We cannot watch her constantly. As for Bera we must find a good woman to live with her and care for her."

"Where will you send the lad?" Liam asked. "I can certainly think of a few places," he added with a chuckle.

"To Sholeh in New Rivalen. She is kin to you both and as head-woman of her village, she has both authority and strength. Cam could be put to work in the fields until the harvest. That should keep him busy and out of trouble," Lara said.

"Aye, he is old enough," Liam agreed. "We will have to send a faerie post to Sholeh and request her aid in this matter."

"Nay, I will go myself, for we are asking a great favor of her and it is in my interests that we need her help," Lara said. She stood up from the table. "Would you mind if I went now, Liam?"

"Shall I have Dasras caught and saddled?" the lord of the Fiacre asked her.

"Nay," Lara told him, and with a delicate wave of her hand she disappeared in a faint cloud of mauve smoke.

Liam stared and then he laughed weakly. How long had he known her, and still Lara's growing magic always surprised him.

But he was no more surprised than Sholeh, the headwoman of New Rivalen, who jumped back as Lara suddenly appeared before her in her chamber. "Gracious!" She jumped to her feet, dropping the brush in her hand for she had been in the middle of brushing her long auburn hair. "Lara! Is it really you?" She immediately embraced her visitor.

"Aye, 'tis me, Sholeh," Lara said.

"How can I serve you, Domina?" Sholeh was suddenly very formal for she was more than aware Lara's visit was hardly a casual one.

"I have come to ask a great favor of you," Lara began.

"Anything!" Sholeh responded.

Lara laughed. "Wait until I have told you what it is I want," she said. Then she explained what Bera and Cam had been doing to her little daughter. "I came to the New Outlands with the express purpose of visiting and then returning with both of Vartan's children to Terah. It is time they were with me again."

Sholeh nodded her agreement and then listened as Lara continued.

"It would be too difficult and cause great dissension between my daughter and me if I had to keep her from Cam. I can only keep them apart if Cam is not there. I would have you take the boy until the Gathering. He is young, but he can be put to work in the fields, and herding cattle. Keep him busy. Hopefully that will keep him from getting into trouble. He will be so charming and polite with you that you will wonder to yourself why I sent him away. But believe me when I say that Cam, son of Adon, is filled to overflowing with wickedness," Lara said.

"I know he is," Sholeh responded. "I saw him with his grandmother as he twisted poor Bera's words and thoughts. I am not fooled by his soft-spoken demeanor, Lara. Aye, I will take him and keep him tightly reined. You will want him gone quickly, I assume. What will you do with Bera?"

"We will find a good woman to live with her for she really is no longer capable of caring for herself. The woman will remain when Cam returns home after the Gathering," Lara told Sholeh. "Will you return with me now to New Camdene?"

"I suppose we will be transported by means of your magic," Sholeh said nervously. "Well, no matter. Come into the hall with me, and we will tell the servants so they do not worry when I am suddenly gone."

The two women left the chamber and went into the hall where, seeing Lara, the servants greeted her with smiles.

"I am going to take your mistress with me to New Camdene,"

she said. "I will return her on the morrow." Then with a wave of her hand they were gone from before the servants' startled eyes.

As they rematerialized beneath the pergola in Liam's hall, Lara said, "There now, Sholeh, that didn't hurt at all, did it?" And she laughed.

Sholeh laughed, too. "It is a convenient mode of transport, I will admit, but it still makes me nervous and you know I fear nothing."

"It is getting cool out here and the sun is setting," Lara remarked. "Let us go into the hall. I smell food and if there is one thing about me that is solely mortal it is my appetite. I am ravenous, Sholeh, and could eat an entire side of one of Liam's cows."

Warned by her husband, Noss showed no surprise when the two women entered her hall. She greeted Sholeh respectfully as an elder of the clan family and as headwoman of New Rivalen. Then she beckoned the two to be seated at her high board. There were only the four adults, Noss's children and Lara's having been fed earlier. They had already gone back outside to play in the long summer twilight.

"Sholeh has agreed to take Cam until the Gathering time," Lara told Liam and Noss. "I will transport them back to New Rivalen in the morning."

"And I know just the woman to care for Bera," said Noss. "She is newly widowed, and her son would like to wed but what woman will come into a house with another woman in it? This will solve both of their problems and when Bera has departed this life we will give the woman her own cottage."

"Make certain she you have chosen is not easily deluded by Bera—and later, Cam. I do not want the history of Vartan's life destroyed by their lies," Lara said.

"You can speak with the woman yourself and make the decision tomorrow," Liam suggested. "It was bad enough when they poisoned little Anoush's mind, but we cannot have their prevarications harming our people. There are always those who are quick to believe the worst or who enjoy blackening the reputations of heroes. It is five years since Vartan's death. His legend remains but his influence has faded from the Fiacre. And there are those, too, who never trusted you, Lara, because of your Hetarian birth, although they have certainly profited by your faerie nature. Any rumor begun among us will eventually spread to the other clan families. We cannot allow divisions to separate us now that we are relatively safe once again."

"Thank you, Liam," Lara said to him. "Your friendship is precious to me. You are as safe as any peoples here, but I am concerned not just with Hetar but with the Dark Lands to our north. Hetar is an ocean away. But the other…" She sighed. "Does anyone know of the people who inhabit that place? It seems to be all mountains."

"None of our folk have ventured north," Liam said. "Those mountains, unlike the Emerald Range that separates us from Terah proper, seem threatening. All the clan families have enough lands where we are. Our territories are at least twice as large as those we held previously. Why do the Dark Lands concern you, Lara?"

"I am not certain, but I sense a threat from them," she

answered. "The first time I saw them, I was on Dasras's back and observing the sea creatures frolicking in the sea we call Obscura. Those mountains drew my eye, and I was almost overwhelmed by the aura of darkness that emanated from them."

"We have never seen any signs of life from them," Liam told her. "I wonder if they are even inhabited. They certainly appear to be inhospitable."

"Aye," Lara replied slowly. Then she shook off the feeling of gloom that had come over her when she spoke of the Dark Lands.

Dillon came into the hall and went to his mother. "Anoush has gone to our grandmother's house," he told her.

"I will fetch her," Sholeh said standing up. "I want to see how Bera is faring."

She hurried from the hall with Dillon by her side.

"You see how it is?" Lara said to Liam.

"Cam will be gone on the morrow," Noss soothed, "and you will not have to see him again. Frankly I'll be glad to have him out of the village. Whenever he ventures out he always manages to cause trouble among the other children. There are several who are fascinated by him, but then there are always those who cannot help being drawn by the darkness and then into it."

"You are such a tattletale," Anoush complained to her brother as they returned together to the hall.

"You were told not to go back there," he countered.

"You are not my master, Brother. I do what pleases me," Anoush snapped.

"You are not old enough to do as you please," he replied.

"I am six," Anoush answered, "and that is old enough."

"Ah, children, here you are," Lara came toward them smiling. "I believe it is time for you to go to bed, Anoush." She took her daughter by her hand and led her away.

Dillon grinned after them. "My mother is surely the cleverest woman alive," he said with a chuckle.

"And you are much too wise for a boy so young," Noss told him, ruffling his hair.

"My soul, I think, is as old as time itself, dearest Noss," he answered.

"You will do well one day with the Shadow Princes," Noss said.

"My mother says I am not yet ready," he replied sadly.

"Do not stop trusting your mother now, Dillon," Noss advised. "She has never failed any of us. If she says you must wait, then accept her decision and be patient."

"I will," he told her but his tone was reluctant.

"Go and fetch the boys for me," she said. "It is time they went to bed, too."

With a quick smile he ran off to do her bidding.

Noss looked out over the darkening landscape. A warm summer breeze touched her cheek and pushed at a loose strand of her hair. It sometimes seemed only yesterday she was a frightened girl from The City sold into slavery by her parents. So much had happened in the years that had passed. She often wondered if her parents still lived, and considered what they would think of the good fortune that had given her a wonderful noble husband, three healthy sons and a respected place in her community.

And Lara. Without Lara she might have ended up a concubine to a Forest Lord, only to be killed when she had delivered a healthy son for her master. She shivered and shook off the black thought. She was the lady Noss, wife to the lord of the Fiacre. She was loved, and she was safe. There was peace and they were far from Hetar. It was enough, she thought as she rubbed her distended belly and felt the child within move lustily. "I am going to call you Mildri," she whispered softly to herself, smiling. And then her three sons came running toward her and Noss laughed with her happiness.

THE CHAMBER WAS A square one. Its walls were black marble veined with silver. Tall silver censers burning fragrant oils lined the room, their flickering flames casting shadows upon the walls. The floors were wide boards of ebony edged in strips of pure silver. At one end of the room, a square throne of gray and silver marble had been placed upon a matching marble dais beneath a silk canopy of purple and silver stripes. To the right of the throne, a colonnade of shining, veined black marble offered a view of the surrounding mountains between its pillars. The sky beyond was reddish-dun colored. On the wall opposite the throne were great double doors of silver. And directly in the center of the chamber had been set a footed silver tripod holding a wide black onyx bowl filled with crystal clear water.

Kol, Twilight Lord of the Dark Lands, waved a languid hand over the vessel. The water roiled for a moment, grew dark and then cleared once again. "Ahh," Kol said, staring down at the beautiful woman revealed to him in the water. "Soon, Lara. Soon you will belong to me and I shall have your magic combined with mine. I shall take both Hetar and Terah, and our worlds will be one." He smiled a dazzling smile.

He was a very tall man, his skin faintly bronzed, his hair midnight-black, his eyes a dark gray that sometimes seemed almost black. His face was a very masculine one, yet he could almost be called beautiful rather than handsome. His cheekbones were high, his nose long and straight, his mouth wide and sensual. He had thick, bushy dark eyebrows and long, dark eyelashes that were tipped with silver. He wore a simple dark robe with a round neck and long sleeves embroidered with silver at his wrists.

"Will it be soon, my lord?" asked the man who stood by Kol. He was a dwarf with the wrinkled brown visage of an old man. His back was slightly crooked, his fingers gnarled with age, but his brown eyes were sharp with curiosity.

"Aye, Alfrigg, soon, for I feel the mating lust beginning to rise within me," Kol answered his chancellor's question. "The Book of Rule says when that happenstance occurs, I must take the faerie woman for my mate. She is destined to give me my son."

"She will not come willingly, for she has a mate whom she loves," Alfrigg said. "And faerie women will not give children to those they do not love."

"I have summoned the Munin," Kol replied.

"The Munin? My lord, that is dangerous. What do you want of them?" Alfrigg looked concerned by his master's news. "The Munin are not easy creatures and can be treacherous if provoked."

"If I steal the faerie woman from her world she will resist me. But what if I have the Munin steal her memories before I take her?"

"What good is she without her knowledge of magic, my lord?" the chancellor asked. "No matter that she is the woman fated to birth the next Twilight Lord, you need her magic, as well. If she has no memory of her magic then she is of little use to you other than as a life bearer."

"The Munin will place her memories in an alabaster jar and restore them to her as I require, but first I must convince her to trust me so completely that when I return her knowledge of magic to her she will be only too glad to aid me in my conquests. Her recollections of her husband and her children, I will not restore to her. She will have no need of them. For Lara her life will begin with me and me alone, Alfrigg."

"She is light, my lord," Alfrigg reminded him. "You are dark."

"She will have no memory of the light," he said with a smile. "And when her fears have been calmed, she will believe everything that I tell her. I will not show myself to be a threat to her in any manner. Indeed, I will be her savior." He gazed down into the bowl. "Is she not beautiful, Alfrigg? Is she not perfection?"

The dwarf stood on his tiptoes and gazed down into the water. "Aye, my lord, she is an excellent specimen of female loveliness," he agreed. "But once you restore her magic to her she may not be as easy to manage as previously. Women should not be allowed to have magic. They are emotional and unstable beings!"

The Twilight Lord laughed at this. "Women do have a certain intelligence, Alfrigg. In Hetar and in Terah they manage commerce and even speak their minds," he told his chancellor who looked properly shocked.

"It is obvious there is no order in Hetar and Terah," Alfrigg replied sourly. "Women of high caste are for breeding purposes only. Women of low caste are meant to be servants but can also be bred if the serving class is to be perpetuated. Only men of high caste can be considered fit to serve the Twilight Lord. As for the others, they serve as they are told to serve. The appropriate order must be kept, and those who would defy it must be punished so others not be encouraged to disobedience."

"You are a hard man, Alfrigg," his master told him with a small smile.

"Thank you, my lord," the chancellor said with a short bow to his master.

The Twilight Lord returned his gaze to the surface of the water. Krell, Lord of Darkness, he thought to himself, I can hardly wait to have her! He felt his rod twitch beneath his robes, and fought back down the feelings of desire that threatened to overwhelm him. *Just a little while longer,* he reminded himself.

"My lord." A serving man was bowing before him. "They have come."

The Twilight Lord nodded. "Let them enter," he said and then turned to Alfrigg. "Secrete yourself behind my throne and listen, but do not reveal yourself."

Alfrigg nodded and did as he had been bid.

The doors to the chamber opened again; suddenly the room was cold. Kol sat motionless watching the Munin as they drifted to the foot of his throne. He had never before seen them and he was amazed by their appearance. They were spectral creatures, almost like shadows. They seemed to have no legs, but he was able to distinguish the arms, hands and faces of the Munin, who ranged in color from the palest to the darkest gray. They traveled toward him in a cluster.

The largest of them now detached from the assemblage, bowed politely and asked in a high, wispy voice, "How may my brethren and I serve you, great Twilight Lord? Your kind has never before called upon us."

"Thank you for coming, and welcome," Kol greeted them politely. "I would ask a great favor of you, lords of the Munin."

"And what will you give us in return for this favor, Twilight Lord?" the Munin murmured.

"You have no home," Kol replied. "You wander the worlds with no place to call your own. Help me and I will give you the valley we call Penumbras for your own. It is set between two of our tallest mountains where the sun's rays never reach. It is a cold, dark and secret place. It will be yours for all time."

"Will you build us a castle there?" the Munin lord demanded.

"A castle and a place beneath the earth where you may store your treasures," Kol promised them.

"The favor you seek from us must be great. Tell me what you desire of us that you would be willing to part with some of your own lands?" the Munin lord said.

"Do you know of the faerie woman, Lara of Hetar, who was first wed to Vartan of the Fiacre and is now the wife of Magnus Hauk, the Dominus of Terah?"

"The daughter of Ilona of the Forest Faeries and the mortal man John Swiftsword? She who undid the curse of Usi upon the men of Terah?"

"The same," Kol replied. "I want you to steal her memories and store them here in this jar that sits by my throne."

A humming sound erupted from among the Munin and then the Munin lord said but one word. "Why?"

"You are aware that the Twilight Lords possess the Book of Rule, brought to us centuries ago by our common ancestress, Jorunn. With each new Twilight Lord, the words and instructions within the book change. It has been predicted since the days of Jorunn that the twelfth generation after Khalfani would take for his mate a woman, half-human, half-faerie, with great powers. Her powers combined with his would allow him to rule over all the lands. Lara is that woman," Kol said.

"Lara of Hetar is wife to Magnus Hauk and Domina over Terah," the Munin lord said. "She is allied with and almost worshiped by the eight Outland clan families. Her mother is the most powerful of all the faerie queens. Kaliq of the Shadow Princes is her mentor. Even Hetar's emperor fears her. Do you mean to steal her, Twilight Lord? She will not come willingly to you. You had best examine your Book of Rule again."

"The book is clear. Lara is to be the mother of the next Twilight Lord. And I know she will not come willingly. That is why I need you to steal her memories and store them in my jar. I will ask you to restore certain of those memories as she comes to trust me. But one memory I would bid you leave her—her memory of how much she enjoys pleasures, for it is not my intent to frighten her when we mate."

"Then, when we have taken her memories, you will steal her

and bring her here to your castle of Kolbyr," the Munin lord said slowly. "Her disappearance will cause an uproar throughout both Terah and Hetar, though for different reasons. A search will be mounted and the Shadow Princes will become involved. And Ilona will not sit by quietly with her daughter missing. There must be no chance of them discovering that we have been involved in your treachery, Twilight Lord. Our powers are small compared to yours and those whom you will go up against. Sooner or later it will be discovered that you have stolen the faerie woman. Magnus Hauk will not restrain himself if you mate with his beloved wife to gain a son. If we agree to help you, Twilight Lord, you must first build us our refuge, for when we have done your bidding we will hide ourselves away there until the matter is finally settled between the Dark Land, Terah and Hetar. *If.*"

"My powers can build you your castle in seven days' time," Kol told them.

An excited murmur arose again from the cluster of Munin as the Munin lord turned back to them to discuss the matter. Some were eager to accept the Twilight Lord's offer. Others considered his plan too dangerous and worried about being blamed publicly for their involvement in Kol's perfidy. But the offer of a castle built for them in a secret valley far from all, with their own vault in which to hoard the memories they stole, was too tempting for them to resist. Even if their participation in Kol's plan was finally discovered, no one would be able to find them. Those belonging to Hetar and Terah did not venture into the Dark Lands. Not even the magic folk.

"Then we are agreed," the Munin lord said to his companions in their own tongue.

"We are," they murmured back.

The Munin lord turned to Kol. "Very well, Twilight Lord. Build us our home. We will give you the specifications as to what will suit us. When it is done you will tell us where to find Lara and then we will do your bidding. But not before."

"I shall start tomorrow," Kol told them. "When it is finished and you have approved it, we will speak again and I will tell you how and when." He stood up and bowed from his waist.

"You have but to call us when you are ready," the Munin lord said, and then the Munin faded away before the Twilight Lord's dark eyes. "You may come out now," he said to his chancellor and Alfrigg crept from behind the throne. "You heard it all?"

"It is a bold plan, my lord," Alfrigg answered him. "How clever of you to know what it was that the Munin wanted. And the Penumbras is a perfect spot for them."

"Aye," Kol said, a small smile touching his lips. "And as they have said, Alfrigg, my power is greater than theirs. Once they have done my bidding, once they have settled in my kingdom, the Munin are mine forever. No longer will they be able to wander at will. I will cast a spell on the valley of Penumbras, so they will not be able to leave it without my authority." He chuckled darkly. "How simple they are. Their weakness is their desire for their own home. That is the trick, Alfrigg, when dealing with others. You learn their deepest desire, and then you use it against them."

The old dwarf looked up admiringly at his master. "Your

wisdom is great, my lord," he said. "You will surely be the greatest of the Twilight Lords."

Kol smiled at his chancellor's words and walked across the chamber to stand between the black marble pillars so he might look out over his kingdom. The reddish sky was now turning purple and black. Bolts of silver lightning leapt from cloud to cloud; his ears caught the distant growl of thunder. Kolbyr, his castle, was built into the highest mountain of the Dark Lands. From its turrets and colonnaded porches you could see nothing but mountains and sky. But beyond those mountains lay Terah and Hetar. Rich kingdoms ripe for the taking. And he would master them all.

Hetar would be first, for its emperor, Gaius Prospero, had already been caught by the lure of the dark and the power it could offer him. But he was a fat simpleton who thought himself more clever than anyone else and who sought only more power, more pleasures and more wealth. *I will replace him,* Kol decided. *He cannot be trusted.* But the man known as the emperor's right hand, Jonah, was a different thing altogether. His heart was already dark, but he was very intelligent. Though he, too, sought power, he knew well how to serve a strong master. *He could be content as my governor,* Kol thought. *And he is clever.* Clever enough to have made Gaius Prospero's number one wife, Vilia, his mistress without that pompous little man knowing. Kol chuckled. Aye, Jonah would be his governor in Hetar. The Forest Lords, the Coastal Kings and the Midlands would fall into line. Only the Shadow Princes could not be conquered, but the Shadow Princes were not known to be aggressive. Left to themselves they were unlikely to thwart his plans for conquest, for they did not involve themselves willingly with others.

Kol watched as the rain began to pour down in thick gray sheets of water. His thoughts turned back to the faerie woman and he drew a deep breath to calm his beating heart. He had already built a luxurious and large apartment to house her and a wardrobe filled with silks and gauzes and furs. She would have views of the mountains from three sides of her rooms. Lara would lack for nothing while in his care. And he would care for her as no man ever had. His chancellor might have little use for women but Kol appreciated their beauty and their charm.

I am already in love with her, he thought. Ever since the Book of Rule had revealed her to him, no day passed that he did not use the reflecting bowl to observe her. She fascinated him with her beauty and manner. He particularly enjoyed watching her with the children she had already borne. It was obvious that she was a good mother. He felt no guilt or shame at robbing those children of their mother. She did not belong to them. She belonged to him. He turned and walked back to the bowl, then waved a graceful hand over it so he might see her once more.

LARA SHIVERED suddenly.

"What is it?" Noss asked her. "Are you all right? You have suddenly gone quite pale, Lara. Are you cold?"

"Nay, but I just had the oddest feeling—as if someone was secretly looking at me. I have had it now and again over this last year. It only lasts a moment or two." She shrugged her shoulders as if to shake off the sensation. "My faerie senses grow stronger. It is, I suspect, nothing more than that," she told Noss with a chuckle.

"The summer is almost over," Noss remarked, "and soon it will be time for the Gathering. I usually look forward to it, but this year I am not. You will leave us after the Gathering concludes. And traveling with a new infant won't be easy for me."

"No, it won't be," Lara agreed. "I keeping forgetting that your daughter will be born shortly. If my son is right and it is a daughter."

"Dillon is correct," Noss said quietly. "When he makes a pronouncement like that he is never wrong, though he is yet a child himself."

"I will be glad to have the opportunity to observe him more," Lara said. "I had not planned to send him to Kaliq until he was twelve but if his powers are strengthening I may have to change my mind. Don't tell him I said so," Lara finished with a small laugh. "He is so anxious to go."

"I suspect he wants to be someplace where his talents are not looked upon with suspicion," Noss remarked. "There are always those who will be frightened of magic, and often he is thought of as more your son than Vartan's."

Lara sighed. "If Vartan were still alive that would not be so."

"I know," Noss concurred. "It is sad, but there it is and we cannot change it."

"I suppose not," Lara agreed. "Has Bera said anything since we sent Cam away with Sholeh? And how is the woman we chose doing?"

"I don't think Bera realizes how many days have passed since the boy left," Noss said. "Pakwa does well with her. Bera enjoys her company and she is a marvelous cook. I actually think Bera is putting on a bit of weight. She seems less intense with Cam gone."

"What a pity we cannot keep Cam from her entirely," Lara murmured. "I hope Pakwa will remain when he returns. If Cam decides he doesn't want her in Bera's house he will make it difficult for her to stay."

"Pakwa has been warned. She will concentrate all her efforts upon Bera and ignore the boy. He will have his lessons to concentrate upon in the Icy Season," Noss remarked. "And he will go to Sholeh again next year. Or perhaps to Rendor or Roan."

"Don't allow him to become close friends with anyone," Lara advised. "He must make no allies among the clan families."

"Lara, he is just a child," Noss said softly.

"He will not always be a child and Bera has put it in his head, you may be certain, that he should one day be lord of the Fiacre. Liam will live long, Noss. I know it. But you do not want Cam causing trouble among the Fiacre as your husband grows older."

Noss nodded reluctantly. "I cannot help but feel if we had been raising Cam it would have been different," she said.

Lara shook her head. "Nay, there is wickedness in him," she replied. "He will need to be kept under control all his life."

NOSS GAVE BIRTH to her daughter in very late summer. Mildri was a pretty baby and gentle of temperament. The time of the Gathering was drawing near. Magnus Hauk would join Lara and the clan families as he had done every year since they had come to the New Outlands. It was at the Gathering that they rendered him their tribute as their overlord. Lara had sent a faerie post to her husband telling him that Dillon and Anoush would be coming home with them. The Dominus wrote back that his sister, Sirvat, had come to help. She was already preparing rooms for the children despite the fact she was great with a second child to be born in late autumn.

Anoush had grown closer to her mother now that she was not in Cam or Bera's company. Having learned from Dillon of Anoush's proclivities for plants, Lara had started a small herb garden with her daughter. They would transplant Anoush's plants to a new garden in Terah, Lara promised. She also taught the little girl small facts such as lavender being an excellent agent for those troubled by sleeplessness and chamomile tea being good for the nerves. One day she took the child up on Dasras with her. They traveled to the Obscura, where they watched the sea creatures playing in the waves. Anoush was fascinated by it all. The angry look had left her eyes, to Lara's relief.

Then, on a perfect late-summer's night, Lara and her two children lay upon a gentle hillock almost all of the evening and watched the flying stars streaking across the black skies before the moonrise. The earth beneath them smelled green and fresh with the early dew. Then with Dillon by her side Lara walked home carrying Anoush, who had fallen asleep.

"It was a perfect magical moment," Dillon told his mother. "Why do the stars fly, Mother? But for this night they seem to be still in the heavens."

"I don't know," Lara admitted. "That is a question we must ask Kaliq when we see him again, my son."

"And when will that be?" Dillon wanted to know.

Lara laughed. "Oh, how you long to go to the Shadow Princes!" she teased. "But this will be the first time you have lived with me in several years. Let me have a little time with you, Dillon. I am certain Kaliq would agree with that."

"You grown folk, magical or mortal, all stick together," Dillon complained.

"'Tis the only way we can survive our young long enough to teach them," Lara told him with a chuckle.

They entered the lord's house, then the servant who had waited up for them barred the doors. Reaching the chamber she shared with her children each time she visited, Lara lay Anoush down in her bed with Zagiri, who was already sleeping, and drew the coverlet over them. She kissed her daughters and then she kissed her son who had already climbed into his own bed.

"Good night, Dillon. Sleep well."

"I don't know if I can," Dillon replied. "It was such a wonderful evening, Mother."

Lara ruffled his hair. "You will sleep," she told him. Then she lay down in her own bed to rest. It had been a perfect summer. In another two weeks, Magnus would join them and they would all go to the Gathering together. She was anxious to see the other clan lords and learn how they were now faring after several years in the New Outlands. Liam said that everyone was content, but she needed to hear it from their own lips. When she had arrived two months ago, the fields below her had certainly looked fertile and green. And the horses belonging to the Aghy had looked fat. But what of the others? Were Rendor's sheep thriving? Were the dwarfs in the Emerald Mountains still getting along with the Piaras and the Tormod? Having brought them all here she would always worry about them, Lara thought. But then her eyes began to droop and she fell into a contented sleep.

In the morning when Dillon awoke, he lay quietly considering the odd dream he had had in the night. It had seemed so very real, yet he was certain he had been sleeping. Yawning and stretching, he saw that his mother was already up. He knew she enjoyed viewing the sunrise and was usually awake before her children. Turning his head, Dillon noted his sisters were still sleeping. He smiled at them. They were both his mother's daughters, and yet they were so very different. Zagiri was adventurous and absolutely sure of herself, which probably came from having a father in her life. Anoush, on the other hand was cautious and defensive, having lost her father before she ever knew him.

Dillon remembered Vartan well and he made it a point to tell Anoush often of how the great Outland lord had taken her up on his saddle and ridden about his meadows with her. He told his sister of how their father had adored his little girl, that he loved both his children with all of his heart. But unfortunately Cam and Bera had told Anoush a different tale of Vartan and confused her. Dillon had to admit that he was glad Cam had been sent away this summer. He was glad that they were returning with Lara to her castle on the Terahn coast. Sadly, without her father, the New Outlands were not good for Anoush. She needed to begin anew. She needed both a mother and a father. Dillon knew that Magnus would love them because they were Lara's children. The Dominus would treat them well.

Dillon arose from his bed and dressed himself. His sisters

would awaken soon. He filled the chamber ewer with water and quickly washed his face and hands. He scrubbed his teeth with a small brush dipped in fine pumice stone that his mother had taught him to use. After rinsing his mouth, he ran his fingers through his dark locks, then emptied the little basin and refilled it for his sisters. The sun was just edging over the horizon. If he was quick he could join his mother.

But he could not find Lara outside and while he pushed back thoughts of his dream he began to wonder if it had been real after all. He had been awakened by what sounded like whispering, yet he could not make out the words. Turning over, he saw a cluster of filmy, almost transparent beings, gray-white in color, hovering over his mother. They drew gauzy golden strands from her head, which one of them wrapped carefully about a large spool. Then the creatures, whatever they were, disappeared into the air itself. Dillon blinked with surprise and when he looked again, his mother was no longer in her bed. *I am dreaming,* he thought, and fell back asleep. But had he been dreaming? It was so very, very odd. It would have had to be magic. He was aware there were magical beings in their world other than his mother, but Dillon knew instinctively that none of her associates would have been involved with what he had seen in the night. Perhaps Lara left because some emergency had called her. But she would not have done so without telling someone. Dillon made his way back to Liam's hall from the hillock where he had gone to watch the sunrise with Lara.

Entering through the kitchen door he bid the servants a good morning, and smiling took the thick slice of freshly baked bread the cook offered him. After a time, Noss came into the kitchens, Mildri in a woven sling about her mother's body.

Noss sat down wearily. "Good morning," she said.

Dillon smiled at his foster mother. "Has Mildri not yet fathomed the difference between night and day, dear Noss?" He touched the baby's reddish head with a gentle finger. "She is such a pretty thing. She will be a great beauty one day and will bring a good bride price to you and Liam."

Noss smiled weakly. "She is also very stubborn," she said. "The boys were so easy compared to this longed-for daughter of mine."

"I cannot find my mother," Dillon replied casually. *Please,* he thought silently, *let Noss say she knows where my mother is. Please let it have been only a strange dream.*

"Did she not go out to watch the sunrise as always?" Noss responded.

"She was gone when I awoke and she was not on the hill when I got there. I have not seen her since we went to bed last night. *Well, that wasn't entirely true, but he couldn't believe what he had seen was real.*

"Oh, she is about somewhere," Noss answered him. "Perhaps she took Dasras and went to visit Rendor."

"But she never said anything," Dillon persisted. "She would have told us if she was going off somewhere."

"Then she hasn't gone off," Noss told him, then turned her attention to Mildri who was now whimpering and demanding to nurse.

Dillon got up and left the kitchens. He headed out into the meadow where he knew Dasras would be with his mate, Sakira, and their foal, Feroz. Reaching the greensward he immediately saw his mother's stallion and went to him. Politely, for manners were most important to horses, he bid Dasras and his family a good morning. Then he told the great stallion that his mother was gone and he could not find her.

"Climb on my back, young Dillon," Dasras told him. "We will search together."

Dillon grabbed a handful of the golden horse's cream-colored mane and swung himself up on the animal's back. Together the two set off to explore the surrounding land. There was no need for Dasras to spread his great white wings, for on foot Lara could not have gotten very far. But when after a time no trace of her could be found, Dasras did indeed take wing. Yet even from above they could not find her. They searched for hours.

I should tell Liam and Noss what I saw, Dillon thought. *But despite their long association with my mother they will be inclined not to believe me. They will say again that I am a fanciful boy. I need to speak with Prince Kaliq.* Dillon sighed.

"What is it?" Dasras asked.

"Nothing," Dillon replied. "I am just disturbed that we cannot find Mother."

"Something is amiss," Dasras said. "Last night in the meadows the other horses were all unnaturally restless for a brief while."

"I think we should go for the Dominus," Dillon answered him.

"Perhaps," Dasras agreed. "But we are guests of the Fiacre and must let them make that decision. Let us return and see if your mother has appeared from wherever she had been."

Back in the meadow, Dasras let Dillon climb down from his back and watched as the boy hurried back toward Liam's hall.

Dillon sought out his foster father and asked if Lara had been found.

"I was not aware she was missing," Liam said, looking startled.

"Did Noss not tell you?" Dillon exclaimed. "I spoke with her early this morning."

"I have only seen Noss in passing today," Liam admitted. "We are getting ready for the Gathering and there is much to do before we make the trek. I could have used your help today, Dillon."

"Dasras and I have been searching all day for Mother," Dillon defended himself.

Noss came into the hall and Liam called to her, "Where is Lara?"

Seeing Dillon with her husband, Noss flushed. Then she said, "I have not seen her today. I have been so busy with Mildri. Did you not find her, Dillon?"

"Dasras and I rode for miles around. We even went skyward but we can find no trace of her. I think I should take Dasras and ride to the Dominus's castle to inform him that Mother is missing, Liam. The night sky will be bright enough, and if I go now I can be halfway there before sunset," Dillon said.

"There is no need to worry your stepfather," Noss said sharply. "She might even have gone to the castle on some mission or another. I am certain there is a reasonable explanation for your mother's disappearance. She doesn't need Dasras to travel. She may have gone to your grandmother in the forest or to the Shadow Princes. Your mother does not answer to anyone, Dillon."

"If she had planned to go anywhere she would have told

someone," Dillon said stubbornly. He had to tell them. "I had an odd dream last night and now I fear it may not have been a dream."

"This is no time for one of your magical tales, Dillon," Noss said impatiently.

"But what if it wasn't a dream?" Dillon persisted.

Both Noss and Liam glared at him and Liam said, "Enough, lad!"

Dillon swallowed back his anger. *Mortals!* he thought furiously. "What about my mother?" he demanded of them. "I have not seen her since last night and neither has anyone else. You have to admit it is strange for her to go off and not tell anyone."

"It is odd," Noss admitted. "But she could have."

"If she has not returned by tomorrow," Liam said, "we will mount a search for her, Dillon, but I am certain this is just a misunderstanding. Besides, Lara has always been protected by her magic and by Ethne."

Something is wrong, Dillon thought to himself. *I feel it. I sense it. Something is not right about this. My mother is nowhere near. I would know it if she were. Do I not always know when she is approaching? But they will not listen to me. They do not understand. In blood I am more mortal than faerie, but my senses are all magical.* "Very well," Dillon agreed reluctantly.

But by the following day, Lara was nowhere to be found, nor had anyone in the village seen her. Over Dillon's objections that he and Dasras had searched thoroughly the previous day, Liam nonetheless mounted a great search that spread out for miles about the village yet at day's end no trace of Lara could be found at all.

The men of Camdene met in their lord's hall that night to discuss the matter. Now even they were becoming worried. It was not like Lara to disappear and not let someone know. Noss, the serving women and Anoush served the men seated at the trestle tables below the high board. Even little Zagiri toddled about offering the men fresh fruit. And then Dillon saw something glitter from beneath the high neckline of his older sister's gown. He caught Anoush by the arm.

"What are you wearing about your neck?" he asked her sharply.

"Just an amulet," she replied.

"Show me!" he demanded.

"It is just an amulet," she protested.

Dillon's hand moved swiftly to his sister's neck and he tore the gold chain from it. "Where in the name of the Great Creator did you get this?" he shouted. "It is Mother's star! The one that holds Ethne. Where did you get this?"

Anoush began to cry. "When I woke up yesterday I found it in Mother's bed," she sobbed. "I have always wanted one like it and she was not wearing it. Give it back!"

Dillon held the chain with its perfect crystal star high for all to see. "Have any of you ever known my mother not to have this about her neck?" he shouted. "I told you yesterday that something was wrong but you would not listen to me! My mother has surely been stolen away! I must fetch Magnus Hauk!" And still carrying Lara's chain and star, Dillon ran from Liam's hall out into the evening.

He ran through the village and into the meadow where he called to Dasras. Quickly he explained all that had happened. Then swinging himself onto the great stallion's back, he said, "Please, Dasras, take me to the Dominus!"

Dasras galloped across the field, his great wings suddenly unfurling and flapping as he rose up into the night sky. The miles beneath dissolved as they flew. The moons of Hetar began to rise one by one as they traveled. After several hours they reached the castle of the Dominus of Terah. Dasras put them down in the middle of the stable yard. It was almost dawn in Terah and Jason, Dasras's personal groom, came stumbling sleepily from the stables.

"My lord Dasras, I was not expecting you," he told the stallion.

"Nor was I expecting to be here today," Dasras replied. "This is the Domina's son. Show him the way to the Dominus's apartments and then return to me."

"At once, my lord," Jason replied. "Come, young master, and I will take you to your stepfather. Is this your first visit to the castle?"

"It is," Dillon replied as he followed the older boy into the castle, then down several corridors and up two flights of stairs.

As they passed each of the guardsmen in the hallways, Jason stopped a moment to say, "This is the Domina's son come from the New Outlands with an important message for his stepfather," and the guardsmen would pass them through.

Finally they reached the apartments of the Dominus and Jason repeated his message to the guardsmen, one of whom asked them to wait while the Dominus was awakened. But Magnus Hauk was already awake. He had not slept well for the past three nights.

"Dillon, what is it?" he asked as he came to the door and ushered his stepson into his dayroom. "Thank you, Jason," he called as he shut the door behind them. "What has happened? Is your mother all right? I have been restless the past few nights."

"My mother has gone missing, my lord," Dillon said quietly. Seeing the look of concern in his stepfather's eyes Dillon liked him better than he ever had.

"What do you mean *gone missing?*" he asked in a tight voice. He was suddenly terrified at the thought he might lose Lara, but he couldn't let the boy know that. Dillon had obviously come to him for help and for reassurance.

"We had been out on the hillside—Mother, Anoush and me—watching the Night of the Flying Stars. Zagiri is too little to stay up so late," he explained lest his stepfather think they were unfairly excluding his daughter. "We returned and went to bed, but when I awoke in the morning, Mother was gone. At first I was not concerned, for more often than not she arises early to watch the sunrise. But she was not outside and no one had seen her that morning. Dasras and I searched for several hours, but we could not find her. I wanted to come to you that night, but Liam insisted upon wasting another day searching with all the men of Camdene. Then last night in the hall I discovered Anoush wearing Mother's star and chain. She said she found it in Mother's bed. I have never known Mother not to wear that star, my lord, have you?" He drew it from his pocket and held it out to Magnus Hauk.

"Nay, I have not," the Dominus said. His chest felt suddenly tight.

"My lord," Dillon started to continue, but Magnus Hauk held up his hand.

"We have discussed this before," he said quietly. "When we are in private you are to address me by my given name. I am your stepfather, but I know you cannot call me Father, for you knew

Vartan. Still, 'my lord' seems so formal and your mother had written me that you and Anoush would be coming to live with us after the Gathering. Now, Dillon, my stepson, continue." He put a comforting arm about the boy.

"My lord stepfather, there is magic here. I know there is. You must come to the New Outlands and you must call for Prince Kaliq to come, as well. My mother is gone, I know it. I feel it! Further searching will not find her there."

Magnus Hauk knew that Dillon favored his mother for she had often enough marveled that he did. "What do you know?" he asked his stepson.

"I can only speak before Prince Kaliq," Dillon replied. "I tried to tell Liam and the others but they would not listen to me. They do not understand!"

Magnus Hauk nodded. "No," he said quietly. "They would not." He did not argue with Dillon. Instead he called out in a firm voice, "Kaliq of the Shadows, I need your aid. Please come to me."

And then suddenly Prince Kaliq stepped from a hazy corner of the chamber. He bowed to the Dominus; an eyebrow raised curiously as he saw Dillon. "How may I help you, Magnus Hauk?" he asked. "Good morning, Dillon."

"Lara has disappeared from the New Outlands," Magnus Hauk said without any preamble. He then quickly explained what Dillon had told him. "There is more, but Dillon will only speak of it to you."

"Let us sit down," the Shadow Prince said. "I can feel your fear, your concern and your exhaustion, Dillon. Sit by me and tell me what you could not tell the others."

The three sat together upon a silken couch that had been placed before a large hearth. The prince raised a hand and snapped his fingers; a fire sprang up in the fireplace, crackling and snapping, its warmth spreading out to touch the boy's thin, chilled frame. Almost immediately, a goblet appeared in the prince's hand and he offered it to Dillon who sipped thirstily. "Now, tell me," Kaliq said gently.

Dillon explained how they had watched the flying stars and then gone to bed. "I awoke because I thought I heard a noise," he said. "I opened my eyes and saw filmy creatures hovering over mother. They were almost silent but for the tiniest of murmurs. My hearing is very acute. I am able to hear the beetles in the grass and the rabbits in the field," he explained shyly.

"Did they have faces or hands?" Kaliq asked the boy. A small smile played about the corners of Kaliq's mouth. What powers Dillon exhibited and he was yet untrained. *One day,* the Shadow Prince thought, *he will be a great sorcerer.*

"I didn't dare look too closely for I was very afraid," Dillon admitted. "I thought I might be dreaming, although something within me knew I wasn't. Aye, they did have faces. Long, somber visages. And thin hands with long slender fingers that they waved over Mother as they floated over her. And then, my lord Kaliq, they were gone. Evaporated into the air, it would appear.

"I stared hard, for I was not even sure I had seen what my eyes were so certain they had seen," Dillon said. "And then as I watched over my mother lest they return—and had they, I would have tried to repel them—my mother seemed to disappear into the very darkness that encompassed our bedchamber.

I got up immediately and went to her bed. It was yet warm with the heat of her body, but she was gone." He sighed. "I went back to bed, sure I was in a dreamlike state, but when I awoke in the morning she truly was gone. Dasras and I searched for her the day long. We could not find her. The Fiacre searched for her the following day. That second night I saw Anoush wearing Mother's crystal star! Mother is never without Ethne. Anoush said she found it in the tangled coverlet of Mother's bed. I realized then my dream had not been a dream, but when I tried to explain to Liam and the others they would not listen to me. So Dasras and I came to Terah."

"You were wise to call me," Kaliq said to Magnus Hauk.

"It was Dillon who asked me to do so. My mind seems not to be functioning," the Dominus replied. "Who has taken her, Kaliq? And why have they taken her?"

"This is a mystery even to me," the Shadow Prince replied. "I must speak with my brothers. After we have conferred I will return to you." But he knew the creatures Dillon had seen were the Munin, although he did not say it.

"I must go to the New Outlands and reassure the clan families that I do not hold them responsible for my wife's disappearance. And then I will return with Dillon, Anoush and Zagiri. I suspect the children are safer here in my castle than anywhere else."

The Shadow Prince nodded. "Aye. I know for a fact that Lara placed a spell I taught her about the castle to repel evil and the darkness. Her children will be very safe with you. Wherever she is, I know that would please her."

"Thank you, Kaliq, for your reassurances," the Dominus said.

"Farewell, my lord. I will find you in the New Outlands. Go to the Gathering, for it will comfort the clan families. Together we will get to the bottom of this mystery." Then the Shadow Prince disappeared into the umbra as easily as he had come from it.

"I cannot wait to study with him," Dillon said admiringly.

"And you will one day," the Dominus assured his stepson. "Has your mother not promised you that you would?"

"Will we find her, Magnus?" the boy asked.

"We will find her," the Dominus assured his companion. "Now I think you must get some rest. If Dasras is up to it we will travel to the New Outlands later today. Come and sleep in my bed, lad. You look fair worn with your worry of these past few days."

"If only they had listened to me," Dillon said sadly.

"Even had they believed you, they could have done nothing. This business is magic and we will need magic to undo it. The Fiacre have no magic, Dillon. You did the right thing. You came to me and we called the Shadow Prince. He and your faerie grandmother will help us." He helped the boy into his big bed and tucked a coverlet about him. "I will call you in a few hours," he promised and then left Dillon to sleep.

Sitting back before the fire that Kaliq had started, Magnus Hauk stared into it. *Where are you, my love, my beloved?* he cried silently. But silence was his only answer. That she had left Ethne behind—or whoever stolen her had—was not a good omen. There was something wicked brewing. He had lived long enough with Lara to sense it.

He needed to speak with his brother-in-law, Corrado, who commanded Terah's fleet. His vessel had just returned last night from a trading voyage. Corrado would have to manage Terah while he was in the New Outlands because the Great Creator only knew how long he would be away. Corrado and his wife, Sirvat, would have to move into the castle to look after the children while he was gone.

And there was the ambassador from Hetar to consider. Jonah had returned to Hetar with Lara away. There was no one who would tell him where she was, for Hetar had no idea that Lara and the Shadow Princes had removed the clan families from the Outlands and brought them to safety in Terah. If he were here now he would be sniffing about for gossip and information as he always was.

The Dominus almost felt sorry for Jonah. He was an intelligent man but he was every bit as evil as his master, Gaius Prospero. And Magnus Hauk knew he was in Terah for the sole purpose of finding a weakness in Terah that he might exploit to his own benefit or Hetar's. Now and again he returned to The City to report to his master on the nothing he had been able to learn. And Lara had laughed, knowing how frustrating that must be to Gaius Prospero. It was better he was gone now, the Dominus thought.

The day went quickly and was coming to a close when Magnus Hauk woke his stepson. They ate a hearty meal and then, as Dasras had agreed he was up to returning to the New Outlands, they departed the castle. They reached New Camdene while it was yet night there and Liam, who had been awaiting them, came from his hall to meet them.

Kneeling before the Dominus he begged his forgiveness for Lara's disappearance.

"It is not the fault of the Fiacre that my wife is gone," Magnus Hauk said loudly, for all of New Camdene's population were gathered around them despite the early hour. "This is dark and wicked magic. You could not have prevented what happened. I have spoken with Prince Kaliq and he will join us shortly. In the meantime, keep to your preparations for the Gathering. I will travel there with you."

Liam arose and kissed the Dominus's hands. "Thank you, my lord. Your words of reassurance are soothing to us. Now come into my hall and refresh yourself after your long ride. The new day will soon begin."

"See to Dasras," the Dominus murmured to his stepson, ruffling his hair.

In the hall, Magnus Hauk greeted Noss and admired Mildri. He sat with them before their fire, and told them that before the trek for the Gathering began he would be sending the children back to his castle. "Lara has a spell about it to protect it and its inhabitants. My sister will be there to see the children's lives continue on uninterrupted. I am waiting for Kaliq, for he can transport them quickly. I may need Dasras."

"You said dark magic," Noss half whispered.

"Naught else could have taken Lara. Kaliq will explain it all to you when he arrives. Until then we must carry on as usual."

"Papa! Papa!" Zagiri came running and climbed into his lap. "Mama is gone."

The Dominus kissed his little daughter and then, reaching out, drew Anoush, who had been standing nearby, into the curve of his arm. "And how are my two girls?" he asked them.

"Zagiri, you are as brown as a little nut! And Anoush, oh my, how lovely you are growing. Come and give me a kiss, too."

Anoush bent and kissed his cheek. "I am so afraid, stepfather," she said, shivers racking her slender little body.

Magnus Hauk drew his stepdaughter into his lap with her sister. "I am, too, Anoush," he told the girl. "But we will find your mother, I promise you. We will find her, and we will bring her home to us."

Anoush lay her head on his shoulder. "May I call you Papa, too?" she asked him shyly and softly.

The Dominus of Terah could feel a prickle behind his eyelids and he blinked hard. "It would please me so much if you did," he said as he placed a kiss on her brow. "But only if you want to, Anoush."

"I have never had a father," Anoush told him. "Vartan sired me but he was gone before I might remember him. I have always wanted a father."

"Then you shall have one in me, my daughter," the Dominus told her. "And I know your mother would be happy with your decision."

"I do not do it for my mother," Anoush replied. "I do it for me."

Magnus Hauk chuckled. "Has the Great Creator given me two headstrong daughters to raise?" he demanded to know in pained tones.

"I am much better at minding than Zagiri," Anoush said primly.

"I am relieved to learn it," the Dominus said.

"Will you find our mother, Papa?" Anoush asked him again.

"I will find her, I promise you, my daughters. And I have never broken a promise," Magnus Hauk told them. "I will find Lara. And I will bring her safely home."

SHE AWOKE, her green eyes scanning her surroundings. She lay in a huge bed of furs in a dim chamber. There was a great hearth opposite which burned high.

She was naked, and as she turned her head, her gaze met the dark silvery one of a naked man next to her. *Where was she?* She wondered. And then a sudden terrible fear gripped her, almost paralyzing her. *Who was she? She did not know who she was!* she struggled desperately to think—to remember—but for the life of her she couldn't. A small cry of panic escaped her and she sat up, clutching the furs to her breasts.

The man sat up, too. "Ah, my precious Lara," he said to her in a deep, musical and very soothing voice. "What is it? Have the pains returned?" He caught her hand in his and kissed it lingeringly.

"I...I...I don't know who I am or where I am," she half sobbed.

"You are Lara, my mate. I am Kol, the Twilight Lord. You have been very ill for many weeks, my precious. You are only just now beginning to recover."

"But why can I remember nothing of it?" she asked him.

"The physician said that your memory could be temporarily lost, for you burned with a deadly fever for many days. He has assured me that it will return. Slowly, my precious, but it will return." Kol wrapped his arms about her, holding her close.

The warmth of his body pressed against hers was comforting. Lara let her head fall against his shoulder. "You will not leave me?" she asked him.

"Nay, my precious, I will not leave you," he promised her. "I have not in all these weeks. I have remained by your side, and governed from this room. Alfrigg has not been pleased with me at all, I fear," Kol told her.

"Alfrigg?"

"My chancellor, sweeting. But he has of course prayed to Krell for your recovery. Everyone in the Dark Land has, Lara. You are my mate, and it has been foretold that you will be the mother of the next Twilight Lord."

"Who is Krell?" she asked him.

"Why, our deity, my precious. Krell, Lord of Darkness," he explained. Then he pressed her back upon her pillows and pulled down the furs covering her bosom. His eyes admired her breasts and leaning down, he kissed each nipple.

Lara shivered slightly.

"Ah," Kol chuckled. "I think you may have a small memory of pleasures," he teased and was rewarded by her blush. "I am relieved, for the mating lust has been upon me for several days now and I long to sink my rod into your sweetness." Bending again, he now began to lick at her nipples, finally taking one into his mouth and sucking on it with strong tugs of his lips. Her little

cries of obvious appreciation encouraged him onward. His rod
began to throb and swell.

Lara felt a corresponding tingle in her nether regions, and
made a small murmuring sound of satisfaction. "Oh yes, my lord!
Oh yes, that is nice." She wasn't quite so frightened now. This was
something she seemed to understand. *Pleasures. Yes, she knew
pleasures. She liked pleasures.* Her fingers threaded themselves
through his ebony hair, then slid down to caress the nape of his
neck.

Kol fought back the mating lust that demanded he impale her
immediately with his burgeoning rod. Instead, he began to
explore the beautiful body he had desired for over a year now.
The flesh of her breasts was firm despite her three children. Her
belly was a soft delicate mound that he covered first with kisses
and then tasted with his tongue. Her thighs fell open to him with
the barest encouragement. He stroked the inside of the tender
flesh.

She pulled her nether lips apart for him and he played with
the tiny lust orb that swelled with his attentions. He rose and
kissed her mouth, his tongue twining itself about hers as he
pushed a single long finger into her. She moaned against his lips
for more and he complied, adding a second finger and finally a
third. She was tight and hot and her juices ran down his hand.
Withdrawing his fingers he looked down into her glittering eyes
and then sucked upon his wet digits.

Her tongue ran quickly about her lips and she smiled up at
him. "I remember pleasures, my lord," she admitted softly.

"Good," he replied, his own eyes blazing. Then he mounted

her and pressed his rod forward until he was totally sheathed within her body. He rested there a moment, letting her feel the throbbing as his rod increased its girth. He let her enjoy his as she had enjoyed other rods. But there were certain features of his rod only possessed by a Twilight Lord; he would later introduce to her to them. Not tonight. Tonight would be about tenderness and sweet lust.

Lara wrapped her legs about Kol so he might delve deeper into her body. Had she ever enjoyed a rod so thick? She didn't think so but her mind was still very hazy. And when he began to move upon her, his rod flashing back and forth within her, Lara lost herself in the fiery pleasures he engendered within her body. She let herself soar and reveled as the stars exploded behind her closed eyes. And then when she could climb no higher and his rod burst forth its juices, Lara screamed with her satisfaction, a sound overpowered by his leonine roar of exultation. She lost consciousness briefly. When she came to herself again her sex was being tenderly bathed by tiny winged elfin-like creatures, as was his.

"Have they been here all along?" she asked Kol.

He nodded. "They are Lustlings. It is their duty to refresh us in the afterwards," he explained. "You have never minded before, my precious."

"I do not recall them, my lord," Lara answered him.

"You enjoyed pleasures? You always did previously," he told her.

She smiled at him. "I think I am hungry for food and then I would take pleasures with you again, my lord, if you would take them with me. I feel safe then, and knowledgeable, which I do not otherwise as my memory is impaired."

"Your memories will eventually return, my precious," he promised her. Then drawing the furs back over her, he clapped his hands and servants began entering the room with bowls and platters of food. "I will feed you but a little, Lara," he advised her. "You have not had solid food in many weeks. Open your mouth now for me," and when she did he gave her two raw oysters before swallowing down a goodly dozen himself. He fed her a bit of poultry, allowed her a bite or two of buttered bread. He dangled asparagus over her open mouth; he groaned as she sucked the stalks. Finally he offered her several plump strawberries he first dipped in cream and then rolled in sugar. As he fed her he told her what each item was. Holding a goblet of something sweet to her lips for her to drink he said that it was frine, a mixture of fruit juice and wine. What he did not tell her was that aphrodisiacs had been mixed into the frine to increase her own natural desires. He suspected she didn't need it but still he gave it to her.

"Tell me a little about myself," Lara said. "Where did I come from and how was I chosen to be your mate, my lord Kol?"

"You come from a faraway land called Hetar," he explained to her. "When I visited it last year I went to a bride fair to see the maidens offered and you were among them. Because you were so beautiful your father was asking a very high price even though you are of peasant stock. It was prophesied that the mother of the next Twilight Lord would be a golden girl from a faraway land. The moment I saw you I knew you were she. So I paid your father's price and brought you home. We were very happy, and then you were bitten by a rather nasty spider and fell into a swoon and have been ill ever since."

"What is a spider?" Lara asked him.

"An insect, a lower species among the Dark Kingdom," he said. He could tell she was trying to piece it all together. Spider. Insect. Low species. He would have to consider restoring some of her memory sooner than later, he suddenly realized. "But not to worry, my precious. I have banned all spiders from the castle."

"Castle?"

"Here. Where we are now," he replied. Yes, some of her memory had to be returned so her references to everyday things would again be intact. He would speak to the Munin in the morning—after he had sated himself with pleasures.

The remnants of their meal were now removed and they began to kiss again, tasting each other with eager lips. His hands wandered over her body, learning it, and her little hands followed suit slipping down his long back to fondle his tight buttocks. She bent her golden head and licked at his nipples. Her little fingers marched across the dark hair covering his chest as she bent lower to kiss his navel.

"You are very furred on your chest and legs," she murmured.

"You are not," he replied.

She giggled, her hands now reaching out to play with his rod and his male orbs. She was gentle but provocative, her fingers teasing, stroking. She bent her head and then her tongue licked about the head of his rod several times. He was afire with his new need for her. He wanted to give her all of him, but would she be ready this first time they were together?

"Careful, my precious," he warned her. "If you suck upon my rod you will arouse its twin. We had not done that before your illness."

"You have two rods?" she asked him, surprised.

"The larger one, the dominant it is called, has a lesser member. When I am at my most lustful it appears. And it must be used along with the dominant when I seed you. The dominant will then also sprout hard sharp little nodules that will but increase your pleasure and guarantee a child for us. The nodules only appear when it is time for me to impregnate you. But my precious, you must regain your strength first."

"Have I ever been pierced by two rods belonging to the same man?" she said slowly. Her brow furrowed in thought. "Was I a virgin when you made me your mate?" she asked him.

"It was not necessary that you be," he said.

Somewhere in the haziness of her lost memories Lara thought she recalled being probed by several male members at the same time, but where and with whom was not something she could remember. Surely she had never known a man who had two rods within one sheath. Her fingers absently stroked him and he thickened beneath her sensuous touch. "I want to see them both, my lord," she whispered provocatively in his ear. Then she licked the curl of flesh. "Show me!"

"Suckle my rod, Lara, and your mouth will help to bring the lesser forth with the dominant," he instructed her. Then he drew in a sharp, almost painful breath as her lips surrounded his flesh and she began to draw upon him. His eyes closed with the bliss she was beginning to engender in his sex. Never in his wildest imaginings had he suspected that Lara would be as adventurous and magnificent a lover as she was proving. It was her faerie blood, of course, but if she treated her mortal lovers with such skill it was no wonder they had all adored her.

Lara could scarcely contain her excitement as she tugged on the swelling flesh, and when he cried for her to stop she ceased immediately, sat back on her haunches and marveled at his size. Then—before her amazed eyes—the lesser rod began to come forward, sliding from beneath the dominant. It was much longer, and slender, with a pointed tip like an arrowhead. Reaching out to touch, she discovered it was as hard as the dominant rod. Her tongue licked quickly around her lips. "I want it inside of me," she heard herself say. "I want them both!"

"You are yet fragile," he pretended to protest. He, too, wanted both of his rods within her heated body.

"Nay! I must have them!" she cried out and meant the words.

"It will require you be put in a difficult position, but we can use the restraints if you will permit it, my precious," Kol said softly.

"Yes!" Her cheeks were flushed and he could see the pulse in her throat beating wildly with anticipation. The lesser rod was iridescent in color with a silver sheen and its arrowhead glowed. She could hardly wait to have her first taste of it.

The Twilight Lord clapped his hands once and two thin silver chains dropped from the ceiling. At the end of each chain was a silver manacle lined in silk and lamb's wool. He fastened the manacles about her delicate ankles and once she was secure her legs were drawn up, back toward her shoulders, and pulled wide revealing both her orifices. Kol clapped his hands a second time and two more restraints appeared. These he fastened to her outspread arms. Lara was now completely subdued and helpless before her lover. He kissed her mouth, smiling down at her as he did so. "Now, my precious, I will obey your directive and you will know what it is like to have two rods within your delicious body."

She could barely breathe as he moved forward, and then she felt the lesser rod, much longer than the dominant, pierce her rose hole. She squeaked with surprise for the head of it was sharp but then it seemed to fold itself as it pushed into her rear channel. And when he had pushed it in as far as it would go he let her sense its power. "Oh, Krell!" she gasped and he was amused to hear her call upon his deity.

Now he thrust with the dominant rod, entering her woman's channel in a single smooth motion. Establishing a slow and sensuous rhythm that grew quicker as he pistoned her, he watched Lara's face as her lust, now fully engaged, rose to a peak. She struggled against the arm restraints. Laughing, he leaned forward and began to suck upon one of her nipples.

She began to moan as wave after wave of passion overtook her. It was utterly amazing. His dominant rod drove in and out of her. The lesser rod lay buried within her rear channel throbbing hotly. Then suddenly both rods were moving in unison and they touched one tiny spot within her body. Lara screamed as her lust threatened to overwhelm her. "No more! No more!" she begged him.

"You wanted this, my precious, and now until both rods have been fully satisfied you must give of yourself to me," he growled fiercely, his lust for her enormous.

She tightened her inner muscles about both rods and he groaned. "Witch!" Then before he had thought he would be ready his juices mushroomed forth in a fierce burst leaving them both in an exhausted and weakened state. And the Lustlings fluttered forth to undo the chains binding Lara before bathing the sex of their master and his mate.

He lay half atop her and Lara wrapped her arms about him. "I remember virtually nothing before today, my lord Kol, but I do know that you are a magnificent lover. I am fortunate that you chose me as your mate." Then she fell asleep again.

Kol's head lay between her breasts and he could hear her beating heart. She was incredible, his beautiful faerie woman. He would never let her go. No other man would ever possess Lara again. She was his and his alone. How had he lived without her?

He allowed himself the luxury of sleep in her bed for a short while, and then he arose and went to his own apartments. There he found Alfrigg awaiting him.

"Have you seeded her, my lord?" his chancellor wanted to know.

"Not yet."

"You have spent all this time with the woman and have not yet rodded her? My lord, that is not like you."

"She has been well rodded," Kol said, "but I am not yet ready to seed her. She is a pleasurable mount, Alfrigg, and I think after waiting a year I am entitled to take a bit of enjoyment for myself before I fill her belly with my son." Then he told Alfrigg the tale he had woven for Lara. "I will gain her trust more easily if I take my time with her. And I will need to call the Munin lord from the Penumbras. Lara needs practical matters restored to her memory. She is like an infant newborn and I cannot be forever explaining what this is and what that is."

"As long as you keep the memories of her faerie nature, her magic and her past life from her," Alfrigg said.

"She still has her magic," Kol replied. "The Munin could only take her memories of her magic, but they could not take the magic itself. They have not the power and neither do I, which is why I must gain her complete trust, Alfrigg. When I stole her from her bed in the New Outlands, I left behind the spirit guardian her mother gave her when she was a child. She cannot hear its voice here. She can hear only mine."

"My lord," Alfrigg cried, "you should have taken it with you! If anyone should find her amulet then they will know she has been stolen and not simply wandered away or gone off by herself as is her wont."

"It is too late now," Kol replied. He waved a hand at Alfrigg. "Leave me now. I must bathe and then speak with the Munin lord."

Alfrigg bowed but his expression was disapproving and dour as he backed from his master's chamber.

Kol clapped his hands and a servant hurried forward. "Tell the bath master that I am coming," he said. "Then bring me fresh garments. When you see me being dressed, ring the black iron bell in my receiving chamber to summon the Munin lord to me." Kol set off for his bath, his servants scurrying quickly ahead to announce his arrival.

The black marble bath was steamy and scented with sandalwood. It was not necessary for Kol to speak with the servants there. They knew what was required of them and performed their functions thoroughly and silently. He was bathed and massaged with sweet oils. Stepping into a small dressing chamber he found fresh garments and footwear awaiting him. Kol stood as his servants dressed him and then without so much as a word he left them and hurried to his receiving chamber where he found the Munin lord awaiting him.

The wraithlike creature bowed. "How may I serve you, my lord?" he asked.

"I need some of Lara's memories restored to her. She knows nothing and it is like dealing with a child. It was amusing when she woke up earlier but I have no further patience for it. Practical knowledge, everyday information, is what I want returned to her," Kol said. "But nothing of her personal history, her magical abilities or her life prior to awakening in my arms may be returned to her. Do you understand?"

"Perfectly, my lord," the Munin said. He flitted over to the great alabaster jar where Lara's memories were stored. He opened it and peering down into the tall vessel he appeared to rummage within, then he drew long golden threads from its depths with his bony fingers and transferred them to his other hand. "I think these are exactly what you desire, my lord Kol," the Munin said in his reedy voice.

"Follow me then," the Twilight Lord ordered, "and I will take you to her. She should be sleeping for she was well rodded but a short while ago." He led the Munin from the chamber and down a dim corridor to Lara's apartments. He cautiously opened the door to the room where he had left her. She still slept.

The Munin drifted over the sleeping woman and, holding each of the long golden threads over her head, individually let them slip from his fingers and back into her head where they belonged. As he did he surreptitiously admired the faerie woman. She was very beautiful. Though he had enjoyed sifting through her memories the night he and his brothers had stolen them, he found himself feeling just the faintest touch of guilt, which was very unusual. Her memories were powerful ones, for she was a powerful woman. But if the Twilight Lord's Book of Rule had said she would be the mother of his son, then so she would be. It was easier for her that she did not know who or what she was.

"It is done, my lord Kol," the Munin lord whispered.

"Then you may go, with my thanks," Kol said. "You are content with your home?"

"It is perfect, my lord Kol," the Munin lord said, "if perhaps a bit cold."

Kol nodded. And knowing he was dismissed, the Munin lord vanished away.

The Twilight Lord sat down by Lara's bedside. He could not get enough of looking at her. It was amazing to realize she was actually here with him. It was unbelievable to find she possessed the same lust for pleasures that he did. The women in his Women's House were all compliant but none were like Lara. Kol felt his need rising and he arose from her bedside. He didn't want to exhaust her, especially after she had demanded both of his rods. She looked pale as she slept. He would go to the Women's House and use several of the complaisant females who spent their lives just waiting for him. It would ease his longing and Lara would not consider that she had a barbarian for a mate. Reluctantly, he left her.

When Lara awoke her mind was clearer than it had been earlier. She felt just faintly sore. Turning over, she looked for Kol, but he was not there. She felt a slight relief. He was a powerful lover and his two rods were extremely talented, but even being fed a light meal between their passionate bouts was not enough to erase her tiredness. Well, she had been ill for several weeks, Lara considered. Still she was hungry. "Hello?" she called out. Almost immediately two serving women entered the chamber.

"What is your desire, my lady Lara?" the taller of the two asked.

"I want a bath and I want food," Lara told her.

"At once, my lady Lara."

"What are your names?" Lara said.

"The master said your memory was faulty after your terrible sickness. I am Macia and my companion is Anka. While I go to fetch your food she will escort you to your bath. The bath mistress will be glad to see you again, my lady Lara," Macia said with a servile bow and a smile. Then she backed from the room leaving Lara with the other servant.

Anka hurried over to the bed and helped Lara to stand, bracing her as she swayed slightly. "It is not far, my lady Lara," she said. Then she led Lara to a pale gray marble bath chamber. "The bath mistress is called Zenda," she whispered helpfully and Lara smiled her thanks.

Zenda came forward to take over as Lara entered. She spoke little except to tell Lara what she wanted of her. Lara sat silently as the nails on both her feet and fingers were pared and then carefully shaped. She stood in a shallow stone basin as two serving women washed her thoroughly with fragrant scented soap and large sea sponges. Then they rinsed her with perfumed water. As they worked, Lara found she was able to identify certain objects in the bath. With relief she realized some of her memory was returning.

Zenda herself washed Lara's hair, marveling at its golden beauty as she rinsed it with lemon. Next, she had Lara lie upon a marble table and using the softest cloth she gently washed Lara's genitals, pushing the cloth into both of her orifices to draw out any residue of Kol's juices. Lara was surprised, but as her memory was not all restored she assumed this was just something else she had forgotten. Zenda flushed the sensitive apertures with a warm solution of alum.

"You will be tight for him each time," she told Lara in a rare spoken explanation.

Lara was finally led to another table where she was massaged with rose oil. The masseuse rubbed the fragrant oil into every inch of her skin. The nipples on her breasts tingled. The golden curls on her mons were crisp and sweetly scented. A tiny bit of the oil was rubbed into her long hair, which was still damp. As she lay upon the table, a serving woman brushed and brushed and brushed her hair until it was at last dry and faintly aromatic with the perfumed oil. When she arose from the table she was clothed in a pale lavender robe, then Anka was there to lead her back to her chamber. A table had been set up for her with a variety of foods. The table was covered with fine linen and lit with candles. There was a black onyx phallus as a centerpiece upon it.

"Where is my lord Kol?" Lara asked Macia.

"I will find his serving man and ask, my lady Lara," Macia answered and hurried off to seek out the man.

"The lord is in the Women's House," Kol's body servant said when Macia found him. "He does not wish to wear the faerie woman out."

"Fool!" Macia snapped at him. "Mind your tongue! You do not know who is listening and the lord's mate must believe she has been here for over a year. If our master heard you he would flay you alive and you would deserve it. The lady Lara is to mother the next Twilight Lord. It needs be done with her consent, not as the product of a rape. All the servants have been told of this and all have acted accordingly but you. If you let your words betray him again, I will report you."

"You demand such exactness, Macia, but I will be more careful in the future, I swear it," the serving man said. "Do not report me to the master! Like all of us, I live in fear of his anger. His punishments are extremely cruel."

"Have I not said that I shall only do so if I catch you at it again?" Macia replied.

Returning to Lara, the serving woman reported, "The lord is speaking with some of his other good servants at this time. He bids you eat, for he may be late or not come until tomorrow. Would you like me to send a message to him that you wish him to be with you now?" She smiled pleasantly and her voice was friendly.

"Nay," Lara replied. "I will await his pleasure." She began to serve herself from the bounteous repast that had been brought to her. She was hungry and the variety of dishes offered was generous. Lara realized as she ate that she knew and understood things she had not upon awakening. She only wished all of her memory had returned. Well, it was just her first day back among the living. When she had finished her meal she arose and walked to the open colonnade that overlooked the mountains. The sky above her was dark but between the mountains she could see a sunset of bloodred, purple and gold clouds. Thunder rumbled faintly behind those clouds. It all had a strange beauty but it was also a bit frightening.

Why couldn't she remember Kol or much of anything else before she awoke in his bed earlier? Still, she had been anxious, nay eager, to taste pleasures with him. If somewhere in her deepest heart and mind he had been a stranger, an enemy, would she have been that impatient, that ardent? The mere act of thinking seemed to hurt her head. And then Lara sensed him enter the chamber. She did not turn about but remained still and quiet where she was. Coming up behind her he touched her robe, which dissolved away. His hands reached about her to cup her breasts in his palms.

"How did you do *that?*" Lara wanted to know. His hands were cool.

He laughed softly. "I do not wish to imagine your beautiful body. I wish to see it and be able to avail myself of it whenever I so desire. What fun is being a great lord if I cannot always have my own way, my precious?" He squeezed her breasts lightly and began to tease her nipples with the balls of his thumbs.

Lara murmured from deep in her throat and leaned back against him. He was naked, too. She rotated her bottom against his groin, feeling his rod already hard and eager for her. "I have been well fed by your servants," she said. His rod was very, very long and she did not believe she had ever known a larger one. It rubbed itself against the crease separating her buttocks.

Kol felt the lust rising again and he moved her quickly to a roll-armed couch upon the open colonnade. His hands left her delicious breasts as he bent her back over the silken arm of the furniture. His fingers foraged between her thighs and he smiled to find her already wet for him. He pushed three fingers deep within her and began to move them teasingly about. "Ohh, such a hot and precious little mate I have," he crooned at her. "Oh, how she likes having my fingers inside her tight and burning sheath. I am glad you are recovering so quickly now, Lara. Soon we must create my heir. You will be my good girl and bear my son, won't you?" His fingers thrust hard and deep.

Lara moaned. "Yes, my lord Kol, I will gladly give you your son," she promised him. "Just don't stop," she pleaded as his fingers pushed in and out of her.

He laughed low and bending forward he grazed her nipples with his teeth. "Not yet, my precious, for I find I will first need to grow tired of rodding you. And I am not ready yet to give up that privilege. The others in my Women's House cannot satisfy my longings. Only you can ease the lusts that overwhelm me."

"You have other women?" she gasped, squirming in his grip.

"While you ate I used up half a dozen of them," he said smiling into her incredible green eyes. "But as you can see my lust is not yet sated, my precious."

"I hate you!" she screamed, and reached out to claw him. "I am your mate! There can be no others, my lord Kol! I will not share you!"

But he caught her wrists with his free hand and pinioned her arms over her head as he held her down with his big body. Laughing into her angry face he told her, "Aye, you are my mate but my appetites are great. I must be able to satisfy them and you will not interfere with me, my precious." Withdrawing his fingers from her sheath he sucked on them thoughtfully. Then he said softly, "Shall I have those women whom I rodded so recently killed for you, my precious?"

"Yes!" she cried. "They shall never boast of having known you. Only I shall have that privilege."

"Ahh, Lara my precious, I knew the Book of Rule was correct when it said you would be my mate and the mother of my son. You have a deep capacity for naughtiness inside you." He turned her over so that she was facedown upon the couch arm and sought her woman's passage. Finding it, he inserted the tip of his rod but a single inch. "Would you like to watch while they are strangled, my precious?" he asked her softly. "One by one by one?" he crooned into her ear.

"Yes!" she gasped. "Oh, please, my lord Kol, rod me. I die for it!"

"You must ask me more politely, my precious," he purred.

"Please, my lord Kol! Please rod me for I long to have you inside of me," Lara cried out. She was burning with her lust for him.

"Shall we kill them first, my precious?" he asked of her.

"No! No! I need your rod!" she half sobbed.

"Nay," he said. "First we will kill my last six lovers, my precious. Then I shall rod you for the rest of the night. You are strong. You can wait." He stood, then pulled her up and when he touched her shoulder she was once more wearing the gown she had worn earlier. "Come," he said.

He led her by the hand from her apartments and across a narrow stone bridge that spanned a deep chasm. On the other side of the bridge was a stone house styled in the same style as the castle. Two giants standing guard at the gates stepped aside to allow them to pass. Once inside they were greeted by another giant. "Ymir, fetch the women I was with earlier and herd them one by one into the execution chamber. Strangle each one in her turn and dispose of the bodies afterwards."

"Yes, my lord," Ymir said and lumbered off.

"Come, we will watch from the secret room," Kol told Lara. He brought her to a small square chamber. Inside was another roll-armed couch facing a stone wall. Kol raised his hand and snapped his fingers; the stone immediately became glass and they were able to view the execution chamber just below. "Now, my precious, we can watch it all," he murmured softly in her ear as he bent her forward pushing the gown up to bare her legs and buttocks. Lifting his own robe he guided his rod between the twin halves of her bottom, finding her woman's passage and pushing in just enough to open the way for his further voyage when he was ready. "Can you see clearly, my precious?" he asked her solicitously.

"Aye," she whispered, unable to take her eyes from the room before her.

Ymir entered with a young woman who was obviously terrified. She cried out, begging the giant for mercy, but he throttled her with one hand and tossed her body into a corner.

The Twilight Lord pushed a short way into Lara's body. "She always smelled of violets," he remarked.

A second girl entered and was as quickly dispatched as the first.

Kol moved further still into Lara's lust sheath. "She always screams when I give her pleasure," he said. "Do you want me now, my precious?"

"*Yes,*" Lara gasped as a third girl was strangled and Kol drove himself deep inside of her. By the time the sixth girl had been dispatched Lara was gasping with her lust and Kol was thrusting himself hard—again and again and again—until the woman beneath him was moaning. Suddenly they cried out simultaneously as their passions peaked.

Kol quickly withdrew from her as the Lustlings appeared to attend to them. "Do you see how much I adore you, my precious? From this moment on I vow I will have each woman I use strangled in your honor. You are my mate and you shall be the only one to boast of having pleasured me, Lara. Come now, let us return to your bed. My rod has only just whetted its appetite for you and there is still a good long night ahead of us." Taking her hand again he led her from the Women's House. As they crossed the narrow bridge over the chasm they saw Ymir ahead of them carelessly tossing the bodies of the murdered women over the edge into the darkness. He had finished by the time they reached him and stepped aside with a bow to allow them to pass.

Back in their bed he asked, "Did you find it exciting to watch Ymir kill the women, my precious?"

"I am not certain," Lara answered him slowly.

"But did it not add to the piquancy of our passions?" he questioned.

"It was exciting," she admitted, "to watch as the deed was being done and at the same time feel your mighty rod within me while knowing that earlier you had rodded them, as well. But I need not such distractions to enjoy pleasures with you, my lord."

He pushed her back among the many pillows upon the bed, his mouth finding hers and kissing her deeply. His tongue slid within her mouth and she noticed with surprise that his tongue was forked. Still, it entwined itself about her tongue sensuously, caressing, taunting, leaving her breathless with her need for him. Had she ever desired a man like she desired Kol? Her fractured memory would not cooperate and give her the answer. Then she decided that she didn't care. She wanted him. She needed him. And he was hers and the great rod impaling her was all that was necessary to her existence.

The long night lay ahead of them and they used it well. If there was day in the Dark Kingdom, Lara hardly recognized it. Her world was now nothing more than satisfying her various appetites. If it had ever been anything else she could not remember, nor did she care. Her surroundings were beautiful and comfortable. She was well served by Macia and Anka. She had a wardrobe filled with exquisite and rich robes. Each time she arose she bathed and chose carefully from among them with an eye to pleasing Kol. On those few days when she could not take pleasures with him he visited the Women's House, and afterwards those he had enjoyed were killed and thrown into the chasm. Lara watched from her colonnaded porch as Ymir deposited them over the balustrade of the bridge and then she welcomed Kol home with a smile.

The Twilight Lord was almost dizzy with his delight in her. Lara the Good, the gracious and generous faerie woman he had stolen, was fast becoming Lara the Wicked. In freeing her from her history and leaving her with just the barest of memories sufficient to survive, by filling her beautiful golden head with his own thoughts he was slowly, slowly, drawing her into his web of darkness.

When he had first stolen her he had let her sleep beneath his spell for two months. It had been difficult but it was important that she believe the tale he had concocted regarding her past. The Munin lord had advised him rightly that the longer she lay unconscious without her memories the easier it would be to convince her of whatever he told her.

For the past two months he had built up her trust in him as he led her further and further away from all she had ever known. Her appetite for lust was incredible. He had never known any female with such desires and such stamina. He could not get enough of her body, her kisses, her hot tight pleasure sheath that enclosed his eager rod over and over again. She was his. All his.

But now the idyll he had woven was coming to an end. He had to impregnate her for the mating lust was ready to peak and at the very moment that it did he must get a son on her, or he would be forced to wait another five years. All his seed would produce in the meantime would be daughters. And once he had made a son, the mating lust would never again come to him. Alfrigg, however, was chiding him daily for his tardiness.

"You must get your son on her, my lord, or we cannot proceed," he said.

"But once she is with child I cannot touch her until after the child is born," the Twilight Lord complained.

"Have you no other women to ease your lusty rod, my lord?" the chancellor asked dryly. "You have more important things to do."

The Twilight Lord laughed. "Rodding Lara is indescribable, Alfrigg. But then if I were mated to your Eitri I should seek other pursuits."

"In her youth Eitri was considered most handsome for a woman," Alfrigg defended his mate. "But when you are over five hundred years old, the first blush of beauty fades, I fear."

"I know you have my best interests and those of my kingdom at heart, Alfrigg," the Twilight Lord said. "I will impregnate Lara soon, I promise you."

"The darkness she carries within her is impressive, my lord. I have watched as you have drawn it forth from her," Alfrigg replied admiringly.

Kol nodded. "Aye, she will teach my son well," he said. And then he felt the mating lust within him, burning him, demanding of him that he do his duty. Alfrigg was right. As much as he regretted it, *it had to be tonight.* And it would be a night Lara would remember for the rest of her life. There would be pain in this particular mating, but she was more than ready to accept that pain. Kol smiled and licked his lips in anticipation. "Good night, Alfrigg," he said to his chancellor.

The dwarf raised a questioning eyebrow to his master and Kol nodded. Alfrigg smiled. "Good night, my lord. I will pray to Krell for your success tonight." And then the chancellor withdrew, bowing as he went.

The Twilight Lord sat for several minutes watching as a great storm began to roll in from the surrounding mountains, over his castle. This was another sign that his son and heir would be conceived tonight. The lightning crackled and the thunder boomed, but there was no rain. None at all. Kol walked between the columns onto the portico. He leaned against the cold marble balustrade and looked out over his kingdom. Within the mountains there lived a race of fierce giants and another of wily dwarfs; the forests covering the mountains were inhabited by the Wolfyn, a race of creatures who could shift their shape from human to wolf. They all owed him their allegiance. And now he had the Munin secure within the Penumbras. Everything was proceeding as the Book of Rule foretold.

He had captured the faerie woman ordained to be his mate. He had her memories, save those few she needed, safe in the great alabaster jar in his receiving chamber. After two months asleep and another two in his arms, she was his alone. She trusted him and tonight he would cajole her into admitting love for him. Then he would mate her, planting his seed deep in her womb. Lara would give him his son. And when she had he would restore her knowledge of the magic she possessed. She would rule by his side and use her magic to help him take first Hetar and then Terah. All the worlds would be his with her help. Kol smiled. *How good it felt when everything was going well,* he thought.

He turned back into the chamber and called to a servant, who immediately hurried into the room and bowed slavishly.

"How may I serve you, my lord?"

"Go and tell my bath master that I shall come shortly. Then go to the lady Lara's apartments and tell her servants that I shall join my mate tonight. I wish her prepared to receive me when I come."

The servant bowed again and then he said, "My lord, may I be so bold as to ask a question? I have not the right but we are so anxious for your happiness, my lord."

Kol nodded. His mood was good.

"My lord…is tonight…" he hesitated, looking nervous.

Kol smiled broadly. He knew what the man was asking. "Aye, it is," he said. "Now go and do as I have bid you."

The servant scuttled out, then hurried to the bath master. "The lord is coming shortly for his ablutions. He has said that it will be tonight!"

The bath master nodded and began shouting orders to the other slaves in his charge. "You are certain?" he demanded of the serving man.

"He said it!" came the reply. Then the servant ran from the baths and hurried to Lara's apartments. He knocked and was admitted by Macia. "Prepare your mistress," the servant said. "The master will come. He has said tonight is the night your mistress will be seeded."

"Indeed," Macia replied. "And how came you by this intimate knowledge?"

"His mood was good, so I dared to ask," the serving man replied. "He said aye."

"About time," Macia said. "Well, go along now. You have delivered your message. The rest is up to them." She shut the door on the serving man and called to Anka. When her companion came Macia told her what the servant had said.

"She is just waking," Anka replied.

"Then let us feed her and then she must go to the baths before she is ready for him," Macia said. She went into Lara's beautiful bedchamber and bowed. "The lord has sent word that tonight is to be a special night for you, my lady," she told Lara. "You must be fed and then bathed. He will come soon."

They brought her raw oysters and juicy capon, asparagus, and berries in sweet cream. Lara's appetite was a good one; she ate it all. Then they led her to her bath where the bath mistress, already alerted as to the importance of this particular night, was relentless in seeing that her mistress was brought to her full beauty. Lara's long golden hair was washed, perfumed and dried, then some of it was braided with bits of glittering silver thread. Finally a gossamer silk gown in deepest midnight-black was dropped over her head. The contrast of the dark silk against her golden hair and pale skin was meant to entice Kol all the more. Then they led her back to her chamber to await him.

And when he came to her, a length of black silk wrapped around his loins, his pale skin glistening with a light coat of oil, her heart began to hammer with excitement. His eyes were a silver-gray tonight. His short ebony hair smelled faintly of sandalwood. Lara reached up and took his handsome face between her two small hands, smiling into his eyes. Then standing on her toes she kissed his mouth sweetly.

"Do you love me?" he asked her low.

"I love you," she replied. "How could I not when you are so good to me?"

"Will you give me my son, Lara?" he questioned. "Will you willingly accept our mating tonight? It cannot be done unless you wish it, my precious," he told her.

"Oh yes, my lord Kol," she breathed with a sigh. "I will gladly bear you your son. I want to give you a son! I adore you, my dear lord! There is none other but you for me."

"There is pain in creation, my precious," he warned her. "Pain in the seeding, and pain in the birth. But from that pain will come the next Twilight Lord. If you love me enough you will accept the suffering. Do you, my precious?" His gray eyes scanned her small heart-shaped face. *Do you love me enough, Lara?*

"Aye, I do!" she declared. "But tell me one thing, my lord Kol. What is pain?"

She did not remember! Krell! She could not recall pain. He had not considered that. But her loss of the memory of pain would make their mating even better. The shock of it when it first happened. The fear she would feel as it continued would breed up a cruel strong heir for him. Kol took Lara in his arms. "It is naught for you to fret about, my precious," he told her gently and he caressed her hair with his big hands.

She looked up at him with shining eyes. "Then let me be the mother of your son, my lord Kol. Let me give you this gift of my love!"

He bent and kissed her mouth, tenderly at first and then with increasing passion as the final and fiercest mating lust wrapped itself about his body. He touched her gown and it dissolved into a silver mist. He yanked the length of silk from his loins. His rod was enormous tonight—and already hard as iron. It would remain that way for several hours until the final culmination of the mating. "On your knees before me," he ordered her.

Lara obeyed and wrapping her little hand about his rod she kissed its fiery tip. Then she began to lick it from stem to tip until finally she took him in her mouth and sucked upon him, her tongue swirling about the tip while his hands kneaded her head.

"Take more," he growled and then moaned as she took him farther. He could feel himself touching the back of her throat and then she opened her throat even wider, half swallowing him. Kol almost screamed as she did. He was not ready to release his juices. "Enough, witch!" he said in an odd hard voice that she had not before heard.

Lara let her teeth gently graze his rod as she drew it from her mouth. She gave the tip a final lick before he pulled her up. "Something is different tonight," she said softly.

"The creation of an heir is a special moment," he told her. "My rod is stronger than it will ever be again. And from the moment I plant my seed I will not touch you again until after the birth. This will be a great sacrifice for both of us, my precious. But we will have other interests to share, I promise you."

"What else will we share?" She wanted to know.

"I will tell you on the morrow. Tonight is meant for our mating only." And he began to kiss her again, his forked tongue caressing her tongue, exploring her mouth as he had a hundred times before. Then he led her to their bed and laying her back, he kissed her breasts and licked her flesh until she was filled with heated desire. His forked tongue played with her lust orb until she was whimpering for surcease. He pushed his tongue into her sheath, stroking the walls of it, preparing her for what was to come. He could feel the sharp little nodules on his rod beginning to surface from beneath the skin. His own lust was almost out of control now and he knew it was time. He slid his tongue from her sheath and licked the soft insides of her thighs. She lay quietly, her green eyes closed, as she enjoyed his tender homage. Then pulling himself up, Kol slipped between her thighs. Leaning forward he whispered in her ear, "Tell me you want me, my precious."

"Oh yes, please, my lord," she told him, opening her green eyes. "Come into me and let us share the ultimate pleasure of creating a child."

He smiled down at her and then in a single thrust drove himself into her eager body. The look of shock and pain in her eyes only whetted his lust for her. Her scream of distress only caused him to begin a relentless rhythm as his rod moved slowly back and forth within her sheath, the sharp nodules stroking her cruelly.

"It is different! Oh, Krell! It…it…it hurts!" Lara sobbed. The hard rod within her was covered with sharp hot spikes that had not been there before. They burned and rubbed against the tender walls of her sheath causing her pain—yet increasing her lust.

"Wrap your legs about me, Lara!" he commanded her. "I must get deeper!" He stopped his motion briefly to force her reluctant limbs up and about his waist. Then he pushed deeper into her, reveling in her fright and agony.

"My lord! My lord! You must stop, I beg you!" Lara sobbed.

"Do not fight it, my precious," he told her. "Let the pain sweep over you. From this pain will come the creation of my son. Trust me! Now scream for me, Lara!"

Lara screamed fiercely and to her surprise the unbearable pain transformed into an incredible sweetness. "Oh, Krell!" she gasped. She could have sworn he was growing in length within her. As her fear subsided she realized that her own lust was being stoked to a fever pitch. He held her arms above her head now. The eyes looking down at her were black, a tiny flame of crimson burned in the center of each orb. As her own eyes closed, Lara knew he no longer saw her. His whole being was concentrated on the pleasure they were struggling to attain and the child that would come forth from it.

He thrust and he thrust and he thrust. Back and forth. Back and forth. Back and forth. So near! They were so near! She could sense it. Outside of their bedchamber the lightning flashed and flashed again. The thunder roared over and over. And then Lara felt the pain returning, growing in momentum, the heat of it threatening to destroy her. But she would not be destroyed! She would not! At the very moment they reached nirvana together Lara screamed as the fierce heat of his boiling juices containing but a single seed exploded and the miniscule life force buried itself deep into her womb. As it dug itself down and into her she felt more pain. Then the pain vanished. Outside, the storm disappeared and suddenly all was completely silent.

They lay together for a short time as their breathing quieted and the strength returned to their limbs. And then Kol arose from her bed. "It is done," he said, and turning he walked slowly from her bedchamber.

"I love you, my lord," she called after him as the door closed.

And Kol smiled at her words. Yes, she did love him. And faerie women did not give children to those they did not love. Even if they had no memory of it. But she loved him and the seed he had just planted within her was already growing. *His son!* Then he felt a small pang of regret. Her body was no longer his. It belonged to his son. And having tasted her passion, having shared pleasures with her, Kol knew that no other female would ever satisfy his lustful nature again. He would slake his desires on the pretty nubile creatures in his House of Women until after the child was born. And he would continue to please Lara by having each woman he coupled with strangled after he used her. Lara must be happy while she carried new life. She must be content. Whatever she desired he would see she obtained.

And while she carried that new life he would continue to draw the darkness from her. Lara of Hetar, Domina of Terah, savior of the Outland Clan families. Lara the good faerie, mentored by the great Prince Kaliq himself. Good, however, was but one side of the coin, Kol thought with a smile. Everyone had darkness in them. And without her memory of the life she had led before he stole her away, that evil could be cultivated slowly like a beautiful flower. Only once before in her past life had she let the darkness touch her briefly but it meant that the cruelty within her could be fostered, cultured and refined. He would enjoy watching it grow even as the belly nurturing and sheltering his son grew. Reaching his own chamber Kol lay down and slept. His duty for now was done.

KALIQ OF THE SHADOWS looked out over the valley of horses where his herd and the herds of his brother princes stood grazing. "It is done," he said, turning to his beautiful companion. "And neither the clan families or Magnus Hauk suspect."

Ilona, queen of the Forest Faeries, nodded. "What will happen now?" she asked. "I pray her memory does not return to her until it is finished."

"Her memories are safely stored and only the Munin can give them back to her. I will not see that done until the child is well along," Kaliq said. "Then Lara will have her memories and will instinctively know what she must do. Kol is besotted with her, Ilona. It has worked out perfectly." He smiled, well pleased. "And Lara will be safe for the interim."

"They still search for her," Ilona remarked. "The clan families are heartbroken. They cannot be convinced it was not their fault. But Magnus believes that Hetar is responsible for Lara's disappearance. He would go to war. Mortals can be so irrational."

Kaliq chuckled. "They can," he agreed. "But does it not prove to you, my fair Ilona, that the Dominus of Terah loves his wife beyond all reason? He is really the perfect husband for her."

"I wish they had met after this. How will you manage to keep what is happening from him when we regain her? And how will Lara cope with what has happened to her? You know how damnably honest she is. A wicked mortal trait! She will want Magnus to know everything and I do not believe he can live with it. It will destroy them both."

"Ilona, Ilona, you surely know me better than that," Kaliq murmured chidingly. "Trust me, my queen. I would never destroy Lara or any she loved."

Ilona sighed. "Inscrutable as always," she replied. "I don't suppose you will tell me what it is you plan to do, Kaliq."

He smiled again. "Nay, I will not. You complain that mortals are irrational, Ilona, but your faerie race can also act without logic or reason."

"Do not act so superior with me, Kaliq," the queen of the Forest Faeries snapped.

"But I *am* superior to you," he said calmly. "And my kind are far older than your race, as well."

"If it had been my choice——" Ilona began but he stopped her mouth with his hand.

"It was your choice when this task was offered to you, Ilona. You might have refused but you did not. It was your choice to take John Swiftsword as a lover and, between you, create Lara. You knew her destiny. There must always be balance, Ilona, and Lara brings that balance."

"But I did not know I would love my daughter as I do, Kaliq," the queen cried. "I thought being separated from her all those years had drained me of any love I might have harbored. Alas! My cold faerie heart betrayed me. I do love Lara and I am terrified of this destiny she has been given." Ilona sobbed. "Look at me! I weep! Faeries do not weep, Kaliq! They should not weep! Yet I do!" She stamped her feet furiously at him.

"Do you believe I do not weep at the thought of the Twilight Lord possessing my exquisite Lara?" Kaliq demanded. "I have observed Lara from her birth. I watched as she grew into the beautiful girl Gaius Prospero, in his pique, sent from The City. She should have been brought to me first and never known the brutality of the Forest Lords, yet even I am not completely privy to the will of the Celestial Actuary. But then I had her in my care and she proved an incredible pupil. I shall be haunted until I finally fade from this realm by the nights we spent together. *You weep, Ilona?* Your tears can be no more heartfelt or bitter than mine, oh queen of the Forest Faeries!"

Ilona reached out a small delicate hand and touched his cheek. "Forgive me, Kaliq. You have always loved her, I know. I am sorry her fate was not to be yours."

He smiled ruefully. "Her spirit could not have been content in the confines of our desert kingdom," he admitted. "And Lara would surely not be pleased with either of us if, in her absence, we allow Hetar and Terah to go to war. I have sent my brothers, Lothair and Nasim, to The City to gather what information they can. The High Council is little more than a mockery of what it once was but if the Shadow Princes eschew it, then it appears as if we are no longer a part of Hetar. With Gaius

Prospero, if you are not with him you are against him. While he will never be bold enough to attack us for he fears our magic, our presence on the High Council alleviates his paranoia. He believes Terah weak without Lara and even now plans to attack Magnus Hauk at the first opportunity."

"The Terahns have a small army thanks to my daughter," Ilona said, "but I doubt they could hold off a full-scale attack from Hetar. The Crusader Knights and the Mercenaries are great in number. Once they see the richness of Terah it will not be easy to hold them back. They could not in a thousand years wear out the land there. And that is only on the Terahn side of the Emerald Mountains. The New Outlands possesses an equal amount of land. Terah offers an invader lands and slaves without number. Do you believe that Gaius Prospero is farseeing enough to dare such an expedition?"

"I do not know if he is farseeing but he is surely greedy enough. It is his right hand, Jonah, who has the greater intellect and instinct. Actually, I consider Jonah a more formidable human than I do Gaius Prospero. The emperor can be tempted from his path and I have already arranged for him to be so subverted. My brothers and I have created a female who will so remind him of Lara that he will do what he must to possess her. Without her he will wither and die. She will hopefully keep him from his own folly long enough for Lara to meet her destiny and then return to her husband and family."

"A woman? You seek to have a mere woman distract Gaius Prospero?" Ilona asked. "And what of the more dangerous Jonah? If the emperor is bedazzled by a mere woman does that not give Jonah his opportunity?"

"Jonah will be far too busy, I suspect, calming the emperor's two wives, Vilia and Anora. And Vilia, who is Jonah's secret mistress, will also be busy attempting to persuade her lover to take this chance to destroy the emperor." Kaliq chuckled.

"If this creature you have created looks like Lara, will not Jonah be suspicious?"

"Come and see for yourself what we have done." Kaliq invited the queen. He led her to a tall mirror. The prince gestured with his right hand and the mirror grew dark.

Then it cleared to reveal a lovely young girl picking spring flowers in a meadow. The girl was petite and slender. As she stood clutching her bouquet, Ilona saw she had a heart-shaped face with two beautiful violet eyes. Her long reddish-gold hair flowed free, contained only by a narrow ribbon. She bore a slight resemblance to Lara but not enough that it would be noticed immediately.

"Her name is Shifra," Kaliq said softly. "We gave her just enough allure and knowledge that Gaius Prospero will be overcome by his lust for her."

"It will do no good," Ilona said. "Remember that Lara cursed his ability to enjoy pleasures any longer."

Kaliq laughed, remembering the incident. "That is true, my dear Ilona, but we have made it possible for Shifra to overcome that curse. For the first time in several years the emperor will enjoy pleasures. And he will enjoy them every time he mounts her. That is why he will want to make her his third wife and his empress. Can you imagine the uproar his decision will cause within his household? Vilia was wise enough to befriend Anora when Gaius Prospero took his second wife. And Anora was content to let Vilia have the authority in the household as long as she was catered to and could practice her painful love with the emperor. But Shifra, being young and innocent when the emperor takes her, will begin to exhibit the pride of a woman who believes herself above Gaius Prospero's senior wives and he will support her at every turn, infuriating the other two. You see, we have made Shifra an amalgam of both Vilia and Anora. The emperor will finally have his perfect woman in one woman.

"The lady Vilia is enormously clever. She will act in her own best interests, for remember, she has Jonah, who actually loves and admires her, though not quite as much as he loves himself. He is a very ambitious man and has just been waiting for an opportunity. Who knows what will happen when he sees the woman he cares for being abused and embarrassed before all of Hetar? As for Anora, she will destroy herself with her outrageous behavior when she realizes her rival has bested her. She has always considered Vilia her inferior in the emperor's heart." The prince smiled. "In the end it is Lara's destiny that will prevail. Remember that from a distant tomorrow will come Hetar's true destiny."

"The prophecy," Ilona said softly. Then she sighed. "I just wish I could have prevented my daughter from the pain she has, and will, experience."

"Look! Look in the mirror," Kaliq said. "Shifra is about to begin her journey!" And the Shadow Prince and the queen of the Forest Faeries watched fascinated as the band of slavers rode into the meadow.

Shifra looked up at the sound of hoofbeats. Recognizing the breed of horsemen bearing down on her she picked up her skirts and began to run. With a whoop of delight the slavers bore down on her until their leader, a man named Lenya, came abreast of the fleeing girl and scooped her up. Shifra fought him, beating at him with her small balled-up fists, and struggled to escape his grasp. "Let me go!" she cried. "Let me go, you barbarian!"

In reply Lenya swiftly turned the girl about so that she now lay face down before him over his saddle. "Be silent, girl!" he told her. "You are caught and there is nothing for it but to accept your fate. It will probably be a most comfortable one, for you are beautiful and young."

The slavers rode on until nightfall when they stopped to make a camp. Shifra was tied to a young tree while the slavers built a fire, found water and began to cook their evening meal. When they had eaten Lenya came with a bowl of stew and began to feed Shifra a small portion. He was pleased to see her eat for often captives did not. And as she ate he began to question her.

"What in the name of the Celestial Actuary were you doing all alone out in the middle of nowhere?" he demanded.

"I am an orphan," Shifra began. "I lived with my old grandmother in a hut in the forest that surrounds the meadow where you took me. She will be alone now and she will surely die." Shifra began to sob.

"If she is old then perhaps it is her time to die," Lenya replied sanguinely. "I believe we passed a hut near the forest road as we came. There was an old hag digging in a garden. She was much too decrepit for us to be bothered with, but you are a nice tender little morsel. We shall get a goodly profit in The City for you."

"That was my grandmother," Shifra wept. "She will wonder what has happened to me now. Oh, my poor Nona!"

Lenya snorted. "Are you a virgin?" he asked her rudely.

Shifra colored at his words and hung her head. "Yes," she whispered.

"I am going to check," he told her. "I cannot represent you as something you are not, despite your beauty. If you are a truly a virgin I will get a much higher price for you than if you are not. What is your name?"

"Shifra," she told him. "I am called Shifra."

He nodded. The name meant *beautiful,* and it certainly fit her. Calling to his men he untied her. "Put her on the blanket and two of you secure her arms. The other two of you, spread her legs wide for me," Lenya said. When his men licked their lips and leered at his instructions Lenya continued. "She says she is a virgin. If she is then she will bring us a much, much higher price at the slave market in The City, you fools. We will make so much coin off of her that you will all be able to spend at least two nights at the Pleasure House of Maeve Scarlet," he told them with a grin. "Now get the girl on her back so I may examine her."

"What if she isn't a virgin?" one of his men asked.

"Then we shall all take pleasures with our little Shifra tonight, my lads, but I hope she has not lied, for the Pleasure Women at Maeve Scarlet's are exceptionally well trained and always welcoming of a hardworking man."

As they brought her down onto the blanket Shifra began to

struggle wildly, sobbing and begging them not to harm her. But she was a dainty girl and no match for the big men holding her prisoner. They quickly had her secure, both of her arms pinioned to either side and her legs spread wide. The tears pouring from her eyes and her little cries of distress would have moved a stone cliff.

Lenya knelt by the girl. He pulled her skirts up, revealing the snow-white skin beneath and a mound of tight red-gold curls clustered upon her mons. He looked admiringly. No doubt about it, she was prime goods. Now if only she spoke the truth. He pressed a single finger past her plump nether lips. Shifra sobbed and begged him to stop. His finger found her passage and he pushed it slowly into her. Shifra shrieked her distress. Lenya's finger reached the barrier of her virginity. Quickly he pulled his finger back and out lest he damage that barrier. He looked up smiling broadly at his men. "She is as pure as the driven snow, my lads. Our fortune is made! Now release her," he said.

Shifra curled herself into a tight little ball, weeping with her shame.

Lenya stood up. "Remember," he said to his men. "I will cut the balls of any of you who touches her *and* make you eat them roasted," he threatened. "Drop another blanket over her. I will be sleeping next to her tonight."

The other slavers knew their leader well enough to know he was not jesting with them so they said nothing more. Two days later they arrived at The City. Shifra was taken to a public bath to be scrubbed. Lenya left his men there while he went to an open market to seek a more attractive garment in which to display his treasure to the slave master. Presentation was, he knew, half the battle when selling a piece of choice merchandise. Finding what he sought, he returned to the bath to find Shifra almost ready. He gave the garment to the bath mistress. "For the girl Shifra," he told her.

"She's a real beauty, Lenya," the bath mistress told him. "Where did you find her? I've done an extraspecial job with her. I hope you'll remember me when you get your price." And she smiled, showing several broken and blackened teeth.

"Have I ever forgotten you?" he replied.

"Aiiii, but this girl is truly valuable," the bath mistress said.

"I will not forget you," he repeated. "Now finish up. I am in a hurry to get to the slave market. The auctions begin at noon. I've been looking forward to an evening or two at Maeve Scarlet's."

The bath mistress cackled and then disappeared back into the baths. She returned a short while later with Shifra, who was now garbed in a pale-green gown of sheerest silk through which her lush and rosy body could be just faintly seen. The skirt of the gown was narrow. One of her beautiful rounded shoulders was bare as were her arms. Her long red-gold hair had been washed and now flowed loose down her back to her buttocks. Her feet were shod in a pair of simple sandals.

"Here she is," the bath mistress said, pleased. "You have an eye for the right costume, Lenya." Then she lowered her voice. "I have given her a cup of Razi so that she will not be so frightened or struggle."

Lenya pressed double the amount he would have usually paid

the bath mistress into her hand. "And there will be more later," he told her.

"You are generous beyond measure, but come back before you and your men go to Maeve Scarlet's," she chuckled.

"I will," he responded with a grin. Then he took Shifra by the hand. "Come now, my beauty, and let us see the excitement you will cause." He led her to a waiting litter, for he would not walk her to the slave market now that she was ready. He followed along as the two bearers hurried through The City's crowded and noisy streets. Finally they gained the slave market and Lenya hurried to find the slave master who, seeing him first, called out to the slaver.

"Lenya! Rumor has it that you have found a treasure for me to auction today. You are in luck, my friend! If the girl is what she is said to be I will sell her in the private chamber rather than here in the open market. I get a much better clientele for choice merchandise there," the slave master explained. He walked to the litter and drawing back the curtains, was stunned by the violet eyes that looked back at him. Reaching into the litter he handed the girl out, then slowly walked about her nodding. "I have not had anything this fine in years," he said admiringly. "Where did you find her? And are there more of them?"

"I doubt it," Lenya said with a chuckle. "We came upon her picking flowers in an open meadow on the forest's edge. We had passed a hut where an old woman lived. Shifra said it was her home and her grandmother."

"In the forest?" the slave master said. "But she has not the look of Forest Folk."

"She is probably Midlands born, but the hut was poor, which

means the farm from which the old woman came was probably bought up or confiscated by the emperor some years ago. She says she's an orphan. Do you really care?" Lenya asked.

"Is it too much to ask if she is a virgin?" the slave master said hopefully.

Lenya grinned. "I verified it myself. The maiden's barrier is there. I did not damage it, knowing its value."

The slave master reached out to squeeze one of Shifra's breasts. Gasping, the girl drew back like a scalded cat, her eyes wide with shock. The man chortled. "I shall want a thirty per cent commission," he said.

"Do not be greedy," Lenya scolded him. "This maid will sell in less than five minutes and the only reason it will take that long will be because the bidding will be hot and heavy. I will give you ten percent."

"Twenty," the slave master replied.

"Fifteen and not a coin more," Lenya responded.

"Agreed!" the slave master said. "And you are just in time, for the private auction is beginning first. Come in and you may view the proceedings. I will sell the girl last, however, in order to get a fair price for the rest of my merchandise but do not fear. There are only five others. Top quality is difficult to come by these days."

Lenya saw Shifra led away and he settled down to watch the auction. Two girls were quickly auctioned off to Pleasure Houses. A third to a wealthy magnate. There was a faint stirring in the audience behind him but Lenya did not bother to turn about. The remaining two slave girls were sold. Then the slave master stepped forward.

"My lords," he said. "I have less than an hour ago received for sale a virgin of such incomparable beauty that it will be many years before I receive such a slave again." He clapped his hands and Shifra was led out to be placed in the center of a small raised dais. "Young, my lords. *Untouched*. Rare."

"And expensive," said a voice in a group of men to appreciative laughter.

The slave master joined in their laughter. "Aye, my lords, expensive."

"Let us see what it is you really offer," another voice called.

The slave master nodded to Shifra and reaching up she undid her gown, letting it fall to her feet. Slowly, carefully she pirouetted about as she had been told to do and she heard the whispering sighs from the men gazing up at her. They admired the small round breasts with the berry nipples. The admired her lush thighs and her plump buttocks.

The slave master allowed them to look their fill and then he said, "What am I bid for this piece of perfection, my lords?"

Lenya held his breath waiting. Would he gain five thousand coins for her? Six?

"I bid fifty thousand gold cubits," a voice called from the audience.

"Fifty thousand," the slave master said as if it were a mere opening bid. His heart was hammering against his rib cage. "I am bid fifty thousand. Who will bid sixty?" He looked about the chamber. "Come my lords, will no one else bid for this rare beauty?"

The room remained silent and so the slave master brought down his small gavel. "Fifty thousand gold. The slave girl Shifra is sold to our gracious and glorious emperor, Gaius Prospero, for fifty thousand gold cubits." The gavel hit the slave master's podium with a loud thunk. "Done for fifty thousand gold cubits!"

It was only then that Lenya dared to turn about. And there was the emperor himself. He was staring intently at Shifra. No wonder no one else had dared to bid against him, he thought. But then, had the emperor not bid, neither he nor the slave master would now be rich men. He almost laughed aloud. He was done with slaving, he decided in that moment. After today nothing he did would compare with this.

A servant of the emperor made his way to the slave master and gave him a scrip with the emperor's seal upon it. "Bring this to the treasury at your convenience. You will be paid there. Send the girl to the emperor's home in the Golden District at once."

Then he turned and departed.

"We do not have the gold?" Lenya said nervously.

"I will put today's open auction in the hands of my son," the slave master said. "You and I shall go immediately to the treasury, my friend, and collect our payment. I trust no one, especially not the emperor. The girl shall not leave this place until we have our coin."

Lenya nodded and together the two men hurried to the large treasury building, a new structure located just inside the gates of the Golden District. Showing the scrip with the emperor's seal they were permitted entry. An officious clerk peered suspiciously at the paper and then without a word called for his superior who in turn called for the assistant treasurer who looked at the scrip.

Then he said, "How do you wish this paid out, sir?"

"In a lump sum," the slave master said.

"No," Lenya interjected. "Pay him his seven thousand five hundred coins. The remainder you will transfer immediately to Avram the Goldsmith in my name."

"You bank with Avram?" The slave master was surprised.

The assistant treasurer turned to the slave master. "Sir?"

"Do as he says," the slave master told him. "He is Lenya the Slaver. The merchandise was his. I will take my commission and go."

"Have my monies transferred now," Lenya told the assistant treasurer. "I am going to Avram to get the coin I will need to pay my men."

"I am curious," the slave master said while the paperwork for the transfer was prepared. "What do you pay your men?"

"They will each get five percent of my profit," Lenya answered. "It is usually two percent of our sales. But I have never before gotten such a sum for a bevy of slaves, let alone one girl. I'm not a greedy man. My men have all been loyal and with me a long time. I shall retire to a small villa in the Coastal Kingdom now and take a wife."

"Here is your record of the transfer of funds," the assistant treasurer said, handing the papers to Lenya.

"Good day to you then," Lenya told them and he was gone from the treasury.

"What did you sell for him?" the assistant treasurer asked the auctioneer, curious.

"A slave girl—an extraordinarily beautiful slave girl. The emperor purchased her," the slave master said. "Fifty thousand gold coins. Not even the legendary Lara earned that sum for Gaius Prospero."

The treasurer handed the slave master a heavy bag of coins. "You shall have an escort back to your establishment," he said. "Courtesy of the emperor, sir."

"Thank you," the slave master nodded. He must be quick. The slave girl Shifra must be delivered immediately now that she had been paid for in full. He hurried from the treasury with the two armed mercenaries. When he returned he discovered that a litter had been sent from the emperor for his new purchase. His assistant, afraid to refuse a royal transport, had already sent the girl along. The slave master did not chide the man. He was actually relieved to be rid of Shifra now. Someone that beautiful was bound to cause trouble sooner or later.

Shifra watched curiously as the litter carrying her passed through the streets of The City. She had been created for loving, Prince Kaliq had told her. She was meant for only a great man. Certainly the emperor was a great man. Did he not rule all of Hetar? She smiled, remembering how she had awakened one day to find the Shadow Princes standing over her. They had tended her lovingly and taught her all about passion and pleasures without once disturbing her virginity, which they assured her was for a great man alone. Who was she, she asked them? An orphan, they told her, raised by her grandmother and when they told her that, her memories of Nona were suddenly there. She had become lost in the forest and they had found her and healed her. Now she must return to her grandmother and let her fate play out. And because she had trusted the princes she had done as they bid her. And now she was to be rewarded. Gaius Prospero, the princes told

Shifra, was going to fall in love with her. She had but to follow her instincts with him.

The litter bearers hurried through the gates of the Golden District. The girl within looked out and saw a beautiful park surrounding the great marble mansions that dotted the landscape. They passed through another set of gates guarded by men-at-arms in elegant dark-blue-and-gold uniforms. Shifra heard gravel crunching beneath the sandals of the bearers, and then they came to a stop. The litter was set down, the curtain was opened and a hand reached in to help her out.

"I am Tania, Lady Shifra, and I have been assigned to care for you," the owner of the hand said. "If you will please follow me I will take you to the quarters that have been arranged for you." She moved quickly away and Shifra had to run to keep up.

They walked through a beautiful rotunda. At its center was a rectangular fountain decorated with a boy riding a bronze dolphin that spouted water from its mouth. There were water hyacinths floating in the pool and benches upon which to sit. Shifra had never seen anything like it and thought it was wonderful.

"It is a very big house," she ventured softly.

"It is," Tania agreed. "And since the master became emperor it has gotten even bigger. The northern wing, which was once used for housing my master's special merchandise, has been rebuilt and enlarged. There is now a throne room, a great room for entertaining, a new dining room for feeding guests and, of course, the emperor's right hand, Lord Jonah, has his offices and living quarters there. Such a man for work, Lord Jonah! Nowadays he spends a several months a year in Terah as the emperor's ambassador, as well. He is probably the only person in Hetar that our emperor trusts."

"Where are we going?" Shifra asked.

"You are to be housed in the west wing," Tania replied.

"Does anyone else live there?" the girl queried.

"Indeed. The emperor's wives, Lady Vilia and Lady Anora, live in the west wing. I will be frank with you, Lady Shifra. Neither will be pleased to know you. They are most jealous of their positions and have squabbled ever since my master became emperor over who should be empress, for neither has been appointed to that position."

"Oh," Shifra said. This was something she would consider carefully.

Ahead of them were tall twin doors covered in gold leaf. On either side of the door stood a man-at-arms. As they reached them the two guards snapped to attention and the doors sprang magically open for the two women to pass through.

"Come this way," Tania said to Shifra, leading her down a corridor.

"Tania! Stop!" an imperious voice called out.

"Aye, do not go a step farther," another voice said.

"Be silent," Tania hissed to Shifra as she turned about. "Yes, my ladies?"

"Is this the slave girl Gaius paid such a ridiculous sum for this afternoon?" came the query.

"Yes, my lady Vilia, it is," Tania replied politely.

"Turn around, girl!" Lady Vilia said. "What is your name?"

Shifra turned slowly, her eyes lowered. She bowed servilely, and responded in a soft little voice, "My name is Shifra, great lady." Her eyes remained lowered.

"Let me see your face, girl," the lady Vilia said sharply. Her hand yanked Shifra's head up roughly. She stared, displeased, but then she said, "I see nothing special in this girl that would have caused Gaius to waste so much coin. He must surely be entering his dotage. What do you think, Anora?"

The other woman, younger and more beautiful than the first, looked Shifra over slowly and carefully. "She has very fair skin, Vilia. I expect the merest cut of my whip would break it. But then I expect we shall soon see, for Gaius needs not only to be whipped, but to whip in order to raise his cock to perform." She ran a nail down the side of Shifra's cheek, laughing softly at the faint weal it raised. "Oh yes, she will mark nicely and easily. Have you ever been whipped, girl? Your master is an expert at it."

"He will not whip me," Shifra startled them by answering. "And he will need no whip to coax his cock to perform with *me*."

Anora laughed. "Gracious, the little slave girl has a bit of spirit. How amusing, and how intriguing, eh, Vilia?"

"You will speak to me with respect, girl," Vilia said sharply.

"Yes, my lady empress," Shifra said softly.

"I am not the empress," Vilia replied. She was not certain whether the girl was insulting her or not.

"You are the emperor's first wife, my lady, are you not?" Shifra said.

"I am," Vilia answered slowly.

"Then you should be the empress," Shifra told Vilia.

"Well, I am not," Vilia answered. Now she was truly confused.

Was the girl mocking her or was she attempting to ingratiate herself? She smiled at the sour look on Anora's pretty face, and decided that Shifra was being polite. "Take her along to her rooms, Tania," she said.

"You are a bold thing," Tania said softly as they went along.

"Why isn't she empress if she is his first wife?" Shifra wanted to know.

"Because he is afraid to make a choice between them," Tania said. "The lady Vilia rarely graces his bed any longer but she is the mother of his children. He will not publicly show her any disrespect for while he has managed to make himself emperor, he still fears the common people. The lady Vilia is well liked for her many charities. The lady Anora, however, gives him relief as no other has been able to for several years since he was cursed by a faerie woman. He no longer enjoys pleasures." She flung open the door at the end of the corridor they had been traversing. "Here we are," she said.

"You know a great deal about this house," Shifra said low.

"I have been a slave here for many, many years," Tania answered. "I serve only Gaius Prospero and my allegiance has never wavered. It never will. I have his trust because I have earned his trust. If I speak candidly to you, my child, it is so you will successfully make your way here. He obviously saw something in you that caused him to spend more money than he has ever expended on anything. And he put you in my charge. It is therefore up to me to see you do not disappoint the emperor. Do you understand me, Shifra? I will guide you and you will follow."

Their eyes met and Shifra nodded slowly. "You will lead me,

and I will follow you, Tania. I would be a fool not to and you will find I am not a fool."

Tania smiled. "I did not think you were, my child," she said. "Now tell me when you last were bathed? The emperor will visit you later tonight and you will want to make every effort to please him at your first private meeting."

"They bathed me this morning in the slave merchant's house before I was displayed for sale," Shifra answered.

"It will have been a hurried affair and the luxuries lacking," Tania told her young companion. "We will begin again." And for the next several hours she personally worked with the bath mistress and her assistants to perfect Shifra's beauty. There was something about the girl, Tania thought, that reminded her of the fabled Lara and yet what it was she could not quite put her finger on. Because she knew him well, she suspected that something was what had caused Gaius Prospero to purchase the slave girl.

Tania questioned Shifra gently as she worked. It was important that she know everything about the girl that she could if she was to help her succeed with the emperor and Tania realized that she wanted the girl to succeed. Her master needed a beautiful young wife to present to the people as his empress. And as she had told Shifra, Gaius Prospero could not choose between Vilia and Anora.

Lady Vilia was intelligent, attractive, the mother of the emperor's children, but ambitious. The empress should not aspire to have her own power. And Tania knew that once Vilia held that kind of power, she would compete with her husband. As for the lady Anora, she was a venal woman whose excesses were beginning to show upon her pretty face. Because she could sexually gratify Gaius Prospero now, when no other woman could, she believed she was superior to other women and considered herself the lady Vilia's equal. What one had, the other wanted. And Anora might have overcome Vilia's influence except that she had been unable to have children.

The emperor had not visited the Pleasure Houses of The City for several years now. He did not want his inability to perform as a man publicly known. There were several houses that specialized in pain, but Gaius Prospero was a proud man. An emperor should show no weakness. So Tania was amazed that her master had bought a slave girl for such an outrageous sum. Why had he done it? Shifra's confidence in her own sensuality was also surprising given her youth and the certificate of virginity she had carried with her. Something exciting, something different, was about to happen. Tania sensed it. If this girl could indeed pleasure the emperor and keep his favor, he might, induced by his humble and long-time slave, make Shifra his empress. Tania secretly loved Gaius Prospero, and always had. She would always seek to further his best interests.

After several hours, she led Shifra from the baths. The girl's skin was like the finest white silk. Her tiny hands and dainty feet had not a rough patch on them. Her long, thick red-gold hair fell in rippling waves down her back. Her plump mons was plucked and as smooth as marble, its slit faintly shadowed. Her small round breasts would just fit in a man's hand. Could she pleasure the emperor without resorting to pain? Tonight would tell the tale, Tania thought.

Shifra was fed a light but nourishing meal. Her teeth and mouth were cleansed and then she was put to bed to rest until her master was ready to avail himself of her. Tania left the new slave sleeping and hurried to find her master in his own quarters. Entering, she knelt before the emperor and said, "Shifra is ready to receive you, my lord. She but awaits your convenience."

"What do you think of her, Tania?" Gaius Prospero asked. "Is she not exquisite?"

"She is indeed, my lord. Your eye was flawless and had Shifra been purchased by a Pleasure House she would have surely become famous. Should she please you well, my lord, a virgin of such great beauty would certainly be eligible for higher rank eventually, would she not? Or do I speak out of turn?" Tania's eyes were lowered.

"As always, Tania, you look to my best interests," Gaius Prospero chuckled. "I think of all my servants, you are the most loyal to me, no matter I sometimes speak harshly to you. You are a perfect example of fidelity."

"I am the most loyal to you of any in Hetar," Tania replied boldly. "I will never leave your side, my lord, though I be but a woman and your slave."

"I should free you," the emperor said softly. "You are worthy of freedom like my good right hand, Jonah."

"Do not, I beg you!" Tania answered him. "I am content as I am."

"I could make you Jonah's wife, Tania. Then I should have both my most faithful servants always by my side," Gaius Prospero said.

"I am more loyal to you than any," Tania repeated. "And if you would reward me then allow me to always be your slave.

I want no other master but you and a husband is master of his wife. I could not divide my loyalties, my lord, and surely Jonah is worthy of a wife whose sole interests were for him and not another."

Gaius Prospero reached out and patted Tania's bowed head as he would a dog's. "You shall have what you desire, my good Tania," he told her. And then, "Tania, tell me, do you think I can be a real man with Shifra? Without the whip?"

"My lord, I am no soothsayer, but you must try. I know that the faerie woman Lara cursed you, but since then you have not even tried one of your women without the whip. Shifra is a virgin but she has a look about her that tells me she knows how to pleasure a man. Let her try and if she cannot then you may resort to the whip. But I believe that lovely girl will pleasure you well."

"I do, too!" Gaius Prospero said excitedly. "It is a feeling I got the moment I looked at her, which is why I bid such a ridiculous sum. I did not want to lose her, Tania."

"You were wise to act as you did, my lord. Now you have had a long day. Eat, then go and bathe so you may come to Shifra. Shall I ask your wives to remain in their own apartments tonight?"

"Yes! And they are not to go near Shifra. I do not want her spoiled and it would be like Anora to do so out of spite. She is such a jealous creature. It is no wonder she needs regular whipping," the emperor said, licking his lips.

Tania arose from her knees. "I will deliver your message, my lord, and then I shall sleep by Shifra's bed until you are ready to join her." She bowed her way from the chamber, hurrying back to the women's section of the emperor's house.

The lady Vilia nodded wearily in response to her husband's message.

"Of course. He will want to play with his new toy," she said. "Perhaps I shall visit my villa in the Outlands for a few days. Do you think he would mind, Tania?"

"I think, my lady, you are as always gracious and understanding," Tania murmured. "I am certain our good lord would fully approve your decision."

Vilia smiled at the response. She was more than aware of how devoted the slave woman was to the emperor. And with luck Jonah would join her for a few nights. It was perfect. He had been spending so much time in Terah of late and she was eager for his talented cock. Gaius rarely, if ever, visited her bed any longer, and Jonah was a far better lover than Gaius had ever been. It amazed Vilia that she had been able to keep the secret of their illicit affair for several years now. But then, they were always careful.

The lady Anora was not as understanding of the emperor's decision. "What do you mean I am to remain in my apartments and away from the slave girl? He will need me to ply my whip on his fat bottom if he is to have any success with her. And this Shifra will need a taste of discipline, too, if she is to pleasure him."

"He says you are to remain here and away from Shifra, lady. I am but the bearer of the emperor's message. The lady Vilia is going to her villa for a few days. Perhaps you would enjoy visiting yours. The Outlands are lovely this time of year, I am told."

"I will remain. When he finds he cannot perform he will want me to come and assist him," Anora said stubbornly.

Tania bowed her way out of Anora's apartments and hurried back to Shifra. She pulled a mat from beneath the sleeping girl's bed and slept, awakening only when the emperor touched her with his slipper. Tania scrambled up and gently shook Shifra by her delicate shoulder. "Waken, my child. Your master has come to be with you." Then Tania hurried from the bedchamber.

Shifra had been sleeping on her side. She rolled onto her back, stretching herself like a young cat. Her violet eyes opened and she smiled slowly as she held out her arms to Gaius Prospero. "Come, my lord, and let me give you comfort," she purred at him. She reached up to draw him down to her.

Mesmerized, the emperor let her lead the way. She settled him in a half-seated position, plumping up the pillows about him. Then seating herself upon his thick and hairy thighs, she leaned forward to kiss him. The touch of her bottom against him caused his eyes to dilate. Her small sweet mouth on his was incredible. She ran a pointed little tongue over his fleshy lips teasing them open and then her tongue slid into his mouth to play with his tongue. Gaius Prospero's head spun dizzily. Reaching out he grasped her two small round breasts in his pudgy hands and fondled them.

She broke off the kiss murmuring softly, then leaning forward, her teeth began to nibble at his ear. Her tongue traced the shape of it, darting into it as she whispered to him, "Do you want to suck my nipples, my lord?" Then she nipped his earlobe with sharp little teeth. "Do you?"

"Aye, my beautiful Shifra, I do," he groaned.

"I am your slave, my dear lord," she told him. "I live to please you." Then she knelt with her legs on either side of his thighs and lifting a breast pushed the nipple into his mouth. With her other hand she took his hand and encouraged his fingers to play between her nether lips. Then Shifra closed her eyes so she might enjoy the sensations of his lovemaking.

Gaius Prospero suckled upon the sentient flesh of her breast. He was startled to taste a liquid sweetness flowing from it into his mouth. It was delicious! He sucked harder and harder until there was no more of the honeyed taste and he whimpered a protest.

"No, my dear lord," she whispered to him. "The other breast is full for you. Take it. It is yours." She invited him. "My body is yours. Only for your delight."

His mouth eagerly closed over the other breast while his fingers played frantically with her. When he had drained the second breast she pulled his fingers away and pushed them into his mouth. The taste was the same, and he licked them clean. As he did he realized that his cock was hard and ready for her. Shifra slid beneath him and kissing him again, smiled as he began to enter her. Her virgin shield was his only impediment. He thrust through it fiercely as she cried out.

Gaius Prospero could hardly contain himself. He could scarce restrain his excitement as he plowed her depths. Shifra wrapped her slender legs about him and whispered little words of encouragement along with her cries of delight. Her arms were tight about his neck. The emperor could not believe what was happening to him. His cock was performing as it had never before done. And he could feel the pleasures welling up in preparation to flow through him until he was weak and replete with satisfaction. The girl beneath him begged him to continue on. And he was able to do so!

And then she sobbed, "My lord! My lord! Ohh, I die!" Her supple body shuddered as she reached the peak of pleasures.

With a groan of delight he followed her down the path, his juices coming in great spurts as Gaius Prospero realized that for the first time in years, for the first time since Lara had cursed him, he was enjoying a woman to the fullest degree. He had not needed Anora's whip turning his buttocks red and hot to perform. He had not needed to give the exquisite girl in his arms pain to raise his lust. *She alone had made it happen.* He rolled off her lest he crush her with his weight and gathered her into his arms.

Shifra laid her head against his shoulder for a brief moment. "Oh, my lord, you gave me such delight. Thank you for permitting me to share pleasures with you." She sat herself up against the pillows and drew him into her embrace. "Now you must rest yourself, my lord, for ruling such a varied realm such as Hetar cannot be easy for you."

She stroked his thinning hair, kissing the top of his head.

"I will want you again tonight," he growled at her.

"I am here for you, my dear lord," Shifra told him. "But catch your ease for a short time and then we shall take pleasures again. To have your body joined with mine is so wonderful. I never dreamed I should find such happiness when I was taken into slavery, but in your arms all things are possible for me, my dear lord."

Gaius Prospero was overwhelmed by her words. She had been torn from her family, roughly handled and sold as a slave, yet she thanked him. "My darling Shifra," he said softly, "you are my treasure." And he meant it. This petite and beautiful girl with her flowing hair was unlike any he had ever known. She was not strong and practical like Vilia. Nor was she cruel and greedy like Anora. She was grateful for his attentions and it was obvious that she cared for him, for his well-being.

Shifra looked down into his face and the emperor thought he would drown in the violet depths of her eyes. "Would I ever be permitted to love you, my lord?" she shyly asked him. "Could one day I be allowed to admit to such feelings, my dear lord?"

"Gaius," he said to her. "You may call me your lord Gaius." Reaching up he stroked her pale cheek, marveling at the soft texture.

"But may I be granted the right to love you, my dear lord *Gaius?*" Shifra asked sweetly. The smile she offered him now was tremulous and bespoke a vulnerability that made the emperor want to protect this girl from anyone or anything who would seek to harm her.

"Aye, my beautiful and sweet treasure, you may love me," he responded. "I do not believe any woman since my mother has ever loved me."

"Surely that is not so, my lord Gaius! You have two beautiful wives who certainly love you."

"Vilia and Anora?" The emperor laughed harshly. "Vilia likes the power that comes with being my first wife and the mother of my children. If she could gain more power, she would. As for Anora, our relationship began in lust and what little is left of it is still no more than that. Neither of them loves me."

"Then I will love you, my dear lord Gaius," Shifra said ingenuously. "You are my world now. I want no more than to be in your heart and in your arms."

"In the most trying time I have ever faced, the Celestial Actuary has rewarded me by sending you to me, my treasure. It is surely a sign that my endeavors will continue to prosper. The moment I looked at you, Shifra, you had my heart. Treat it gently."

"I am yours," Shifra told him. "Everything I do will be for you, to please you. Only for you, my dear lord Gaius."

And the emperor of Hetar smiled a smile that none before had ever seen.

KALIQ OF THE SHADOWS LOOKED into the Viewing Mirror and was pleased with what he saw. The beautiful girl Shifra was performing just as he and his brothers had hoped. Her genuine sweetness, her innocence and her incomparable sexual skills were already bewitching Gaius Prospero. Hetar's plans for conquest would be held in check for a brief time while Gaius Prospero reveled in his newly revived ability to enjoy pleasures. As much as Kaliq had regretted undoing Lara's curse upon the Hetarian overlord it had been necessary if Shifra was to succeed and the girl was well on her way. The emperor was as bedazzled as a youth with his first love.

For the moment, his first wife, Vilia, didn't care. She was too busy riding Lord Jonah's lusty cock. As for Anora, the Shadow Princes had curbed her jealousy by giving her a rather uncomfortable and most stubborn rash that at first kept her sexual organs in a heated and itchy state. And just when Anora had managed to get this difficulty under control, the rash appeared anew upon her breasts, belly and face in the form of hard purple and red bumps that when they broke, oozed stinking yellow and green pus. Anora closeted herself within her chambers allowing no one but a single unfortunate servant to share in her misery.

Kaliq could not help but chuckle although he felt a small frisson of guilt. It was a harsh punishment, but Anora had a talent for mischief, especially when she felt she was being thwarted. If she irritated the emperor enough he would leave Shifra and all of his women, returning to his plans to go to war against Terah. The only thing that could stop him would be Lara's return and that, Kaliq knew, was many months away. The Shadow Princes and the Forest Faeries would do what they must to keep the tenuous peace among the various worlds. And so Anora suffered a plethora of bumps and rashes keeping her from Gaius Prospero who was so besotted by Shifra he wanted nothing more than to be in her company all day and all night long.

Vilia, at her villa in the Outlands province, had a corps of spies among the imperial household who reported to her as necessary. She quickly learned of her husband's deepening passion for the slave girl, Shifra, and considered how best to use it to her advantage. Vilia was a beautiful woman, with thick, lustrous, dark brown hair and amber eyes. Her best feature was her flawless creamy skin. She had given Gaius Prospero his only son and two daughters, but her form was still shapely. She was some years his junior, and he had divorced a wife to wed her. Hetarian law allowed a man of wealth to have as many wives as they wanted, but most of the magnates kept only two or three and usually cast off older wives to take younger.

When she had agreed to marry Gaius Prospero, who in those days was the head of the Guild of Merchants, Vilia had asked of him but one thing and he had agreed for he had been in love with her then. He could take no other wife without her express approval. And he had wanted no other wives until he had met Anora, a fair beauty, who plied her trade in one of The City's finest Pleasure Houses. Vilia had agreed to his desire for Anora as she had long ago become bored with her husband and she had secretly taken a lover. A dangerous lover.

He was Lord Jonah, the emperor's right hand, who had long ago been the emperor's slave. But Jonah was far more clever than his master. He had not sprung from the lower classes of Hetar, despite his unfortunate circumstances. Indeed, he was the son of Sir Rupert Bloodaxe of the Crusader Knights and his lover, the lady Farah, a Pleasure Mistress who was now rumored to be the next headmistress of the Pleasure Guild. His mother had come from a wealthy Midlands family and was blood kin to its governor, Squire Darah. Though sold into slavery by his father's wife when his sire died, he had purchased his freedom and then remained by the emperor's side, encouraging Gaius Prospero in his plans, gently reining him in when those plans became foolish or risky, and all the while making his master believe that Gaius was the creator of the great destiny that was Hetar's. Jonah was tall and slender with dark hair and burning black eyes. He had schemed to take Vilia for a lover only to learn to his delight that she wanted him. They were an ambitious pair ideally suited to one another.

As Hetar's four moons rose over the Sea of Sagitta, the lovers lay sprawled together on a wide double chaise that was set upon a tiled terrace overlooking the water. Jonah's slender fingers twirled themselves within Vilia's female passage as they spoke together. Vilia murmured with each little burst of pleasure he drew forth from her.

"They say he is completely infatuated with his new toy," she told Jonah.

"Has Anora not been able to interfere between them?" her lover asked.

"He does not need her!" Vilia exclaimed excitedly. "It seems his ability to enjoy pleasures has returned. I always thought his hysteria over that dream he had of Lara was ridiculous although I would not have thought Gaius had that much imagination. Umm...oh yes, my darling, that is nice." Vilia shuddered delicately.

"But surely Anora would want to join them in order to protect her own status," Jonah murmured as he licked her juices from his fingers. "After all, she is his second wife and you are not there."

"Anora has come down with a rather unpleasant rash. She will only allow one of her servants to tend her. It is obviously quite dreadful. She can hardly interfere under those circumstances." Then she nipped at his earlobe as he mounted her and his talented manroot slid deep. "Oh, darling, yes!" Vilia yelled as he began to use her vigorously and when he had both taken and given pleasures they lay together contentedly. Or so Vilia thought.

It is too convenient, Jonah mused. He knew Gaius Prospero did not have the imagination to have created what Vilia believed a dream. Lara had indeed cursed the emperor and now someone had lifted that curse. And a beautiful slave girl had appeared beneath the emperor's nose and his ability to enjoy pleasures had returned with her. And Anora, the deliciously perverted Anora, was suddenly unable to interfere. No; something else was going on here, but Jonah could not figure it out. *Yet.* He shrugged to himself. It was probably something magical and Jonah was wise enough to know he could not fight magic. Perhaps Lara had had a change of heart. Well, someone had.

"Perhaps," he said to Vilia, "it is time to return to The City, my darling. If we are to plan a campaign against Terah, then we must begin soon. Before summer begins."

"There is time," Vilia replied. "We do not often have the luxury of time together, my love. I could wish it were otherwise. I am tired of hiding our passion!"

"Vilia, my adorable Vilia," Jonah gently scolded her. "Listen to me and heed what I say to you. If it was known we were lovers we could both be executed. And frankly, Gaius cannot do without us, although he doesn't know it. In time I will take his throne from him and you, my Vilia, will rule by my side as my empress. I will have no hesitation as he has in placing you there. And I will take no other to my bed, Vilia."

"And I will give you a son to follow us, Jonah," Vilia told him. "Together, you and I will found a dynasty. In a thousand years the name of Gaius Prospero will not even be remembered, but the Jonah dynasty will still rule!" She kissed him passionately.

The Jonah dynasty, he thought and felt a thrill run through him. This was why he adored the woman in his arms so much. She had an eye on the future, and it was not a small future but a great one that would last at least a thousand years. "You do not want your son, Aubin, to rule one day?" he asked her.

"Nay," Vilia told him. "Aubin is too much like his father. And he is both young and foolish enough not to need anyone else's council. I know that without you, my darling Jonah, Gaius Prospero would not be emperor of Hetar. It is you who have advised him, led him and put him on his throne. But he has been but a means to an end for you, my darling. Now we must begin planning your future." And she kissed him again.

He kissed her back with equal passion and finding one of her plump breasts he squeezed it hard. "Yes, my Vilia," he told her. Then his manroot sought for her again and Vilia welcomed him with a glad cry into her body.

In the morning when she awoke, he was gone. He was so very discreet in his comings and goings that none of her servants ever knew he was there. He would have returned to his own villa. She knew he would go from there to The City today for he would not have left her so early otherwise. Vilia sighed. She longed for the day when they did not have to hide. The day she would sit by his side and rule over Hetar.

JONAH HAD INDEED returned to his own villa before the dawn even began to hint of itself in the Outlands sky. Disciplined, he slept for two hours, then awoke, bathed and was served the first meal of the day by the attending servant. As he ate he gazed out through the great arched windows in his bedchamber at his vineyards. The rows stretched as far as the eye could see. Soon the vines would begin to show tiny snippets of green. Then the leaves would begin to form, followed by the clusters of grapes which would ripen beneath the hot summer sun. His vineyards were his greatest joy and the wines his vintner made each year would soon make him an extremely rich man. The vintage was rich, rare and very special. It had quickly come into great demand among the magnates of Hetar. But true power lay in the wealth a man might amass, Jonah knew. *That* was a lesson he had learned from Gaius Prospero.

Jonah called a servant to him. "I am returning to The City," he said. "I shall not return for several days. Tell Lionel he is to remain here until I come back."

"Yes, my lord," the servant bowed and then went off to do his master's bidding.

About Jonah's neck he wore a chain from which hung a milky-white oval jewel. It was a sorcerous means of transporting its owner from one place to another, given to him by the great Shadow Prince Kaliq. It had been magically imprinted with Jonah's essence and would not obey anyone else's command. This way he might come and go between Hetar and Terah easily. Jonah took the gem between his fingers and rubbed it gently. "The City, my rooms," he said, and was instantly transported to his own apartments within the palace.

A serving woman cleaning in his bedchamber gave a startled cry as he appeared.

Waving his hand impatiently he left her and hurried to find Gaius Prospero, who was having his morning meal in his own dayroom. The emperor looked tired but he had a distinct air of contentment. Remembering his night with Vilia, Jonah almost smiled but managed to restrain himself. "Good morning, my lord," he greeted the emperor, bowing politely.

"Where have you been?" Gaius Prospero demanded. "I sent for you yesterday and you were not to be found. Were you in Terah?"

"I was in the Outlands at my vineyards," Jonah answered. "I needed to confer with my winemaker, for the growing season is upon us."

"Be careful, Jonah, or you will become a rustic." The emperor chuckled. "Did you see my wife while you were there?"

"Nay, but which one is there now?" Jonah said pleasantly.

"Vilia. She is a most thoughtful woman and went off to allow me the leisure to enjoy my new slave, Shifra. Anora, of course, stayed. She is so fiercely jealous. Once I found it charming and amusing. I am not so certain I feel that way any longer," Gaius Prospero grumbled. "However I was told she has developed a most disgusting rash and has been forced to keep to her own rooms."

"Then you have been free to dally with your new slave girl, my lord. I can see it has done you good," Jonah told him. "You appear more at ease than you have in many months. Your responsibilities weigh heavily upon you, I know. I am delighted that you have someone with whom you can enjoy life, my lord."

"Jonah, it is a miracle. I am once again able to enjoy taking pleasures with a woman! You know that ever since I had that dream where that wretched faerie woman cursed me, I have not been able to do so. Anora's whips could arouse my manhood but even her most skillful abuse could not cause me to enjoy pleasures. But with Shifra it is all different! Ah, Jonah," the emperor gushed, "she is beautiful and kind and sweet, yet she is intelligent. She seems to exist merely to please me and make me happy. Over these last few days I have offered her whatever she wanted to show my satisfaction with her but she refuses to take anything from me. She asks only to be allowed to be with me. How different is that from my two wives? Both are always eager for some new acquisition. And what one wants the other must have or I am allowed no peace in my own house."

"But the lady Vilia is the mother of your children, my lord, and she has always had your best interests at heart," Jonah murmured. "And you loved the lady Anora enough to ask the lady Vilia's permission to marry her."

"I don't want either of them any longer!" the emperor declared forcefully. "What can I do, Jonah, to get rid of them without the people thinking badly of me? I want to free my sweet Shifra and marry her. I want to make her my empress! Think, Jonah! *Think!*"

"My lord, this is a serious decision that you propose making," Jonah said softly. "With the lady Anora, while she will protest mightily, the solution is a simple one. I believe she would be content owning her own Pleasure House in The City. If you can arrange that along with the license to operate it in her name, if you will settle an outrageous amount of gold upon her, if she may keep her villa with its farm in the Outlands province, along with all the jewels and other luxuries you have settled upon her and if she may take her servants and slaves with her, I believe she could be persuaded to allow a divorce especially if no fault in the matter was laid at her door.

"And while I have always been respectful of the lady, I have also felt she was your bête noire, my lord. You will lose naught by ridding yourself of her. But the matter of the lady Vilia is another thing altogether, my lord. She is the mother of your children and is greatly respected among the people. You must think on this most carefully before you decide to move forward," Jonah advised.

"She has always preferred the country to The City," Gaius Prospero said slowly. "Even when we had that little farm in the Midlands where we would go to escape The City's heat in the summer. And with our daughters wed and Aubin grown, she seems to spend more and more time at that villa of hers in the Outlands."

"Ridding yourself of her will cost you dearly, my lord," Jonah said. "You cannot free and wed your slave girl and then make her your empress if you are still wed to the lady Vilia. The people would not stand for it. But first the lady Anora."

"Anora would cost me less if she just died," Gaius Prospero said softly.

"Indeed, my lord, she would," Jonah agreed, "and as you say, she has been ill these past few days. If you truly mean to rid yourself of her this might be a most convenient time," he suggested.

"I have paid little attention to her since she grew sick," the emperor noted. "Perhaps I should send her some special treat. She has developed a taste for Razi of late, the peach-flavored in particular."

"Will you allow me to send her some from one of my Razi kiosks, my lord?" Jonah suggested. "In your name, of course."

"It will be a most special blend of Razi, will it not?" Gaius Prospero asked. "It must be the best for I will have only the best for my dearest Anora." He lowered his voice so that only Jonah might hear it. "It should be quick. There ought not be any suf-

fering to draw attention to the sad event, Jonah. This illness she
has been suffering must be blamed for her untimely end. She is
not well-known among the people. A small period of official
mourning to show respect should suffice."

"It will be just as you wish, my lord, and a short public
mourning will more than suffice," Jonah told Gaius Prospero.
"But let us now consider the rest of the matter, my lord. The slave
girl is yours and she is going nowhere. You must move slowly and
carefully in the matter of the lady Vilia. In another month at the
Spring Festival, free Shifra in public gratitude for Anora's life and
service to you. The girl then becomes your private Pleasure
Woman. The people begin to know her and are happy for their
emperor who is so obviously content and happy himself.

"Then you will speak with the lady Vilia about dissolving
your union. And over the following months we will work out
the agreement between you with all its many details. You will
be very, very generous, both with your fortune and with your
words. At no time will you show disrespect, my lord, to either
your lady wife or the children she has borne you. While your
offspring are grown you must nonetheless make provisions for
them. This will please the lady Vilia and reassure her that you
mean her children no ill will. And by year's end the lady Vilia
will no longer be your wife, and you may do what you will with
your beloved," Jonah concluded softly.

"Jonah, as always you voice my very thoughts so succinctly,"
the emperor said.

"I have learned much from you in your service, my lord,"
Jonah murmured with a small bow. "If you will permit me I shall

now go and arrange for that gift to be delivered to the lady Anora so all of your plans may be set into motion." And he quickly withdrew, leaving Gaius Prospero chortling with delight.

A discreet and clever man, the emperor's right hand left the Golden District on foot and found his way into the Quarter. He was well cloaked, for he wanted no one to recognize him. He sought out one of his own Razi kiosks and purchased a full skin of the beverage, a mixture of frine and several herbs that gave the drinker dreams. Razi had become very popular in The City, especially among the poor who used it to quell the effects of their poverty. But the well-to-do also found it pleasant to drink when they sought to escape the tedium of their own world.

Returning to the Golden District, the wineskin concealed beneath his garments, Jonah sought out his own apartments. Within, there was a small interior chamber where he kept certain items. Carefully emptying the skin of Razi into a magnificent cut-crystal pitcher with a engraved gold lid, he then poured a small vial of clear, odorless liquid into the Razi and mixed it about. Then he personally carried the pitcher to the lady Anora's apartments and knocked.

The door opened just a small crack and a servant's head came into view. "Yes? What is it?" she asked. "Oh, it is you, Lord Jonah. I am sorry but my mistress is not well and will receive no one."

"I have just come from the emperor who informed me of your mistress's unfortunate illness. The emperor wished me to deliver this pitcher of peach Razi from one of my own kiosks, which as you know serve the best Razi in The City. He thought that as the lady Anora has been so indisposed she might enjoy this small treat. And he wished me to convey to the lady Anora that he has missed her good company and hopes she will soon be well enough to join him again." Jonah handed the pitcher to the serving woman, then with a small nod of his head, turned and left her.

The door had barely closed when Anora was nagging at her servant to deliver her the Razi for she had been listening to the exchange. "Bring it here! Bring it here! And fetch me a goblet," she said. "So, he is finally bored with his little slave girl and thinks to wheedle back into my good graces, does he? When this damnable rash finally recedes, his fat bottom will burn fire for his neglect of me, I promise you," Anora said, licking her lips in anticipation of the whipping she planned to give her husband.

"But the rash seems worse today, my lady," her servant pointed out. "It has crept down your legs and is even between your toes now. And there are more bumps erupting on your face and belly. And nothing the physician has prescribed has worked to ease your difficulties. Those little lumps ooze each time one breaks and it takes forever for them to dry up. And many that have broken have just been raised anew from the pus itself," she observed.

"The Razi, you stupid cow!" Anora snarled. "If I must bear this torture at least I can escape into a dream." She flung herself onto a low couch.

The serving woman fetched a large goblet and brought it along with the crystal pitcher to a small table by Anora's side. She poured the Razi into the goblet, smelling the delicious fragrance of peaches as she did. Anora snatched the goblet from her and drank it down, almost immediately holding the goblet out for more.

Anora looked at the large pitcher. The Razi sparkled within its crystal container. It would take her most of the afternoon to drink it all, but she would. And in between she would doze and dream. The stink of her sores and the appalling itching wouldn't plague her at all. Razi was what she needed to relax, for Anora had been terribly distressed by the nasty rash and evil pustules that had afflicted her. She swallowed down half the gobletful and felt generous. "Go and get some rest or just do what pleases you for a few hours," she said to her servant. "I will be all right here with my Razi. And do not ask, for I want no food. My belly is still distressed with this illness."

"Thank you, my lady," the servant replied. "If you are certain you do not need me I do have some things to do. And a walk in the garden would be pleasant."

"Go along," Anora waved her away, sipping at her goblet, her eyes closing.

The servant scampered from her mistress's chambers sighing with relief to finally be free of Anora's usual bad temper and the stink of her open sores. When she returned late in the day she wondered if she had stayed too long and if Anora would be angry at her. But the emperor's second wife was content. She even asked for some soup, which she drank down, returning then to her pitcher of Razi which was now almost empty. The serving woman helped her mistress to bed. Anora clutched her cup as she lay back, the last of the Razi in it. After washing the empty pitcher the servant dried it, set it among her mistress's things, for it was very beautiful, and found her bed.

When morning came the serving woman looked in on Anora. She appeared to be sleeping still, and as sleep had eluded her these past few days the servant decided to allow her mistress more rest. But when the noon hour came and there was no indication that Anora was awakening, the servant crept into her mistress's bedchamber. Anora looked beautiful despite the rash covering her body but the serving woman saw that she was not breathing. She put a small hand mirror to Anora's nostrils to be certain, but the mirror remained unblemished by even the faintest breath. Dropping the glass the servant ran from Anora's apartments screaming.

The emperor was informed that his second wife had died, apparently in her sleep. A physician came and seeing the rash and weeping sores announced that the poor lady had died of an infection, the cause of which was unknown to him. Criers went through the city announcing the untimely death of the emperor's beautiful second wife, the lady Anora. Because of the nature of her death the body would be cremated and the ashes buried in the family's burial ground. A public memorial would be held so that all the citizens of The City might mourn with the emperor who would host a grand feast for all of his good people.

The lady Vilia returned from her villa in the Outlands genuinely shocked by Anora's sudden death, but Gaius Prospero's apparent distress over his second wife's demise soothed any suspicions she might have had. Jonah said naught to her and he, too, appeared surprised by what had happened. But when on the first month's anniversary of Anora's death, at the Spring Festival, Gaius Prospero publicly freed his beautiful new slave girl, Shifra, Vilia began to wonder if Anora had not been murdered—and if her own life was now in jeopardy.

In the dark of night she made her way through the palace and sought her lover's quarters. All was quiet. She had managed to come to him using a series of hidden passages, thus avoiding the guards and the fierce panther cats that were brought in at night to prowl the palace with their keepers. Jonah was surprised to see the hidden door in his bedchamber open suddenly and Vilia step through.

"This is unwise, my love," he told her.

"I want the truth," Vilia said. "Was Anora murdered, Jonah?"

He smiled a rare smile. "I wondered when you would decide to ask me that question," he said, drawing her into the comfort of his arms. "The answer is yes, but I do not consider it murder, my love. The emperor wished to rid himself of her. He outlined to me the generosity he would show to Anora, for you know his fear of not being considered generous and benevolent. And then suddenly it occurred to us that perhaps there was an easier, a quicker way. You know her weakness for Razi. I indulged it."

"You poisoned her," Vilia said softly.

"With the illness she has been suffering I could be almost assured that the rash and pustules would be held to blame and they were," Jonah replied. "She did not suffer."

"And am I to be disposed of next?"

"Yes," he answered her candidly.

"Jonah!" She gasped.

He laughed gently and caressed her head. "In a far more humane way, my love. He holds you in high esteem, Vilia, but he wants to divorce you while at the same time not giving the appearance of cruelty or ingratitude for he knows that the people admire and respect you."

"To wed Shifra? He can have as many wives as he wants," Vilia exclaimed.

"To not just wed her but to make her his empress," Jonah said quietly.

"Never!" Vilia replied furiously. "The pig! That wretched little man would not sit so high were it not for us. He would take a nameless slave girl and make her empress of Hetar? He would put that soft girl in *my* place? I will kill him first!" Her eyes flashed angrily and there was high color in her cheeks.

"I have never seen you like this," Jonah murmured low and then pushing her to the carpet he fell upon her, his hands shoving her gown up. "You are surely the most exciting woman ever created, my darling Vilia."

"Get off me! Let me up!" she ordered him.

"No!" he growled and thrust himself into her female passage.

Vilia beat at him with her knotted fists. "Stop! I do not want you! This is no time for pleasures, Jonah. Stop!"

"Liar! You are already wet with your desire and I must have you!" He forced her arms above her head. Finding his rhythm he began to pleasure them both despite her protests, which waned until the only noise within the chamber was the sound of their rapid breathing and their moans of delight.

"You cannot make me forget what you have told me by wielding your manroot so skillfully," Vilia told him when they had finished indulging their passions.

Jonah stood, pulling Vilia up. Sitting down in a large chair by the hearth he drew her into his lap. "I don't want you to forget, my darling," he said. "But the time has not yet come for us to act. Gaius Prospero and his little *empress-to-be* will not rule Hetar for very long, Vilia. But we do not yet have the wealth we must to buy the allies who will help us successfully achieve this coup."

"I want him dead!" Vilia said. "And his pretty plaything, as well."

"Be patient, my darling." Jonah soothed the angry woman. "If we act too quickly the magnates will choose one from among them to rule or worse, go back to the republic with its High Council. There is no other man in Hetar besides me who can rule and there is no other woman who should grace the empress's throne but you, my darling Vilia. But we must proceed slowly. First, you must agree to the divorce that the emperor desires. Then you will negotiate under my guidance for an equitable settlement."

"And what is equitable?" Vilia wanted to know. Her anger was easing and suddenly the idea of ridding herself of Gaius Prospero was very appealing.

"Half of his wealth," Jonah said, smiling at her gasp of astonishment.

"He'll never agree!"

"He will agree, for his need to marry this girl and make her his empress will override everything else for him. I will see to it. The emperor believes himself secure and safe upon his throne. But once his wealth is halved he will be weakened."

"Gaius's one great talent," Vilia said, "is his ability to gain profit. He will rebuild his wealth quickly."

"Not quickly enough," Jonah replied. "I have amassed a small fortune during my years of service to Gaius Prospero, and you have also amassed a small fortune of your own. Our combined assets added to the settlement Gaius Prospero will fix on you will make us more powerful than the emperor. And that is when we will act to seize his throne. After all, the throne is part of his wealth and he has stolen it from you in order to put another in your place."

"How do you know I have amassed a small fortune?" Vilia asked him.

He smiled. "I know everything about the emperor and his family, my darling. I would not have survived this long did I not. You possess almost five million gold cubits along with considerable land holdings."

She nodded in acknowledgement of his words and then said, "And what do you possess, Jonah?"

"More. Much more," he said and the corners of his mouth turned up just faintly in reply to her question.

"How much more?" she demanded.

"Do not be greedy, Vilia. I am going to help you to become the richest woman in Hetar—as well as its empress," Jonah told her. "But since I see you cannot be satisfied until you know what you will know, I *will* tell you that I possess over one hundred million cubits of gold. You have more land than I do but I could not appear to be gaining wealth lest the emperor become suspicious."

"How in the name of the Celestial Actuary did you ever amass such a fortune?" Vilia wanted to know. She did believe him and she was enormously impressed.

"Mostly from the Razi kiosks," he told her. "Remember, I hold the monopoly on Razi in Hetar. And I have more kiosks throughout the country than anyone else. And if someone wishes to open a kiosk they must come to me first and apply. Of course I gain a fee when an application is filed. And then another fee when I issue a license. And the kiosk builder must pay me a fee for every kiosk he builds and there are only two builders who may build kiosks in the land. And the independent Razi vendors cannot own their kiosks. They must pay me a monthly rental, as well as thirty percent of their profits—collected daily so they may not cheat me. Razi has turned out to be a very lucrative business for me, my darling. And of course my vineyards are profitable and becoming more so each year."

"And my husband has more than that?" Vilia wanted to know. She had never paid a great deal of attention to Gaius's wealth. She had her own and her husband had never denied her anything she wanted for herself or their children.

"My wealth is equal to the emperor's now although he does not know it, my pet. But when you gain half of what is his and we combine our assets, we will be able to gain control. Cubits are power and the more one has the more powerful one is. We will marry, my dear Vilia, and you shall be Hetar's empress."

"When will we wed?" she wanted to know.

"I must consider the timing," Jonah told her. "It would appear suspicious should you divorce your husband, then turn about and wed too quickly."

"Will it not look suspect under any circumstances, Jonah, my love? If I aid you in gaining your goal I will not allow you to set me aside."

"Never!" he swore to her. "You will be my empress and my wife, Vilia, but be patient. First you will divorce Gaius Prospero and retire to your villa in the Outlands province. You and I both know that the only way to gain the throne must include the disposal of the emperor and his empress. And when I have been acclaimed Hetar's new emperor, my darling, I shall announce to all that as I have admired you from afar for many years, I have now asked you to be my wife and sit by my side as Hetar's empress. You are of an old and distinguished Hetarian family, Vilia. And your charities among the poor as Gaius Prospero's wife are well-known. Many gossip now that it is a disgrace he has not made you empress. You will be welcomed as my empress."

"What will happen to my children when Gaius is over-thrown?" Vilia wanted to know. "Especially my son, Aubin?"

"Aubin has no taste for the political life," Jonah said. "He is merchant-born as his father once was. And he enjoys a slightly decadent life, as do many young men of wealth. I will never harm any of your children, my darling. I swear it! But I will want you to give me an heir of my blood, Vilia. You are young enough yet."

"Aye, I am," she agreed. "I love my children, Jonah, but Aubin reminds me too much of his father. He is already running to fat."

"Then we are agreed as to the order of things," Jonah said.

"You will obtain your divorce and retire to the country. After I have overthrown Gaius Prospero and gained the throne, we will wed and you will be my empress."

"We are agreed, my love," Vilia told him. But she did not agree. She would wed him sooner. "I had best return to my apartments, Jonah. Sleep well, my lord." She kissed him softly, running a finger down his narrow face.

Jonah remained seated, staring into the fire burning in the hearth. His time was coming. He could smell it! He could taste it! Within two years he would be Hetar's ruler and Vilia would be by his side. He was surprised to realize that he really did want her with him. Was it love? He had no idea, but she was beautiful and clever and would make a perfect empress. But Vilia was also impatient. It would take all of his own skills to keep her from ruining everything. He would be more at ease once the divorce had been settled and she was back in the Outlands.

During the next few days Jonah carefully steered Gaius Prospero toward the emperor's goal. He coached his master carefully as to his meeting Vilia in order to tell her that he was divorcing her. "You must lay no blame for this decision upon her," he advised the emperor.

"I am bored with her," Gaius Prospero whined. "She does not excite me any longer and she is unable to take pleasures with me. Only Shifra can please me."

"And how fortunate you are, my lord, to have found this wonderful maiden," Jonah enthused. "But on the rare occasions I have been in the lady Shifra's company she has appeared a gentle and kind girl, my lord. I know she would not want you to hurt the lady Vilia."

"My Shifra is the soul of courtesy, Jonah. No, she would not want me to harm Vilia in any way. Ahh, Jonah, may you one day find such perfection," the emperor enthused with a gusty sigh.

"Indeed, my lord, I wish it myself. But we must also consider the people in this matter of your divorce, for what they think is important to you," Jonah continued.

"How shall I please the people, then? They love Vilia," Gaius Prospero said.

"The first step must be to speak with your wife," Jonah advised.

The emperor visited Vilia. Her delight in his arrival within her apartments almost made him feel guilty. She was still a handsome woman and far younger than he, Gaius Prospero considered silently. Was he doing the right thing? And then a vision of Shifra arose in his head and he knew that right or wrong, he must have Shifra for his wife and for his empress. If he kept Vilia and then supplanted her with Shifra as his empress the people would not stand for it. No. He had to divorce Vilia. There was no other way.

They were seated in the privacy of Vilia's dayroom. She had dismissed the serving women and was serving him herself. She poured him a large goblet of sweet wine and placed a wooden board with bread and fine Midlands cheese before him. "I am certain you are famished after your long day, my lord," Vilia said pleasantly. "We have hardly spoken since Anora's tragic death. You seem to have born up well, Gaius."

"I have had Shifra to comfort me," he answered her.

"It was kind of you to free her from her slavery in Anora's honor. The people very much liked such a generous gesture on the part of their beloved emperor," Vilia remarked with a small smile.

He drank half his goblet down and she quickly refilled it. "I have come, my dear Vilia, to speak with you on a most sensitive and serious matter," the emperor began. Tiny beads of moisture were beginning to dot his smooth forehead. "Over the past months we have barely seen one another and it is long since we took pleasures together. Your life seems to be spent more and more at your villa in the Outlands province, Vilia, while mine must of necessity be spent here in The City."

"You wish to divorce me," Vilia said and she almost laughed when he paled at her words. But then she reached out and put a comforting hand on his arm.

"I have not said it!" he cried.

"But it is what you wish," she answered. "If you wanted me to spend more time with you, Gaius, you would have asked me directly. You have found love, I am told, with the young Shifra. You have not loved me as a husband should for a long time. I think I realized it when you asked to marry Anora."

"Do you love me as a wife loves a husband, Vilia?"

"No longer, Gaius, but you know that without asking. We have grown apart and while that is sad there is no help for it," Vilia told him frankly. "We can remain friends."

He could feel the waves of relief rolling over him at her words. "I think of you as I would a dear friend," he told her. "I want us always to be friends, Vilia. We have children in common."

"Indeed, Gaius, we do," she said with a small smile. "But as long as I am your wife you cannot wed Shifra without my approval and knowing you as I do, you want her for more than a wife. You want her for your empress, Gaius."

"I have not said that!" he protested but she waved his denial aside.

"Gaius, Gaius, I am not a fool. If you wanted Shifra only for a wife I would give you my permission and you would wed her. But you want to make her your empress and you cannot do that while you are still married to me. The people would not stand for it. You are clever enough to know that. You must rid yourself of me first. And you cannot have another wife conveniently die, can you?" She laughed at the look of shock and surprise and yes, even a little fear upon his fat face.

"I...I don't know what you mean," he said nervously.

"I mean what I say, Gaius, but do not distress yourself. I am perfectly willing to give you the divorce you desire and to make certain that the people know we are both of a single mind in this matter. And because of your great generosity to me I shall sing your praises to the skies and publicly pledge my loyalty to both you and your new empress wife. But as a good merchant, my dear husband, you realize that there will be a steep price to pay for this unique gift I am prepared to give you." She smiled at him but he saw no warmth in her amber eyes.

"What do you want?" He finally gained the courage to ask her.

"Half of all you own, Gaius. That is my price for your happiness and for the privilege of allowing your beautiful Shifra to have what should have rightfully been mine several years ago—had you not been such a fat coward," Vilia said in an icy voice.

The emperor grew red in the face. "You are mad!" he shouted. "Totally and completely mad to believe that I would give you half of what is mine!"

Vilia shrugged. "Then enjoy your Pleasure Woman, Gaius, for unless you give me what I desire, I will not give you what you desire and Shifra will remain nothing more than that." She smiled at him again. "I thought you were enjoying your wine, *Husband*."

"You play a dangerous game, you bitch!" he snarled.

"Had I not stood by your side all these years, had I not curried favor with the magnates' wives and given the lavish parties and entertainments that brought you to prominence, Gaius. Had I not given you children and an air of respectability. Had my respected family not allowed you to marry me, the daughter of a prestigious Hetarian house when you were not truly worthy enough of my bloodlines, where would you be today? My support and my wisdom guided you, Gaius. And now you wish to cast me off as if I was an old slipper? Well, you shall not. You shall give me half of all you possess and in return you will gain all I have previously promised to you. Is your Shifra not deserving enough of half your wealth, Gaius? Does the gold mean more to you than the woman you claim to love?"

"I must think on it," he said putting the goblet down, for his hand was shaking.

"I have sent faerie posts to our children telling them you seek to divorce me," Vilia said. "They will, of course, be extremely upset."

"You would turn them against me!" he shouted at her.

Vilia smiled. "If you treat me properly and with respect," she said, "that will not happen. Have you considered that Shifra might give you a child? You are not too old to sire another child and Shifra will do naught to prevent it if she believes it will please you. And if you would put this girl in my rightful place, Gaius, what is to prevent you from disinheriting my children in favor of hers? No, this is not just for me, it is for our children, too. I must protect them and see to their inheritance."

The emperor stumbled to his feet. "I need to think," he said and he headed for the door to her apartments on visibly unsteady feet.

"Think well, my lord," she warned him. "Shifra might even now be breeding."

Gaius Prospero fled his wife and hurried to his own quarters. Once there he sent a servant for Jonah who quickly answered his master's call. Stammering and stuttering, Gaius Prospero told his good right hand of his visit to Vilia and what had transpired between them. "She will beggar me!" the emperor complained, gasping for breath.

For a brief moment Jonah almost felt sympathy for Gaius Prospero. Vilia at her coldest was a formidable opponent. He put a comforting hand upon the emperor's arm. "You will not like what I have to say, my lord, but the lady Vilia is indeed entitled to what she asks. You are clever, my lord. Your enterprises will quickly make back the half of your wealth that you give her. And even with the loss of that wealth you are surely the richest man in Hetar. She has not dissembled with you but has been honest and open in her wishes. Accept her terms and within the month the deed will be done and the lady Vilia will be gone from The City. You need never again set eyes upon her if that is your wish. And then when summer ends you may wed the lovely lady Shifra with a happy heart and a clear conscience. This matter might have taken many months to negotiate but the lady Vilia is a reasonable and wise woman."

"But what if my Shifra gives me a son, Jonah? I already have a son," Gaius Prospero said. "Is not Aubin my rightful heir?"

"Indeed my lord, he is, but I am certain that if his mother reasons with him he will step aside. But if you ask that of the lady Vilia then you must accede to her demands in return," Jonah advised. He would not have thought to push Gaius Prospero so hard and so fast but Vilia obviously knew her husband better than any. Vilia was going to be a magnificent empress, Jonah thought admiringly. She had incredible instincts.

The emperor's eyes narrowed as he considered Jonah's words. Then he said, "Do you really think she can convince Aubin to relinquish his place in the succession, Jonah?"

"I think she is the only person who can," Jonah replied. "Half your wealth, my lord, will buy you the woman you love for your wife and your empress and a clear line of descent. Isn't it worth it?" Following Vilia's lead he pushed the emperor, but gently.

Gaius Prospero sighed deeply. Then he said, "Go to her, Jonah, and tell her if she will convince Aubin to give up his place as my heir, then I will agree to all of her demands. You are right! I would end this as quickly as possible. As the bitch pointedly reminded me I cannot have another wife die suddenly merely for my convenience. I think she knows about Anora, though how I cannot be certain. But I will not allow Vilia to spoil my happiness. Nor will I allow any harm or slander to touch my Shifra."

"I shall go at once, my lord," Jonah told him, and he hurried off. Reaching Vilia's apartments he was ushered into her presence. She received him seated in a high-backed chair. "Lord Jonah," she said formally. "What is it my husband wishes of me?" She waved a hand at her serving women. "Leave us. I will call if I need you." Then she turned her attention to Jonah, waiting until the women had left the chamber. "Well?" she demanded. "Has he recovered from his shock?"

"Your proposal is painful for him, my darling, but if Aubin will agree to give up his place in the succession, then the emperor will agree to give you what you want. He wants it done quickly and you gone from The City as soon as possible."

"I will send for my son at once," Vilia said.

Aubin Prospero came with all haste and listened to what his mother had to tell him. He was a younger version of his father, of medium height and stocky. When his mother concluded her tale he said, "I will want to be named your principal heir in your will, Mother. My sisters have husbands to provide for them. And if I am to find a rich wife it must be known that I am your heir. The wealthy do not give their daughters to poor men. Give me ninety percent of what is left when you go to the Celestial Actuary and the girls may each have five percent."

"Is that not just a trifle greedy, Aubin?" Vilia asked her son.

"Nay, 'tis not. It isn't likely my father will leave me anything, Mother. I was at the auction where he bought his new Pleasure Woman. Shifra is incredibly beautiful and she will probably give the emperor children. I don't care about being his heir and inheriting his throne one day," Aubin Prospero said. "I would not want to be in his shoes. I am content with my activities with the

Merchants' Guild. I should not like to have the responsibilities of Hetar upon my shoulders."

"I will give you eighty percent, Aubin, and your sisters will each gain ten percent. That is fairer, my son."

The young man laughed. "Done!" he said, holding out his hand to his mother.

Vilia took her son's hand, shook it and then kissed it. "Thank you," she said. "You will, of course, have to sign some sort of legal document, won't he, Lord Jonah?"

"Aye, my lady, we must observe the legalities of the matter to the nth degree," Jonah answered. Then he turned to Aubin Prospero. "You are certain, young lord?"

"I am certain," Aubin Prospero answered him.

"I shall go and tell the emperor, my lady," Jonah said and departed the room.

"What will you do?" Aubin Prospero asked his mother.

"I am going to my villa in the Outlands province," she told him. "I love it there and have since the moment I saw the property. My home is spacious and comfortable. You must come and see it, Aubin. If you like it I will give it to you one day."

He smiled at her. "You are not unhappy, are you, Mother? I suspect you are glad to be getting your divorce from my father."

"He is going to marry her and eventually declare her the empress," Vilia said. "I can hardly remain under those circumstances, can I, Aubin?"

Aubin Prospero shook his head. "He is giving her what should have been yours," he said slowly. "I do not like that he shames you in such a fashion."

"I can only be shamed if I allow it," Vilia said. "He will marry her by summer's end, but he will not create her empress until the people are used to her. He would destroy his credibility with the people if he crowned her while the ink was still fresh on our divorce papers." Vilia chuckled.

"You are an amazing woman, Mother," Aubin Prospero said. "What a shame my father could never see that. If I cannot find a woman like you I shall never marry," he told her with a smile and then he kissed her cheek.

Vilia laughed. "You will marry one day, Aubin," she told him. Then she took his hand in hers. "When the news of our divorce becomes public and it soon will, you will be queried by friends and acquaintances alike. Do not fault your father in the matter. You are right when you say I am not unhappy. I am not. Actually, by freeing me your father has done me a great kindness, so let none speak ill of him."

"I hope he has made a decent settlement upon you, Mother. You have served him well all these years," Aubin said.

Vilia laughed. "If you want to know what I have taken from him, my son, then just ask it of me. When this is over and done with and the papers signed, your father will be poorer by half his wealth," she told him, laughing again as his eyes grew wide with his surprise. "You will be a very rich man one day."

When Aubin Prospero got past his shock he said, "Amazing! You have earned every cubit of it, Mother. Who negotiated the settlement for you with father?"

"I did," Vilia responded. "Do you think I would pay some legal counsel when I was perfectly competent to do it myself?"

He laughed. "Amazing!" he repeated. Then he arose. "With your permission I will depart. I have an assignation at Lady Gillian's tonight with an enchanting creature and I do not want to keep her waiting." He caught his mother's hand up and kissed it. "Goodbye, Mother. Do not leave The City before you have seen me again."

"I shall not, Aubin," Vilia said and watched as her son left her. He was a dear boy, she thought. Yet he could never imagine the plans that she and Jonah had and perhaps that was just as well. She would keep her bargain with her son, for any child she gave Jonah would inherit his father's wealth.

HROLLEIF, CHIEF OF THE Wolfyn, looked about the table at his companions—Skrymir, chieftain of the Dark Land giants; Dain, chieftain of the Dark Land dwarfs; Alfrigg, the chancellor of the Dark Land; and the Twilight Lord himself. Why, Hrolleif wondered, had they all been called into the great Kol's presence? Then Kol spoke.

"The time for conquest draws near," he began. "I have the faerie woman in my power. She ripens with my heir. The Munin have been slowly restoring her memory. Soon I will return the memory of how to use all of her magic."

"But will she wield it for you?" Hrolleif growled in a deep voice. The Wolfyn were creatures with the heads of wolves and the bodies of mortal men. They were fierce fighters and savage in their conquests, which had been few in recent decades.

"She has no memory of her past other than that which I choose to allow her," Kol said. "She loves me. If she did not I could never have impregnated her with my son. She will do whatever I wish, for she trusts me. She believes I taught her the magic she now remembers. She believes I gave her the knowledge so she might help me."

"I have heard it said that when you mate with other women you have them killed afterwards in order to please Lara," Dain of the Dwarfs remarked.

"That seems a shameful waste of female flesh," Skrymir muttered.

The Twilight Lord laughed. "I only killed a few to gain her trust," he replied. "If she continues to believe that I kill more, it is all to the good, is it not, my lords?"

"Is it possible that your own black heart has been engaged by the faerie woman? It is said that her charms are irresistible," Hrolleif growled. "Love is a deterrent to power, my lord, as you well know."

Kol shot the Wolfyn chief an angry look. "If anything," he replied, "Lara has strengthened my powers. Whether I love her or not matters little, for our magic combined is unstoppable. Do you question my vision now, Hrolleif?" The look Kol gave the Wolfyn caused Hrolleif's pointed ears to twitch.

"Nay, my lord Kol!" he protested. "I am merely concerned for your well-being. Perhaps it is natural that you feel tenderly toward this faerie woman who has been chosen to bear your son. I recall a similar emotion when my mate dropped her first litter."

"Aye," Skrymir added soothingly in his rough voice. "We all have felt tenderly toward our mates when they are breeding. It is natural."

Dain nodded in agreement.

"My lords, can we please get back to the matter at hand?" Alfrigg said sharply.

Kol hid his smile at the irritation in his chancellor's voice. Alfrigg was not a sentimental man. "The timing will be crucial," he said. "The planning, however, must begin now for the key to keeping our casualties low and the damage to the land at a minimum will be in that foresight."

"We will want the forests of Hetar and the cattle pastures of the Fiacre for ourselves, my lord," Hrolleif said.

"And *we* will want the mountains in Hetar and Terah for ourselves," Dain remarked. "And the dwarfs there for our slaves."

Kol held up an elegant hand. "My lords," he said. "This can all be worked out. I shall leave you with Alfrigg to begin your work." Then with a cold smile he left them.

Kol moved swiftly through the corridors of his castle. He was anxious to be with Lara, a fact that surprised him every time he realized it. In just a few more months she would deliver his son and heir. And then they might take pleasures together again. He had missed their couplings, but it was tradition that once the Chosen One was with child her lord did not use her body even casually. Strangely the lustful urges that generally overcame him were few of late and he rarely visited his House of Women where there lived a variety of beautiful females from his own world and others.

Reaching Lara's quarters he swept into her dayroom. "Good morrow, my precious," he greeted her with a small smile.

"My dearest lord!" Lara held out her arms to him in welcome. She was lounging upon a purple velvet couch with but one rolled arm. "What have you been doing today while I missed your company?" One graceful hand lay upon her swollen belly.

"Beginning the plan for our conquest of the other worlds," he told her. "I have gathered Hrolleif of the Wolfyn, Skrymir of the Giants and Dain of the Dwarfs, all bound to me by oath. I left them with Alfrigg. What have you been doing?"

"I spent some hours looking into the reflecting bowl as you suggested. The fat emperor of Hetar seems to be a wife short from the last time I looked. He still does not know that his first wife is betraying him with his right hand." She laughed. "And he has fallen in love, Kol! That obnoxious little man is in love!"

"Is his lover beautiful, my precious?" Kol asked Lara.

"Oh yes, very beautiful! I have planned a delicious entertainment for us when we take The City, my lord. Before we kill him we will bind this fat emperor to his throne and make him watch as this pretty creature he loves is forced to give pleasures to you as Hetar's conqueror. And you will use both your dominant and lesser rods with the girl. Then you will pass her to the Wolfyn chief, the Dwarf chief and finally to Skrymir. If his love rod does not split her in two then we will give her to whichever of your legions fought the hardest. Her screams should drive the fat emperor mad," Lara laughed.

Kol smiled broadly. "My precious, what delicious darkness bubbles within you. May our son inherit it. But what of the emperor's unfaithful wife? Should she not also be punished for her naughtiness?"

"Not as severely, for her wickedness is dark. Is that not good, my lord?" Lara purred. "Let her be forced to take pleasures with her lover in the emperor's sight. And then we will kill the fat slug. But slowly. We will cut his rod and balls from his body. I will prevent him from feeling the pain of it. Then we will roast them over a slow fire and force him to eat them." She giggled. "With each bite he takes he will feel the pain. His screams, however, will become tedious then, my lord, and so we will have to garotte him." She caressed his cheek. "Do you like my program, my lord?"

"Aye, I do, you charming witch. How I wish we might take pleasures together, for when you speak of such delightful evil I am filled with my lust for you, Lara, my precious. But my son must be protected." He lay his hand on her belly and smiled into her icy green eyes. "You are such perfection, Lara. I adore you!"

"I am so glad the knowledge of my magic has returned," Lara told him, smiling back into his eyes. "Now, my lord, there is something we must discuss. I will need a wet nurse for this child. A healthy woman with big breasts overfull with milk to suckle our son, for I will have no time for such common labors. Find me such a woman and have her ready for the day I give birth. Tell her to wean her own child within the next two months. Then she must come to the castle and you will suckle her daily until your son is birthed. It will keep her milk fresh and sweet, her breasts overflowing and ready to nourish your son. Is that not a perfect idea?"

Kol found himself more and more astounded by Lara as each day passed. The faerie woman of Hetar and Terah was known for her kindness, her goodness. But Lara, devoid of all of her personal memories, this Lara that he was helping to shape and create was a creature of pure darkness. She was indeed his mate and for the next several hundred years they would enjoy one another, for it appeared the mortal in her had been overridden by her magic. She would not die young as humans did.

IN THE WORLD BEYOND the Dark Land the spring passed, another summer came and Magnus Hauk grew more and more despondent. His magical allies appeared to be completely stymied by Lara's mysterious disappearance and their inability to find her was maddening. The Dominus's only solace was the three children in his home. Zagiri was now four years old and would have forgotten her mother had it not been for her half sister, Anoush. The Dominus had come to love Lara's two offspring by Vartan, but he especially loved Anoush, for even with little real personal knowledge herself of her mother, the girl wove a history of Lara that kept her alive for Zagiri.

"When will our mother return to us?" Magnus Hauk heard his daughter ask her half sister one day.

"Very soon, I am sure, little Zagiri," Anoush assured her younger sibling. "Her destiny will soon be realized and she will return to us."

"Really? Truly?" Zagiri asked wide-eyed.

"Oh yes," Anoush replied with certainty.

"How do you know that?" Zagiri said.

"I just do," Anoush responded. "Do not forget, Zagiri, that our mother is a magical being and we have all inherited certain of her talents, I am sure."

Dillon, who had been standing in the shadows with his stepfather, smiled and said softly, "Aye, and now I see that Anoush has been given the gift of sight along with her budding abilities as a healer."

Magnus Hauk drew in a sharp breath. "And Zagiri. What will her talent be?"

"I do not know, Magnus," the boy replied. "It is too soon."

"Walk with me," the Dominus said. "We need to talk. It's almost a year now since your mother was stolen away. Answer me honestly. Do you believe that Kaliq does not know where she is? And what of Ilona? It has been weeks since I have heard from either of them and when I do, they say naught but that there is no hint of where Lara is. I think that they lie and I wonder why it is that they do. My suspicions grow daily."

Dillon nodded. "I cannot say that I do not agree with you, Magnus. It has seemed odd to me that the Shadow Princes, the most powerful beings in our world, are ignorant of my mother's fate. But I am yet a boy and my talents have not been trained. Still, I believe it is now time for you to request Prince Kaliq's presence. Ask him directly what it is he knows and why he has kept it from us. We have all been patient but we are all suffering from Mother's absence. Verica, my mother's staff, has ceased speaking even to me. Andraste, her sword, hums incessantly from her place above the hearth in my mother's rooms. Dasras yet sulks in the New Outlands with Sakira, and the clan families mourn without ceasing and blame themselves. But we know that they are not responsible for Mother's disappearance."

"Is it, do you think, her destiny?" the Dominus asked his stepson fearfully.

"It must be, but we will not know until we have summoned

Kaliq," the boy said. "You must do it, Magnus. You must call for the Shadow Prince to come to us."

Magnus Hauk nodded. "Then let us go to the interior chamber from where your mother and I summon him. It is private."

"First let us see the girls tucked into their beds," Dillon suggested. "It will be better for us all in the quiet of the night when we are less apt to be disturbed. I will find Mila and see it done."

The Dominus nodded and sought the little chamber to wait for Dillon. *Lara!* Her name echoed softly in his head. What had happened to his beloved wife? Where could she be? His first thoughts were that Hetar had somehow managed to gain custody of her. If so, he was ready to go to war over it. But Kaliq assured him it was not and Magnus Hauk had trusted Kaliq—although now he was not certain that he still should. And if the great Shadow Prince knew where Lara was, why had he kept the knowledge to himself? Questions, questions. He had far more questions than he had answers.

Finally his stepson joined him.

"All is secure. It is a quiet night, Magnus."

"Then we are ready to summon Kaliq." He turned and faced a blank wall opposite the door to the chamber. *"Kaliq of the Shadows, heed my call. Come to me from out yon wall,"* the Dominus intoned.

"Good evening, Magnus. Dillon," the Shadow Prince said as he stepped through the wall and into the chamber. "It has been some weeks since we last spoke. You are both looking well, I am pleased to see."

He was as handsome as ever, Dillon thought. The Shadow

Prince's bright blue eyes blazed with light. His ebony hair showed no silver despite his many centuries.

"We are not well," the Dominus replied. "None of us. We all suffer Lara's loss. Our children. The clan families. Dasras, Andraste, Verica, the Terahn people. I think you know where my wife is, Kaliq, and the time has come for you to be forthright with me."

Kaliq's eyes touched Dillon lightly. "And you, young Dillon? What think you?" he asked the boy.

"I agree with my stepfather, my lord prince. While I realize you have your reasons for keeping silent, I also think it is past time for us to know the truth."

Kaliq smiled a small smile. "Use your instincts, young Dillon," he said. "Concentrate and use them now! Tell me where Lara is!"

Dillon's eyes closed slowly. He was silent for some few minutes and then opening his eyes he said, "My mother is in the Dark Lands, my lord."

Kaliq nodded. "She is," he agreed.

Magnus Hauk felt hot anger welling up within him. Forcing that anger back he said, "If you knew Lara was in the Dark Lands, why did you not tell us a year ago?"

"Come now, Magnus, you know the answer to that as well as I do. You would have mounted an expedition and warred with the Dark Landers. We could not allow it. Had you attacked them you would have loosed the forces of darkness upon both Terah and Hetar. Your worlds would not have known real peace for centuries. The darkness must always be contained, Magnus. We cannot wipe it out entirely for there must always be a certain balance between good and evil, but we can contain the worst of it. When we do not, war, pestilence, cruelty and famine roam the worlds and cause havoc."

"But the Dark Land has always remained to itself," Magnus Hauk said.

"Yes, but as there is prophecy here and in Hetar, so there is prophecy in the Dark Lands. Lara has always known that she had a special destiny. Part of that destiny is in the Dark Lands. When she has fulfilled it she will be returned to you. Shortly, that part of her destiny will be met. And it must be met or the worlds of Hetar and Terah will suffer. That is why you could not know where she was. You must trust me in this. I will allow no harm to come to Lara. I would forfeit my own life first."

"When she returns to us, will she tell us of where she had been and what she has done?" Dillon asked the prince.

"Nay, young Dillon, she will not. Her memory of her time in the Dark Lands will be completely gone from her, and it is better that it is. She will be told that part of her destiny has been implemented and she will be satisfied with that knowledge," the prince explained.

"Why will you not tell us what she is doing?" Magnus Hauk asked.

"Because it is not necessary that you know," Kaliq responded quietly. "I will tell you only that Lara is helping us to keep the balance between the darkness and the light. Anything else would be too much for you to bear, Magnus Hauk. Why are you so suddenly insistent on meddling in matters of magic?"

"Because it is *my wife* whom you are using as your tool," the Dominus said angrily.

Kaliq laughed aloud although he had tried not to. "Ah, my poor friend. How fortunate Lara is to have you for her husband. No other mortal could possibly love her as you do." He put a comforting arm about the Dominus's broad shoulders. "Please trust me, Magnus. Your time of separation is almost over. I swear it."

"It would seem I have no choice unless it is to amass my armies and go into the Dark Lands," the Dominus replied.

"You would be advised not to do that for many reasons but probably the one that would concern you the most is Hetar's plan to attack Terah shortly. They believe that you have been weakened by Lara's disappearance and they have convinced their people that Terah poses a threat to Hetar. Their proposed war against you is being undertaken to *protect* Hetar, or so it is being said. The Coastal Kings have been building great ships of war. I suspect you had best prepare to defend your own kingdom while Lara completes her destiny and balances the light and the darkness."

"So that is why we have seen so little of Jonah of late," the Dominus muttered. "Can you close the portal so he may not return? That way he cannot report when we reinforce our defenses along the sea and at the fjord entrances."

Kaliq smiled. "The portal is already closed, Magnus. And now I must go. I wish to take Dillon with me for a time—with your permission, of course. I will return him shortly," Kaliq promised.

Dillon's green eyes grew wide with his excitement. "I am to be allowed to go to Shunnar?" he said and then his look swung to the Dominus. "Magnus?"

"I do not know," Magnus Hauk replied. "Your mother did not want you going until you were twelve, Dillon."

"Going to be *taught*," the prince quickly interjected, "and I certainly agree with Lara, but this is just a little visit to quell Dillon's curiosity and to ease his anxiety over his mother. I will return him in three days' time, I promise you."

"Oh, please, Magnus!" the boy begged. *"Please!"*

"No more than three days, Kaliq, for I need him by my side," the Dominus said.

Kaliq nodded. "I understand," he said, and he did. Dillon with his budding magic was the closest thing Magnus Hauk had to Lara now.

"Very well then, but three days only, Dillon. Do you understand?" the Dominus told his stepson. "If your mother returned while you were gone I should have a great deal of explaining to do about this."

"Thank you, Magnus," the boy said as Kaliq enfolded him in his robes. And then they were gone in a magical and shadowy mist.

Magnus Hauk stood silently for some minutes after they had disappeared. He was very curious about what the Shadow Prince had said. A balance between good and evil that must be maintained. What had that to do with Lara? He wondered if he would ever really know what Kaliq had meant. He found himself impatient sometimes with the magical world that lived alongside of him.

Magnus Hauk left the chamber and sought his lonely bed. He had other matters to consider now, namely Hetar. He had hoped the clever Jonah could keep that fool who called himself emperor under control. But either he could not, or like his master he believed Terah was weak without Lara. The thought irritated the Dominus. Terah had been strong before Lara and would remain so in her unfortunate absence. *I hope I have done the right thing allowing Dillon to go with Kaliq,* he thought to himself just before he fell asleep.

DILLON HAD CLOSED his eyes when the Shadow Prince had wrapped his cloak about him. Now Kaliq's voice bade him to open those eyes. It was morning and the air was warm. Nay, hot. Seeing a sculpted balustrade across the chamber, he remembered his mother's tales of her mentor's palace of Shunnar. Unable to help himself, Dillon ran to the balustrade and looked down in the green valley below where several herds of magnificent horses were now grazing.

"Oh, my lord, it is just as my mother said!" he exclaimed excitedly. Then he turned about. "Why have you brought me here now?" he asked softly.

"I thought it was time for you to choose one of my horses for your own," the prince answered smiling. "You need a like companion, for you are a unique boy in your world, Dillon. I will call the giant Og, your mother's friend who is my horse master, and he will take you down into the valley. You will like him."

"Mother has told me all about Og," Dillon responded. "I have always wanted to meet him. She says he is a small giant but most kind."

The prince smiled and called to one of his servants to request that Og join them.

The giant came and while Lara might say he was small, he

seemed very large to Dillon. He might have been afraid were it not for Og's gentle blue eyes. "Do not tell me! Do not tell me!" Og exclaimed. "I would know you anywhere—Dillon, son of Lara."

Reaching down he lifted the boy up and settled him in the crook of his arm so they might speak on a more even level. "Welcome to Shunnar, young master. I did not expect that we would meet for another few years." He smiled cheerfully at Dillon.

"Take the boy to the valley, Og," the prince said. "Find him a horse that will be his own, and together, begin to train it."

"I will, my lord prince," Og said and then looked at Dillon. "Tell me, young master, have you any particular color horse in mind?"

"Well," Dillon said, "I thought perhaps a dappled gray, Og. Do you think there is one in the valley that would be suitable for me?"

"We will have to go and look," Og said. He set Dillon down again. "Follow me then, lad, and we will see where your horse is." He bowed to the prince. "How long would you like me to keep him, my lord? We really should have the day."

"You have it," Kaliq said smiling, and he watched as Og moved off with the boy running in his effort to keep up. The prince then turned to his waiting servant. "Bring me the reflecting mirror," he said and when the servant had complied he withdrew from the chamber. Kaliq placed the oval, set into a golden frame, into a polished wood stand. Then standing before it he said quietly, "Come to me, lord of the Munin." At once, the wraithlike creature who spoke for his brothers appeared in the glass.

"Help us, Kaliq of the Shadows," the Munin lord said, his filmy arms outstretched.

"What help do you require of me?" Kaliq murmured. "Are you not content in the Penumbras in the castle the Twilight Lord created for you?"

"He has imprisoned us here!" the Munin lord cried. "We are unable to harvest, to retrieve or to restore memories, which is our function in this world. Help us!"

"If I help you, then you must do what I ask in return," Kaliq told the Munin lord.

"What do you want of us?" the Munin asked.

"The balance must be restored between the light and the dark," Kaliq began. "You must return *all* of Lara's memories to her. Only then can she act to fulfill her destiny. It must be done."

"If we do as you ask, Kol will destroy us," the Munin lord said desperately.

"If you do not do as I ask, I will leave you in the Penumbras and you will be forced to serve at Kol's command for eternity. Do you really want the Twilight Lord using your gifts to his own advantage? You know what that would do to the balance. But if you do what I ask of you, I will give you another homeland and you will be free to roam at will as you should. You will have the protection of the Shadow Princes and Kol will not be able to harm any of your brothers ever again."

"Returning all of her memories may destroy her, for in Kol's charge the light within Lara has dimmed almost entirely. Her aura has grown purple. Even I am afraid of her," the Munin lord said. "And if the shock of her restored memories should harm Kol's heir, he may very well kill her."

"She will survive and so will her offspring," Kaliq said. "But that is not all I require of the Munin. My second request I will make at another time, however."

"Where would you raise up our castle?" the Munin lord asked slowly.

"On the most remote shore of the Obscura. A tunnel would run from deep within your castle beneath the sea to your storage facility. No one in Hetar is even aware of the Obscura's existence. This sea is wide and on its other side live the clan families of the New Outlands. They are not mariners but people of the land. We will render your castle invisible to all but magical eyes so you will be safe. Kol can see nothing in the blazing light of the desert," Kaliq pointed out. "What say you?"

"You will protect us from his revenge, Shadow Prince?" the Munin lord asked.

"I will protect you. Even as I speak your castle stands awaiting you, the storage chambers beneath the sea cool and dim and ready for the memories you possess," Kaliq said. "What is your answer, Munin lord?"

"I must speak with my brothers," came the reply.

"You have five minutes," Kaliq replied and he watched as the Munin lord disappeared from his sight in the mirror.

When the Munin returned he said, "First you must release us and then we will do your bidding."

"I will move your brothers but you must remain," Kaliq said.

The Munin lord nodded his agreement. "Very well," he said.

"Then it is done," Kaliq murmured. "I have filled your castle with images of the Munin so Kol will not know that you are gone. Now I will send you to Kol's throne room. It is the

sleeping hour there, so no one is awake. You will take the remainder of Lara's memories from the alabaster jar by Kol's throne
and give them back to her. I will be by her side upon the dream
plain while you do, so she is not frightened."

"And when I have done your bidding?" the Munin lord asked.

"You will join your brothers," Kaliq said.

"And the other request you would make of us?"

"In time, not yet," Kaliq replied. "Now, prepare to enter the
castle of the Twilight Lord." Kaliq waved his hand and the Munin
was transferred from his castle in the Penumbras into the great
receiving chamber of the Twilight Lord. Kaliq watched as the
mirror reflected exactly what was happening.

The chamber was quiet and dark but for two censers
burning on either side of Kol's throne. Silently, the Munin
lord drifted to the tall alabaster jar. Carefully he removed the
golden threads of Lara's remaining memories and slipped
them into his robes while drawing out a sheaf of empty
memories which he placed into the jar. Kaliq watched and
nodded. The Munin was clever. Now the creature drifted
from the room and, making his invisible way down a series
of corridors, finally entered Lara's apartments. He moved
past her sleeping attendants upon whom Kaliq had placed a
deep sleeping spell so that there would be no chance of them
awakening.

Entering Lara's bedchamber the Munin lord floated over the
faerie woman and reaching into his robes for her memories,
allowed the slender golden strands to slide from his fingers and
back into her head. When it had been done the Shadow Prince

gestured quickly with his hand and the Munin was gone. Then Kaliq closed his own eyes and prepared to enter the dream plain to speak with Lara.

She stirred, then opening her green eyes, realized she stood upon the dream plain. About her, the warm mauve mist swirled. "Who is it?" Lara called. "Who seeks me?"

"It is I, my love," Kaliq answered her and then he was at her side.

"What has happened to me?" Lara asked him.

He took her into his arms to comfort her. "Be still for a moment, my love, and it will all return to you. You are shortly to fulfill a portion of your destiny, Lara."

"How can this be?" Lara suddenly cried, pulling away from him, her eyes dropping to her very distended belly. "Ohh! Ohh! How could you do this to me, Kaliq?" Her eyes were filled with tears. "Do you know what has happened to me? Do you realize who this child I carry is? And *this* was my great destiny? To be bred to a lord of the darkness? To give him a child?"

The Shadow Prince held up a hand. "Stop!" he said to Lara.

She grew silent and looked despairingly at him.

"Hear me out, my love, and all will be well, I promise you. There must always be balance between the light and the dark, for the mortal races seem unable to choose good over evil. Those of us in the magical world must therefore keep the balance between the two when the darkness threatens to over-whelm the light, which it does with certain regularity. If only it would go the other way—but it never does so we toil to counterbalance discord with harmony.

"We have known for some time what was written within the

Twilight Lord's Book of Rule. That in the twelfth generation after Khalifa, the lord would sire a son on a faerie woman. That this child would be the strongest Twilight Lord ever, possessing great and terrible magic, magic that could allow the darkness to forever eradicate the light in this world. We could not allow this to happen, Lara."

"But you allowed my memories to be stolen from me so I would be compliant!" Lara cried.

"You are faerie," he replied. "You cannot give a child to one you do not love and it is necessary for you to bear Kol's heir. You could not have loved him if you had retained your memories, Lara, and you know that is the truth." She looked so distraught that he wanted to hold her again but he knew now was not the time.

"I do not love him!" she said angrily.

"Not as yourself, you do not," he agreed, "but as Lara, the frightened amnesiac, you did. Kol needed you. And he needs your magic, for without it he is not strong enough to do what he must do, nor will his child exist."

"What of Magnus and the children?" she asked as she forced herself to be calm.

"They know nothing of this, nor will they ever," Kaliq said.

"And just how will you accomplish that or is that something else I need not know, my lord? And how will I return to my own life, to my husband, and not feel dirtied by this *adventure?* How can I go on knowing what I have become under this creature's influence, Kaliq? Tell me how you will make it all right once again?"

"I can *and I will* make it all right, Lara," he swore to her.

And in spite of herself, in spite of her anger and her feelings of betrayal, Lara believed him. She didn't want to, but she did. This was Kaliq, her one-time lover, her mentor, her beloved friend. She drew a deep breath. "Tell me what I must do."

"Only you, Lara," he told her, "can overcome the darkness in this matter. Remember what the Book of Rule has decreed from its inception. Each Twilight Lord will only produce one son. By doing so they have managed to keep their line of descent straight and without controversy. There has never been an argument over who any Twilight Lord's heir would be. And it is against their own law and culture to raise a hand or allow another to raise a hand in violence against any offspring born to a Twilight Lord. You can hold back the darkness with your magic, Lara, and you must do it now before you awaken. When you awake it will take every bit of your skill to continue to play the woman Kol has come to love, for he loves you as that girl loves him."

Lara nodded. She knew now what she needed to do and she placed both of her hands over her belly. *"One divide. One is two. Become selfsame in all but name,"* she intoned. And she felt the child within her dividing itself, morphing into two babies as she spoke the spell. "Kol will not be pleased," she murmured with a touch of her old humor.

"Nay, he will not," Kaliq agreed. "Since he cannot be there when you give birth—and you will do it so quickly that the women attending you will be totally confused—no one will be able to say which of the boys came first. No one will think to make any kind of provision to identify the firstborn. And Kol's sons will quarrel with each other from the moment of their birth. While Kol and his minions will follow the law of the Dark Land, his sons will not. They will spend their lives attempting to do away with one another. Kol will be so beset by them that he will not be able to carry out his plans for conquest or enjoy that wicked program you planned for the taking of Hetar."

"Do not remind me," Lara replied with a shudder. "How could I have even contemplated such things, Kaliq? What evil I planned to spawn! And the worst thing was that I actually enjoyed thinking about it."

"The darkness was threatening to overcome you, my love, but all will be well now," he said soothingly and held out his arms to her again.

Lara went into the comfort of his embrace, her golden head resting against Kaliq's shoulder. "Tell me when I may leave him?" she asked.

"Remain long enough after you have given birth to help stoke his confusion over this turn of events. When you call my name I will transport you to Shunnar, where you will heal from this time you have given us. And then, Lara, I will wipe away your memory of these months you have spent with Kol in the Dark Land."

"But what of Magnus, of my children, of Terah and Hetar?" she queried him.

"Trust me, my love. I will take care of it when it is time," he promised her.

"Where is Ethne?" Lara wondered, her hand going to her neck where the chain she usually wore hung.

"Left behind when Kol stole you away," Kaliq explained.

She nodded. "Kol has been good to me for all his evil nature,"

Lara said softly. "He was never cruel nor did he deny me anything I said I desired. And he has been a passionate lover, I must say." She smiled mischievously. "I never thought to know another after I wed Magnus."

"He loves you," Kaliq responded. "And the girl you have been has loved him. He made her feel safe. I believe you actually brought out a small bit of light in him despite the deep darkness of his soul. As for his amorous skills, he is certainly unique," he teased her wickedly and then he kissed the top of her golden head. "I must leave you now, Lara."

He did not tell her that because of her faerie blood she would live far longer than Magnus Hauk and one day know other lovers. This was not the time for it. "You must be strong over these next few weeks," Kaliq advised her gently, "and you must not allow Kol to learn that all of your memories are intact. You must become the woman he believes he has created—his mate, his equal, and filled with more wickedness as each day passes. But if he asks you to use your magic for evil, refuse him, saying you are weakened with the life you carry and would not harm his son."

"I am a little frightened by this now," Lara said.

"Lara, my love, you outwitted the Forest Lords. You will outwit Kol, too," Kaliq assured her. And then the shadows and the mists began to swirl about him and suddenly Kaliq was gone from her.

Lara stood a long few minutes upon the dream plain. He had left her to gather her own courage before she descended and awoke. She breathed slowly, clearing her mind, banishing her fears, gathering her courage. Within her womb she felt her twin sons beginning to stir and she sensed them quarreling already. She almost laughed when she considered the look on Kol's face when he learned his mate had given him not one, but two sons. Most men would be delighted by what they considered their prowess but Kol would not think of it in those terms. Then she felt herself slipping into sleep and finally Lara awoke to hear the rumble of thunder outside of her windows. The icy autumn rains had come, not that the summer rains had been much better.

How had she borne the Dark Lands over this last year? The sun never shone directly on them. She had never seen a sunrise or a bright day here. But many days she could see between the tall sharp-peaked mountains a slash of blood red sunset above which a purple-and-black sky glowered. It was the only color she could recall in her time here. It was always gloomy with its landscape in half light. It rained most days in the more temperate seasons and snowed every day of the winter. And there was always thunder. Rain or snow, the thunder pealed out accompanied by silvery forks of lightning.

Kol's castle of Kolbyr was built into the rock of the mountainside. The rooms were all square or rectangular. There were shades of black and gray marble everywhere. Everyone wore dark colors. The serving people were relegated to deep brown. Her own robes were in Kol's favorite silver and varying shades of purple, the lightest of which was a deep lavender color. Kol himself was usually clad in black or silver. Now that she was restored to herself Lara found the whole place gloomy because she could recall all the other colors of the rainbow. She vowed silently to herself that when she escaped this dark land she would never again wear a dark shade. Lara opened her eyes and turning her head, looked toward the windows. Aye, it was raining. Her ears had not deceived her.

"Ah, mistress is awake," Macia said, coming to hover over Lara. "How may I serve you, great lady?"

By not hanging over me, Lara thought irritably. Instead she said, "I am famished. Why is my morning meal not ready for me? I think that you are derelict in your duties of late, Macia. Perhaps a good whipping will help you to attend to your chores. Now go and fetch my food for me at once. And where is Anka? I think your bottoms both need a good beating. Yes, after I eat I shall whip you both. It is obvious to me that you are both in need of some discipline."

"Not I, mistress," Anka said as she hurried in with a tray of food for Lara. "But if Macia has been inattentive of late it is because she is spending more time with her lover," Anka tattled. "I caught them taking pleasures the other day on your bed when you were walking with your lord." Anka smirked at Macia.

"*My* bed? You took pleasures on *my bed?*" Lara demanded of the red-faced Macia.

"He caught me unawares, mistress," Macia blubbered. "I could not help it!"

"*He?* Who is he? And what was *he* doing in my private chambers, Macia?" Lara said coldly. It was not difficult, she realized with shock, to slip again into the persona of the amnesiac Kol had stolen away. But she dared not back down. "You will be sent to the Punishment Master. How many lashes you receive will depend upon whether you are willing to name your bold lover," Lara told the sobbing woman. Then she threw Anka a cold look. "Do not dare to speak his name," she warned the servant. "This must be Macia's decision." Lara's green eyes glittered. "You will receive twenty lashes with the biting whip, Macia, but if you will name your lover you will receive only ten."

The biting whip was several lengths of leather braided with live stinging thorns that bit into the flesh of its victim.

"What will happen to him?" Macia wept.

"If you give me his name he will receive the ten lashes I will relieve you of," Lara said in deceptively sweet tones. "Surely he is man enough and cares for you enough not to allow you to take the whole blame for your behavior? But if you do not tell me, Anka will and you will both receive twenty lashes of the biting whip. The choice is yours to make, dear Macia. Tell me your lover's name." She smiled, horrified by her own behavior and the fact that Anka was bursting to tell on her friend.

"His name is..." stammered Macia.

"Alvar!" Anka was unable to contain herself. "He is one of the men-at-arms who guards your door, mistress."

Macia began to sob hysterically now. "I was trying to tell you, mistress! I was!"

Lara took Macia's hand patting it. "I know you were, dear. You and Alvar will only receive ten lashes each," she said. Then she turned her gaze to Anka. "But you who know no loyalty to your friend will receive twenty lashes of the biting whip. Then the two of you will offer pleasures to your master who I know has hardly visited his House of Women at all in my absence from his bed. Go and fetch him to me now." She began to eat now, savoring a peeled blood orange and lavishly buttering her black bread.

Kol came and Lara told him of Macia's fall from grace. "You would punish them for taking pleasures?" he asked.

"Nay, my lord, but I would punish them for defiling our marital bed. I must have a new one at once! I cannot spend another night in a bed where my servant has entertained her lover. She has sullied the few memories I possess, for I can no longer think of the magnificent times I lay in your arms in this bed and received the homage of your passion. I can only see this low servant female enjoying her lover's rod on my sheets. His juices will have surely stained the mattress! Their essence will linger despite the fresh linens, my lord." She put her face in her hands and sobbed convincingly. "The distress of this will injure your son!"

Kol put his arms about his mate. Lara and his son were the only things that mattered in this situation. "A new bed will be installed in your bedchamber within the hour, my darling," he promised, brushing the tears from her cheek. "Come, let us go and watch as the punishment is executed, my precious."

"And when they have been well whipped," Lara purred at him, "you will use them thoroughly to take the edge off of the lust you have been storing up for me."

"Which deserves the most of your sweet anger?" he asked her.

"Anka, for she knows not the meaning of loyalty," Lara said.

Kol smiled. "Then after I have taken pleasures of her I will give her to the Punishment Master for an hour."

"Oh, my lord," Lara murmured, looking up into his face with

a smile. "You do know how to please me well. May I watch while he abuses her? *Please?*"

Kol laughed and caressed her cheek. "You are becoming so deliciously naughty, my precious. I find it more and more difficult to adhere to the rules of your confinement as set forth in the Book of Rule. I think after today I shall not seek your company until our child has been born. Your growing wickedness piques my lust for you, my beautiful mate." He placed a lingering kiss on her lips.

Lara sighed. "I want the brat born quickly, my lord, for I long for your love rod and wish to spend my life pleasing only you. Have you found the wet nurse for me?"

"She arrives at the castle today. You will see. She is perfect," he told her.

Lara finished her breakfast, her two serving women helped her to dress and then in the company of the Twilight Lord she escorted them to the Punishment Master. Kol watched with a mixture of both pride and amusement as she carefully instructed him as to what she wished done. The two men-at-arms guarding Lara's door had accompanied them and Lara surprised the hapless Alvar by ordering him to be punished, as well, but only after he watched as his lover received her due.

Then Lara and Kol reclined upon a double chaise as Macia was stripped naked and hung between two marble pillars and the biting whip cut into her flesh. As her screams rent the air Kol slowly stroked Lara's belly and felt the life within moving with apparent excitement. He smiled, well pleased.

Next, the man-at-arms was to be punished. When he was

naked the Twilight Lord called to the Punishment Master and murmured something in his ear. The man nodded and returning to his victim turned him about to face his lord and his lady. The Punishment Master took a small jar from a nearby shelf and drew a wad of thick cream from it with three thick fingers. He rubbed the man-at-arm's love rod with the cream and within minutes the love rod thrust itself hard and tall from its owner's body. Now the Punishment Master raised the biting whip and skillfully drew it across Alvar's torso, the tip wrapping itself about his love rod. Surprised, Alvar did not cry out until the second blow touched that most sensitive organ. Then he howled with his pain while Macia wept bitterly to see Alvar so abused.

Finally it was Anka's turn. She was sobbing with her fear and howling even before the Punishment Master raised his whip to strike. The man, who was masked, grinned with obvious delight at her terror. Ten blows fell on the screaming woman's back and then she was turned about to receive ten more blows on her breasts and belly.

The Punishment Master managed to skillfully nip her nipples several times with just the tip of his whip. It was enough to sting her, but not to break the skin. When he had finished both women were ordered upon their hands and knees and Kol took his pleasure of them. Then Anka was given to the Punishment Master for an hour of pleasures. The man thanked his lord and lady for their generosity, licking his lips as he gazed on Anka.

Lara had been revolted by the whole thing, but she knew she had further impressed Kol with what he believed was her burgeoning darkness. And his decision not to see her until after she gave birth was a great relief to her. He escorted her back to her apartments where the new wet nurse was awaiting them. Lara looked the woman over. She was a big-boned creature with two enormous breasts that reminded Lara of cows' udders. She stood, eyes lowered before the Twilight Lord and his mate.

"You have weaned your child?" Lara demanded of her.

"Aye, mistress, as I was ordered to do," the woman replied.

"My son will not be born for another few weeks," Lara told the wet nurse. "I do not want your milk drying up. The solution for that is to have you suckled by your master at least twice daily. Do you understand me? You are being given a great honor."

"Aye, mistress," came the response.

"You have a name?" Lara asked.

"Ema, mistress." The woman never lifted her head.

"I have had a room fitted out for you, Ema. It is next to my bedchamber. Take your master there now and suckle him so that your milk remains sweet and fresh for our son." Lara turned to Kol. "Go with her now, my dearest lord. I will keep to my chamber when you come and we will not see one another until the child is born." She stood on her toes and kissed his lips sweetly. "Farewell until then, my lord Kol." Then turning Lara entered her own bedchamber and closed the door behind her, sighing with relief. As long as she didn't have to interact with Kol, or see him, she could hold the darkness in her to a minimum. *Oh, Great Creator,* she prayed silently, *forgive me all the terrible wickedness I have done these past days. Forgive, too, the wickedness I will do in the coming days that Kol not know I have been restored to myself. Help me to return safely to my beloved Magnus. Never let him learn of this terrible interlude in my life! Let Kaliq keep his promise to me so that I forget this time in the Dark Lands.*

Had the children missed her? Well, Dillon would have. Anoush had probably come to hate her again and Zagiri would not even know who she was. *I don't care what I have to do,* Lara thought, *I am never leaving my children again!* It was past time she gave Magnus his son. A little boy with his father's deep golden hair and turquoise-blue eyes. She winced suddenly as the life within her protested her thoughts. One child squirming within her womb was bad enough but two was awful. They would be pale-skinned and dark-haired as their father was, she knew.

Ema came to tell her when the Twilight Lord had left. She looked drained and tired and Lara felt sorry for her. She told the woman to rest. Macia was whimpering with the stripes upon her back. Lara took pity on her and devised a spell that took most of the pain away, leaving just enough to remind Macia of her sins. Anka returned bruised and battered. Lara later heard her whispering to Macia that the Punishment Master was the finest lover she had ever known and that she would be visiting him again when she could find the time. Lara let Anka live with her pain, which did not seem so great, leading her to suspect the Punishment Master had put some soothing ointment on the woman himself. As for Alvar, he would not wield his love rod for several weeks.

Macia did not complain, instead she served her mistress with devotion. When Lara asked her why this sudden change in her attitude, Macia said, "Because I can now see you are more than just a woman upon whom our lord's son will be gotten. You are his equal in every way, mistress. You know how to punish. I am proud to serve you. And forgive me if I have spoken out of turn."

Lara slapped the woman's cheek hard and smiled. "You think too much, Macia. Remember, you come from the lower orders. But I do forgive you for your boldness. You are almost a perfect servant. Some day soon you will help me to correct Anka's continuing impertinent behavior."

"Whatever you require, mistress, I will do it," Macia said, rubbing her cheek and returning the smile Lara had given her. She was thrilled her mistress obviously cared enough about her to personally punish her. The slap was a badge of honor for Macia.

And then, on a black night when not a star shone upon the Dark Land, Lara went into labor. The Twilight Lord was notified but he would not come until the child was born. It was tradition. Another tradition they would observe was her healing. After their son was born she would be given special herbs and ointments that would be rubbed on her sexual organs. In exactly one week from her delivery Lara would be completely healed and Kol would pierce her with his love rod. They would take pleasures publicly before his chancellor, his underlords and other invited guests to show them that both he and his mate were fit again and that the child who had come from their loins was a strong infant who would one day lead his people. Kol concentrated upon that ceremony as he waited for word of a successful birth.

Lara's labor was the worst she had ever had. She knew, thanks to Kaliq, that it would not be long. But Great Creator! It was hard and painful. Only Macia and Anka were there to attend her. She hadn't wanted anyone else. Knowing it was not her first child, Kol allowed her to have her way but a midwife waited outside of Lara's apartments in case she was needed.

The woman winced, hearing Lara's shrieks of pain. Finally she could bear no more and entered unbidden, pushing the frazzled Macia and Anka aside. Looking down she swore, "Great Krell, help us!" seeing two thin little legs pushing from Lara's body. The child was coming backwards and there was now no help for it. Without a word she reached up, inserted several fingers and helped the baby's buttocks and torso to move down the birth passage. Lara screamed as the shoulders and head burst forth from her body, but then that the midwife cried out. "Great Krell, what is this?"

"What is the matter?" Lara gasped, then shrieked again and pushed as hard as she could. It had to be done quickly to keep the three women in a state of confusion. She could already hear the first child crying.

The midwife said nothing at first and just caught the second child as it shot forth from his mother's body grasping the arm of the sibling who came before it. "There are two boys, great lady," the midwife finally said. "Such a thing has never happened!"

"See to my sons! See to my sons!" Lara cried out to them.

The trio of amazed servants quickly did as they were bid, cleaning the evidence of the birth from the twins, swaddling them tightly. The two children were identical in every way. Tufts of ebony hair adorned each head. Dark blue eyes were now but barely visible. Milk-white skin revealed not the faintest hint of color. They were brought to their mother and shown to her.

Lara nodded. She was astounded that she felt nothing for these children. "Take them to their father," she told Macia and Anka.

The two women obediently departed, each carrying a baby. The midwife then turned to caring for Lara who quickly passed the placenta. Then the woman began preparing Lara for the ceremony that would take place in exactly one week. Lara was silent under her ministrations for she was considering what Kol was going to say when he learned that he had not one son, but two.

Kol watched as his mate's two serving women came into his privy chamber where he was seated with his chancellor, Alfrigg. They hurried to him and presented the bundles they carried. Kol stared in shock. "What is this?" he demanded, realizing even as he asked how stupid he sounded.

"Your mate has given you two sons, my lord," Macia half whispered.

"Which one came first?" the Twilight Lord demanded.

The two women looked at him startled and shook their heads. "We do not know, my lord," Macia said.

"How can I distinguish between them?" Kol wondered aloud.

Alfrigg came to his side and the serving women bent to show him the babies. "They appear identical, my lord. Undress them," Alfrigg snapped.

Macia and Anka complied with the request, and immediately the two babies began to scream and flail their limbs in protest. Ignoring them both Kol and his chancellor sought some sort of difference that would distinguish the children but neither man could find anything. The infants were indeed identical.

"Wrap them up again," Kol said to the two servants.

"This presents a problem, my lord. Was there nothing of this in the Book of Rule?" Alfrigg asked.

"Nothing," Kol replied. "It just said I would get my son on Lara."

"Look in the book now, my lord," Alfrigg suggested.

Kol reached for the book kept by his chair. Opening it he gazed down, and stared hard. The book's pages were blank beyond the prophecy regarding Lara.

"There is nothing," he said.

"You must kill one of these children, then," Alfrigg said.

"I cannot and you know I cannot," Kol exclaimed. "It is against our law. This event is confusing enough. Nothing like it has ever occurred before. What if I kill the wrong son? Nay. They must be allowed to grow up and only then will I be able to tell which is the true heir, Alfrigg."

The chancellor shook his head. "I fear for the days ahead," he said. Then he turned to the Twilight Lord. "What will you call them, my lord?"

"Kolbein and Kolgrim," the Twilight Lord said. Then he took a dagger from his belt and made a small cut on one infant's cheek. The wound bled fiercely but after a few drops had fallen Kol touched it with a single finger and a thin scar immediately covered the cut. The baby, who had screamed at the piercing of his skin, grew silent as his father's finger healed him and removed the pain. "This is how we will tell Kolbein from his brother." He then marked the other twin in the same manner on his opposite cheek with the same result. "Kolgrim is marked on the left cheek, and Kolbein on the right cheek," he explained.

"Cleverly done, my lord," Alfrigg said.

"Return the twins to their mother and tell her I will come to her shortly to tell her what I have done and why. Notify Ema that those hefty dugs of hers will nurse both my sons and put them to her breasts while I speak to their mother," Kol ordered his wife's serving women, who hurried from his presence with the infants.

"What you have done is impressive, my lord," Alfrigg said. "With your permission I will notify all the lords of your prowess and the success it has led to with these births. The invitations will be sent immediately for the Completion Ceremony." He bowed and withdrew from the chamber on his short legs.

Kol sat for several minutes taking in the fact that he had fathered two sons instead of the requisite one. It was obviously the will of Krell or it would not be. Rising from his chair he hurried from his privy chamber to congratulate his mate on their incredible achievement. It never occurred to him that anything might be amiss.

7

KOL FOUND LARA exhausted with her labors when he entered her bedchamber. Bending he kissed her lips gently. "You are amazing, my precious," he told her. "Have they shown you how I marked the twins yet?"

Lara nodded. "What are their names, my lord?"

"Kolbein and Kolgrim," he told her. "Kolbein is marked on his right cheek, and Kolgrim on his left."

"Oh, my lord, I am so sorry," Lara said feigning a sob. "Why has this happened? Why did my womb birth two sons instead of the required single child?"

"I do not know," Kol admitted to her, "but it can only be Krell's will, my precious. Do not fret yourself. When our sons are grown men I shall set them to several tasks, and the one who succeeds in completing them all will be my heir. If they both succeed then they shall battle to the death for supremacy. Whichever of them lives will rule the Dark Lands after me."

"Oh, how clever you are, my darling," Lara told him.

"You must rest now," he said to her. "I will not see you for seven more days. We will meet at the Completion Ceremony."

"What is the Completion Ceremony?" Lara asked him.

"A celebration of our sons' birth that you and I will perform for our high lords," he answered. "You will enjoy it, I promise you, my precious."

She drew his head down to her and kissed him again. "Then until that day, my lord," she said smiling at him. "I am relieved not to have displeased you."

"You could never displease me, Lara," he said softly. Then he arose and left her. Outside in her dayroom he called Macia and Anka to him. "Your mistress, not being born a Darklander, does not know the particulars of the Completion Ceremony. You will not tell her anything. I want it to be a surprise for her. And if you behave yourselves, I will permit you both to take part in the Afterwards. You will choose any of the lords present for your lover that night.

"You understand that this is an honor. But if Lara is not amazed and delighted by her part in the Completion Ceremony I will have you both slain and fed to my dogs. Do I make myself clear? Macia? Anka? If my mate learns beforehand of her part, you will both die."

"Yes, my lord!" the two women chorused.

"We will say naught," Macia swore.

"Any of the lords?" Anka boldly asked.

"It will be your choice. You favor the Wolfyn, don't you?" Kol chuckled. "You are a lustful creature, Anka." Then he left them.

"The Wolfyn frighten me," Macia said.

"Then whom do you favor?" Anka asked her.

"Perhaps a sturdy giant lord or mayhap two of the dwarf lords. Surely I may have two of them, as two equal one Dark-lander," she said thoughtfully.

"How do you think the mistress will enjoy taking pleasures before the high lords?" Anka wondered. "She is a delicate creature. I suspect she will not like it at all, but if we do not tell her and obey our master, she will be well repaid for beating us, will she not, Macia?" And Anka laughed.

Macia laughed, too. She would not tell Lara what awaited her, either, but only because she feared the Twilight Lord more than she feared Lara. She did not doubt for a moment that he would kill them and she suspected it would be a nasty death.

Two nursemaids were found to watch over the twins. Several times a day they would bring their charges to Ema to nurse. Although Ema had unusually large breasts, the twins were vo-racious eaters and emptied each breast at each feeding. Lara realized that if Ema was to survive her nurslings she would have to set a firm schedule for the wet nurse's comfort. She saw that the woman was fed six times a day so that she might keep her strength up. Ema was also to rest in between the feedings. Her only duty, Lara told her servants, was to feed the twins. She would be burdened with nothing else.

And each day of the first week of her sons' life, Lara was bathed daily, her sexual organs treated with salves, and she was given herbal draughts to drink down several times a day. She was not unhappy to find herself completely healed so very quickly and feeling quite well by the sixth day. She began to consider when she would call out to Kaliq and make good her escape. But she sensed that she must wait until after the Completion Ceremony was celebrated lest she break any taboo that would render the twins' birth irrelevant and permit Kol to seek another mate with whom to create another male heir.

And each morning the twins she had given Kol were brought to her. It was not difficult to be indifferent to them. They were oddly adult and a little frightening. Unlike most infants, who slept much of the first few months of their lives, Kolbein and Kolgrim were lively boys whose dark eyes were forever scanning everything in their view even in their first week of life. When they looked at her there was a certain knowing in their gaze that always surprised her. She did not like them. She and Kol had created them. She had carried them within her body and pushed them from it to give them life. But she did not like them.

The Completion Ceremony was to be celebrated on the seventh night after the twins' birth. Lara was bathed and her hair dressed in several braids that were looped and curled about her head. Her gown was a deceptively simple violet silk robe sewn all over with tiny seeds of black onyx. On her feet were placed slippers of silk covered with thin sheets of beaten silver. A silver crown studded with amethysts and topped with a silver crescent moon was fitted over her head.

Macia and Anka had been given simple robes of dark purple silk and wore silver crescent moons in their hair. They had been designated to lead her into the ceremony. Both were trembling with their silent excitement at taking pleasures with the lords. Conceiving a child with one of those lords would give them the opportunity to be freed of their service and taken into the lord's household as a concubine. It was a chance rarely offered to the lower orders.

"Where are we going?" Lara asked them as they ushered her from her apartments.

"We cannot tell you, mistress," Macia said. "It is not permitted."

Through the dim corridors they led her until finally before them a large silver door loomed. The double doors opened silently as they reached them and the three women entered a great domed chamber. Macia and Anka stepped back, allowing Lara to go forward to greet the Twilight Lord awaiting her in the room's center. She had been told to take his hands in her hands, pressing them first to her forehead, next to her heart and finally to her lips as she knelt before him. She did. The Twilight Lord gave a cold smile of approval. Lara spoke the words she had been taught to say.

"I thank you, my lord Kol, for permitting me to nurture your powerful seed within my unworthy body and to safely bring forth from that body your sons. Praise to Krell!"

"Praise to Krell!" The voices of many erupted, and glancing up Lara saw that a great balcony encircled the whole chamber. It was filled to capacity with the Twilight Lord's subjects. This was the first time she had seen anyone else but for the castle's servants. Her quick peek showed her giants and other creatures she could not identify and through the open balusters she spied the faces of many dwarfs.

Remembering her part Lara continued, "Before your subjects, my lord Kol, I now stand ready to prove my worthiness as the mother of your sons. Command me as you will! All praise be to Krell!" His hands drew her to her feet again.

"All praise be to Krell!" the spectators shouted eagerly.

"Remove the garments I wear, my mate," the Twilight Lord said and flung wide his arms to facilitate her efforts.

His words surprised her but Lara nonetheless unfastened his black robe, pushing it back to allow her two attendants to slide it down his sinewy arms. From this moment on she was not certain what would transpire. She knelt, slipped his silver slippers from his big feet. Then she stood again.

"Take her robe," Kol commanded Macia and Anka.

Lara was not pleased to be rendered naked before a balcony full of bystanders, but it was obviously part of the ceremony and she could hardly protest. A sigh of obvious appreciation at her nudity arose and she felt her cheeks warming beneath the sound.

Then a deep voice called out loudly. *"Show us your strength, my lord Kol! Show us the strength of your mate. Complete the cycle!"*

"Complete the cycle!" came the shout.

Kol waved his hand and the floor beneath them rose to make a dais. A double couch with one open end and one rolled end appeared. Kol took Lara's hand and led her to the couch. "Lay back upon it," he said softly.

Lara realized that she had no choice. The twins' legitimacy must not be questioned. She suspected now what was coming and was not pleased, but it had to be done. She positioned herself in the middle of the couch and lay back. Almost at once Macia and Anka came to stand on either side of their mistress, each taking one of Lara's feet in their hands. At a flick of Kol's eyelash they slowly raised Lara's legs up, moving back until her limbs were practically over her shoulders and she was spread wide for all to view. Above her she could see the eager faces of the spectators waiting. Lara now understood that as the creation of Kolbein and Kolgrim had come about because she and Kol took pleasures with each other, their first week of life would end with their parents taking pleasures together for the first time since that moment. The Completion.

Kol knelt between Lara's outstretched legs and leaning forward began to lick at her sweet flesh with his forked tongue. She knew her response to him this night must be one that brought him more respect than he had ever had of his subjects. Closing her eyes Lara released all thought of dismay and displeasure at her current situation, and sighed audibly. The flickering tongue poked and prodded at her, touching her lust orb, making it tingle with excitement. She moaned with appreciation, a little cry escaping her as the tongue slipped into her love sheath to tease her more. Slowly, for Lara understood that this was a moment that must be savored by the spectators, she let her juices begin to pearl and then she screamed as his teeth nibbled upon her aching lust orb, causing it to burst forth with a sweetness that sent a shudder through her body. The spectators cheered this event, and cried out, *"All praise to Krell!"*

Kol stood up and posed before the balcony. His great dominant rod sprang forth to enthusiastic clapping and more cries of *"All praise to Krell!"* He strutted about the dais, allowing them all a long look at his mighty rod. Lara held out her arms to him as if pleading. The look in his eyes told her that her act pleased him.

And then cheers and more clapping as the thin and pointed lesser rod appeared, glistening with its silver sheen. The females accompanying the lords screamed with excitement and once again the cry, *"All praise to Krell!"* was shouted enthusiastically.

Kol preened once more before his subjects and then turning his attention to his mate he slipped onto the couch and began to slowly impale her on both of his great rods. Open-mouthed, the spectators in the balcony watched as Kol's enormous dominant rod slid into Lara's waiting sheath even as the pointed tip of his lesser rod pierced her rose hole. Then, both rods fully sheathed, his dominant rod began to pump her with slow, majestic movements while the lesser rod remained throbbing within her narrower passage and the spectators leaned forward to gaze upon the strength and magnificence of the Twilight Lord and his beautiful faerie mate. Macia and Anka struggled to maintain their place. Both women were near to swooning with their own lust as they watched their master and mistress perform before their subjects.

Kol's movements began to quicken and then his dominant rod was flashing fiercely in and out of the hot, tight love sheath that had been so perfectly prepared over the last week to receive him once again. He bent forward and suckled and bit her breasts. Lara screamed with delight and her nails clawed at his back, going deep, drawing blood. The crowd roared its approval. Their lord's mate was no weak female to be easily overcome by her master. When he finally triumphed over her it would only be after a great battle had been fought between them.

For over an hour the two lovers writhed upon the couch as

above them their subjects watched with favor as Kol's strength and that of his mate was more than proven to them. And then Lara reached around her lover and two of her fingers found their way between his buttocks to caress his hidden flesh. Kol howled with surprise and delight. His two rods, but a small wall of flesh separating them, sought together for that tiny spot that when touched would send Lara into a paroxym of joy. He found it. The two rods caressed it from either side and her pleasure began to peak. Lara shrieked with her satisfaction as the tremors began to race over her. Her head spun. Stars exploded behind her closed eyelids into a myriad of dazzling colors while around her the roar of the crowd grew louder and louder. And then blackness. Silence.

Kol arose from the unconscious body of his mate. "All praise be to Krell!" he shouted and they shouted it back at him. *"Am I strong enough to rule you?"* he demanded of them. *"Does my mate meet with your approval?"*

"Yes!" the spectators roared with one voice. "All hail to our lord Kol! All praise be to Krell!"

"Lower her legs," Kol ordered the two women. "You are free to choose whom you will from among my lords." The Lustlings appeared and began to cleanse the tired sexual organs of the Twilight Lord and his mate. When they had finished he picked up his robe, wrapped himself in it and then lifted Lara from the couch that they had shared. Leaving the rotunda the Twilight Lord carried his mate back to her bedchamber and lay her upon the bed. The rest of the night would be spent in a carnal celebration by his lords and the women who accompanied them. He would eventually join them in the banquet hall, but not quite yet. He lay down next to Lara and gathered her into his arms.

It was almost a full hour before she began to stir. As she came once more to her senses Lara smelled his fragrance and opening her eyes saw he was cradling her. "Did we please the lords?" she asked him softly.

"We pleased them well. As I left the rotunda with you many of them were already rodding their women. I gave Macia and Anka leave to stay and seek pleasures if they chose. Anka is a very lustful creature and sought immediately for a Wolfyn lord. I think Macia had finally decided upon a giant. Let us hope her lover does not split her in two." He chuckled. "You were magnificent. You have an innate understanding of how to deal with the lower orders, my precious." He began to caress her breasts.

"Are you already hot again for pleasures?" she said. "I think it is you who are a most lustful fellow." Lara entwined her fingers into his dark hair.

"We did what we did for the lords," he said to her. "Let us now do it for ourselves, my precious. Then I will leave you and join the lords in the hall."

"May I not go, too?" Lara asked him.

"Will you feel strong enough?" he asked her solicitously.

"Will you?" she teased him wickedly.

Kol laughed.

"Take pleasures with me like the Wolfyn lord will do with Anka," she tempted him seductively. Lara rolled over and leaning forward drew herself up on her knees, resting her head upon her folded arms, her pretty bottom pushing up at him. "Are they as fierce as you, my lord?" she taunted.

Kol covered her body with his and growling he leaned forward to bite the nape of her neck sharply. "I am fiercer," he told her and thrust his dominant rod into her woman's passage. Then holding her hips in his grasp he began to piston her until Lara was moaning with undisguised pleasure. She had roused his lust to a fever pitch and he could not seem to stop with her. Twice he brought her to a peak only to continue, his great rod delving deeper until she was begging him to stop. But he knew she could be challenged once more and he was not quite ready. His hands moved from her hips to grasp her dangling breasts. He squeezed them hard, pinching the nipples cruelly, making her whimper with the pain. Then he felt her shuddering a third time, his rod quivered, his juices exploded and Lara screamed softly as she collapsed beneath him.

Kol rolled away from her, turning her over to face him. "Am I not fiercer?" he demanded of her.

She laughed weakly as she opened her green eyes to look at him. "I cannot know, for I have never taken pleasures with a Wolfyn," she told him mischievously.

"Little bitch," he said to her. "Perhaps I should give you to Hrolleif. He could curb you of your insolence, my precious."

"But you would not enjoy a mate less spirited than I, my lord Kol," Lara said softly. "You love my insolence." Her fingers reached up to caress his saturnine face. "Don't you?"

He laughed, but he did not answer her.

The Lustlings appeared and did their duty. Then the Twilight

Lord and his mate arose, dressed themselves and went to the banquet hall to join the lords. Their entrance was met with cheers. They took their places at the head of the large banqueting table and the feasting and drinking began. The various lords were enchanted by Lara as this night was the only opportunity they had to view her and speak with her. Even Alfrigg seemed pleased, which Lara found amusing, having heard from Kol of his chancellor's normally sour disposition.

A young Wolfyn lord came to Kol and murmured low into the Twilight Lord's ear. Kol then leaned over to Lara and said, "He wants to keep Anka. Will you allow it?"

"Where is Anka?" Lara asked. "I would speak with her first."

The Wolfyn lord went off, then returned dragging Anka with him. She was not happy. Indeed, she looked a bit frightened. Seeing this, Lara said, "No, he may not have her, but I will allow him to amuse himself with her for three days, my lord. I suspect it will cure her of her boldness."

The Twilight Lord relayed his mate's message. The Wolfyn lord bowed to Kol, gave a polite nod to Lara and dragged Anka off with him. Macia returned barely able to walk from her adventure with a young giant lord. There was nothing for it but to take to her bed for the next few days as she could not stand for more than five minutes. Anka returned subdued and would not speak of her time with the Wolfyn lord.

Lara knew that Kol prepared to loose his armies on Hetar soon. It was now time for her to leave him and bring further confusion and discord to the Dark Lands. The twins, not even a month old yet, had already made adherents among the Dark-landers seeking to position themselves for the day when Kol would declare one of them his heir. That it was many years hence did not deter them from choosing sides. And Kol encouraged their behavior and their rich gifts to Kolbein and Kolgrim. Each petitioner was permitted to personally present his gift to the twin involved. Lara could have sworn that these infant boys knew exactly what was going on and were marking down their supporters within their memories. She found it disturbing.

Kol came to her each night now, and it was harder and harder for her to keep up the pretense of being his willing mate. She had to leave, yet something about this dark creature called out to her. She was having moments when she wondered if she could go. Finally one night she fought back the unseen forces she sensed about her and cried aloud, *"Kaliq!"* And he appeared before her just as Kol entered her bedchamber, stepping back stunned by the sudden brightness there.

The Twilight Lord's dark eyes blazed with fury. *"She is mine!"* he roared at the Shadow Prince. "And you, creature of light, have no place in my kingdom! Begone!" His eyes hurt.

"Nor does Lara, daughter of Swiftsword and Ilona of the Forest Faeries have any place in your kingdom," the Shadow Prince said quietly.

"She is my mate. The mother of my sons," Kol replied. "She belongs to me! She is now my creature, Shadow Prince. Darkness fills her soul completely."

"Not completely," Kaliq replied. "You had the Munin rob her of her memories but for those you wanted her to have. But all of her memories have been returned to her, Twilight Lord.

Now she will leave you and return to her world, which needs her more than you do." He glowed with light.

"She will remain with me, Shadow Prince," Kol said in a fierce voice. "Tell him, my precious! Tell him that you love me and will stay."

"I do love you, Kol," Lara said quietly, "but I will not remain with you. Did you not hear what Kaliq told you? I have my memories once more. You cannot hold me by the force of your magic any longer. I cannot bear another day in your dark and dreary kingdom. I am faerie. I need the heat of the sun upon me, a warm breeze blowing my hair. I need color, and flowers and most of all I need Magnus Hauk and our children!

"Do you really believe that you could have succeeded in your nefarious scheme had not higher powers than yours permitted it? All my life I have moved toward a destiny that I neither knew nor understood. Now I do. It was my destiny to give twin sons to a Twilight Lord whose predecessors could sire only one son in a lifetime. Your laws will not permit you to kill one of your offspring, Kol. And besides, you cannot be certain which one is the true heir and meant to follow you. Until you can learn that secret the Dark Land will be kept in a turmoil by Kolbein and Kolgrim as they struggle for supremacy. They may even seek to destroy you, for you will learn that in their quest for power they will not be governed by the rule of law.

"You sought to loose the forces of darkness upon our worlds, Kol, but there must always be a balance between the dark and the light. That balance is now restored and will remain so for some time," Lara told him. "You have great magic, my lord, but so do I and without my magic you will not succeed with your plans to conquer either Hetar or Terah. I suggest you consider what you will tell your lords now as I am certain that they have been planning for the riches these conquests would bring them. You will have to placate them in some fashion if you hope to retain their loyalty." Lara turned to Kaliq. "I am ready now," she said and reached for his hand.

"No!" the Twilight Lord said. "I will seek you out again, Lara. You will return to me or I will kill you, for no other shall have you."

Kaliq shook his head. "Your reflecting bowls are gone, for I have taken them. You will make no others, for that knowledge was lost to your kind centuries ago. My brothers and I have sealed off your kingdom from the rest of the worlds for at least a hundred years. Until then, neither you nor your body servant can leave Kolbyr. You are trapped here where you can do little harm. Farewell!" Kaliq wrapped his golden brocade cloak about Lara and together they disappeared in a shadowy mist, Kol's shriek of fury echoing in their ears.

As Kaliq removed his cloak from his companion Lara slowly collapsed against him. "The strength has gone out of me," she said and she began to sob.

The Shadow Prince quickly scooped Lara up in his arms and carried her out to the great open corridor where there was morning sun and warm air. For months she had been penned within Kol's dark castle in the chill and dank. Such an atmosphere was anathema to her faerie soul and it had slowly begun to shrivel. Back in her own realm, however, she would soon be revived. "Breathe," he instructed her.

Lara drew a deep breath and the scent of flowers filled her nostrils. "Roses," she murmured with a sigh and relaxed against him. She sniffed again. "And lilies, and woodbine and yellow primroses, which are the sweetest." The sunlight seemed to revive her and she said, "Put me down now. I think I can stand. I want to see the horses."

Kaliq set her gently upon her feet and helped her to the balustrade, but his arm remained about her waist.

Lara looked down into the great green valley where the Shadow Princes' herds grazed. It never failed to amaze her that in the center of the desert this magical place existed. "Is Og here?" she asked Kaliq. "Does he know what happened?"

"Og is here and so is your son, Dillon," Kaliq informed her.

"Dillon should not be here yet," Lara cried, turning to look up into his handsome face. "I said you might have him when he was twelve but not before, my lord."

"I brought him to Shunnar but a short while back, Lara, and I did because he suddenly knew that you were in the Dark Lands. I needed to distract Dillon before your husband took him too seriously, marshaled his army and marched north. Hetar is threatening Terah. Your old friend Gaius Prospero has disposed of Anora and is divorcing Lady Vilia so he may wed his lover, a creature of our creation. But he will, I fear, be disappointed for all of his plans will come to naught. We will retrieve the lady Shifra when she has served her purpose for us."

"And what has her purpose been, my lord?" Lara asked him, curious.

"To distract Gaius Prospero from his nefarious plans to invade

Terah, which he believes weakened by your absence," Kaliq told
her. "And to break his heart."

"Will Jonah take Vilia to wife?" Lara wondered aloud.

"Aye, he will and while it will greatly discomfit the emperor
to learn of the marriage, he will believe Jonah's explanation.
That he has wed the lady only to prevent her from falling into
the hands of those who would depose Gaius Prospero and to
prevent her from being shamed and seeking to wreak revenge
upon her former husband. Her family is a prominent and con-
servative one."

"And the emperor will be grateful to his good right hand,"
Lara replied with a small smile. "And then the creature you have
given Gaius Prospero will disappear. Not right away, I hope. He
needs to be punished for all his wickedness. If the emperor is
content with this female then you have removed the curse I
placed upon him, Kaliq, so he might enjoy pleasures with her.
It is the only reason he would revere her, for his tastes have long
since been jaded."

"It was necessary," Kaliq said, "and you should really have never
plagued him in such a manner, Lara." He scolded her with a smile.

"Magical or mortal," Lara replied dryly, "all men stick
together when it comes to matters of pleasure."

The prince laughed. "You are feeling a little better," he said.

"Aye, but I am also very tired, Kaliq."

"I know," he replied sympathetically. "Being in the Dark Lands
for so many months has drained you of your strength. You will
remain with me until you are fully recovered, my love." His
elegant fingers caressed her face.

"May I see Dillon?" she asked him.

"I do not think it wise," he told her. "I am going to return him to Magnus today with the message that you will soon be home again. He knows now that your disappearance had to do with fulfilling your destiny."

She nodded. "And when I do go back to my husband and children?"

"Your memories of those months spent in the Dark Lands will be gone, my love," he said quietly. "As for those affected by your disappearance, they, too, will not remember. It will be as if you had never been gone, Lara. Magnus will remember coming for you in the New Outlands and bringing you home. The past months for you all will be recalled as any year in your lives. Nothing special will have happened. In Hetar, the war that Gaius Prospero plans will be based solely upon his fears of Terah and his need to do *something* to keep in favor," Kaliq explained. "Your lives will go on as they should."

"You can do this?" she said.

"My brothers and I, working with the Munin, can do this," he replied. "The Munin owe us one more favor for rescuing them from Kol and the Dark Lands."

"But Kol will not forget what has happened," Lara said.

"Nay, he will not," Kaliq answered her. "It is a punishment for him that he will remember that once he possessed a most beautiful faerie woman called Lara. No other will ever please him again. But he will be too busy with the sons you gave him to spend much time grieving. He must hold on to the Dark Kingdom from within his prison and in the face of the growing threat Kolbein and Kolgrim will present to him. And without the presence of their lord to hold them in check, the giants, the dwarfs and the Wolfyn will run rampant throughout the Dark Lands," Kaliq said.

"Then I am safe," Lara murmured. She was growing very tired and slumped against Kaliq's shoulders. "I need to sleep," she told him.

"Come," he said and led her to the magnificent apartment that had once been hers.

"We will eat our evening meal in your garden." Then he left her.

She was truly alone for the first time in months. And she was in a familiar place. Slowly Lara looked about her. She stood in the little antechamber where he had first brought her all those years ago. And then Noss had come in, and they had been so glad to have found one another again. Lara smiled with the memory. Could either she or Noss have ever imagined the future before them then? She doubted it.

Everything seemed to be the same within her apartment. It was a spacious accommodation with a dining chamber, a dayroom, a small bedroom where Noss had slept and a large bedchamber that had been hers for little over a year. There was also a small tiled bath with its own bathing pool. Lara looked down to see the same fine wool carpets in shades of ruby, sapphire, amethyst and emerald adorning the marble floors. The sheer, pale golden silk curtains blew in the soft warm breeze and beyond was a lovely green garden. Lara knew that Kaliq's chambers were on the other side of that garden. The furniture was ebony accented with gold, as well as plush covered in silk, and was strewn with plump pillows. She walked into her bed-chamber and smiled again. She had always loved this room with its pale wood walls painted with all manner of desert animals. Curious, she opened the wardrobe to see it filled as it had always been with silk robes and little leather sandals in just her size.

Her bed beckoned and pushing aside the gossamer draperies that shielded it, Lara lay down. Her destiny had been fulfilled and she was amazed by what had happened. Recalling how she had always disliked the oblique mysteriousness of her peers when that destiny was referred to, she had to laugh. Despite the magic in her, despite the powers she now possessed, Lara knew that had she ever been asked directly to do what needed to be done, she would have refused. She would not have left Magnus and her children.

And yet it had been necessary for her, for their worlds, that she fulfill that destiny. Without her the deception could not have been played out. She wondered if Kol's Book of Rule had actually said that he would take a faerie woman for his mate, or if that had been but another part of the deception. Perhaps what had been written had not even mentioned a faerie woman at all. Perhaps that was just something that had been inserted by a power far greater than the Book of Rule's magical author. *And who had that author been?* she wondered. His essence would have had to have been completely erased from memory for another to overcome the magic in the book. She had so many questions to ask Kaliq and she wondered whether she would ever receive her answers. Her eyes felt heavy suddenly, then Lara lapsed into a deep and healing sleep.

When Kaliq had left her he had gone down into the valley below to find his horse master and young Dillon. He found them in a paddock. In the few days his visitor had been in Shunnar, Og had helped the boy by getting the yearling Dillon had chosen to accept him as his master. Kaliq watched as Dillon, holding a long rein, cantered the animal about the enclosure. He had a natural ability with horses, the prince could see.

Spying the prince Dillon brought the animal to a halt. Together he and the horse bowed to Kaliq. "My lord prince," Dillon said, "I thank you for my fine mount." His hand reached up to rub the beast's muzzle.

"What is his name?" Kaliq asked.

"Amir," the boy replied. "It means king."

"Dasras may have something to say about that," the prince noted with a smile.

"He descends from Dasras!" Dillon said excitedly. "Both his sire and his dam were born from Dasras's seed, although on different mares. I am certain Dasras will be very pleased to meet him!"

"Provided he acknowledges Dasras's superiority, lad," Og remarked. "Dasras is a great stallion. None finer."

"My lord, does Amir have the gift of speech?" Dillon wondered.

"He will one day," Prince Kaliq said. "He is still young. Now, Dillon, today you are to go home to Terah. You will carry a message to your stepfather for me. Amir will be here awaiting you when you come to me for a visit or for your schooling. You must tell your stepfather that your mother will shortly be returning home to you all."

"She is here now," the boy said. "I always sense when she is near."

Kaliq was surprised by Dillon's words, but then he said, "Yes, she is resting. You will not tell the Dominus she is here for she is in a weakened state and needs to remain in Shunnar for a short time in order to recover and regain her strength."

"She was in the Dark Lands, wasn't she?" the boy said quietly.

Kaliq nodded. "She was and for a faerie woman to exist in that dark, cold place is difficult. She has fulfilled part of the destiny to which she was born and when she is well she will be returned to Terah." Telling Dillon the truth now did not matter for when the spell was woven to eradicate the year past he would not remember any more than Lara, who had lived it, would recall. But for now, the boy's natural curiosity was satisfied. "It would be wise, however, if you did not repeat what I have told you to your stepfather. Magnus Hauk is a passionate man and his anger could lead him to act foolishly, I fear. All he needs to know is that Lara will soon be with him."

Dillon nodded. "I understand," he replied. "Magnus is a good man and his love for my mother is deep. While she is perfectly capable of handling any difficulty that comes her way, Magnus wants to protect her." Dillon smiled. "Are all men in love like that, my lord Kaliq?"

Kaliq laughed. "Aye, to one extent or another, we are. You will be, too, one day when you fall in love. Love is paramount."

"I hope that will not be for a long time, my lord," the boy responded. "I have much magic to learn and I do not want to be distracted."

"Then be content with lust, which can be a great deal of fun," the prince chuckled.

"My lord!" Og gently scolded his master. "The lad is too young for such talk."

Kaliq laughed again. "Come to my library in an hour, Dillon. I will give you the message for the Dominus then and send you home."

"May I continue training Amir?" Dillon asked.

"Yes," the prince said. "Enjoy your time with him now, then say goodbye. He is a fine animal." Kaliq patted the dapple gray yearling with a gentle hand.

When the boy had gone off into the valley with the animal, Og spoke. "She really is here, my lord? May I see her?"

"She is here, but she is exhausted by her ordeal in the Dark Lands. She needs to rest, but she does want to see you, Og. Perhaps tonight, briefly."

"So her destiny is partly fulfilled," the giant murmured. He was dying to ask the prince what this part of Lara's destiny had been, but did not dare.

"It was necessary for Lara to restore the balance between the light and the dark in our worlds, Og," Kaliq told him knowing the giant's thoughts. "The dark was becoming stronger and would have soon reached out to overcome us all. Thanks to Lara, that danger has vanished for the immediate future."

"But it will come again," Og said quietly.

"Sadly it will," the prince replied. "But not for many years. The Twilight Lord who rules the Dark Lands is now confined to his castle and without him little can be done. His subjects are at a loss without strong leadership, and will quarrel with one another."

"It was a great task then that Lara undertook," Og said thoughtfully.

"It was a terrible task," Kaliq replied, "but she was successful."

"Praise the Celestial Actuary for that," Og answered.

"Come to my garden at moonrise," the prince instructed the giant and then he left. Returning to his library he took out a parchment, picked up his stylus and considered what he would say to the Dominus of Terah. Finally he began to write. He kept it simple and to the point. Magnus Hauk was not an easy man and his love for Lara was great. Kaliq considered how the Dominus would feel in the years to come when he began to age as all mortals did and Lara, being faerie, did not. When he had completed his brief message he rolled the parchment tightly and sealed it closed with hot wax into which he had impressed his seal.

Dillon arrived exactly on the hour. "I have said farewell to Amir for now," he said. "Anoush will be very jealous when I tell her that you have given me a horse of my own, my lord. Perhaps one day you will give her one. Og tells me that Amir's dam has just given birth to a little white filly." He looked hopefully at Kaliq.

The prince laughed, ruffling Dillon's dark wavy hair. "We shall see," he replied. Then he drew out the rolled parchment and handed it to the boy. "For Magnus. Now, I will return you to the little chamber from whence you came, Dillon. I hope you have enjoyed being with me in Shunnar."

"Very much, my lord prince, but I am disappointed that I learned naught of magic here," the boy replied.

"It is not yet time for you to be educated by me, Dillon,"

Kaliq said. "Remember that you were not to come to Shunnar at all until you were twelve. Your mother was not pleased when I told her you were here. But perhaps you can visit now and again."

"But it does not really matter, does it, my lord? You will remove the memory of my stay from both of us shortly," Dillon said with a grin.

Kaliq laughed. "I can see that you will be a fine pupil," he told Dillon. "Are you ready now?" When the boy nodded, the prince gave a wave of his hand and his companion was gone from him. Kaliq sighed. He had enjoyed Lara's son very much. He would miss him but the time would come soon enough that Dillon would return to be taught by the Shadow Princes. Leaving his library, he went to see if Lara was comfortable.

Entering her apartments silently he went directly to her bed-chamber and saw that she was sleeping peacefully. He sat by the bedside and watched as she slumbered. Of all the women he had ever known, of the few he had loved, she was the most unique. It was not simply her delicate beauty, it was her indomitable spirit that reached out to him. Had he not been fully aware of the destiny that had been chosen for her he would have never let her leave Shunnar all those years ago. He loved her, a fatal flaw for a Shadow Prince, for while his race believed in love above all, they rarely gave their hearts to any one woman. Yet he had been fortunate in that her faerie nature had allowed her to accept him not just as a casual lover and friend but as her mentor. Kaliq slipped from the room as quietly as he had entered it.

When Lara awoke she could see, looking out into the gardens, that the day was almost finished. She stretched lazily and realized that she felt more rested than she had in months. Since the night she had been stolen away by Kol. The air about her was warm with the desert heat and fragrant with flowers. And then she saw Kaliq coming across the garden that separated their apartments. Rising, Lara went to greet him.

"Have you slept well?" he asked her, taking her into his arms and kissing her forehead. "I looked in on you and you appeared at peace."

"I slept amazingly well considering my ordeal," she told him.

"I am going to bathe you," he told her with a smile.

"Magnus would not like it."

"Magnus is not here and you will not remember this interlude," he told her. "It is up to me to treasure you and help you to regain your equilibrium. Come!" He took her hand and brought her to the little bath that was part of her quarters. "We will not go to my palace's baths. It will just be the two of us as it used to be."

"I well remember how it used to be," Lara replied with laughter.

"Do you?" he asked her, and his bright blue eyes scanned her face.

"I remember *very* well," she said softly. "There is not a moment of that year I spent with you that I cannot recall if I choose to recall it," Lara told him. "I was happy here with you and your brothers, Kaliq."

He reached out and unfastened the robe she wore, his supple fingers undoing the embroidered front closures. And when they were all opened he pushed the garment from her. Then he removed his own robe and they stood together naked as they once had done. The bath was silent; there was no servant to aid them. The prince took Lara to a small indentation in the marble floor and stood her there. Then he took up a large sponge that he dipped in a large bowl of soft soap. He began to wash her, slowly, thoroughly, drawing the sponge across her shoulders and down her back. Rotating it about her buttocks and then stooping to do her legs. Lara lifted each foot for him, setting it back down again when he had finished. He brought the soapy sponge back up the front of her legs, over her belly, around her breasts, her chest and slender neck. Her mons had grown a bushful of golden curls over her months in the Dark Lands. Kaliq had always preferred his women denuded there, so he spread a creamy depilatory upon her mons. It would remain until he rinsed her body free of the suds now caressing it. Lastly he washed her long golden hair.

When he had finished, Lara took the sponge from him and dipping it into the bowl of sweet smelling soft soap began to wash him. It was not easy keeping her mind on the business of cleanliness, she found, when his manhood began to burgeon and swell with her touch. "Kaliq," she scolded him, half laughing.

"We are going to make love, Lara, and you know it," he said, pulling her against him and kissing her mouth with soft little but-terfly kisses.

"I am Magnus Hauk's wife," she reminded him.

"You are more faerie than mortal, my love," he reminded her. "And faerie women take lovers. Besides, as I have previously told you, the memory of this interlude will be gone by the time I return you to the Dominus. There is no harm in what we do. But come and let us rinse the soap from our bodies."

They stepped from the bathing area and into separate indentations in the marble bath floor where small geysers of warm water rinsed their bodies and hair free of soap and the depilatory that was smeared across Lara's plump mons. Lara closed her eyes as the water sluiced over her head, freeing it of its lather. Stepping from the small rinsing hollows they made their way to the little square bathing pool and soaked in the warm, perfumed water for a brief time. Lara had brought a thick drying cloth with her and now toweled her hair before pinning it up with a small gold pin she snatched out of the air. Then she dried Kaliq's dark wavy locks.

"You never change," she said. "You are as handsome as ever."

"And you, my love, do not change, either," he told her. "You are as beautiful as the first time I brought you to Shunnar."

"I feel cleansed of the Dark Lands now," she told him. "The baths there were dark and over-humid. I did not have the lovely soaps, creams and oils, or even the thick drying cloths that a civilized house would have. I'm afraid I am a very spoiled faerie woman, Kaliq," Lara said with a little laugh.

"There is one more thing we must do, my love, to complete your transformation," he told her. "Come, stand in the center of the pool with me." And when he had her there he took her arms and raised them up, bringing her wrists together.

Suddenly Lara found her wrists bound with silk padding and her body was raised up just slightly above the water. She was not afraid, for she had perfect trust in Kaliq, and was more curious as to what he was up to now. Her curiosity was quickly assuaged as he took each of her feet in turn and began to kiss them, his tongue pushing between her toes. Then his hands slipped up her wet body, sliding around to clasp her buttocks. He drew her toward him and kissed her newly smooth mons, his tongue slowly following the shadowed slit separating her nether lips. Pushing his tongue between those lips, he sought and found her love bud, teasing it until it grew swollen and tingled.

"Ahhh," Lara said as a frisson of delight raced down her spine. "Oh, Kaliq, that is lovely! Don't stop." She closed her eyes and enjoyed the sensations he was engendering within her heated body as she hung above the bathing pool.

The prince snapped his fingers and she was lowered just slightly. Lifting his head from her sweetness he sought her breasts, laving them with slow strokes of his tongue. One hand freed itself from her buttocks. The other repositioned itself to hold her steady as he began to nibble and suck upon her nipples. His free hand moved to push between her nether lips. One finger. Two fingers. Three fingers thrust into her love sheath, swirling about, moving in a leisurely fashion.

Lara murmured. "I want more of you," and as the fingers withdrew from her she was lowered back into the bathing pool and the padded manacles about her delicate wrists dissolved. Lara put her arms about the prince's neck. She wrapped her legs about his torso and felt his talented manhood sliding into her love sheath. "Ah, yes, my lord Kaliq," she purred in his ear as they caught the rhythm and pleasured each other until they were both drained.

Her golden head then fell upon his shoulder, and he carried her from the bathing pool, and laid her down upon a thick drying cloth that had been spread upon a high bench. Patting her dry, Kaliq then poured a dollop of fragrant oil of lilies into his palm and rubbing his palms together he began to massage her as she sighed with delight. "I want to do you next," she said, "as we used to do."

"Not tonight," he told her. "Tonight I will erase all the suffering you endured at the hands of the Twilight Lord. Tonight I will teach you the joys of passion once again.

"There will be nothing left burrowing in the deepest corner of your mind, Lara, that will ever niggle at you with a questioning. You will never wonder if something happened that you cannot recall. You will only remember that love between two people who genuinely care for one another is a blessing," Kaliq said quietly as he continued to massage her.

Lara grew silent and let his strong fingers do their work. Her memories of Kol's hot and endless lust were indeed beginning to slip away. There was only Kaliq and the sweet passion that they had always shared together. For the briefest moment she thought of Magnus Hauk, but then she realized that now was not the time to think of her husband. When he had taken a faerie woman as his wife he had sworn that he understood what that entailed. But he really did not, Lara knew. Magnus was a mortal with all of a mortal's strengths and flaws. Soon she would be home again and her memories of the last year would be gone from her. In the meantime, she meant to enjoy this respite from the world.

She had earned it. Soon enough she would pick up her responsibilities as Domina of Terah, as Magnus Hauk's wife, as a mother and as the daughter of Ilona, queen of the Forest Faeries. But now that she had fulfilled a part of her destiny, did she have any other purpose, Lara wondered? She must remember to ask Kaliq.

LARA REMAINED in Kaliq's palace at Shunnar for several days. The desert sun warmed the chill of the Dark Lands from her bones, her mind and her heart. She spent the days being pampered by Kaliq and his servants. She and Og enjoyed several hours renewing their acquaintance. Lara told him of the giants who lived in the Dark Lands. "I did not see them a great deal, but Kol spoke of them, for they are bound to him in fealty. I recall he told me the name of the giant lord was Skrymir."

When she said this Og grew pale. "Did you say Skrymir?" he said.

"Aye. The giant lord was Skrymir," Lara repeated. "Kol told me that the giant race was a small group of about fifty—and more men than women. Why?"

"Where do they live in the Dark Lands?" Og asked.

"One mountain with its forests belongs to them," Lara explained.

"My father's name was Skrymir," Og said. "He was not there the day the Forest Lords came to slaughter my kind. He and a party of hunters, both male and female, had gone hunting several days prior. My mother, although she was a fine huntress, did not accompany them that day, for her belly had begun to show. They never returned to the forest or my mother would have been saved. Or if they did return, they did not come near where my mother hid herself and so she did not know." Og sighed. "Skrymir is not a common name among giants and is only used among the Forest Giants. How odd that in a forest so far from Hetar there should be another giant race and a lord who is called Skrymir as my father once was."

"If your father and some of your people were not there the day the Forest Lords came, perhaps this giant lord who is called Skrymir is your father, Og. If your mother told you that the hunting party did not return, then perhaps they did, saw the murder done and fled Hetar. Giants can possess magic, too, Og. Who knows how they reached the Dark Lands? But it is possible these giants are your own race."

"I shall never know," Og replied sadly. "I would not go there, Lara. It is too dangerous and I am a small giant who is not very brave. I will live out my days here in the desert of the Shadow Princes with the horses I care for, and with my wife and my children. It is a better fate than I ever anticipated," he said with a little smile. "I never knew the Skrymir who fathered me on my mother. I know of him only through what my mother told me. She always said he was a good man. It is a better memory to hold on to to than that of a giant lord who gives his loyalty to the Twilight Lord of the Dark Lands."

"I never met him, so other than a name I can offer you no information," Lara said. Nay, she had met none of Kol's people but for the servants. Alfrigg, Skrymir, Dain and Hrolleif were but names to her. She had never seen them except at the Completion Ceremony. Lara shuddered at the potent memory and understood why Kaliq was keeping her in Shunnar and had become her lover once again. He wanted to soften those memories for her before he had them entirely erased from her mind and her heart. Lara doubted that she would ever truly forget. But to her surprise, as the next few days passed, the trauma of her sojourn in the Dark Lands did begin to fade.

"It will soon be time for you to return home to Terah," Kaliq told her one evening as they sat together across a game board playing Herder. "Your husband grows anxious for you."

"How will you erase what has happened, Kaliq? You can let the Munin take those memories away from me but what of the rest of Terah?"

"It is as simple as I have already told you," he began. "For all of you, all of Terah, there will be no definitive memories held by anyone of the year that has just passed. There will be nothing you can quite put your finger upon and say, 'last month when we went to…' Nothing will seem out of the ordinary, Lara, for any of you. You will pick up your life where you left off. As for Hetar their memories of your disappearance will be taken from them, too. It was never public knowledge to begin with."

"And what of the threat Hetar poses to Terah?" Lara wanted to know. "What reason will Gaius Prospero give his subjects for wanting to invade Terah?"

"You are still the reason," Kaliq said with an amused smile. "Your magic has grown to such an extent that Terah now poses a danger to Hetar. You must be captured and stopped before you can conquer or destroy Hetar's independence."

"That's ridiculous!" Lara cried. "Terah wants nothing to do with Hetar, and nor do I. They are a decadent and decaying society whose legendary greed has brought them to the brink of their own destruction. How can Hetarians believe such babble?"

"Since you led the Outlands to their victory over Hetar in the Winter War nothing has really been the same for them. There was already too much poverty and unemployment, not just in The City, but in the surrounding provinces, as well. It was you, Lara, who marshaled the Outland clan families into fighting back. It took Gaius Prospero over five years to regain his people's favor and another two years to get himself declared emperor, thus weakening the High Council. But even acquiring the territory that had belonged to the Outlands did not solve the problems that beset Hetar. The magnates and merchants have gotten more wealthy. The poor suffer worse than before.

"Until almost two years ago when it was announced that no more mercenaries were required for the interim, every farmer's son who chose not to farm came to The City to make his fortune. And once they discovered there were no fortunes to be made, each of those young men joined the Mercenaries. Their ranks have grown over the years, but there was no work for them until the Outlands were opened up for settlement. The mercenary ranks thinned a little then. And they are the constabulary of the Outlands which has taken some pressure off Gaius Prospero.

"But there are the Crusader Knights to consider. With no wars to fight there has been no tournament to select new candidates for seven years now. The tournament where your father won his place was the last one held. Their income grows scarce. Too many in their ranks are aging and need care. The upkeep of their homes in the Garden District is not what it once was for there are more important needs to consider now. And the Crusader Knights, like the Mercenaries, sit idle for the most part.

"The City decays around them all, Lara. The wealthy do what little business they can and continue to play. The poor drink Razi from Lord Jonah's insidious kiosks in order to forget their troubles, and the fact that their bellies are empty and their children are crying. They steal from whoever they can, even each other," Kaliq said. "The Hetarians are beginning to murmur against their emperor, but even ridding themselves of Gaius Prospero will not solve their problems."

"People always believe that changing the government will bring them a change of fortune," Lara pointed out. "Yet it rarely does because it is the people themselves who need to change first."

"Exactly!" Kaliq declared. "But people don't want to change, don't want to make the effort. What they want is the *good old days* back so they may go on as they always have. So to save himself, to save his power and to direct the people away from their miseries, Gaius Prospero must first work on their fears and then offer them a solution to those fears. In this case he has spent months convincing Hetar that Terah poses a great and imminent threat to Hetar because you are the Dominus's wife.

"It is no secret that your powers have grown over the last few years. Gaius Prospero has most Hetarians believing that unless you are *stopped,* you will use your power to invade Hetar, slaugh-

ter and enslave its population, destroy the very fabric of its civilized society. Of course, to slay the daughter of a Hetarian hero
and a faerie queen would not be wise. So the emperor wishes
to reeducate you in Hetarian ways. But to do that the threat of
Terah must be removed," Kaliq concluded.

"That is the most convoluted reasoning I have ever heard,"
Lara responded. "Terah has not threatened Hetar, nor is it a
danger to Hetar. The problems facing Hetar have been created
by their society and by their emperor. Even taking the Outlands
territory has not solved Hetar's problems, although it might have
had it been managed properly. There is more than enough land
in the Outlands for generations to come. But Gaius Prospero
and his friends were greedy as ever. The poor might have been
easily resettled with farms large enough to earn their living and
there would still have been much land left for the rich. But of
course that wasn't what happened. And now the poor, growing
poorer and even larger in numbers, are beginning to complain
more loudly with each passing day. And so another diversion
must be planned."

Kaliq smiled at her analysis. As much as he adored Lara's
delicate beauty and lush body, it was her facile mind that intrigued
him most. She was quick like a faerie but also more analytical like
a mortal. "So," he said, "what is the solution, my love?"

"I do not know yet," Lara told him. "First I must return home.
You are right. It is time for me to go, Kaliq. Not," she said with
a wicked grin, "that it has not been delightful being with you
again as your lover." Her green eyes twinkled at him. "I am sorry
you must take my memories of this time with you from me but

alas, I do not believe my conscience could bear knowing for I do love my husband."

"I understand," he replied with an answering grin.

"Do you, I wonder?"

"Oh yes, my faerie love, I *really* do," he responded. "I know your love for Magnus Hauk is true but I also know that sometimes your faerie nature wants to overcome your mortal nature. But as long as you have your Terahn lord it will not. Forgive me, Lara, for wanting to be in your arms once more."

She reached out to caress his smooth tanned cheek. "I suspect, Kaliq, that I am capable of forgiving you almost anything."

"You will return to the New Outlands exactly when you left it," he explained. "And your husband will arrive that same day to escort you to the Gathering. Oh, I have forgotten," and he reached into his robes to draw out the gold chain with its crystal star that she had worn her entire life until Kol had abducted her.

"Ethne!" Lara cried and reaching for the chain slipped it about her neck.

I am relieved to see you safe once again, my child, Ethne murmured. *We are proud that you have begun to fulfill your destiny.*

Hearing the voice of her beloved guardian spirit within her head, Lara felt a tear slip down her cheek. *I am so glad to be with you again, Ethne. Will you remember that I have been away? Or will it also be for you as if naught has happened?*

We in the magic realm know the sacrifice you have made, my child, but it is better that you forget it. When Prince Kaliq returns you to your husband, to Terah, all references to your destiny will be forgotten and gone, Lara. The light has once again triumphed over the darkness, thanks to you, Ethne told her.

Lara nodded. *I am content that the memories will soon be gone. I do not believe the mortal side of my nature could live with those memories, or having to keep them from Magnus. Will you leave me now that I have completed part of my destiny, Ethne?*

I will never leave you, my child. Because you have completed part of the destiny set forth for you by the magical realm does not mean you do not also have a mortal destiny. I was given to you by your mother to be there always to guard, to guide and to protect you. I will not fail in my duty, Lara. I am with you always.

And I am glad for it, Ethne! Lara told her spirit guardian. Now she turned back to Kaliq. "When?" she asked him.

"Now, if you desire," he answered her. "It is almost dawn in the New Outlands, my love, and time for you to awaken from your slumbers." Leaning forward he kissed her lips gently and Lara immediately fell into a somnolent state. He caught her as she fell toward him over the game board, and standing up, carried her into her bedchamber. Placing her gently upon her bed Kaliq called to the Munin lord. *"Lord of the Munin, hear my plea. Cease all else, and come to me."*

The Munin lord appeared in his filmy robes. "I am here, my lord prince."

"You and your brothers have completed the tasks I set for you?" Kaliq asked.

"It is done, my lord. None in Hetar or Terah will recall this last year as anything special nor will they remember this lady's absence. Is it time for me to remove those memories we discussed from her? You have the container you wish to store them in, I presume," the Munin lord said in his whispery tones.

"I do," the Shadow Prince replied. "And when those memories have been taken from her and sealed away, you will take it with you and store it in your vaults beneath the Sea of Obscura where none will have access to it but you and I."

"You trust us to hold those memories, my lord?" the Munin said, surprised.

"I do," Kaliq responded, "for you know that my powers are greater than any, now. You will not betray me."

"Nay, I will not," the Munin lord said quietly. "My kind are best at keeping memories stored away. We know how to properly care for them."

Kaliq languidly swirled his elegant hand and a small round jar fashioned from silver and gold appeared in it. It had a crystal stopper. "The memories are dark," he said to the Munin lord, "but they will need a little light to survive and they should survive in their captivity. I carved your storage facility from a sea cave and gave it a glass roof. The water reflecting the diffuse light will suffice these memories. Too much light would harm them." He unstopped the jar and handed it to the Munin lord.

The wraith took the lovely round jar in his palm and then with his other hand thrust carefully into Lara's head, drawing the memories of her time in the Dark Lands from it. The thin strands were like silver threads but they glittered darkly with tarnish in the light of the chamber, twisting and squirming with an apparent life of their own. The Munin lord slowly pulled them one by one from Lara's golden head and lowered them with great care into the gold-and-silver jar. The last thread glittered brightly, for it contained Lara's memories of her recent days with the prince. Kaliq reached out and took that one strand from the Munin, who, when he had completed the task, put the stopper firmly into the mouth of the jar. A faint murmur of protest came from the jar as he did so and then all was silence.

Something passing for a faint smile touched the Munin lord's lips. "You have kept that one memory for your own, my lord. Be careful, for the strands are very fragile."

"It did not belong with the others," Kaliq said as he slid it into the pocket of his white robe where it glowed through the fabric. "I have a small crystal container to house it and will keep it in the sunlight."

"My task for you is completed, my lord prince," the Munin lord said. "May I return now to that fine castle you built for us? It is even better than Kol's and warm, too."

"You may go, with my thanks, Satordi," Kaliq said softly.

"You know my name!" the Munin lord cried, distressed.

"And knowing it I hold you in my power always," the prince answered him. "Farewell, Satordi of the Munin."

The Munin lord was gone even before the sound of Kaliq's words had died.

The Shadow Prince laughed softly. Knowing the Munin lord's name guaranteed his fidelity. In the magic world names were sacred. But then Kaliq turned to look down at Lara. *Just for a moment more,* he told himself with a sigh. She was his one weakness, though he kept it from everyone, even his brothers. Lothair, in particular, would be very annoyed that he had not been told of her visit. Had he known, however, Lothair would have wanted to share pleasures with Lara. He had always admired her passion. Kaliq now bent and kissed Lara's lips lightly a final time. "Farewell, my heart," he murmured and then he whispered the spell necessary to transport the sleeping woman back to her own bed in Liam's hall in the New Outlands. *"Send her back through time and space. Returned now to her rightful place."* And Lara vanished before the Shadow Prince's bright blue eyes. With a sigh Kaliq turned and left the bedchamber. As he walked down the wide corridor he stopped to look over the balustrade down into the valley where the horses were settling themselves for the night. The copper desert moon was almost full and it shimmered in the skies above him. He sighed again. She would be awakening shortly, he knew. And Magnus Hauk would be coming soon to take his wife home again to his castle high above the Dominus's fjord. Sometimes being immortal was painful.

He sought his reflecting mirror, and saw it would be a beautiful day in the New Outlands.

THE HARVESTS had been good and were already gathered for the winter to come. The rising sun was warm, the air clear and crisp. Lara's eyes opened slowly. Rolling onto her back she yawned and stretched. It was not quite dawn and she had time to reach the hillock near the village to watch the sunrise. She arose, pulling a loose medium blue gown over her chemise. Not bothering with sandals Lara exited the chamber where she slept with her three children. The servants were drowsily preparing for the day in the hall, sweeping and setting the board for the morning meal.

Lara gave them a friendly wave and hurried outside, drawing a deep breath of fresh morning air. Above her the sky was a clear blue and the horizon was beginning to hint of sunrise. Gaining the top of the hillock, Lara sighed with pleasure. Then looking up she smiled and silently greeted the Great Creator of them all. Her eyes turned now to the impending sunrise, the edges of the sky beginning to color faintly. Above her, one large morning star blazed brightly. It would soon fade into insignificance with the sun's rays. A hand suddenly slipped into hers and looking down she saw her son. Lara smiled.

"I heard you get up," he said. "I love sharing the sunrise with you, Mother. I love it here and I love it at the Dominus's castle."

"Aye," she agreed. "I love going with you to the Morning Garden that faces the sunrise. Even on those bitter Icy Season mornings, my son."

"I do, too," the boy told her. "The Dominus has been so very welcoming to Anoush and to me. We are not of his blood. Nor are we even Terahn. Yet he loves us."

"Of course he does. You and Anoush are my blood," Lara told her son. "And you both share my blood with the daughter I bore Magnus. Magnus Hauk is a strong and respected leader, Dillon. He loves you and Anoush not just because you are my children but because his heart is a great one. Ahh, look! Here is the sun."

They stared at the golden-red orb as it pushed its way above the horizon into the palette of colors flooding the blue sky. All around them the sun's entrance into the New Outlands was greeted by a profound silence. It seemed as if every living thing was perfectly still for that brief moment. Mother and son stood silently in quiet admiration.

"I love this time of day," Lara said softly. "I love the warmth and light of the sun. I should die if I were forced to live in a world without the sun."

"Is there such a world?" Dillon asked.

"I don't know," his mother answered, "but if there is I hope never to go there."

They walked back together to the hall. With the sun now risen the chatter of birdsong filled the air. By the looks of the baggage carts before each house it would appear that the citizens of Camdene were just about ready to depart for the Gathering. She thought the date was on the morrow. She must transport Magnus today so he might join the trek with the Fiacre. Perhaps next year they would travel with the Felan clan. Lara didn't want to give the impression that she favored the Fiacre. As mentor to the clan families she needed to remain impartial. Entering the hall, she was greeted by Noss.

"Sholeh has just sent a faerie post," Noss said. "She wants to know if they should allow Cam to come to the Gathering or leave him behind with those too infirm to travel?"

"As much as I don't want to see him or have him see Anoush," Lara replied, "it is best they bring him with them. At least they have a better chance of knowing where he is, and what he is doing. Sholeh must never leave him on his own. Do you want to bring him back with the Fiacre when the Gathering is over? Or leave him with her for a few more weeks?" She sat down at the high board with Noss, saying to Dillon as she did, "Go and wake your sisters. It is far too beautiful a day to be lying in bed and soon enough the Icy Season will be on us."

Dillon ran off.

"Nay," Noss said to her, "we might as well bring him back with us, as you originally planned when you sent him to Sholeh. It is almost time for learning again and with Pakwa tending to Bera and Anoush gone, he is well isolated, though it saddens me."

"Watch him carefully. He will always seek to make allies among the other children. One or two is all he really needs, Noss, to cause trouble. Cam must be carefully observed at all times and his friends, as well. No child is to be told not to associate with him for then that is the one thing they will desire above all. The children will soon learn that Cam is not be trusted. They will eventually shun him without being told," Lara said quietly.

"He is just a boy," Noss remarked sympathetically.

"He is the son of Adon and Elin," Lara replied. And then she reached for the freshly baked bread that had just been put upon the table and tore off a piece to butter.

"When is Magnus coming?" Noss wanted to know. "We leave tomorrow."

"I'll transport him later today," Lara answered. "I've missed him and I do not think I can stay away from him so long again. I've been here with you for over a month."

Noss grinned. "You just miss taking pleasures with your husband," she teased. "I do believe you are considering giving him a son, aren't you? After all, Zagiri is now four years old. And Dillon will soon be gone to Prince Kaliq to be trained in your magic ways. Terah does need an heir to follow Magnus."

"Aye," Lara agreed with her best friend. "I think it is now time to give the Dominus a son. It is probably past time," she smiled, "and I have always been a woman for doing her duty. Yes, today is a good day to bring Magnus to me." Her eyes twinkled.

Noss laughed aloud.

Dillon returned to the hall with his sisters trailing in his wake. Lara directed her children to the lower end of the high board to eat their morning meal. She was tired and realized that her night had been a restless one although she could not recall dreaming at all. She missed Magnus. She would send the children out to play with their cousins and friends, and then take a little nap. And when she awoke, Lara decided, she would bring Magnus to her. She smiled. It seemed a good plan.

Dillon, Anoush and Zagiri all ran out into the sunshine. Like the rest of the village children they would not be seen for the remainder of the day, for these last days of summer were precious. Having asked Noss if there were anything she might do and receiving an answer in the negative, Lara returned to her chamber and lay down to sleep. When she awoke the long shadows of afternoon were streaming into the room. She was quickly alert and rising, washed her hands and face in the little basin on the table. She took up her hairbrush and unbraided her long hair, brushed it, then replaited it neatly. It was time. Standing in the middle of the chamber she chanted. *"Come to me, my love, my life. Come and now be with your wife."*

Magnus Hauk appeared in a puff of white smoke. He shook himself impatiently. "You might at least warn me when you are going to do things like that, Lara," he said.

"Have you not missed me these past few weeks?" she pouted at him.

The Dominus of Terah grinned. "I have missed you very much, my darling," he told her. Then he took her into his arms and their lips met in a burning kiss. When they broke off the embrace he said to her, "Bar the chamber door, Lara, and I will show you just how much I have missed you." His turquoise-blue eyes met her green ones.

Lara did as she had been bid. Then she returned to the warmth of her husband's arms. "Show me now," she whispered to him, her hand caressing his strong face with a delicate graze of her knuckles. A single finger traced a path down the bridge of his long nose and then dragged across his lips. Reaching up she ruffled his dark gold hair. "Just how much have you missed me, my lord Dominus?" she teased him, pressing herself against his hard, masculine body. *Tell me!*"

"Obviously as much as you have missed me," he teased her, reaching up to fondle her plump breast. His thumb and his forefinger found the nipple and pinched it suggestively, sending a bolt of pure lust through her.

Reaching down she found his manhood beneath his long robe. She began to draw his robe up so she might take him in her hand. He took her hand away and in response pulled his robe off first and then hers. Then he removed his camise and her chemise. Lara began to giggle, her eyes dancing with mirth. Magnus Hauk looked puzzled and said to her, "What do you find so amusing in the midst of our mutual seduction, my darling?"

"You are wearing your boots," Lara told him.

"Then take them off," he told her.

"Can you not take off your own boots?" she demanded of him.

"I like it better when you take them off," he leered at her suggestively. "I love seeing your perfect little bottom when you bend to pull my footwear off." He sat down on the big bed.

"You are a most lustful man," she told him, but turning her back, she took one shod foot between her two legs and drew the boot off and then she took the other. All the while his two big hands fondled her buttocks, squeezing. When both boots had been removed along with his foot coverings Lara made to stand, but her husband pulled her back into his lap, his hands sliding around her torso to capture her two plump breasts. She squealed with surprise, but then feeling his manhood beneath her wiggled against it, teasing him as he was now teasing her. His breath was hot in her ear.

"I am a lustful man," he agreed with her cheerfully. "And I have kept my lust well in check these past few weeks you have been here in the New Outlands. But now I am here. And you are here. And I find no reason to restrain myself. *Do you, Wife?*" His lips found the nape of her neck and he began to nibble and kiss it. The warm fresh scent of her was intoxicating to his aroused senses.

"Nay, my lord," Lara replied amiably, closing her eyes and enjoying the feel of his big hands on her breasts, his lips on her neck. The hardness beneath her was very exciting, and she was almost embarrassed at how eager she was to have him sheathed within her. The past few weeks had been lonely without him. Whatever had possessed her to spend time in the New Outlands? Now that Dillon and Anoush were living with her it really wasn't necessary. The children could come next year if they wanted but she was not going to leave Magnus Hauk again.

He took her nipples between his fingers, pulling and pinching at them. Lara leaned back, her head resting against his shoulder. "I love your breasts," he murmured in her ear as he licked the curl of flesh, then blew warm breath upon it.

"I love seeing your hands on my breasts," she told him breathlessly.

His big strong hands slipped from her bosom and caressed her belly. "I want the son you promised me," he told her.

"I am ready to give you that son, my lord and my love," she answered him.

He reached down and touched her mons, sliding a finger between her nether lips to find the center of her. She was already creamy with her need for him. She sighed as his finger played with her, and the longing in the sound made him turn her about so that they were facing one another. He lay back and she sat atop him licking her lips in anticipation of the passion to come. His manhood stood straight and tall before her.

Reaching out Lara caressed it first with delicate fingers that trailed down the thick pillar of hard flesh. Then she grasped him in her two little hands and slowly, slowly, pushed his foreskin down and then up again several times. The ruby head of his manhood glowed like a beacon and when a small pearl of his juices appeared Lara bent herself over him and lapped it up with her tongue. Then her tongue carefully encircled the tip several times before she took him in her mouth to suck upon him.

Magnus Hauk groaned, and for just the briefest moment he

thought that his head was going to explode along with his manhood. "I won't spill my juices down your greedy maw," he told her in a tight voice. "My seed is strong and we can create a son with it."

Lara immediately released him, looking to him for direction.

"I have to taste you," he told her as he lifted her up and lay her on her back. "I need the taste of you flooding my senses." He yanked at several pillows upon the bed and pushed them beneath her so that her hips were elevated high. Then he pushed her legs apart and put his head between her shapely thighs. She drew her nether lips apart for him and he began to lick eagerly at her. His tongue moved slowly over the insides of her nether lips. It found her center, her jewel, and he nibbled at it. Then taking it into his mouth he sucked hard upon it and Lara's body spasmed beneath him as her juices flowed copiously. "I can't wait," he apologized as he mounted her.

"Neither can I," she said softly and then gasped with delight as he filled her heated body with his throbbing manhood. Lara wrapped her legs about her husband's torso, clinging to him as he began to piston her with long, slow strokes, which quickened and grew more powerful in intensity. Her nails raked down his back, and raising her head she bit down on his shoulder hard.

"Vixen!" he growled at her and then he groaned as his pulsing manhood felt her sheath tightening about him, as he sensed the climax of their lust beginning to quiver within her. He waited, waited, and then released his juices, shuddering as they attained pleasure together in each other's arms. "I love you, my faerie wife!" he told her.

"And I love you, my mortal husband," Lara murmured, reluctant to allow the pleasures to fade away as they eventually must.

A knocking came upon the door as they lay recovering in each other's arms.

"Mama! Let us in," they heard Zagiri calling. "I want to see Papa!"

Magnus began to laugh and Lara called out, "Papa and I are busy, Zagiri. We will see you later." She struggled not to giggle.

"No, Mama! Now!" Zagiri shouted.

"Zagiri," they heard Anoush say, "come away. They are taking pleasures now and do not want to be disturbed. Come with me, Little Sister."

"What are pleasures?" Zagiri demanded to know.

But whatever Anoush told Zagiri they did not hear. It was obvious the two girls had moved away from the bedchamber door.

Lara's eyes were brimming with her mirth.

"What can Anoush possibly know about pleasures?" Magnus demanded of his wife. "She is still a little girl. And Zagiri is certainly too young to understand."

Lara laughed softly. "Aye, Anoush is a little girl but in the summer months she runs with all the village children. Some are older and some younger. And they all listen to adult conversations because adults speak carelessly before children, not believing that the children could be possibly interested. That is how they pick up knowledge of things beyond their ken," she explained.

"We will have to learn to be careful in future, my love," Magnus told her.

"We will," Lara agreed solemnly but her eyes were still dancing.

He chuckled. "I suppose we should get up and join the evening gathering in the hall like a respectable Dominus and Domina."

"Perhaps it would be a good idea," Lara agreed, "but I did enjoy this little interlude with you, my lord. I think I will not leave you again for several weeks' time."

"I think I will not let you," he agreed as he stood up.

They bathed quickly and dressed. Upon entering the hall they were greeted warmly by the Fiacre.

"Ah," teased Noss, "I see you are blooming with happiness to have your husband with you again. And he looks like a large yellow tomcat who has just enjoyed a very large bowl of warm, sweet cream. When did he arrive?"

"Earlier in the afternoon," Lara replied, watching as her three children now swarmed the Dominus. He hugged Dillon and Anoush first and then picked Zagiri up in his arms, kissing her cheek before putting her back down again.

"Anoush said you were taking pleasures with our mother," Zagiri began. "Do you take pleasures with Mama often, Papa?"

The Dominus looked perplexed. He flushed.

"Really, Zagiri," Dillon spoke up, coming to his stepfather's rescue. "Pleasures are something private between adults. They are not discussed with little children, as you will understand someday."

"Do you take pleasures, Dillon?" Zagiri asked him.

"I am too young to take pleasures or even discuss them," Dillon said sternly. "And if I am too young, then you certainly are too young."

"But Anoush said—"

"Anoush," her brother said, glowering at his blushing sister, "knows even less about pleasures than I do, so I would not listen to any of her chatter, little one."

"Oh," Zagiri responded.

"Thank you, my son," the Dominus said. "I could not have put it better myself."

Dillon swallowed the grin that threatened to explode across his face.

The evening progressed with food, frine and song, but ended early, for the trek to the Gathering would begin at first light. Many of the Fiacre would travel to the autumn festival held every year. The most elderly and fragile, however, would remain behind. This year it had been decided that Bera would not go.

"I want no discord," Liam, the lord of the Fiacre, said quietly.

"She is quiet, poor lady," Noss protested.

"Most of the time now, aye, but if something distresses her, and one never knows what will distress her, then she becomes very vocal and abusive," Liam said. "I do not want her among us this time. And, too, Cam will be there with Sholeh. He is sure to attempt to arouse her to a frenzy for his own amusement. Nay. Bera remains in Camdene this year. She does not go out now except to sit in her back garden. She will not even know that we are gone."

The next morning, Lara, Magnus and their three children arose early and ate quickly. Then they gathered with the others and mounting their horses, moved off. While Dillon and Anoush rode their own horses, little Zagiri rode with her father, seated before him on his saddle. It was two days' travel to the site, and when they arrived the Fiacre found two of the clan families just arrived, the Felan and the Aghy. Roan of the Aghy came forward to help Lara from her saddle, his hands lingering about her waist just a moment longer than they should have. She laughed down at him and shook her finger in remonstrance. He grinned back. Magnus Hauk glared at the Horse Lord but as always Roan of the Aghy wasn't in the least intimidated. He stepped forward, shook the Dominus's hand and bid him welcome to the Gathering.

Eventually all the clan families arrived, and for the next few days they feasted and socialized with one another. The annual meeting of the New Outlands High Council was held but there was virtually nothing to report. After several years the clan families had put down deep roots and were content to be freed from the threat of Hetar. In a short ceremony each of the clan families paid their annual tribute to the Dominus, who accepted it graciously.

Afterwards, Magnus asked his wife, "Should we tell them of Hetar's planned aggression against Terah?"

"Nay, not yet," Lara said. "If we need to confer later with the clan lords we can bring them to our castle, but the Icy Season is coming. It is unlikely that Hetar will cross the Sagitta until spring. We have the watchtowers on the heights to warn us of any approaching vessels. We have an army now that is well trained. The Emerald Mountain Range separates us from the New Outlands. There is no need to fret the clan families, but I would tell one of the lords. Rendor should know."

"Not Roan? He is the warlord of the clan families."

"That is true," Lara agreed, "but if you tell Roan, it will not remain a secret, for he will immediately begin planning for a battle that may never come. To plan a battle he needs to recruit more troops and then the secret is out. Nay, Roan need not know, but Rendor must, for he is the High Lord of the High Council. If we need to call upon the clan families he should be aware in advance of that possibility." She sighed. "I regret having to place this burden upon him but it would seem we have no choice, my lord."

The Dominus nodded. "Speak with him then, Lara," he said.

"Will you not be by my side when I do?" she asked softly.

"If you wish it," he replied, "but it is you that the clan families revere, my love. They have accepted me as their overlord only because I am your husband."

"You are the Dominus of Terah, Magnus Hauk. Who and what I am or what I have done for the clan families would not matter were it not for your generosity in allowing them to be relocated here. They do not forget that you are lord of this all. Nor do I," Lara said quietly. She well knew her husband's dignity and pride in his position. She would not damage it or allow anyone else to. "You are a good ruler, my lord."

He smiled down at her. She was clever and generous of heart, his faerie wife.

"Thank you," was all he said.

They sought out Rendor of the Felan, and together told him that Hetar was considering a war against Terah.

"Why?" was the first thing Rendor wanted to know. He had ever been a practical man. "Is not the Outlands enough territory for him that he must cross a sea to war with a peaceful people?" Rendor shook his grizzled head. "Gaius Prospero was ever a fool."

"But a dangerous fool," Lara said. "He is like a child standing before a large sweet who wants every bit of it for himself. He knows he cannot devour it all, yet his eyes are too big for his stomach and he must attempt it nonetheless. This emperor knows naught of Terah, but he has convinced Hetar that we pose a threat because I am the Domina. He bleats that my magic threatens them all, and preaches war."

"Can he take Terah?" Rendor wanted to know. He was a shrewd man who knew that if Hetar took Terah they would be unlikely for many years, if ever, to come over the mountains. Hetarians were not adventurous folk by nature. Greedy. Overproud. Tradition bound. Aye. But they were not by nature explorers.

"He cannot take Terah," the Dominus said firmly. "But unless he can be dissuaded from his path he will cause great misery, mostly in Hetar."

"He has converted many of the Coastal Kings' trading vessels into ships of war," Lara said. "But his naval force of men, but for the officers, is conscripted and not well trained. I can put up a fog bank to keep him at bay if he actually has the nerve to set sail.

"And the fjords can all be blocked to prevent his sailing up them. The cliffs descend directly to the beach below, and the beaches are only narrow strips of sand covered by water in high tide. Without a way up he will be caught."

"And we may shoot them easily from the heights with our bows and arrows," Rendor replied with a grin. "It will be like wolf-hunting season," he chuckled.

The Dominus laughed. "Aye, just like wolf-hunting season," he agreed. "I am relieved that you are not distressed by this news, Rendor, but I do apologize for burdening you with this information."

Rendor shook his head. "Nay, it is better I am kept fully informed in this matter. I will keep it secret from the others, for there is no need for them to know about something that might not come to pass. Roan would want to prepare for a war that at this moment does not exist. And Floren of the Gitta would start to dither about some new species of plant or tuber he didn't want destroyed by an invading army."

Lara laughed. "Yes, Floren would indeed dither," she agreed.

"In that case we will return to Terah on the morrow," the Dominus said. "I am, I fear, a man who enjoys his comforts and I long for my own bed."

"No more than I do," Rendor said with a grin. Then he embraced Lara, kissing her on both cheeks. "I will look forward to seeing you at the next Gathering," he told her.

"You could see me before then," she reminded him. "Next year we will stay in your hall with you and your wife, Rahil."

"We shall be honored," Rendor replied. Then he bowed to Magnus and Lara. "Farewell, my lord, my lady Lara. The Celestial Actuary keep you safe."

"And the Great Creator keep you safe, Rendor," Magnus Hauk responded.

Rendor left them.

"I will go and gather up the children," Lara said. "Tomorrow they will return home and their schooling must begin anew."

They found Dillon watching over his little sister, Zagiri, but

Anoush was not with them. When Lara asked where her eldest daughter might be, Dillon frowned.

"Cam sought her out," he said.

Lara swore softly beneath her breath. "Do you know where they are?" she asked her son. "Could you not stop her from going off with him?"

"Nay, I could not," Dillon answered quietly. "It is time that Anoush learned to control her own actions. She knows you do not approve of Cam."

Lara grimaced. Dillon was right, of course, but there was something about being lectured by one's young son that grated on her nerves. "At least save me the trouble of stamping about the encampment," she said.

The boy grinned at her. "There is a stream on the edge of the camp, Mother. You will find them there," he said.

Lara hurried off. Her first instinct was to turn Cam into a snake but if she did he would probably bite someone and poison them. She had won Anoush back last year and she was not going to let Adon and Elin's son spoil that. She would not confront the boy, for that was precisely what he wanted of her. He was not capable of driving a wedge between Lara and Anoush. Only she could do that if she acted foolishly. Spying her older daughter, she called to her.

Anoush turned at the sound of her mother's voice, looking guilty that she had been caught. But to the little girl's surprise Lara did not scold her. Instead her mother put a loving arm about her and smiled.

"'Tis time for us to leave, my darling," she said in a sweet voice. "Good morrow, Cam. Sholeh tells me you are becoming a fine cattle herder." Lara looked down at her daughter. "Magnus, your brother and sister are waiting for us, Anoush. The Learning Season begins in a few days and you need to be ready. Say goodbye to your cousin now, and let us go." Her arm remained about her daughter's thin shoulders.

"I don't know why you have to live in Terah," Cam said, his tone sulky. "Isn't the New Outlands good enough for you and your brother anymore? You are Fiacre, not Terahn, after all."

"Oh, but Cam, Dillon and I are half-Terahn. We love the castle of the Dominus. We are happy to be living again with our mother and our stepfather is good to us. And we are learning so much. I actually love the Learning Season. We have a wonderful old scholar, Master Bashkar, for our teacher. He is a Devyn who left his clan family to travel beyond the old Outlands to see what he could see."

"You just like being rich and the stepdaughter of the Dominus who is so all-powerful," Cam replied irritably.

"Farewell, Cam," Lara said softly.

"Yes, farewell!" Anoush said and turned away with her mother. The two walked back across the encampment to the tent where they had sheltered during the Gathering. "I think Cam is jealous of Dillon and me," Anoush said. "And he does not like the fact that he cannot lead me about by the nose any longer," she noted. "I'm so glad you came to get me, Mama. I was about to leave him when you did."

Lara smiled, but said nothing. Inside the tent she gathered her family around her. "I will send you home now," she told them.

"Then Dasras and I shall come back together. We will see you shortly. Dillon, tell Jason that Dasras will be coming so he can prepare his stall." She kissed her husband who let her lips leave his only reluctantly.

"Tonight," he murmured in her ear.

Lara smiled into his eyes and nodded. Then with a quick wave of her hand and a short spoken spell, *"Send these four back to their home. No longer to roam."*

Magnus Hauk, flanked by Anoush and Dillon, Zagiri in his arms, disappeared in a flash of light and a puff of greenish smoke. Lara sighed. She loved the picture they had made waiting for her to work her magic. Leaving the tent she made her way through the encampment where all the clan families were in the midst of departing for their own territories and homes. In the green field beyond the camp, horses grazed. "Dasras!" she called and the great golden stallion separated himself from the herd and galloped over to her. "Time to go home, old friend," Lara said to him. "I have sent the others on ahead."

"Climb on my back then, mistress," Dasras said.

Grasping a handful of his creamy mane Lara pulled herself up onto the horse's back. Her slender leather-clad legs grasped the beast's sides. Her fingers wrapped around his mane, making a little fist as Dasras galloped across the green field, his great white wings unfolding slowly as they took to the skies. The horse circled the encampment below while many members of the clan families, looking skyward and recognizing Lara and Dasras, waved at them. Lara waved back. Then her mount turned to the Emerald Mountains and Terah which lay beyond. They would be home even before the midautumn's early sunset.

The cold air stung her cheeks as they traveled. The winds had begun to come from the north. Lara briefly glanced in that direction as she rode. The Dark Lands beyond did not seem as threatening to her as it once had. She laughed to herself. Even a faerie woman might have her fantasies, she thought, wondering why she had once considered those mountains so ominous. Turning away, she leaned forward, eager to get home. The brief month she had spent away from her husband seemed longer than it normally did. Perhaps next summer she would not, after all, return Dillon and Anoush to the New Outlands to live among their father's people.

Then she had a somber moment. Perhaps next summer they would be at war. She would need to consult with her mother who knew everything that was happening in Hetar. She would have to speak eventually with her mentor, Kaliq of the Shadows, who was also a font of information. Terah did not want war. She would have to do everything in her power to try and prevent it. But Lara knew that even faerie magic could not solve everything. And while she disliked admitting it, Gaius Prospero was a force with which to be reckoned.

9

"YOU ARE GOING TO MARRY Vilia?" Gaius Prospero looked astounded at the news. "Why? She is certainly past her prime now, Jonah."

"My lord, I do this for you," Jonah said. "Despite all your kindness to her and your great generosity of heart, she feels ashamed that you have cast her off to wed the beautiful lady Shifra. And now that you have announced that you plan to make Shifra Hetar's empress, the lady Vilia's shame is slowly turning to anger. We must stem that anger, my lord. Quickly!"

"But how does marrying a freed slave help Vilia's anger?" the emperor wanted to know. "She is a proud woman, born into one of Hetar's finest and most ancient families."

"My lord, it is true that I served in my early years as your slave, but did you never once consider my heritage? It is a respectable one. Perhaps not as fine as the lady Vilia's, but 'tis naught to be ashamed of, I assure you," Jonah said.

"You know who your parents were?" The emperor was both surprised and curious. "Who were they then?"

"My father was Sir Rupert Bloodaxe of the Crusader Knights.

He is long dead, as you know. My mother is the lady Farah, a Pleasure Mistress. Sir Rupert Bloodaxe paid the Pleasure Mistress for the privilege of my mother's company for a full year.

"After I was born and put to a wet nurse, also paid for by my sire, my mother returned to her duties. As you know, she became a famous Pleasure Woman and eventually was given charge of the house in which she served. You may question her. My mother will not deny me, my lord, and my blood is good."

"But why were you a slave?" Gaius Prospero wanted to know.

"Sir Rupert died when I was sixteen. Illegitimate children of a Crusader Knight belong to them as much as any piece of property. Usually these men make a provision in their wills freeing any children they may have sired outside of their marriage. Sometimes they don't even know if they have sired children, but make the provision anyway. Unfortunately, my father simply forgot.

"So I became the property of his estate and Sir Rupert's wife was a jealous woman. She had borne her husband five daughters but no son. It impeded my father's advancement and he was not pleased.

"My poor half sisters were no beauties. Our father had paid a fortune in dowries to see them married properly. But worse, Sir Rupert truly loved my mother. I had been sent to an academy of learning by my father. On the day he was buried, a mercenary came and took me from my classes. I was sold in the slave market without delay. My mother was furious, of course, but it was your house, my lord, into which I was sold. I asked her to keep her peace because I wanted to serve a man that I admired,"

Jonah said and the emperor bridled with pleasure at the compliment. "And that is what I am attempting to do now, my lord. Serve you as I always have served you."

"Vilia knows of your connections?" Gaius Prospero asked.

"She does, my lord," Jonah answered.

"And she will have you as her husband?"

"Her heart will always be yours, my lord," Jonah lied with facile charm. Vilia didn't give a damn about Gaius Prospero. She was completely his. "Despite your generosity to her, there have begun to arise some rather unpleasant murmurs regarding your behavior toward the lady," he continued. "By quickly remarrying, she disproves the rumors. And we certainly cannot have her uniting with someone from an ambitious family who might use her to further himself and threaten your throne, my lord. I cannot permit it! And so I have offered myself to the lady Vilia as a husband. She will not accept me, however, without your personal permission and approval. So I have come to you on bended knee, my lord. Give us the favor of your approbation, my emperor."

"Shifra and I will give the wedding!" the emperor burst out. "All of Hetar shall see how generous I am toward the mother of my children. But your heritage must be announced for the people to know," he continued. "I want no one believing that I have insulted Vilia by forcing her into a marriage with a former slave. Perhaps it might even help if the two of you admitted that after her divorce you were attracted to one another. Then you came to me and I gave you my benediction. Yes! Yes! That is what we will do, Jonah. It is perfect and shows the people that my heart is a good one." He beamed with pleasure at the thought.

"It is brilliant, my lord, and I thank you!" Jonah said, kissing his master's hand.

Soon the word spread throughout The City. The emperor's right hand, although he had spent ten years in slavery, was actually the son of Sir Rupert Bloodaxe and the famed Pleasure Mistress, Lady Farah. Sir Rupert's daughters admitted it was true. Their mother was dead and if the truth were known, their father's mistress had made him happy in his last years. It was she who had convinced him to increase their dowries, making each of them far more desirable. They had not approved, they declared in a loud and united voice, of their mother selling the poor boy into slavery.

Jonah smiled to hear this. His half sisters hadn't given a damn about him. But he made public visits to each of them, embracing them and eating at their tables. They had all wed influential men and it would not hurt to have those men in his corner when the time was right. Vilia's family was also vocal in their approval of her impending marriage to Jonah. So at last, he went to visit his mother.

Lady Farah publicly greeted her son at the door of her Pleasure House. Then she led him into her very private chambers. "How clever you are, Jonah," she said to him with a warm smile. "And your patience is absolutely astounding. How long have you been planning this marriage?" She was a very beautiful woman with long straight ebony hair that she wore simply pulled back, and slightly slanted dark eyes like black cherries.

He gave her a brief smile. "For some time," he replied.

"I hope you have made her fall in love with you, my son."

"She is devoted to me and my manhood keeps her more than satisfied," he answered his mother. "I have obviously inherited your passions."

"Excellent! You have the key to controlling her. If she is content and happy, her family will be content and happy. They can be of great use to you one day, I suspect."

He said nothing and his dark eyes were inscrutable, revealing nothing of his plans or his emotions. *Did he have any?* Lady Farah wondered and then laughed at herself. Of course he had plans. From birth Jonah had been a calm and thoughtful being. But Farah knew in her heart what his plans were for she too was ambitious.

"I will help you when you ask me," was all she said.

"And I will ask," he told her with the tiniest of smiles.

She offered him frine and they spoke on mundane matters for a brief time and then Jonah departed his mother's Pleasure House. He must learn who owned it and purchase it for her. He would be generous and the house's master would sell it to him in order to gain favor with the emperor's right hand. Jonah knew his mother was an honorable woman. He would not divide her loyalties between her son and her Pleasure Master. She would be free to give him all of her loyalty once the sale was complete. And when the lady Farah was elected new head-mistress of the Pleasure Guild, his power base would expand even further. He hurried home to Vilia, who was already awaiting him.

She came eagerly into his arms and he gave her a small smile.

"I have visited my mother," he told her. "She is pleased we are to wed."

"May I meet her?" Vilia asked him. "We could have her here."

"A most excellent suggestion," Jonah approved.

"I am so proud of you," Vilia said softly. "What ambitions you have! Not at all like Gaius. We had to push him every inch of the way to the throne."

"And now together," Jonah replied, "we will tumble him off that throne. The war with Terah will be the final straw for the people of Hetar."

"Terah is not really a danger to us?" Vilia asked.

"From what I have observed as Hetar's ambassador, the Terahns want nothing more than to live in peace. Will they defend themselves against us if we attack them? Oh, yes, Vilia, my dear. They will most certainly defend themselves," Jonah said. "But that is all they will do. They will beat Hetar back and leave us to lick our wounds. And while the emperor directs this misadventure, we will undermine him."

"Will we kill him?" Vilia asked excitedly. "And his little empress?"

"Of course we will kill him," Jonah told her. "He will still have friends among the powerful, but killing him will turn their loyalty to us, for the magnates are ever mindful of their own interests. One does not fight a war and then leave the enemy alive to rebuild his fortunes. That is madness."

"There are some who will say you are cruel," Vilia murmured.

"They will not say it aloud nor will they have the authority with which to back up their words," Jonah told her. "But enough of strategy, my dear. I have bought you a present in the slave market today." He clapped his hands and immediately a naked young slave was led into the chamber.

He was very tall and shapely. His manhood was the largest that Vilia had ever seen and she could not keep her eyes from it. But then she turned to Jonah questioningly.

"Do you like him, my dear?" Jonah asked her.

Vilia nodded slowly.

"Examine him," Jonah suggested. "Touch him, my dear."

She walked about the slave whose head was respectfully lowered. She raised his head with her hand. He was a beautiful creature with velvety brown eyes, but they held no expression. He lowered his head again when she released it. Vilia ran a hand down the slave's hard bicep. She caressed his buttocks but then her hand could not resist the enormous manhood that hung between his sinewy thighs. She looked up at Jonah.

The faintest smile touched his lips and he nodded encouragingly.

Vilia ran her hand down the slave's length. She cupped the large seed sac behind it. It was cool to her touch. Cool with his virility. She felt heat suffusing her body, and when the slave's manhood began to burgeon beneath her touch Vilia gasped softly, looking again to Jonah, but she did not remove her hand. "Why?"

"You are a woman of great appetites," he began. "There will come a time when the press of governance will prevent me from being with you and I do not want you unhappy, but neither do I want you cuckolding me as you did Gaius. This slave has been trained to give pleasure. It is his only function. He has no other. He is perfect for you, my dear. He is mute but he will answer to your commands. And, my dear Vilia, I am told you will find both his manhood and his tongue skillful. If you do not, then I shall return him and find you another."

Vilia was astounded. "Oh, Jonah, my love," she said to him. "How can you know me so well? We are truly well mated. I would have remained true to you, Jonah, even though at times it would have been difficult for me. That you should consider my needs and give me this beautiful slave is beyond kindness." She caught his hand and lifting it to her lips, kissed it fervently. "Thank you!"

"Let us see if he pleases you," Jonah said wickedly.

"Here? Now?" Vilia didn't know if she should be embarrassed.

"Why not, my dear? If he does not please you, the sooner I return him, the better."

"Jonah, I do not think…"

"I want to see him using you, Vilia. I need to know that you are happy," Jonah told her in a hard voice. "Lift your gown up now and bend yourself over the arm of that couch," he told her, pointing. "Look at Doran, for that is his name. His great member is eager to sheath itself in you. If you are to be my wife you must be more amenable to my wishes, my dear, for while I value your sage council, I value your obedience equally," Jonah said, his tone softening a bit now. "Come." He led her to the couch, and when she had bent herself over it he pushed her gown up himself, baring her shapely white buttocks. Then he signaled Doran. "Do your duty by your new mistress," Jonah instructed the sex slave.

Doran walked over to where Vilia waited. He positioned his enormous manhood. Then grasping the woman's hips with strong fingers he thrust hard into her.

She felt the entrance to her love sheath being stretched wide and then his great length pushed with a single smooth motion into her. He was so thick and yet she found to her surprise she was able to contain him. Never in all her days had Vilia entertained such a large member. Gaius had been average in size. Jonah was a large man. But Doran was huge. And then he began to ream her with his manhood, slowly at first and then with increasing speed. Her passions peaked once, twice, a third time. Her moans rose in intensity until she was almost weeping.

"Enough!" she heard Jonah command the slave, and Doran immediately withdrew from her.

"No!" Vilia cried. *"No! No! No!"* And then she felt Jonah entering her and skillfully bringing them both to a perfect conclusion. "Oh, my darling," she sighed gustily with her total and utter satisfaction. "Thank you!"

He withdrew from her lush body, then turned her over so he might observe her. "For the slave, my dear, or for the other?" he asked seriously.

"For both!" she said enthusiastically.

Pulling her gown down he drew her to a standing position. "Then the slave pleases you, my dear?"

"Aye, but you please me more," she admitted.

He nodded. "You will use him then when you need him, Vilia?"

"Aye. It was a most thoughtful gift, my lord," Vilia told him, smiling.

"I am glad the gift delights, my dear." He kissed her brow and turned to the slave. "Go to the slave quarters, Doran. Your mistress will call you when you are needed. You have done well today and I am satisfied with you."

Turning, the slave ran out of the chamber, and taking Vilia by the hand Jonah led her to a seat large enough for both of them.

"The emperor wishes to give us our wedding," Jonah told her.

"I shall make certain then that it is a most extravagant one," Vilia said and he laughed aloud.

Vilia considered that she had only heard Jonah laugh perhaps once or twice before in all the years she had known him. Today had given her a new insight into her lover. She had realized from the start that he was clever and ambitious. But never until today had she known that he was a dangerous man. Vilia felt a frisson of fear travel down her spine. Jonah knew her too well, perhaps; still, that knowledge was rather exciting. Yet there were things he did not know about her and perhaps he never would. For now, caution was the better path for her to travel. She did love him and she had never really loved Gaius Prospero.

"Do not let Gaius spend so much coin that our wedding is vulgar. And we must also remember that if I am to replace him, eventually I must seem more a man of the people and less a magnate," Jonah advised Vilia. Giving her a kiss upon her cheek he arose from her side. "I must go and speak with the Pleasure Master of my mother's house," he told her. "I intend to purchase it."

"How wise of you!" Vilia cried, clapping her hands delightedly.

"I think it more prudent for both of our sakes," he remarked and then he left her.

Vilia considered recalling Doran to her side but she thought better of it. The sex slave was a comfort to be used sparingly except when Jonah could not be with her. She decided instead to send a faerie post to Lady Shifra so that they might meet and discuss Vilia's impending wedding preparations. Calling a servant to her, she sent the woman for a scribe to come and take her dictation.

THE FAERIE POST was delivered to the lady Shifra as she sat before her mirror having her long red-gold hair brushed by her favorite servant. She took the missive, noting with surprise Vilia's seal on the folded parchment. "What can she want of me?" Shifra said aloud. She broke the wax seal and, opening the message, read it slowly, carefully. Then summoning a servant, she said, "Go and tell my lord the emperor that I would speak with him as soon as possible."

"Yes, my lady," the servant said and hurried out.

"Brush some oil of lilies into my hair," Shifra instructed Tania who resumed brushing her locks. "You know how he likes the scent of it."

"Ahh," Tania said, "you want something of him."

"Not just something," Shifra replied with a small smile. "Lady Vilia is to marry Lord Jonah and she says that the emperor has offered to give the wedding. She asks that I give her my aid in the planning."

"Of course he would offer to host such a wedding," Tania responded. "It is a clever move on his part."

"Why?" Shifra wanted to know.

"Because the people will see it as generous," Tania said.

"To host a wedding for his ex-wife and his ex-slave?" Shifra remarked. "Does not the lady marry down, Tania? I was told her family is an ancient and proud one."

"And so it is, my lady," Tania replied. "But Jonah's lineage is almost as good and the fact that he served ten years in this house as a slave cannot tarnish his line. His father was a well-known Crusader Knight and his mother is a Pleasure Mistress. In fact, rumor has it that when the lady Gillian retires, the lady Farah will be elected headmistress of the Pleasure Guild. She is a blood kin of Squire Darah," Tania concluded.

"How do you know all of this?" Shifra demanded to know.

"I know because when Jonah first came into the House of Prospero he told me in a very rare moment of weakness and then swore me to secrecy. As such knowledge would not harm my lord Gaius I swore an oath to keep his secret. I could see then he would regain his freedom one day and be a great man. And so he has. This marriage is clever on his part for it allies him with some very important families."

"Will that make him a danger to my dear lord?" Shifra asked astutely.

Tania shrugged. "I have never doubted Jonah's loyalty and neither has the emperor, my lady mistress. You should not doubt it, either," she warned.

Gaius Prospero came into Shifra's chambers, beaming as his eyes lit upon her. "My darling," he said and she went immediately into his arms to offer her lips. He kissed her and then his nose twitched. "Lilies! You smell of lilies, my darling. When you called me I came directly from the council, for your wish is my pleasure."

Shifra took him by the hand and led him to a wide couch to

sit by his side. "I have received a message from Lady Vilia. She said you have given your approval to a marriage between her and Lord Jonah."

"I have," Gaius Prospero replied. "And I have learned the most amazing thing about my good Jonah." He went on to tell Shifra what he had learned and she listened, pretending to be amazed by his disclosure about Jonah. "I always wondered about his breeding," the emperor said. "He has never had the look of a common Hetarian."

"We are to plan their wedding," Shifra said.

"Yes!" the emperor said enthusiastically. "Is it not brilliant, my darling? Together we will host this festive event."

"Nay," said Shifra. "I cannot."

Tania stifled her gasp. What was the matter with the little fool that she would defy Gaius Prospero's grandiose plans to appear the most benevolent and tolerant of rulers?

"Nay?" The emperor looked surprised. "Why would you refuse me, Shifra? You have never refused me anything, my darling. What is the matter that you would now?"

"You wed me quietly on the day your divorce was declared legal, my lord. There was no pomp about it yet I was happy simply to be your wife. But I have not yet been crowned your empress, my lord. Did you not promise me that I would be crowned empress of Hetar? How can we stand side by side to do proper honor to Lord Jonah, who has served you so faithfully all these years, and to Lady Vilia, who also served you with such devotion and gave you children, if I am nothing more than your wife and not Hetar's empress?" Shifra wanted to know.

Tania's mouth fell open with her surprise at her mistress's words. She quickly closed it and her gaze went to Gaius Prospero.

The emperor digested Shifra's words and then he said, "You are right, my darling! Before Jonah and Vilia can wed you must first be crowned Hetar's empress. Then we will host this marriage and as Hetar's supreme rulers, the honor we do those two will be considered incredibly generous." He jumped up from her side. "I must go and begin making preparations for your coronation this very minute!"

"I will want the lady Vilia to serve me at my crowning," Shifra murmured. "She must carry my train and then be my footstool as Jonah will be yours when we sit upon our thrones together before our people."

He turned, his face wreathed in smiles. "What a perfect picture you paint, my darling. I knew there was a reason I could not choose either of my two former wives as my empress. They were not worthy of the honor. They had not your majesty or vision," Gaius Prospero complimented her, then he left.

Shifra smiled, well pleased. But Vilia, when she learned why her wedding had been delayed, was furious.

"How dare she!" she almost screamed at Jonah.

He stepped quickly up to face her and clapped a restraining hand over her mouth. "Do not proclaim your emotions to everyone, Vilia," he warned her. "I will see what I can do to mitigate some of this. But if the emperor wishes to crown his wife empress before he hosts our wedding, he can do it."

Vilia tore his hand from her mouth. "I will not be her footstool," she hissed low. "I will carry the little bitch's train and I will smile broadly at all to see, but I will not serve as a footstool!"

"Nor will I," Jonah answered her quietly. "Trust me, Vilia, I will get this changed before Shifra's crowning day. I promise you that."

"But I like the idea of you and Vilia serving as our footstools," Gaius Prospero said to his right hand when Jonah brought up the subject several days before the coronation of Shifra. "It displays my ultimate power over all."

"Indeed, my lord, it does but is it not just a bit vulgar, a bit obvious? And it could easily diminish my authority when I speak for you," Jonah suggested slyly. "I know you would not want that. You do not need me beneath your feet to prove to Hetar that you are a great emperor or that I am devoted to you and your cause. And have you considered that putting Vilia beneath the feet of the young empress might appear cruel? The beautiful new wife swaggering over the older cast-off wife? Vilia is popular among the masses. She does not deserve such from you, my lord."

"Why, Jonah," the emperor said softly. "Are you coming to care for Vilia?"

"She will be my wife, my lord," Jonah answered him. "I will always treat her with respect and dignity for it will speak well of me as her husband—and well of you as my master, for have you not been my example of what is right and correct?"

"I have, it is true," Gaius Prospero answered him. "Oh, very well, Jonah, you shall have your way in this matter, for you are right. My passion for Shifra had blinded me to sensible behavior."

"I would not be the cause of any breach between you and the young empress," Jonah said softly.

"Nonsense!" the emperor chuckled. "Shifra will see reason."

Shifra, however, did not see reason until her husband promised her a golden footstool studded with gemstones to replace Vilia's silk-clad back. "But it will not be nearly as dramatic and meaningful as my suggestion," she pouted.

"Even people like us must occasionally compromise, my darling," the emperor told his young wife. "Vilia is quite thrilled to be carrying your train."

"I shall bear the emperor's scepter," Jonah told Vilia afterwards when he returned to tell her of his success with Gaius Prospero.

She sniffed. "This young wife he has taken will cause Gaius Prospero more trouble than Anora and I together."

"And is not that to our advantage, my dear one?"

"I suppose it is," Vilia admitted. "As long as he is besotted by her he will make mistakes, he will not pay attention and eventually he will bring about his own downfall."

"Precisely!" Jonah said.

"But when will we move to attack Terah?" Vilia wanted to know. "The longer we wait the more dangerous these Terahns become to us. Or so the people must believe."

"Our most advantageous time will be late next spring when the seas are favorable for our vessels to cross the Sagitta. Terah may be primitive, but it is a magnificent land. However, it is not like Hetar. Its people live along seven fjords which are arms of the sea. The fjords, called Dominus, Silk, Jewel, Ocean, Star, Green and Light, push up into the land. On either side of them are great green cliffs. And beyond those cliffs is a territory so vast even the Terahns do not know how big it is. And it is cut in two by a range of mountains called the Emeralds. Who knows what lies on the other side? If the Dominus knows, he certainly never shared that information with me."

"And the faerie girl, Lara, is his wife still?" Vilia wanted to know.

"She has become a great lady," Jonah replied.

"A child raised in the Mercenary quarter? A halfling with a faerie for a mother?" Vilia said scornfully. She had not liked the sound of admiration in Jonah's voice.

"You have not seen her in many years, Vilia. She has grown in beauty, as well as magical skills. Like you, she is beloved of her people. She is wise and the Dominus depends greatly upon her, my dear. But she will not use her magic against Hetar unless Hetar strikes out at Terah. I think you know as well as I do that Terah presents no real threat to Hetar, Vilia. This war the emperor plans is but a means to an end for us. And when he fails and the young men of Hetar are killed, the people will turn against him and cry out for a new leader," Jonah said. "They always do. Remember when he blundered into the Winter War with the Outlands? It took him five years to regain the trust of the Hetarian citizens. But this time he will have no second chance."

"But the High Council was stronger then," Vilia reminded her lover. "And they had always governed Hetar well. What if the people demand a return to the High Council? Remember, Jonah, that you are called the emperor's right hand. You are very much identified with him and his policies. How can you gain the trust of the people under those circumstances?"

"You must leave that to me, my dear," Jonah told her softly. "I will not fail."

Vilia looked into his face and then she smiled. "No," she said. "I do not believe that you will, my darling. Now tell me, when is this coronation of Shifra to take place?"

"Are you so anxious to see her crowned then?" he asked.

"Nay, but I am eager to be wed to you and if that cannot take place until she has been crowned then aye, I am impatient to have it over and done with, my darling," Vilia told him with a small smile. "You see, I would like to have a child. *Your* child. Your heir, my darling. And I do want his birth to come as soon after our marriage as possible. I want us to have an heir before Shifra may give the emperor a son. I want people to think Gaius was a fool for casting off a fecund wife to marry a barren girl."

She had surprised him and briefly, Jonah was speechless. He had always intended to wed her, for her family connections were important to him. But he had not stopped to consider that he would eventually need an heir. But of course he would! "Vilia, my dear!" He took her into his arms. "This is most generous of you and I thank you for considering this. Yes! We must have a child." Jonah's mouth took hers in a hard kiss.

His reaction to her determination delighted Vilia. She had not been certain at all how he would take her plans. She knew that she might prevent conception for she was now in her thirties and had not borne a child in almost twenty years. And she did not intend to spend the rest of her life out of the limelight. She had been born for greatness, as her mother had promised her from birth. Vilia kissed him back and then, pulling away, said, "I will do whatever I have to so you may attain your goals, my love."

"Is it safe for you?" he asked, finding he was actually more concerned for her well-being than her family ties. "I should not want to lose you, my darling Vilia."

"I married Gaius when I was thirteen and had our son, Aubin, when I was fourteen," she answered him. "He is a man now and my daughters are wed. But I am still young enough to be seeded and bred, my love. I could give you our son—for it shall be a son—by late next year." Vilia smiled at him, pleased by his caring.

"Then I shall convince the emperor that Shifra's crowning must be done before the coldest months set in, in order to bring the people into The City to see it. I shall then plan our wedding for the week after. Our union will be a great event which will be remembered far longer than the crowning of that insipid girl," Jonah said.

"And when you overthrow Gaius Prospero, my love," she purred at him, "when will I receive my coronation?"

"We will be crowned together, my dear," he told her. "I would not have it otherwise. And it will be a far grander affair than either of our predecessors has had. That I promise you, my clever and fertile Vilia."

Vilia smiled up into his face. She had known from the first time she had seen Jonah that he would be great one day. By binding them together with a child, Vilia instinctively understood that this man, unlike Gaius Prospero, would never cast her off. Jonah looked at the larger picture. He looked ahead. And while he enjoyed pleasures, he enjoyed power far more, as she did. They were really the most perfect couple. Perhaps even as perfect as the Dominus and Domina of Terah.

True to his word, Jonah cajoled Gaius Prospero into an immediate coronation for Shifra. And in the next few weeks he also negotiated a marriage contract with Vilia's uncle, Cubert Ahasferus. The wealthy magnate was a canny man not easily brought to a settlement.

"She's a wealthy woman in her own right now," Cubert said slowly as he sat with Jonah over goblets of wine from the Outlands vineyards. "What can you offer her in exchange for her fortune and her blood ties?"

"What can any man offer such a woman?" Jonah replied carefully.

Vilia's uncle smiled broadly. Then he said softly, "*Power.* You are no fool like our beloved emperor, who believes as all old-fashioned men believe that women are of little use but for pleasures. You appreciate my niece's intellect."

"Of course, she will have a certain amount of respect as my wife, and aye, I do value her wisdom," Jonah replied quietly.

Now Cubert Ahasferus laughed aloud. "You do not fool me, my lord," he said. "You have ambition. Do you think I cannot see it?"

"The emperor once had ambitions," Jonah answered.

"To be emperor, to take pleasures with beautiful women." His companion sneered. "But you, my lord, see beyond the end of your nose. You want more, and if you would wed my niece I must be certain that when you get what it is you want she will share equally in your glory. Guarantee me that and I will draw up the marriage contracts between you," Cubert Ahasferus said.

Jonah considered his request and then he said, "How is it possible for me to do such a thing, my lord? Anything we put in writing, no matter its innocent intent, could easily be misinterpreted as treasonous. Such a covenant between us could endanger not just my life and Vilia's, but the entire Ahasferus family, as well."

"You are cautious and right to be so," Cubert Ahasferus said approvingly. "Your reputation proceeds you, however. It is said you rarely give your word, but when you do that word is as good as gold. Take my hand and swear to me a blood oath."

"Whose blood would we swear upon if indeed I decided to take you up on your proposal?" Jonah asked curiously. The answer stunned him.

"Swear to me on the life of your unborn child," Vilia's uncle said.

"What child?" Jonah replied, hiding his surprise.

Cubert Ahasferus smiled again. "Why, the one you will put in her belly, dear boy," he said. "I know you will keep your word to me if you swear on his young life. You will not endanger your heir. He will, I suspect, be your one weakness."

"Nay," Jonah said. "I have no weaknesses."

"But you will swear, will you not?" came the reply. "You will give me your blood oath and Vilia will be yours along with all her wealth and the favor of the Ahasferus family. We have many friends, my lord, but then you already know that."

Jonah was silent for a short time as he considered what Cubert Ahasferus had proposed to him. He wanted Vilia. She was as pleasant a bed companion as he had ever enjoyed. He wanted her wealth. He valued her advice. Her connections were important to him. When he became emperor he would crown her his empress. Did all of that not make her his equal? If it re-assured her family to have him swear a blood oath on the life of his unborn son that she would be that equal, then where was the harm in it? He considered the suggestion from all angles, but it always came back to the fact that without Vilia Prospero, born Ahasferus, his plans would not come to fruition.

"I will have my secretary write up the contracts with the necessary dower portion. Did you know that my niece has a quarter share in our trading company?" Cubert Ahasferus said.

"Aye, I knew," Jonah replied. But he had not. He could see he was going to have to speak to Vilia about keeping things from him. "Have the agreement drawn up between us, and set a day for the signing. If I decide to accept your terms I will swear my oath on that day, my lord." He arose from his seat. "I must leave you now. I hope you will forgive me, but the empress's coronation is in just two more days. I have a great deal to oversee for the emperor."

"Of course, of course," Cubert Ahasferus responded jovially, offering Jonah his hand. "I will have the contracts ready the day after the coronation."

Jonah shook the pale white hand, which was surprisingly strong. "Excellent!" he said and hurried off.

Jonah had hardly departed the chamber before Vilia entered the room by means of an inside passage.

"Were you listening?" her uncle asked. "Of course you were."

"I heard it all," Vilia replied. "Did I not tell you he was clever?"

"Let us hope he is not too clever," Cubert Ahasferus said. "Will he sign? Will he swear the blood oath? And are you sure he can get you with child?"

"I am certain," Vilia said. "And he will both sign and swear.

Gaius never loved me, Uncle. He loved the support my family gave him over the years. Jonah, for all his coldness, does, I believe, love me."

"Perhaps," her uncle agreed, "but do not be blinded by your love for him, Niece. This man you are taking as your second husband is as cold as ice. Were there a better opportunity, he would seize it and cast you aside, Vilia. Make no mistake about that."

"But you will protect me, Uncle, will you not?" Vilia murmured.

"Aye, Niece, your family will protect your interests first and foremost," Cubert Ahasferus said firmly.

Vilia smiled. "Then I have naught to trouble myself about, Uncle."

"You are taking part in the empress's coronation, are you not?" he asked.

"I will carry her train," Vilia said.

Cubert Ahasferus snorted. "What presumption!" he grumbled.

"Uncle, had not Jonah intervened I should have served as her footstool as she sat upon her throne. And Jonah, the emperor's footstool. But my clever lover convinced Gaius that such an *honor* could undermine his authority to speak for the emperor. I understand that our soon-to-be empress was not pleased and the footstool upon which her dainty feet will now rest is an expensive concoction of gold and jewels," Vilia said.

"What outrageous effrontery!" her uncle snapped. "The wench is most sure of herself that she would demand such concessions from the emperor."

"He has been besotted by her from the moment he saw her in the slave market," Vilia admitted a bit sourly. "She is very beautiful and reminds me a bit of the faerie woman, Lara, except Shifra's hair is red-gold."

"Who is she?" Cubert Ahasferus demanded to know. "Who are her family? What connections does she have that can be useful?"

"She is a nobody and claims to have lived with her grand-mother on the edge of the forest bordering the Midlands," Vilia replied. "But I sent my own agents to find the grandmother and the hut in which she lived, and they learned nothing, nor could any in that region help them. No one seemed to know Shifra or her grandmother, Uncle. My agents searched all along the forest border but could find no trace of her relations at all."

"Interesting," Cubert Ahasferus mused.

"So then I sought out Lenya the slaver, who had sold her. He swears he found her where she claims he did. He even said he saw a small hut that Shifra said was her grandmother's home. And he did see the old woman, but spoke not to her, for he feared she would refuse to sell Shifra to him. He simply made off with the girl. I am certain he was telling the truth."

"Then who is this creature Gaius Prospero would crown?" Cubert Ahasferus wondered. "Is she magical? Can she protect him?"

"I doubt she is magical herself," Vilia said. "She would appear to be just what she is. A beautiful, simple-minded girl, who exists solely to please Gaius. She really is his ideal woman." Vilia laughed softly.

"Not so simple that she did not attempt to thwart your dignity," her uncle noted.

"But she did not protest too greatly when she could not. She simply persuaded Gaius to have a gold and bejeweled footstool made for her instead," Vilia replied. "I see no malice in her. A budding greed perhaps, but no malice, Uncle." Leaning forward she kissed his cheek. "You must go now," she said.

"Aye, I want those contracts drawn up by tomorrow. I will have them sent to you for any omissions or corrections."

She nodded her understanding.

"Do your part well at the coronation ceremony," Cubert Ahasferus advised her. "The family will all be there watching. I have had a great deal of difficulty calming them down over your divorce and the emperor's decision to crown this young wife of his. I suspect that he had Anora disposed of although such a thing would be difficult to prove. I have told them we are fortunate he did not murder you, as well."

"He never intended to, Uncle," Vilia told him. "He simply wanted me out of his life. It was Jonah who warned me and told me what to ask for in the settlement."

"While standing by to snap you up like a tasty morsel dropped from his master's table," Cubert Ahasferus remarked dryly.

"Uncle, he could not have had me had I not wanted him. We have been lovers for several years now," she told her relation, who wore a look a complete surprise on his face.

"You were cuckolding Gaius Prospero, Vilia?" he gasped.

"It was very exciting, Uncle." She laughed.

He looked at her now with something almost akin to admiration. "And he never knew or even came close to catching you? Well done, Vilia! Ah, what a pity you are not a man. You could rule the world!"

"And can a woman not rule the world, Uncle?" she responded softly.

His mouth fell open in surprise at her question.

"What difference should it make that I have a love sheath and a man has a manhood? Why is one considered more dominant than the other? How ridiculous," Vilia told him, secretly amused by the different emotions drifting over his features.

"You are an interesting woman," Cubert Ahasferus finally told his niece. "I can but hope this new husband of yours will appreciate you." Then with a quick bow to her he departed.

Vilia chuckled. She had surprised her uncle and that was a good thing. She would allow her family to broker her marriage as was Hetarian custom, but she did not want him thinking that she was weak or foolish. She had been very young when they had seen her married to Gaius Prospero, but now she was well into her thirty-fourth year. She would rule through Jonah. But rule she would. Was not the faerie woman, Lara, now ruling in tandem with her husband, the Dominus of Terah? The daughter of a mercenary—well, a Crusader Knight now, Vilia allowed—and a faerie ruled a land vaster than Hetar.

Jonah had said that Terah was no threat to Hetar, but how could it not be? Perhaps not now, but eventually it would be. Primitive, Jonah said, but Lara had been raised in Hetar. How could she not miss the elegance of Hetar's ways? Eventually she would want those ways for Terah and so it would begin. Terah would eventually become a danger to Hetar. Better it be conquered quickly before it turned the tables upon them all. Jonah would have to be convinced and she would convince him, Vilia decided.

But not yet. There was too much for them both to accomplish before they looked to Terah. A coronation, and here Vilia allowed her true feelings to surface briefly. How could Gaius Prospero dare to give *her* crown to that creature whose only accomplishment was to open her legs and give the fat fool pleasures? It was galling! He had refused her that crown which was rightfully hers, murdered Anora, oh yes, she knew he had, and then divorced her. She was fortunate, Vilia thought to herself, not to be dead.

Well, she would repay the fat fool in kind. She would dutifully carry Shifra's train at her coronation in two days' time. She would be gracious to all those who saw her and knew the crown should be on her head. Then she would marry Jonah and give him a son. Then when Hetar went off to war next spring she would pray to the Celestial Actuary that Terah wreak havoc on the Hetarians. She felt a small twinge of guilt at that thought but she pushed it aside. It had to be if Jonah was to overthrow Gaius Prospero.

And when he had, Vilia thought, she would be Hetar's empress. Jonah loved her. He would not refuse to have her crowned. She would rule by his side and their son would one day be Hetar's emperor. And Hetar would absorb Terah into its fold as it had absorbed the Outlands. Vilia's hand went to her belly. *I will carry a son,* she promised herself. *I will give my lord Jonah a son.* She smiled. Everything was proceeding exactly as they had so carefully planned.

"SO GAIUS PROSPERO HAS had his young wife crowned empress of Hetar," Lara said.

"And Lord Jonah has wed the cast-off Vilia," Magnus Hauk replied.

They were seated in their small family dining room with Lara's mother, Ilona, queen of the Forest Faeries, who had materialized in her usual mauve cloud several minutes prior to bring them the news.

"It was disgraceful," Ilona said, her beautiful face showing her distaste. "Never among mortals have I seen such a show of gaudy and expensive waste. What is the matter with Hetarians that they did not rise up in anger over both of these celebrations? The ordinary folk grow poorer while the magnates grow richer, especially with Hetar's acquisition of the Outlands."

"I thought the land was suppose to have been distributed to those willing to work it," Lara remarked. "Was it not?"

"They gave small plots to those who asked, but then those gaining such land were forced to borrow in order to build shelters and purchase seed and equipment. Vast tracts, however, were parceled out among the wealthy. They have planted large vineyards and produce fine wines. They graze cattle upon it not for milk, but for food, which is then sold at outrageous prices in the markets of The City."

"Who works the land?" Magnus Hauk asked. "They gained no slaves from their hollow conquest of the Outlands."

"They have transported thousands of poor from The City," Ilona said. "They give them shelter and food, both scant I might add, in exchange for their labors. The death rate is high, but the magnates care not, for The City is filled with those willing to toil for food and shelter from the elements." Ilona's leaf-green eyes grew misty. "Even I cannot help but feel pity for Hetar's poor," she said. "There are so many of them now, my children. Even the forest is being affected by conditions in Hetar."

"They cannot just bring the poor in to till, plant and harvest," Lara said.

"Those from the Midlands, from families no longer able to sustain them, are employed to supervise the workers. They are treated just slightly better in that they are paid a small wage," Ilona replied.

"And those working the fields are not?" Lara was shocked.

"Aye, they are given a wage, but then what they eat and the shelter in which they live is deducted from that wage. Little, if anything remains after that."

"Then they are slaves," Lara said.

"Nay, they have the right to walk away," Ilona responded, "but if they do, then they have naught. They are not even returned to The City. They are driven from the large farms where they have toiled with only the clothes on their back. And the small plot holders will not take them in for they cannot afford to feed them or pay them to work for they are so burdened with debt themselves. Most eventually die on their own and unless someone finds them they are left to rot where they fall."

Lara's eyes filled with tears. "Once Hetar was a place of laws and fairness. It was an orderly world. Each citizen had his place in it. The quarter where I grew up was peopled by the Guild of Mercenaries. We were not rich, but our hovels were kept in good repair. We were kept warm in the cold and we always had enough to eat even if our food was not the choicest of viands. When Magnus and I were last there I saw homelessness and true poverty, Mother. And those awful kiosks selling Razi so cheaply that even the poorest could purchase it. And those drinking it, even the children, felt neither cold nor hunger. They would fall into a stupor and just dream. I found it horrifying. And now they transport the poor to slave their short lives away in the Outlands." She sighed sadly. "What do the magnates do with all the profit they make? Why has Hetar's society grown so greedy and venal that it cares nothing for those who cannot care for themselves? Given learning, skills and opportunity most people will gladly work. Everyone needs a purpose in life. Everyone needs to be useful."

"Yet there will always be those among the mortal races who lack good fortune," Ilona pointed out, "and who will always be poor."

"But they should not be penalized for it," Lara said. "I do not suggest coddling those who are lazy, but those who are genuinely helpless need to be cared for, and once Hetar did so. This lack of charity is shocking."

"And now, having crowned an empress and seen to Jonah's marriage, Gaius Prospero thinks to sail across the seas and attack Terah," Magnus Hauk said. His handsome face was dark with his anger. "I am a peaceful man by nature, but I will resist Hetar and if I must I will destroy it. Why does the fat fool do this, Ilona?"

"While in part his greed drives him," Ilona told her son-in-law, "it is more from fear. You see, my dear Magnus, you possess what he does not—my daughter, Lara. Gaius Prospero and his minions have spent months convincing Hetarians that Terah is dangerous because Lara is its Domina. That her magic is certain to reach out and strike at them, and so Hetar must strike first. That Lara, Hetarian by birth, must be returned to Hetar, and her power used for Hetar and not Terah." Ilona could not help but smile at the look of outrage on her daughter's face.

"If Kaliq had not given that fat fool back his abilities to enjoy pleasures," she grumbled, "this should have never happened. He was a broken man when I put my spell upon him. Now look what has happened. I am no danger to Hetar and Gaius Prospero well knows it, but let them come to Terah with conquest upon their minds and I will be!"

"The young empress is a creation of the Shadow Princes and was generated by them to distract the emperor. When the time is right the princes will remove her from him," Ilona said. "There is a greater purpose here."

"Can you tell us?" Magnus Hauk asked her.

Ilona nodded slowly.

"What!" Lara teased her mother. "You will actually tell us? But you will couch your words in mystery, of course, and we shall have to discover their meaning for ourselves, won't we?"

Ilona laughed. "Nay," she told them. "I will not cloak my words in hidden meanings. Magnus, I am sorry, but Hetar and Terah must struggle against one another until one of you overcomes the other. This world that you both inhabit must be made one world for the sake of peace. I will tell you things now that you have never known—but you must know if you are to survive."

The Dominus of Terah reached for the decanter upon the table and slowly poured frine into each of the three goblets. Then setting the decanter back in its place he said, "Tell us, Ilona. What must we know to make a difference?"

Ilona nodded. "This world you all inhabit floats in the skies as do many other worlds. It is naught but a speck of light in what we in the magic kingdoms call the Cosmos. The star you call Belmair is another populated world of great culture and prosperity. But eons ago they were much like this world of yours. Once their many clans and peoples came together as one, peace ensued, and only peace as you in Terah know can bring true happiness. But before this came about, there was much discord on Belmair until the good and the light overcame the greedy and their spiral into wickedness and evil," Ilona explained. "While there must always be balance, that balance cannot be toward the dark. It must be toward the light, for the Cosmos is vast and there are many worlds floating within it. We who labor for the good are not always in the majority in every world. Sometimes the darkness is even too much for us. But we never give up trying to bring the light into every corner of the Cosmos."

Magnus Hauk struggled to wrap his brain around her words. *Other worlds? In the skies above them?* How could it be possible?

"Do not attempt to understand it all," Ilona advised him, seeing the look of puzzlement on his face, with his brow wrinkling in concentration. "Just know that you and my daughter have been chosen in this time to unite your worlds and it will not be an easy task, Magnus. Hetar is mired in the muck of its own creation. It will take a great effort to draw it out but together you can do it."

"Will you in the magic realms help us?" the Dominus wanted to know.

Ilona nodded. "We will, but even our powers cannot always overcome hearts that have been turned to stone, as the heart of Hetar has. You will have to soften that heart by winning its people over to you. Right now their fear of Terah, of Lara, is very great. The people have been told over and over again that she is dangerous to them, to Hetar. It is the same tactic they used when they sought to conquer the Outlands. Then, with the help of magic, you were able to save the clan families of the Outlands. Now you must save yourselves for there is nowhere you can flee."

"We will never flee!" Magnus Hauk said, his turquoise eyes blazing fire.

"Yet," Lara said, speaking up at last, "Hetar will never allow itself to be called Terah, nor will the people of Terah permit themselves to be Hetar. With such a passion for one's history as both lands possess, how will we be able to unite into a single nation?"

"The people of Belmair call the large bright star that your world appears to be to them *Thare*," Ilona murmured.

"There is time for names later," the Dominus said impatiently. "Can we not attempt diplomacy before this situation degenerates into war, Ilona?"

"Diplomacy is a good beginning," she agreed, "but you would have to win over Hetar's High Council and right now only the Shadow Princes will support your cause. Squire Darah and fellow members from the Midlands Province, the Coastal Kings, the Forest Lords and the two new councilmen from the Outlands province will not."

"But surely they know I am not dangerous," Lara said.

"In their hearts they do, but to admit it would be to go against Gaius Prospero. And he holds the key to all the riches they plan to acquire when Hetar conquers Terah."

"There are no women on the High Council," Lara mused almost to herself. "Perhaps it is time women began to speak up. Perhaps it is time for women to become involved in the matters of government. These wars are never quite as simple as they are purported to be. *It will be over and done with quickly,* Gaius Prospero always tells the people, but certainly they can be reminded of the Winter War. How many carts of Hetarian dead did we send into The City? It will be far worse this time. How many husbands, fathers and sons will die on our shores and be buried here? How many women will be widowed? How many children orphaned?

"The women of Hetar must be made aware of the bleak future they face without their men. And the High Council must understand that if they send their citizens into a battle with Terah, that a future generation will be lost. When that happens Hetar will become a hapless prey for Terah and their great history will be lost forever. The women will understand that. I must speak with Hetar's women," Lara said.

"If you go to Hetar," Magnus Hauk said, "Gaius Prospero will take you captive. He has convinced everyone that if he has possession of you he can conquer Terah easily."

Lara laughed softly. "Then you still love me, my lord husband?" she teased him, and her mother smiled. It was such a faerie gesture, Ilona thought.

"Of course I love you!" he shouted at her. "And I will not allow you to put yourself or Terah in danger. Let Gaius Prospero come. We will repel him and his Crusader Knights and his mercenaries."

"What? Do you think I am foolish enough to make a great public show in Hetar, Magnus? Nay, I will use my magic. The hearts of those who are good, and there are many women in Hetar whose hearts are good, can be appealed to, my lord. The emperor will not send his forces against us until the late spring when the Sea of Sagitta is calm and easy to travel upon once again. We have the Icy Season in which to appeal to the women of Hetar. I must seek among them the bravest and the boldest, who will be the first to speak up among their friends. These will give the other women the courage to follow them. There is time, Magnus."

"And meanwhile we will continue to enlarge our army," the Dominus said.

"And I will place a thick fog bank off Terah's shores," Ilona told them. "If Gaius Prospero sends his fleet toward Terah before we are ready they will have a terrible time once they depart the shores of the Coastal Kingdom. Thanos, my mate, is most adept at storms. It is a talent your brother, Cirillo, has inherited."

"You must be so proud of him, Mother," Lara replied. "But I have not asked at all of your kingdom and its well-being. What of the forest? Is it still being cut back?"

"Nay, now that the Outlands are available for pillaging they have left the forest in peace. And they never got close to the deepest part of the wood where we reside," Ilona responded. "We have caused new trees to spring up where the old were and the Foresters have cultivated more growth. They have become more ingrown if such a thing is possible. My mother's curse still plagues those of them with pure Forester blood, but they are fewer now and the sons born of the new blood will have no difficulty in reproducing. The Forest Lords are as arrogant and small-minded as ever, but at least the women who give them sons now are not slaughtered. They are treated as concubines."

"And the children?" Lara asked curiously.

"The children are taught to call their fathers' formal wives *Mother*," Ilona said.

"At least the concubines are not killed any longer," Lara remarked.

"Will you attempt to reach out to the forest women?" Ilona asked her daughter.

Lara shrugged. "I do not know," she said. "I must think on it, but I believe the women of The City must be stirred to action first."

"Then we are agreed on our plan of action for the next few months," Magnus Hauk said quietly.

They nodded and then Ilona said, "I must go now, my children. I can just hear Thanos calling me. All these years now and he worries if I am not with him, the foolish faerie man." Then with a smile she was gone in her cloud of mauve smoke.

Lara arose from the table where they had all been sitting. She held out her hand to her husband. "Come, my lord, it is time for us to take pleasures of each other," she told him with a small smile.

He stood, taking her hand. "When will you give me a son, Lara? When will you give me an heir for Terah?" His turquoise eyes searched her face for the answer. "But months ago you said you would."

"The time is not right now," Lara told him. "We must settle this matter with Hetar first. Remember, my lord, that while my faerie powers have grown stronger over the years, I am still half-mortal. I cannot do all my mother can do. Carrying a child will drain me, and I need all of my strength for what lies ahead. Besides, women can rule, Magnus. Do not discount little Zagiri just yet."

He took her in his arms, and kissed the top of her golden-gilt head. "After what you did to repel the curse of Usi and banish his shade from Terah, I really have no right to ask anything of you."

"But Terah will have an heir," Lara said. "I know it. I promise you, Magnus, that when we have finally settled this matter I will give you your son." Reaching up she caressed his handsome face. "He must have your features and your turquoise eyes." She smiled into those eyes she so loved.

"Come," he said and he led her out into their favorite of the gardens that hung over the Dominus's fjord. The air was almost cold and the night sky above was black.

"Look," Lara said, pointing up. "'Tis Belmair. After what my mother told us tonight I shall never again look at it in the same way."

"Nor will I," Magnus Hauk admitted. "I am still not certain I believe it. Another civilization, other people. It is very far away, isn't it? Do you think we will ever know more?" he asked her.

"I cannot say," she answered him. "Tonight I learned for the first time in a great while how little I actually know, Magnus. There always seem to be more questions than there are answers." She laughed. "It is humbling."

"Do not grow too humble," he advised her. "I like your arrogance, wife."

"Arrogant? I am not arrogant!" Lara exclaimed, and she hit him a little blow upon his arm. "Why would you say such a thing? You are the arrogant one!"

"I am the Dominus of Terah," he responded reasonably.

"And the Dominus is arrogant!" Lara told him. "He always has been."

"*I am Lara, Domina of Terah, daughter of Swiftsword and Ilona, queen of the Forest Faeries,*" he teased her wickedly in a falsetto voice, his eyes dancing with amusement, but his amusement turned quickly to surprise as Lara reached out and yanked on his dark-blond hair. "Ouch, you faerie witch!" he yelped.

"Serves you right," she told him, and then turning she scampered off.

Grinning, Magnus Hauk chased her across the garden. "You'll

pay for your disrespect, wife," he told her, but when he reached out to grab her arm Lara disappeared and he was left grasping at air. Then he heard her tinkling laughter.

"Come and find me, my lord," Lara called mischievously.

The castle door opened and closed quickly, and he knew she was gone from the garden. He followed in haste. As he hurried down the corridor the fire bugs in the globes lining the hallway dimmed ahead of him. The door to their apartments flew open of themselves and closed before he could reach them. Gaining the entrance at last he pulled the doors open, walked across the spacious dayroom and entered their bedroom, where he found Lara sprawled upon their bed.

"What kept you?" she asked him teasingly.

He flung himself down next to her and pulled her head to his. "You do not always play fair," he said softly.

"I am Lara, Domina of—"

He stopped her mouth with a hard kiss. "Of Terah, daughter of Swiftsword and Ilona, queen of the Forest Faeries," he finished for her. "But first you are my love and my life, Lara, Domina of Terah," Magnus Hauk said and kissed her again.

Lara wound her arms about his neck. "And you are my only love and my life, my beloved husband," she told him.

Their lips met again, this time in a long sweet kiss, lips tasting, tongues dancing. Their bodies molded themselves against one another as they stretched themselves upon the bed. His big hand caressed her small heart-shaped face tenderly. Her fingers kneaded the back of his neck, her body quivering as she anticipated what was to come.

Lara pulled her mouth from his but briefly. *"Robes, evaporate!"* she said and they were naked.

His big hand immediately went to one of her breasts, fondling it, pulling the nipple out, gently pinching it. Shifting positions he raised himself just slightly, and then lowered his head as his mouth closed over her breast. He suckled on her and Lara was suddenly awash in sensation. She sighed deeply with the beginnings of pleasure. When he left her first nipple wet and puckered he moved to the second one, but this time one of his hands held the breast while the other began to play between her thighs.

The tips of his fingers began to stroke the soft sensitive flesh, making her shiver with anticipation. He pushed through the delicate folds, finding her jewel, playing with it until she was squirming beneath him and moaning low as the heat began to permeate her body. He watched the play of emotions across her face. Her eyelashes fluttered upon her fair cheek as he pushed first one, then two and finally three fingers into her body. His fingers swirled about her love sheath, mimicking the rhythm of his manhood, faster and faster until she was sobbing with a mixture of both pleasure and desire. His voice whispered hotly in her ear. "Tell me what you want, Lara."

"You!" she cried. "Oh, hurry, Magnus! *Hurry!*"

Covering her writhing body he entered her slowly as Lara gasped and clung to him. She was so delicate, yet she was strength itself as she wrapped herself around him and caught the rhythm of his passion. He thrust hard. She rose up to meet him. Their mouths met and tasted. They sucked and licked at each other as he drove himself in and out of her love sheath. Her fingers dug into his shoulders. Her nails raked down his back. Lara cried out softly and Magnus groaned as they met perfect harmony in the pleasure dome. And then their bodies fell away from each other, though their limbs remained intertwined.

"If I accepted your offering tonight and gave you a son," Lara finally said, "then we should not enjoy pleasures until he was born."

"Why not?" he demanded to know. "We enjoyed occasional pleasures while you carried Zagiri." He leaned over and kissed her breast. "And I am not yet satisfied, wife."

Why had she said that? Lara wondered to herself. She had never denied either of her husbands her body when she was with child. Oh, yes, they had to be careful but she had indulged her lusts right until the last moment. It was the weeks afterwards when she had been healing that she had not wanted to take pleasures. *Why had she said it?* She shrugged to herself, then pulling his head down kissed him again. "You are a greedy man, Magnus Hauk, but when you have sufficiently recovered your strength I will feed your appetites once again," Lara told him.

She dreamed later that night. Dreamed of a dark place and heard a voice calling her name. She awoke with a start, drenched in her own sweat, while Magnus snored by her side. She could actually feel her mind grasping at something that didn't seem to be there. Lara arose and went into her private bath to sponge herself with cool perfumed water. When she went back to sleep, it seemed a dreamless one, yet in the morning she remembered that odd little scrap of dream.

In the days that followed Lara began to devise a spell that would allow her to summon certain women of Hetar to the

Dream Plain, where she might speak with them freely and convince them that Terah and she were no threat to Hetar. That Gaius Prospero sought only more wealth and power, at the expense of the people and even Hetar's survival. She gathered together the dried leaves and blooms of strong yet gentle herbs and flowers. Clover. Lavender. Camomile. Mint. She ground them into a fine powder in a bowl carved from dark-green agate. Removing most of the powder and storing it in a crystal flacon, she lit a small leaf of sage and dropped it into the mortar. The mixture flamed quickly with a small puff of smoke as Lara spoke.

"Lady Gillian, headmistress of the Pleasure Guild,
Through the magic of this spell
I summon thee to come to me.
Do not take fright, for all is well,
And we two shall like sisters be."

Lara then quickly lay upon the simple cot in her apothecary and closed her eyes. Almost immediately sleep claimed her. When she opened her eyes she stood in the mists of the Dream Plain and through the beclouded haze she saw a figure approaching.

"Who summons me?" Lady Gillian said. She was a tall woman of regal bearing with dark auburn hair and bright blue eyes.

"Lara, Domina of Terah," Lara replied quietly to the woman now facing her.

A look of not quite distress, but concern, passed quickly over Gillian's beautiful face. "What do you want of me, Domina of Terah?"

"I mean you no harm," Lara quickly responded. "I merely wish to speak with you. The choice to remain here on the Dream Plain with me is yours, my lady. I cannot, nor would I, force your will to mine."

"They say you would use your magic to harm Hetar," Gillian said.

"Terah has no quarrel with Hetar," Lara answered her. "Nor would I use my magic for a dark purpose, lady. The problem lies, as I think you know, with those who govern Hetar. Hetar is not meant to be an empire. It has always been a benevolent republic. The High Council ruled fairly by majority agreement, not through the will of one man alone. But now self-interest rules Hetar and he who calls himself your emperor is about to lead you into another war, lady. Does no one in Hetar remember the Winter War? The toll it took on Hetar was small compared to what will happen if Hetar attempts to wage war on Terah."

"Do you threaten me?" Gillian demanded to know. Her look was severe.

"Nay, lady, I do not threaten you. I simply ask you why the women of Hetar choose to remain silent in the face of looming tragedy."

Lady Gillian looked startled at the question, so Lara continued.

"Why is it that women have no voice in the governance of Hetar, lady? Women have certainly shown that they are capable of rule. Women manage the Pleasure Houses in Hetar. There are women who keep shops and several who qualify as merchants and do successful business despite the fact that the Merchants' Guild will not allow them to become members. Women are healers and teachers of our young, and even the simplest women in the quarter keep their hovels and families in good order. Yet there is not one woman on the High Council from any of the provinces.

"You stand silent while the emperor and the magnates drive up the price of bare necessities. As headmistress of the Pleasure Guild I know you are aware that the Pleasure Houses are proving less and less profitable, because the cubits needed for an evening's entertainment these days must be used to feed a family. You have seen the quality offered in the shops and markets of late. These goods are not nearly as fine as they once were, lady. But you remain silent."

"The shoddy goods in the markets now are *your* fault," Lady Gillian said. "Ever since we learned that the Coastal Kings were merchant traders, not the craftsmen we believed them to be, you have sent us items of poor quality."

"Nay," Lara told her. "The trade between our nations has grown smaller. Gaius Prospero has confiscated much of the open lands belonging to the Coastal Kings. He and the magnates have set up factories in an attempt to reproduce what Terah has been sending to Hetar for centuries. But you have no craftsmen nor artisans to do this work, lady, and the goods they manage to finish are awful. As for the little trade between our lands now, those goods are retained for only a few in favor with Gaius Prospero."

Lady Gillian's look was one of outrage at Lara's words. "But the Pleasure Houses should be given the best of everything," she said. "And in return we offer the men who come to us the best of everything. We sing and we dance, and we hold intelligent discourse with our patrons. We have always been treated well, but if the truth be known, Domina of Terah, we have not been treated as well in the last few years."

"And you have said nothing," Lara remarked quietly. "Why?"

"Why?" Lady Gillian looked puzzled and then she answered, "I don't know why. The life of a Pleasure Woman, a Pleasure Mistress, has always been circumscribed by its rules. You certainly know that, Domina."

"Rules can be broken, lady. Especially when the enforcer of those rules is not keeping up his end of the bargain. It is up to the owners of the Pleasure Houses to see that the women who manage the houses and the women who inhabit them are kept comfortable. But I will wager that you have of late had many complaints from the Pleasure Mistresses in that regard," Lara said.

"How can you know that?" Gillian demanded.

But the look on her face told Lara that she had guessed correctly. The hard times in Hetar were hitting at higher levels.

"I know," Lara said quietly, "because if the cubits are finding their way into fewer hands, lady, then everyone will suffer. And now your emperor proposes a war. To what purpose? He promised Hetar's citizens land and slaves when the Outlands were taken. But there was naught in the Outlands but emptiness, and now the choicest parcels of that territory belong not to the people, but to the emperor, his friends and the magnates.

"Now Gaius Prospero once more promises the citizens of Hetar great wealth if he can gain Terah. How truthful are his words, lady? You know he lies again, and but seeks profit for himself. Hetar cannot survive under such conditions. But the women of Hetar say naught. They sit while their world is crumbling about them, while their men are either worked to death or sent off to war to die, while their children cry from hunger.

"Are the carefully circumscribed rules of Hetarian society so ingrained into the women of Hetar that they will remain silent and die rather than speak up? *They must demand change!*"

Lady Gillian was silent for several long moments while the mists of the Dream Plain swirled about the two women. Finally the older woman spoke up. "I cannot disagree with much of what you say," she began, "but how can the women of Hetar be united to speak with a single voice? There is so little time in which to act. Spring will break but three months after Winterfest, Domina of Terah."

"I know that the time is short," Lara agreed. "Already a thick fog lies off the Terahn coast. It will be difficult, if not impossible for Hetar's fleet to penetrate it. But eventually they may and then the men of Hetar will die upon the narrow sands bordering Terah. And those who manage to escape the beaches will be slain by the Terahn armies. But we do not want this. We want peace, as I know Hetar's women do."

"You are asking me to raise my voice against Gaius Prospero," Gillian said. "Perhaps I could but then shortly my power and authority would be given to someone else. And speaking out against this emperor may prove to be an exercise in futility."

"Why?" Lara wanted to know.

"The truth?" Gillian smiled as Lara nodded. "Lord Jonah is planning to overthrow Gaius Prospero. The emperor is one of the few not to have divined that fact. Of course none of us would voice such thoughts. But already the magnates secretly align themselves with Jonah. It is his mother, Lady Farah, who will soon sit in my seat. He will then have unspoken control of the Pleasure Guild."

"The majority of whom are women," Lara reminded her.

"Jonah wants a war," Gillian said. "He knows it will be a disaster and when it is, Gaius Prospero will once more be blamed and easier to remove from his throne."

"I cannot believe that Gaius Prospero does not see what is going on beneath his nose. He was always extremely clever," Lara remarked.

"The emperor is besotted with his young empress," Gillian said. "He sees nothing but Shifra. And now there is a rumor that she might be with child. Gaius Prospero envisions creating a dynasty that will rule forever."

"What of Aubin?" Lara wanted to know.

"Aubin renounced any claim to his father's throne when the emperor divorced Vilia. He is a member of the Merchants' Guild," Lady Gillian said. "Vilia is very duplicitous, Domina. And dangerous, as well. I believe, though I have no proof of it, that she seduced Lord Jonah long before her divorce. She is extremely ambitious for her new husband and the truth is that he is a better prospect for her ambitions, for his own ambition is equal to hers. They make a dangerous pair, I fear."

"Are there those among your Pleasure Mistresses or other women whom you can trust with your life?" Lara asked the headmistress of the Pleasure Guild.

"Aye," she answered slowly, her blue eyes wary.

"Meet with them. Discuss with them the possibility of joining with other Hetarian women to speak up with a single voice to make the emperor cease in his plans for another war. I will create a spell that I will weave about you to protect you so that no one can overhear the dangerous words you will speak to others," Lara said.

"And are these women to be the only voice decrying this proposed war of Gaius Prospero's?" Gillian asked Lara.

Lara smiled, certain now that she had won the headmistress to her side. "Nay, there will be others who will speak up after you do, but you must lead the way, for you are deeply respected among the women of Hetar. And that knowledge will also save you in the early days of your rebellion from any retribution, for the emperor, Jonah and the magnates will be very surprised by what is happening. They will have to decide if they dare to silence you," Lara told her.

"And will they?" Gillian wanted to know.

"I cannot answer that," Lara replied candidly.

"You do not lie," Gillian responded, an amused smile touching her lips.

"Not often," Lara said. "I can tell you that this revolt of Hetar's women will also cause many men of the lower orders to rally to your side. The farmers cannot plant and bring in crops without help."

"The women who ordinarily might help in the fields will not," Gillian said and now she was smiling in earnest. "And the small merchants will not like a war. They cannot earn a living if their sons are gone fighting. There will be no cubits to purchase their foodstuffs or other goods. You are a clever woman, Lara, Domina of Terah."

"Then you will help me to prevent this war?" She felt her spell beginning to weaken.

Lady Gillian nodded. "Will we speak again?"

"Soon," Lara promised and then she let herself fade away into sleep as her companion disappeared, as well.

Over the next few weeks Lara burned the magic powder she had formulated and slipped onto the Dream Plain during the night to speak with other women in Hetar. By observing Hetar in her reflecting bowl she was able to find women of intellect and backbone who were not at all content with the status quo. Many were located in the quarter where the wives, mothers, sisters and daughters of the Mercenaries were housed. Others she found, to her surprise, among the women who lived in the Garden District, the area inhabited by the Crusader Knights. Her stepmother, Susanna, was not among those, however; Susanna would speak up only in defense of her husband and sons.

Lara sought discontent among the women of the Midlands, and there she found a hotbed of anger to serve her purpose. In the Coastal Kingdom the women were feeling like second-class citizens as Hetar's magnates took their lands and polluted the air with their factories. Even in the forest the concubines of the Forest Lords were becoming more and more unhappy with their lot in life. The women in the Outlands, however, were too beaten down to be appealed to. They would have to see women in the other provinces of Hetar rise up before they would join their own voices to those already protesting.

Having found these women and seen their unhappiness, Lara began bringing them to the Dream Plain to speak with them.

Winterfest had come and gone and it was but another month to spring. Now Lara brought not just one woman at a time, but groups of women whom she encouraged to speak up before their lives and those of their families were completely destroyed by the greed of their emperor and his cronies. But having found their voice, the women of Hetar were not certain what to do with it.

"You must march to the emperor's palace," Lara told them.

"In the Golden District?" one woman said. "The guards will stop us."

"Nay, they will not. They will be so surprised by a great mob of women that they will be confused and not certain what to do. And Gaius Prospero's greatest fear will be for his empress, Shifra the Fair," Lara told them.

"We must have a list of demands drawn up," Lady Gillian said.

"And if all we seek at first is to put those demands in the emperor's hands," another woman from the Midlands spoke up, "who can fault us?"

"But you must be certain that you see the emperor. Do not let Lord Jonah intercede for him," Lara said. "He will attempt to prevent Gaius Prospero from hearing your voices. Remember that the war is to his advantage," she reminded them. "It is rumored that he seeks to take Gaius Prospero's place."

"A wily snake in exchange for a fat rat?" the wife of a Coastal King said. "'Tis not a good trade, I'm thinking."

And the other women laughed.

"Do not be distracted by that rumor," Lara told them. "Your single purpose is to stop a futile war, to force Hetar to deal with Terah diplomatically. I have told each of you individually and I tell you as a group, I mean no harm to my native land, and my husband, the Dominus of Terah means no harm to you or to Hetar. He is a man of peace and loves his own land. To be honest, he does not like Hetar," she concluded with a small smile. "I don't think he'd have you even if you offered yourselves to him."

To her relief the women clustered about her on the Dream Plain laughed aloud.

"How can you live in Terah when you have known the glory of Hetar?" a mercenary's wife asked frankly.

"I love my husband," Lara told them simply, allowing them to believe that she was making a great sacrifice.

There was much nodding among the group, but Lady Gillian caught Lara's eye with her own, a small smile touching her lips. She had come to like Lara over the past weeks on the Dream Plain and realized now that, while she once might have made a magnificent Pleasure Woman, her true talents would have been wasted. Perhaps it was fortunate that Lara's beauty had caused such dissent among the Pleasure Guilds that they had had to forbid the sale in an effort to keep the peace. If women could indeed rule as men ruled, Lara would make a great leader, Gillian thought.

IN THE CITY THE TIME was drawing near for war with Terah. There were parades every day. Crusader Knights in their armor on their great war horses, squires and pages going before them with flags and music. The Guild of Mercenaries marched wearing their leather breastplates and helmets, carrying their weapons. But oddly, there seemed to be little enthusiasm for these displays of military might.

And then upon a bright and sunny spring morning an enormous crowd of women left their homes and their hovels to march through the streets of The City. They were women of all classes and ages, done up in their very best clothing. They were led by the lady Gillian, and the fact that they were silent as they marched was just the tiniest bit menacing. Only the stamp-stamp of their feet could be heard echoing through the narrow streets and across the open market spaces. When they reached the gates of the Golden District the guards, as Lara had predicted, fell back in the face of their might and allowed them through.

Silently the women marched on toward the emperor's palace, tramping down the graveled paths of the Golden District beneath the budding trees with their new yellow-green leaves. And when Gaius Prospero's enlarged house, which was now a palace, came into view, the women stopped briefly, amazed, for few of them had ever even seen it. Then as one they moved toward it, and the men guarding the entrance to the palace gaped in surprise to see the huge crowd of women approaching. But the women were quiet and, while menacing, did not seem violent.

"Halt!" One of the guards said as the women stopped before them, "Why has this mob assembled?"

"I am Lady Gillian, headmistress of the Pleasure Guilds," Gillian said. "We wish to see the emperor. Tell him the women of Hetar are not pleased with him. We are not pleased at all." She waved her hand at the guardsman. "Go! Hurry!" And she almost laughed, as did many of the women, as the guard scampered away, leaving his mate to protect the entrance to the palace.

After many long minutes, as Lara had predicted, an official appeared from inside the palace. He glared at them——as if his look could quell them. "What is it you want?" he demanded in a high-pitched voice.

"We wish to see the emperor," Lady Gillian replied.

"The emperor cannot take time from his day to see a bunch of noisy women," the official said to them. "Be gone back to your husbands and masters!"

"We wish to see the fat slug who calls himself our emperor and who would lead us once again into misfortune," Lady Gillian said firmly. "We will wait until he completes his *important business.*"

The official's mouth fell open in surprise. He recognized Lady Gillian and was horrified to see her a part of what appeared to be a undisciplined rabble.

And then Lady Gillian raised her hand and pointed a single finger at him. "Go!" she said in a stern voice, and the official turned and hurried off.

Seeking out the emperor's right hand, the official told Lord Jonah of the women now waiting before the gates of the palace.

"Who are they?" Jonah asked the man. *What mischief was this?* he wondered.

"They seem to be women of all classes, my lord," the official said.

"Do you recognize any?"

"The headmistress of the Pleasure Guild," the man replied. "There are other women of high caste, as well as those who are poor. I even thought I saw Maeve Scarlet."

"And exactly what do they want?" Jonah asked.

"They say to see the emperor. I told them the emperor was busy but they refused to leave. My lord, it is as if they are all bewitched. I have never seen women behave as they are behaving. It is quite shocking," the official said.

Jonah considered for several long minutes during which the official shifted his weight from one foot to the other. Finally he said, "I will speak with them myself," and hurried from the chamber. He moved swiftly through the palace, exiting through the atrium where all guests entered. And then he gasped audibly at the great crowd of women standing before the building. Catching himself up again he stalked forward, looked at them with what he hoped was icy hauteur, and said, "How dare you cause a disturbance before the palace of Hetar's emperor?"

"We dare because the women of Hetar have had enough!" Lady Gillian shouted back at the vulpine creature before her. She knew Jonah well enough to realize his mind was even now considering ways of punishing her for this breach of etiquette. "We wish to see the emperor, my lord."

"The emperor cannot see you," Jonah said, as those before him had said.

"Then we will wait," Gillian replied.

"It will be a long wait," Jonah retorted.

"What is he so busy at?" a faceless voice in the crowd called out. "Taking pleasures with his beautiful and vapid empress, who surely is young enough to be his daughter? Shame! Shame!"

Jonah found himself completely stymied. The group numbered at least a thousand women. Where had they all come from? Why were they here? "What is it you desire from the emperor?" he finally asked them. "Perhaps I can help you." He had softened his tone and was making every effort to sound sympathetic to the women.

"We will speak only with the emperor," Lady Gillian said implacably.

Jonah shrugged and walked back into the palace.

The spring sun grew warm as the day passed, beating down upon the heads of the women who waited. The day ended and still the women remained, though seated now. Wisely they had brought water with them but there was little food. They carefully rationed what they had. The night was damp and chilly as the dew fell, but they waited on until finally the dawn of a new day broke and the sun rose to warm them once again.

The emperor had finally been informed by Tania, for no one else dared to tell him, of the crowd of women waiting outside his palace.

"What do they want?" Gaius Prospero asked.

"They will not say, my lord, to any but you," Tania answered.

"Are they armed?" His voice quavered nervously and he put a protective arm around the lady Shifra.

"They do not appear to be, my lord," Tania said.

"How many of them are there?"

"Hundreds, my lord."

"And they waited all night?" Gaius Prospero was surprised.

"You must see them, my lord," Tania told him. "They will not go away otherwise, I fear. They are women, nothing more."

"Has Jonah spoken to them?" Gaius Prospero wanted to know.

"He has, my lord, but they want you," Tania responded.

"You must go then, my dear lord," Lady Shifra said. "I will come with you."

"Nay," he protested. "I do not want you in danger."

"We will garb ourselves in our finest robes, and your trumpeters will proceed us as we go," Shrifa said. "It will charm the women to see that both their emperor and empress have come before them. They probably want nothing more than for you to release some grain from your storehouses so the price of bread may be lowered. They are thinking of their children and their oldsters, my lord. Let us go and treat them with courtesy and with kindness."

The emperor looked first to his wife and then to Tania.

"The empress is wise. You should follow her advice, my lord," Tania said.

Gaius Prospero nodded and immediately Tania called to the servants to fetch the royal garments. The emperor and his wife were garbed in cloth of gold embroidered with rubies, sapphires, diamonds and emeralds. Shifra's long red-gold hair was topped with a small crown while her husband wore a larger headpiece. And while they were being dressed Tania found the imperial trumpeters, who hastily gathered up their instruments.

Jonah saw the preparations and attempted to dissuade the emperor from his course of action. "If you give in to this rabble of women, then other groups will come with an endless stream of complaints they want you to correct. And when you cannot they will be angered, my lord. I but try to protect you and the empress."

"It is the empress's suggestion that we greet these women and treat them with courtesy," Gaius Prospero said. "You have not, despite the authority I have given you, been able to disperse these women. If seeing me will do so then they shall see me and my gentle empress. And arrest a half dozen of them when they go back through the gates of the Golden District."

"Lady Gillian is among them," Jonah said. "She has, so far, done much of the talking."

"Indeed," Gaius Prospero replied. He made a *tch*ing sound of disapproval. "Arrest her first," he told Jonah. "Her term of office ends at Summerfest and Lady Farah is already prepared to take over the business of the Pleasure Guild. What do a few weeks matter, eh? We cannot have Hetarian women behaving badly and they will ape their betters, won't they? If Gillian is not stopped immediately and publicly punished then others could easily grow bold. I cannot permit such a thing to disturb the order of Hetar, Jonah. The women must follow the example of my obedient Shifra, who thinks only of my welfare. Her womanly behavior is to be commended, don't you agree, my lord?" Then turning to his beautiful wife the emperor offered her his arm. "Come, my dear, and let us greet our subjects."

They walked together through the wide gates of the palace. Gaius Prospero's eyes widened momentarily as he viewed the great crowd of women before him. But then, Shifra on his arm, they stepped forth into the late morning sunshine. The women were silent as they had been all along. It was eerie. The emperor held up his hand in greeting to the assembled. Then he spoke.

"Women of Hetar, what is it you desire of your emperor that you would put all manners aside and besiege my palace?"

And they answered him with one great voice. *"No war! No war! No war!"*

GAIUS PROSPERO FELL back, aghast at the great sound the voices of the women made. Did they not understand? he wondered silently to himself. But then he realized that of course they could not possibly understand. They were only women. A paternal rush welled up in him. He held up his hand to still them and they did indeed grow silent.

"Women of Hetar," he began, "you must understand that we are threatened by the terrible magic forces of Terah. If we do not strike first, if we do not bring the battle to Terah, they will fall upon us like rabid wolves. We go to war to protect Hetar. To protect you and your children. And Terah has much land to be settled, many riches to be shared. Hetar is a peaceful land. We do this to keep the peace."

"You do it to enrich yourself and your friends further!" a voice in the crowd called out.

"We do not want our menfolk slaughtered needlessly!" cried another voice.

Lady Gillian stepped forward and the women grew silent

again. "My lord emperor," she said politely and she bowed to him. "There is no real proof that Terah threatens Hetar. The Coastal Kings have traded for centuries with them and at no time did Terah ever evince hostility toward Hetar. Rather, they strove to avoid us. Our ships have never been permitted to sail into Terahn ports. Indeed, no Hetarian other than Lord Jonah has even been allowed to visit Terah.

"You promised the citizens of Hetar that the colonization of the Outlands would bring us all prosperity. It has not happened because, rather than distributing the land fairly, you have parceled it out among the magnates and you have transported the poor into positions upon their farms that make them little better than slaves. The few who have gained their own land have fallen into debt with the high prices needed to purchase equipment and build their shelters. We have problems here in Hetar that need correcting. We do not need another war. We will not support another war," Lady Gillian told him implacably. "Will you send your son, Aubin, into war, my lord? How many of the magnates' sons, the sons of the Crusader Knights, will be sent?"

"What has that got to do with the threat that Terah poses to us?" the emperor demanded.

"You are quick to send our sons into battle!" one of the women cried out. "But not your own lad. Why is he better than our boys?"

"The emperor's son cannot be compared with a mercenary's son, or a merchant's son or the son of any common Hetarian citizen," Gaius Prospero said in lofty tones, as he looked down upon them from the steps where he stood. *Stupid women,* he thought, irritated.

"We will not send our sons into your war this time, Gaius Prospero," Lady Gillian said quietly. "The women of Hetar will not support your foolishness any longer."

"The women of Hetar will do as they are told!" the emperor burst out, his fury evident.

Suddenly an angry murmur arose from among the crowd and the women once again chanted, *"No war! No war! No war!"*

The young empress stepped forward and held up her hand for silence.

The women stopped to listen, for she was an unknown commodity.

"Women of Hetar," her girlish voice cried out to them, "you surely cannot comprehend, for I know that I do not, the greater good our emperor brings by his actions. Trust him. I do."

"We thank the empress for her kind thoughts," Lady Gillian said, "but she has not the experience of many years or sons to protect as we all do. Know this, Gaius Prospero. The women of Hetar will stand against you in this matter. Think carefully before you commit us to a futile endeavor." Then Lady Gillian turned, and the crowd parted for her and then followed her as she walked back down the gravel path, across the greensward and toward the gates enclosing the Golden District.

When she reached the gates, the guards, already alerted by Jonah, attempted to take her into custody, but the women protested and their numbers physically overcame the guards pushing them back with great shouts of outrage. Lady Gillian walked on proudly. The guards tried to snatch several others, but their companions would not permit it. Finally, the great crowd of women had exited the Golden District and they walked through the streets chanting. *"No war! No war! No war!"* Now and again the protesters would stop and one of their number would speak. Soon other women in the streets were joining them.

From the safety of his palace Gaius Prospero was still stunned by what had just occurred. He hurried back to his library, his young wife running behind him with Jonah. "How could this sort of thing happen?" he demanded of the man he called his right hand, slumping into a chair while Shifra poured him a goblet of wine and mopped his forehead, which was beaded with moisture. "Women in revolt against *my* authority? *The authority of Hetar?* If it had been ten or even fifty or a hundred I should have taken no heed of them. But there were over a thousand women certainly, Jonah!"

"Surely not a thousand, my lord," Jonah said in silky tones. "And now they have all gone home. They have had their say, my lord, and that will be the end of it." He offered his master one of his rare smiles.

"A thousand or more," Gaius Prospero said firmly. "And who encouraged them to this rebellion? There were women of all castes, Jonah. From the highest to the lowest. Most were bold and showed their faces, but I saw others who were well cloaked that their faces not be seen. Those garments were of the richest fabrics. They were surely wives of Crusader Knights and magnates, as well as Pleasure Women of high rank."

"Many were from among the mercenary class," Jonah soothed. "The poor always complain, my lord. It is in their nature."

"This revolt crosses class barriers, Jonah," Gaius Prospero said.

"'Tis a little revolt, my lord," Jonah answered.

"From little revolts come bigger revolts," the emperor replied. "But no matter. I want to know who is behind it, Jonah. How many were arrested at the gate?"

"I will inquire," Jonah said.

"I want Gillian questioned. Do what you must but find out what we need to know. I will put a stop to this resistance against my authority immediately," the emperor said.

"Of course, my lord. Your will is mine to obey," Jonah told him, then bowed himself from the emperor's library even as Shifra slipped into her husband's lap to soothe him, her little hand caressing his face with a gentle touch.

Jonah sent a messenger to the gate to inquire about those arrested. He then directed his personal servant, Lionel, to find his most useful spy, Arcas, and bring him to the palace. He was not pleased to learn that no one had been arrested. And when Arcas finally arrived, Jonah, who knew the emperor would not be pleased to learn this, rounded on the man who was his spy and in Jonah's debt.

"You have heard what happened?" Jonah asked grimly.

Arcas nodded nervously. "I have, my lord."

"Women in revolt, Arcas, and you knew nothing of it? The booth in the market where I placed you to toil as a scribe is next to a most popular women's destination. A large booth dealing in scents, lotions, soaps of the finest quality. It is always filled with women chattering. And you heard nothing of this rebellion? It has been months since you brought me anything of value,

Arcas. I wonder if you have lost your ability to be useful," Jonah murmured, the threat veiled but unmistakable.

"I did hear something in the last few days," Arcas admitted nervously. "But my lord Jonah, they were babbling women. I did not think it was of any importance."

"It is not up to you to decide what is important or unimportant," Jonah said angrily. "You are in my employ to gather information. *Everything* you hear. I will make the decision if it is important or unimportant. Now tell me what you heard, you useless fool!"

Arcas, who had formerly been a Coastal King and was now exiled from that province, served Jonah as a gatherer of information. Some of that information Jonah passed on to his master, the emperor. But some of it he did not. Arcas suspected that Jonah planned one day to overthrow Gaius Prospero or at least make an attempt. But he had no proof at all that the man known as the emperor's right hand was disloyal and until he did he dared not speak out. "Recently," he began, quickly gathering his thoughts, "I have heard women speaking of their dissatisfaction with the emperor's plans to pursue another war. They say he does it to enrich himself and the magnates. They complain that the ordinary folk gain nothing from these wars. Rather they lose husbands, fathers and sons. That more poor are created by Gaius Prospero's wars as the women of Hetar and their children are left without their men to support them and protect them. They say that it is time the women of Hetar stood up for their families and told Gaius Prospero that they will not let their men be killed and crippled by his blind ambition and greed." Arcas stopped a moment to see if Jonah was pleased by his tidings.

Obviously Jonah was, for he said, "What else?"

"They gossip that Terah is no danger to Hetar. That Gaius Prospero lies when he says that they are," Arcas replied. "They say that in the few years since they learned of Terah's existence it has remained as it was before. Invisible."

"Do they mention the faerie woman, Lara?" Jonah wanted to know.

"They do not believe her powers are strong enough to harm Hetar. Besides, she is Hetarian-born," Arcas answered. "Even I who am her enemy know she would not harm Hetar."

"Do they not remember her part in the Winter War?" Jonah asked.

"They know the Winter War was won by the Outland clan families by better tactics, not by magic," Arcas said. "As I told you, my lord, foolish chatter."

"That foolish chatter brought over a thousand women to the emperor's palace," Jonah said softly. "From this moment on you will report to me daily and tell me what you have overheard. As I have told you, it is not up to you to decided what is relevant and what is not. Leave me now." Jonah impatiently waved his minion away.

Alone he began to consider how this turn of events might play into his hands. He did not believe for one moment that Hetar's docile women had considered the advantages and disadvantages of war. Someone had planted the idea in their heads, but who? The emperor was eager to arrest the lady Gillian, but Jonah thought not. This burgeoning movement was too volatile right now and it wasn't just Gillian who was leading it. Besides, her influence would soon wane as his mother, Lady Farah, became the new headmistress of the Pleasure Guild.

Jonah wondered if a war could be avoided. If this women's conspiracy were allowed to grow, could it be used to topple Gaius Prospero from his seat? He needed to know more and he needed his wife's counsel. Vilia was a clever creature. She would look at this situation from a completely different point of view. He left the palace and walked the short distance to his own home. Vilia had insisted when they married that they have their own house. While living in the emperor's palace had been convenient, he understood his wife's desire to be away from her former husband and his girlish new wife.

He found Vilia in her bath and she invited him to join her, dismissing the bath attendants. Jonah was always surprised at her ability to arouse him so easily. Long ago, when she was still Gaius Prospero's wife, he had planned to seduce her. She had seduced him instead and while he was still able to detach himself from his lust for her when he was away, it was impossible to do so when she slipped her arms about his neck and pressed her lush body against him, smiling up into his cold eyes.

"I have missed you today," she purred at him. Her teeth nibbled the lobe of his ear. "You are tense, my lord, and appear weighed down with your duties. Let me help you to relax, my darling Jonah." Reaching down into the water she cupped his seed sac in the palm of her hand. Her tongue ran about the outline of his mouth.

He felt her hand holding him but she did not fondle him. The simple subtlety of it was the catalyst for his arousal. Jonah kissed his wife a long slow kiss as his manhood burgeoned. He pressed it against her belly, his hands on her buttocks pulling her closer to him. Reaching out he pinched first one nipple and then the other. Vilia gave a little squeal of excitement. He kissed her again, his tongue pushing into her mouth to play with her tongue. "I want your ass," he growled at her, and he turned her about, helping her to brace herself upon the steps that led into the bathing pool, her bottom just out of the warm water.

Jonah reached out and with one hand lifted the lid from a jar that held a pure white cream. "Open!" he said, and reaching back Vilia drew the cheeks of her buttocks apart for him. He rubbed the white cream generously in and around the puckered flesh, grazing it seductively, pressing his thumb against it, feeling it give beneath the pressure. Removing his hand he directed his manhood to the same spot and patiently pressed against it until he felt it giving way to allow him entry. Slowly, carefully, he sheathed himself fully within her rear channel.

Vilia moaned. "I can feel you throbbing," she murmured to him. "It is so exciting, my love!" Then she gasped as his hand reached beneath her to play with her love bud. "Ohh, Jonah!" she sobbed as he brought her once, twice and a third time to perfect pleasure while his pulsing manhood beat a tattoo within her. Then he moved, just two strokes, and groaned as Vilia felt his juices being released. "Such a waste, my darling," she sighed.

He withdrew from her saying, "This is no time for you to give me a child, Vilia. Soon, but not yet. Now let us get out of our tub, for I have need of your wisdom, Wife."

They dried each other off with thick toweling, then donning

simple cotton robes over their heads, they exited the bath and entered their bedchamber. At once a servant came forward, and Vilia told her to see that the evening meal was served in the dayroom.

"Let us eat first," Vilia suggested. "Then we will talk."

"When the meal is served, dismiss the servants and we will speak over our food," he countered. "We have decisions to make, Wife. And time is of the essence."

"I am intrigued, my lord," Vilia said.

Their food was quickly brought and the servants sent away. They sat eating and Jonah told his wife of what had transpired over the last several days at the palace when he had not come home to her. Then he explained how he had had Arcas brought to him. "The fool kept hearing things, but thought it just women's talk, and did not report it," Jonah grumbled irritably.

"A few women complaining before Gaius's palace," Vilia said. "Why are you so upset?"

"It was not a few women, Vilia. There were well over a thousand women there. Did you not hear them chanting 'no war'?" he asked her.

"I spend a great deal of time in our gardens by the waterfall," Vilia told him. "Perhaps I heard some sounds when I was in the house, but they did not seem threatening so I dismissed them. Women have virtually no real power in Hetar, Husband. Why do you fret about the wives of farmers, mercenaries and merchants?"

"Aye, there were many farmers' wives there, but there were also Pleasure Women, including the lady Gillian who is obviously one of the leaders. And I saw wives of Crusader Knights, as well. This is a serious movement, Vilia, and now I must decide how to use this to our best advantage. You know as well as I do that there is no need to pursue this war with Terah."

"You still believe that the faerie Lara is no danger to us?" Vilia asked.

"Nay, I do not," Jonah replied. "Do not make the mistake, Vilia, of taking seriously the gossip we have been putting out about the Domina Lara."

"If this movement of women grows," Vilia now said thoughtfully, "it might prove more of an advantage to us than a war. A war will cost us lives, even fought across the sea. Women do not fight wars. Men do. But without men to seed their women Hetar's population will not increase and we could be seriously vulnerable to Terah or another predator sometime in the future. If we did not know of Terah, my lord, what else do we not know?"

"Tell me how these women could be used to our advantage?"

"Could we not use them to bring down Gaius?" she asked him. "Then we should not be involved in his demise at all, Husband. A new emperor would have to be chosen and you have been building your alliances for some time now, Jonah, my love," Vilia said. "Would you not be the logical choice? Especially if you had these women behind you."

"If I am to gain the influence of these women," Jonah said slowly, "I will have to be most careful else the emperor learn of it and I am destroyed. I must think on it, Vilia."

"If I were to secretly aid these women," Vilia said softly, "it would certainly put you in their favor, my lord. You and I cuckolded Gaius for several years and he never caught us. We can do this as well, Jonah."

"Trying to stop Gaius Prospero once he has made up his mind is impossible," Jonah said.

"Don't try to stop him," Vilia said.

Jonah smiled. "Aye, let him start his war and we will help the women to quickly stop it before too many are killed. Just enough to put a bad taste in the mouth of every Hetarian wife."

"He must be killed," Vilia said. "Gaius and his little empress must die."

"The High Council will want to hold a trial," Jonah replied. "But you are right, Vilia. He must be slain quickly—and his lady Shifra with him. If he is not then the few friends he has will seek to free him and restore him to his throne. We could have a civil war in Hetar. That would not do at all, Vilia. We must prevent that at all costs."

She nodded. "You say the lady Gillian is involved in this movement?"

"Aye," he replied. "The emperor wants her arrested but I will prevent that. Making her a martyr would be very foolish."

"I agree," Vilia said. "Better Gillian become a heroine of Hetarian women."

"Aye, we do not want to destroy this movement," Jonah said, "but use it."

"True. Let me see how strong these women are and if I learn Gillian is truly their leader I will help stoke their passions even hotter, my dear Jonah."

Vilia sent her most trusted servant to investigate over the next few days. It took time however, for the women were cautious, as was Vilia's serving woman, Kigva. She visited the kiosk of a famed maker of perfumes in the Grand Marketplace and listened. She went to the public baths and listened. Finally one day she dared to approach a woman she overheard at a Razi kiosk speaking in low urgent tones to her companion. "Please," she said, "I have heard of this women's protest. Can you tell me more?"

"I do not know of what you are speaking," the woman said nervously and moved away from Kigva, who followed after her and tugged on her sleeve.

"My mistress is the wife of an important man," Kigva said low. "She wants to help, but dares not do so publicly. I know there are women of importance involved in this for I saw them marching in the streets that day you went to the emperor's palace. My mistress has sent me to learn more and to aid you."

"Who is your mistress?" the woman wanted to know, but Kigva shook her head.

"I dare not say her name for her well-being, but you would be surprised if you knew it."

"Say nothing," the woman's younger female companion said, trying to draw her friend away. "This could be an attempt to harm us all."

"Please," Kigva pleaded, "I mean you no evil."

Turning, the two women hurried away from her.

Sighing, Kigva was about to move away from the Razi kiosk when another woman there murmured, "There is a meeting tonight in the house of the widow of the feather merchant, Aja."

"When?" Kigva asked without even reversing herself.

"At sunset," came the reply.

"Thank you," Kigva said, but the woman had already moved off. She found the feather merchant's house by watching in the street for the cloaked women hurrying into one particular dwelling. She joined a small party of them, pulling her hood up over her head to shield her face as they were all doing.

The meeting began. Kigva was surprised to see the head-mistress of the Pleasure Guild step forward, throw back her hood and address the gathering.

"Women of Hetar," Gillian said, "it is past time that our voices were heard. For too long have we been silent and docile while our leaders have brought the people of Hetar to poverty. Meanwhile, they have grown richer. Now Gaius Prospero, whom I well know, claims that this land across the Sagitta is a danger to us. That we must attack them before they attack us. He lies! And we all know he has lied to us before. This is not to protect Hetar. It is to enrich the emperor and his friends. We must resist this latest assault on Hetarian families that will only weaken us.

"Terah is a peaceful land. For centuries the Coastal Kings have traded with them, but never have the Terahns allowed any Hetarian to put a foot on their soil or even sail within sight of their coast. And yet Gaius Prospero claims they are a danger to us? How? He would risk the lives of our men for a war that need not be fought. But the Crusader Knights and the Mercenary Guild grow restless and he fears them.

"Our emperor is also a greedy man. He seeks the wealth of Terah. Not for Hetar and its folk, but for himself and his cronies. Look how we were told that the Outlands posed a danger to

Hetar. That if we would conquer it, its lands would be divided among our citizens and its people would give us cheap labor as slaves. Its herds, its flocks, its mountain wealth would be ours. But they are not ours. The clan families of the Outlands were gone. Their herds and flocks were gone. And Gaius Prospero and the magnates have taken the majority of the land for themselves.

"Now this emperor tells us that Terah is a threat to us, but we will conquer it and its lands, its people, and its wealth will be ours. I do not believe Terah is a threat to us, nor do I believe that its lands and wealth be ours if we conquer it. They will be Gaius Prospero's and the magnates'.

"Many men will die in this attempt and there is no guarantee that Hetar will prevail over Terah. Our men must sail across the Sagitta, and they do not know what awaits them when they get to the other side. We know so little of Terah, my sisters. But I *do* know that if we attack this peaceful place they will resist. Whether we take it or not matters little. Our men will be killed. Who will take care of us when that happens?

"The other provinces are divided in this matter. The Shadow Princes will not aid us, nor will the Forest Lords. The Coastal Kings do not like Gaius Prospero, especially now he has taken their lands for himself and his friends and their vessels for this ill-advised venture. They cannot defy him openly, but they will do their best to thwart him. Only Squire Darah, the governor of the Midlands, sits in the emperor's pocket."

A woman stood up. "I am from the Midlands. Most of our sons have been conscripted to work in the factories of the Coastal

Kingdom or as servants to the Mercenaries or the Crusader Knights. Our farms are old and the land tired. We were promised new lands, but few have been forthcoming for us. My brother and his family died last winter in the Outlands because they could not afford to keep the little house they built warm. Now my two oldest sons slave in the factories for the magnates and my younger one was recently taken to serve the Guild of Mercenaries as a servant lad. My daughters and I are left to work our land with my crippled husband. They would have taken him, too, but for his infirmity. Where is the justice in that?"

"There is no justice in Hetar any longer," another woman said sadly.

"No, there is not," Lady Gillian agreed. "Our once-proud country with its laws and its customs no longer exists. But why should we stand idly by as Hetar slides further into chaos?"

"We are but women," came the answer. "It is not our duty to rule or to instruct our men in that manner. It is tradition in Hetar that women are the lesser."

"Why should we be?" Lady Gillian asked her audience. "We manage the Pleasure Houses. We manage our families. Those of you wed to men of business more often than not are involved with your husbands' work. We bear the children of Hetar and teach them. A life of pampered and privileged leisure may be fine for some, but even those women will lose all they have if we do not stop Gaius Prospero and his minions from forcing us into a war that need not be fought. Will those men care for Hetar's widows and orphans? Have they done so in the past?" Lady Gillian looked out at the other women. "You know they have not. How many of you have taken in your sisters and their children? We do not need another war!"

"You say that this Terah is not a threat to us," a voice came from the crowd. "But how do you know that for certain? Do the men who are our leaders not know better than you?"

"Nay, *they do not,*" came the quick reply. And then Lady Gillian held out her hand to a shrouded figure who had been standing near her. "I bring you proof positive, women of Hetar. I bring you the Domina of Terah herself. Lara, daughter of Swiftsword and Ilona, queen of the Forest Faeries. She is a child of Hetar as are we all."

Stepping forward, Lara pushed back the hood on her cloak, smiling at the gasp from the large group of women crowded into the feather merchant's house. "I come in peace, my sisters, and bring you greetings from my husband and dear lord, Magnus Hauk, Dominus of Terah. As Lady Gillian has told you, Terah is a peaceful place. We wish no war with Hetar. If the truth be known the Terahns desire nothing more than to be left alone to pursue their crafts, which have been sold here in Hetar for several centuries. We are not a warlike nation, but we will protect ourselves if we are attacked."

"You say you are of Hetar, yet you speak for Terah," said a woman.

"I was born in Hetar and lived my early years here, but I am now the wife of Terah's ruler, and it is fitting that I take his land for my own."

"You have magic," another voice said.

"I do," Lara replied, "else I should not be here tonight to greet you all and answer your questions. My magic has grown stronger over the years, but I have used it only for good—except once when I used it to punish someone who was most wicked."

"You say Terah is a peaceful place and means Hetar no harm," a woman near the front said. "Why should we believe you? It is said you betrayed Hetar."

"And who tells you that?" Lara said with a small chuckle. "Gaius Prospero? Do you know why he speaks ill of me, my sisters? Because he lusted after me and I refused him. Now he would lead the men of Hetar into a war as he led them into the Winter War. Do you recall the seven carts piled high with the dead that were driven to his door when that debacle concluded? There are surely some of you in this room tonight who lost loved ones then."

A murmur of assent arose from among the crowd.

"It is said your magic caused those deaths," a woman finally said.

"I used no magic in the Winter War," Lara told them quietly. "But I did fight by the side of my then-husband, Vartan of the Fiacre, who was later murdered in a plot fostered by Gaius Prospero. Hetar invaded the Outlands and tried to enslave two of the clan families. Gaius Prospero believed they were weak and disunited, but they were not. The five other clan families came to the aid of their brothers and sisters and drove Hetar from their lands."

"You fought by your husband's side?" a voice asked, disbelieving.

"She lies! The clan families are a myth. There was no one in the Outlands when we reclaimed it. It was empty and fertile land," another voice cried out.

"Land confiscated by Gaius Prospero and his friends," a third voice said.

Lara shrugged off her long enveloping dark cloak. She was garbed in the leather pants and the cream silk shirt she had once favored. "I do not lie," she told the gathering. Then reaching back over her shoulder she withdrew Andraste, her sword, from her scabbard and swung it over and around her head. "Sing, Andraste!" she commanded the sword. "Sing for the women of Hetar, I pray you!"

It was then that the women saw in the exquisitely decorated hilt of the sword the head of a woman whose emerald eyes opened and fixed them all with a fierce stare. Then the sword began to sing in a deep and dark voice. *"I am Andraste! I will drink the blood of the invader, and the unjust as is my right! Let Gaius Prospero and those who follow him beware my sting!"*

Lara placed the sword before her, Andraste's stern face looking out at the women. "I was taught to use this weapon by Lothair, a Shadow Prince," she explained. "I am a woman first, but when I must be I am a warrior. As for the lies told you about the Outlands, it was my magic that removed the clan families to a place of safety from the danger Hetar posed for them. They, too, were peaceful folk, content to care for their flocks and herds, their gardens and mines." Lara did not mention the Shadow Princes' part in taking the clan families to the New Outlands. If the women believed that she alone was responsible for the rescue they would believe her magic even stronger than it was, and that was not a bad thing.

A deep silence enveloped the room as the women took in all Lara had said to them.

Lady Gillian finally broke the quiet. "We must force the emperor to put aside his plans to invade another peaceful land. If Gaius Prospero would govern us, then he must do so fairly and justly. He and the High Council must spend their time working to overcome the problems we have here in Hetar, not in planning wars that only enrich them and impoverish us."

Lara slipped Andraste back into her scabbard. She looked out at the women. "My sisters," she said, "I beg you to dissuade Gaius Prospero from this tragic mistake. Do not invade Terah. My husband and our people stand ready to defend our lands, and we will prevail." Then she turned to Lady Gillian. "Thank you for letting me speak," Lara said. She reached for her cloak, putting it about her shoulders. "May the Celestial Actuary give you wisdom and keep you in peace," Lara said and with a flourish of her hand she disappeared in a pale mauve haze.

Moments later she reappeared in her own chambers. Mila, her serving woman, jumped at her mistress's appearance. "I don't think I will ever get used to you doing that," she said with a nervous chuckle.

Lara laughed. "I'm sorry. I didn't mean to startle you." She handed Mila her long cape, and removing Andraste from her back, set the sheathed sword in her place above the hearth in the dayroom. "I'm going to lie down for a little while," she told Mila. "Being but half-faerie, I am sometimes exhausted by the appearing and reappearing."

Mila nodded. "I put a decanter of fresh-squeezed juice by your bed," she said.

Lara nodded her thanks, and entering her bedchamber

changed into a loose robe and lay down, falling into a slumber almost immediately. But her sleep was troubled, as it had been in the last few weeks. She kept hearing a voice calling her name and twice now she had found herself summoned to the Dream Plain only to sense another presence but not be able to see it or communicate with it, whatever it was. Awakening after a restless few hours she poured herself a goblet of juice and sipped it thoughtfully. Something was missing, she realized, and she knew that there was only one person who could help her. She needed to speak with Kaliq, but he had been avoiding her summons. That in itself was odd and only increased her curiosity. She sensed she could not remember something—what it was escaped her.

Magnus entered her bedchamber. "How goes your campaign to undermine Gaius Prospero?" he asked her with a small smile. He flung himself down next to her.

"You're back," she said. "How is Uncle Arik? All is well at the Temple of the Great Creator? And aye, my campaign goes well, I believe."

"My uncle sends his regards," the Dominus said. "He wants to know when you will give me an heir. No female can inherit the title of Dominus, as you well know." He ran a finger down her arm. "You are looking impatient with me," he grinned.

"There will be no more offspring until I am certain Terah is safe from Gaius Prospero and his ambitions," Lara told her husband. "We have spoken on this before."

"Will we ever really be safe from Hetar?" Magnus Hauk asked his wife.

"Probably not," Lara admitted, "but carrying a child weakens my powers. You do not want me weakened right now, my lord. There is more going on in Hetar than meets the eye. The lady Gillian has reached an age where she must give up her power to another. Her successor will be the lady Farah, who is the mother of Lord Jonah, who has, as you are well aware, married Gaius Prospero's divorced wife, Vilia. Tonight I saw Vilia's serving woman among those gathered to listen. Her hood fell back a moment. I have only seen her twice but I recognized her. It is obvious that this movement of women is growing in power, and Vilia has sent her servant to learn what she can and gauge the danger. But to whom? Vilia can have no loyalty left to Gaius Prospero, which can only mean she does whatever she does for her new husband. I believe Lord Jonah is positioning himself to overthrow Gaius Prospero."

"How is it that you can see all these machinations after simply glimpsing a lady's servant, Lara? Are you even certain this woman was who you say?"

"I never forget a face," Lara replied quietly. "And as for how I see what I do, my lord husband, it is because I am Hetarian-born. Deception and subterfuge are in every Hetarian's nature, Magnus, even one who is half-faerie. Never forget that."

"Do you warn me?" he asked softly.

"I should never betray you or Terah," Lara replied as softly.

He pulled her down into his arms and kissed her mouth in a slow and leisurely fashion. "Give me a son, my faerie wife," he said.

"Not yet," she told him again as she had every time he had asked. She loved him, but his trusting Terahn nature would not allow him to fully understand the dangers they faced. It was up to her, Lara realized, to protect him and in doing so, to protect Terah. She pulled him back down to her and kissed him fiercely. "Do you want to take pleasures with me, Magnus?" and she smiled when his turquoise eyes lit up in answer to her question.

Her fingers began to unlace his shirt carefully. Anticipation, Lara knew, was always stoked by going slowly. Pulling the shirt over his head Lara pushed him onto his back and smoothed her hands over his broad chest. Bending her golden head she first nibbled at his nipples, scoring them lightly with her teeth, and then began to lick at his flesh with long sweeps of her tongue. "Ummm," she said. "You taste salty and smell of leather and horse, my lord." Her head moved lower as her fingers began to undo his leather riding pants. She slipped a cool hand beneath the leather, reaching down to fondle him. Then she moved to draw the riding pants down over his slender hips and long legs.

Lara wiggled her way back up his body until they were level again. Then sitting up she pulled off her sleep robe and climbed atop the Dominus. "Now, my lord, we shall begin again," she said. Lowering her head and bending her body she began to lick and nibble at him, sending little shivers up and down his spine. She was very, very thorough. Reaching up, she unbound her long gilt-colored hair and trailed it slowly up and down his torso. He shuddered. Straddling him, her buttocks toward him, Lara began to caress his rod, which had already burgeoned. Her fingers reached beneath him to cup his seed sac in her palm. She gently squeezed it, careful not to give him any pain. Her supple fingers fondled the pouch and he groaned. His rod stood straight and tall. Lara bent to kiss its head, drawing the flesh back to view the garnet-colored head. A tiny bead of moisture glistened in its single eye.

"Enough!" he growled, pulling her down and onto her back. His lips met hers in a fiery kiss, his tongue chasing hers about the cavern of her mouth. "You're a wicked temptress, my faerie wife," he told her. His fingers now sought her core, pushing past her nether lips to bury themselves within her. She was very wet and deliciously hot. Soon he would sheath his love rod inside her, but for now he wanted to tease her a bit. The three fingers moved slowly back and forth in a leisurely manner. "I love taunting you," he whispered against her mouth.

"I love it when you do," she murmured back, her green eyes closing as she enjoyed the sensations he was creating within her. "But do not be long," she said. "I need you inside me."

He played with her for a short while more, and then withdrawing his fingers he mounted her and thrust deep inside her. Lara sighed and raked her nails lightly down his long back. Magnus Hauk began to move, slowly at first and then with increasing rapidity. What was it about Lara that, no matter how many times they coupled, he could not get enough of her? He groaned with the pleasure his body was receiving from the simple possession of her.

Lara thrashed beneath him. He was very hard, long and thick. And oh so skilled with his love rod. Never had she known a mortal who was so proficient in passion. He forced a hand between them and played with her already excited love bud. But when he next reached beneath her to push a single finger into her other channel Lara gasped with a mixture of utter pleasure and a trepidation that she did not understand. "Magnus!" she cried out and then she was overcome with pleasure as her juices crested, bathing his love rod as his own juices mushroomed forth to fill her with his heated tribute.

Afterwards they cuddled in a mutual embrace until finally Lara said, "The sun is setting, my darling, and we promised the children that when we were all home together we would eat the evening meal together. I know they have not forgotten. They will be expecting us."

Grumbling, he arose from the bed, gathered up his garments and departed through the door that connected his private chamber with hers. Watching him go, Lara smiled to herself. She loved him so very much. Rising, she went to the silver ewer on the table and poured some perfumed water into it from the matching pitcher. Lara bathed herself free of his juices, then called to Mila to bring her a suitable gown. Once dressed, she sat down to restore her hair into a semblance of order once again.

But as she brushed her tresses she thought back to just a short while before. When he had pierced her rear channel with that single finger a wisp of something—was it a memory?—had assaulted her. There was something wrong but she did not know what it was. If Kaliq would not answer her call then she must go to her mother. Whatever was troubling her, Ilona would know, for she and the Shadow Prince were hand in glove. Reaching down, her fingers touched the crystal star that hung between her breasts. *Ethne,* she called out with her mind to the protective spirit her mother had given her.

I am here, my child.

I have lost something, Ethne.

For a brief moment Ethne was silent and then she said, *I know.*

What is it? Lara begged her spirit protector.

'Tis not for me to enlighten you, if indeed you should be enlightened at all, Ethne responded quietly.

Kaliq will not answer me, Lara said.

Ethne laughed softly. *He is a man for all he is a great and magical lord, my child. He wishes to protect you, for he loves you dearly.*

Then I must go to my mother and learn what I need to know, Lara replied. *My dreams are restless. Haunted. I go to the Dream Plain, and I can see no one though I sense someone is there. I do not know whether to be frightened or not, Ethne.*

The golden flame in the crystal star flickered and then Ethne spoke again. *Then you must certainly go to Queen Ilona and learn what it is that troubles you, my child. But do not tell the Dominus why you are going to visit her. Use whatever excuse you must to justify your decision.*

Joining her family for the evening meal Lara was quick to notice how happy the three children were to see her and the Dominus. They had been so involved in preventing this war with Hetar that the children had taken second place in their lives. Lara felt badly about it, but this was important to the future of her offspring. She and Magnus needed to know they were safe. And she needed a peaceful time in which to give her husband a son. She was pleased to see how close Vartan's children were to their stepfather. Dillon was growing faster in his wisdom. She had always been able to speak to him as an equal. She would miss him when he went to study with the Shadow Princes. Anoush, having no memory of

Vartan, adored Magnus as any daughter would her father. She and her little sister, Zagiri, had become very close. It had been the right decision to bring the children to the castle of the Dominus. Their meal together was a happy one. After tucking the three children into their beds Lara and Magnus sat together in their dayroom.

"I want to visit my mother," Lara told her husband. "I will not stay long."

"You have been away so much of late," he complained. "I missed you. The children have missed you. Did you not see how happy they were tonight?"

"I will stay only a few hours," she promised, "while they are all at their studies and you are going about the business of running your kingdom."

"Ask your mother to come here," he suggested.

"Nay," Lara told him. "I need her advice on the Hetar dilemma and it is only polite that I go to her to seek it, Magnus. Besides, I have never seen her palace and am curious. I will go tomorrow. While I am gone you will write to Rendor and update him on our situation."

"I suppose I cannot stop you," he grumbled.

"Nay, you cannot," she agreed cheerfully with a mischievous grin. "I will bring you back faerie sweets," Lara promised. "You have never tasted their like."

When morning came, and the children were settled with Master Bashkar, Lara went to the hidden private chamber she used for summoning. "Ilona, queen of the Forest Faeries, I would come to you," she said three times. Then she waited and almost immediately the wall before her opened to reveal a short golden tunnel beyond which a green forest beckoned. Lara stepped through, walking the length of the tunnel and as she stepped forth into the late winter woodland, she found herself within a room with invisible walls that shimmered in the moonlight of evening.

Ilona came forward smiling. "Daughter! To what do I owe the honor of your visit?" The queen took her into her arms and kissed her. "Are you well? Is Magnus well? And the children?"

"I need your counsel, mother," Lara said.

"Come," the queen replied, leading Lara to a comfortable seating area. "It must be serious, for never before have you come into my realm." The two women sat and reaching out, Ilona took a cup that had appeared in midair and gave it to Lara before taking one for herself. "Sip your faerie wine slowly," Ilona said. "It is very potent, my daughter. Then tell me what it is that has brought you to me."

Lara sipped the liquid in her cup. It was delicious, and tasted of raspberries. "Of late, Mother, my sleep is troubled," she began. "I hear a deep and dark voice calling my name. I am brought to the Dream Plain, but though I sense someone, I can see no one. There is something that has been taken from me, but I know not what it is."

Ilona had grown pale. Tears sprang up in her beautiful emerald eyes. "You are more faerie than even I had realized," she said. "You must have faerie blood from your father that we did not know about. This is why you are as you are, Lara." The queen sighed. "You were born, my daughter, for several purposes. You have a destiny. You have fulfilled part of that destiny, but because it was such a difficult task, Kaliq and I called the Munin lords to remove your memories of those months."

"What was the task?" Lara asked.

"I fear to tell you, my daughter," Ilona responded. "There is still enough mortal blood in you that you will react with loathing, guilt and shame. Kaliq and I want to protect you, Lara. You still have much to do to bring peace to Terah and Hetar. We cannot have you discouraged and deterred by what was necessary and is now past. We need you to be strong."

"If you took my memories from me, Mother, then why does my mind seek for them?" Lara asked quietly.

"The memories of faerie folk should not be stolen. Because we believed your blood was half-mortal and half-faerie, we believed we could take those memories and hide them away where they could not harm you anymore. But it would seem your blood is more than half-faerie, my daughter. It might not have sought to regain your memories were he not calling out to you."

"My memories must be returned to me, Mother, and who is *he* that seeks me?"

"There must always, as you know, be a balance between the light and the dark," Ilona began. "But sometimes the dark grows stronger and stronger, threatening to overcome the light and all that is good. Part of the reason for your birth was to push back that darkness and the evil that it brings. To do this it was necessary that you go to the Dark Lands and mate with its lord."

Lara shrank back, horrified, but then her faerie nature took control. "Tell me," she said.

"The Dark Lands is ruled by the Twilight Lord, and each Twilight Lord's path is dictated by the Book of Rule which has been handed down to them for five hundred years. The masters of this realm can only produce one son in each generation. The book speaks differently to each Twilight Lord. In this case it told its master that you were the wife he must take and that the son you bore him would conquer both Hetar and Terah, bringing them into the darkness."

"Why did you not protect me from this creature?" Lara demanded. She was not certain if she should be angry or just sad at being manipulated.

"Because it was necessary for you to fulfill the Twilight Lord's destiny as laid out in the Book of Rule. He is a cruel creature and he stole you away, Lara, after having the Munin remove the memories of who you were. When you awoke with no memory, he convinced you that you were his wife and that you had been ill. Little by little he returned the knowledge to you that you needed, everything but who you were and your family. He impregnated you, and because you believed you loved him, you carried his child. And then Kaliq came to you and restored all of your memories, explaining why we had allowed you to be used in this manner. You cast a spell creating two sons from the one child. And when you gave birth to identical twin sons, the Twilight Lord was horrified, but the Book of Rule would not permit the spilling of one child's blood in favor of the other. These children are chaos personified and they have already set the Dark Lands against itself. Factions have formed around each of these boys, for who knows which of them will be the next lord? This is what was meant to be in order to defeat the darkness for the next hundred years, Lara. And only you could do this for us all. I am sorry," the queen concluded.

"Why take my memories of this, Mother? Did you think me so weak that I could not do what needed to be done?" Lara demanded to know.

"You were gone a year, Lara. The clan families were in despair that you had disappeared while there. They felt responsible for your loss. Magnus and your children were frantic and heartbroken. When we stole you back we put a spell on the Twilight Lord to prevent him from coming after you. We took the memory of that year from everyone in Terah and Hetar. Do you truly believe your husband could have overlooked what happened to you? Do you believe he would have ever forgotten that you gave twin sons to another man, an evil man, especially when he wants a son of you himself? He could not have forgiven you, even knowing the circumstances of your abduction, for he loves you beyond reason, Lara. It is the nature of his mortal soul. To assuage his honor he would have declared war upon the Twilight Lord, a magical being, and brought destruction upon Terah even as Hetar was planning to attack you. It is very unwise to fight a war on two fronts, my daughter."

"I understand all you tell me, Mother, but I want my memories of that time returned to me. It is obviously this Twilight Lord who calls to me in my dreams. How can I fight him if I know nothing of him or our time together? You have said I am stronger than either you or Kaliq knew. I am. The prince has been avoiding me, Mother. We must go to him together and convince him to return what is mine."

"But when those memories return you will suffer with the

knowledge of the time you spent with the Twilight Lord. Like all magical beings he is far more carnal than mortal men."

"And being faerie, I responded enthusiastically," Lara remarked dryly.

Ilona was forced to laugh. "He possesses two manhoods," she said, "and sometimes he used both together."

"Ahh," Lara replied. "That is why..." She remembered her lovemaking session with Magnus the day before.

"Why what?" her mother asked.

Lara briefly explained.

"And that touched a chord in you, as well?" Ilona inquired.

"Aye, it did," Lara responded.

"Then I must go with you to Kaliq," Ilona said. "Your memories must be restored. If we do not those memories may attempt to rebuild themselves and do you harm."

"I promised Magnus that I would only remain away a few hours," Lara said.

"Go home then," her mother advised. "This can wait another day. Tell Magnus that you are going to visit Kaliq with me because we wish to discuss Dillon's schooling next year. That I have decided to involve myself in my grandson's education, but that you need to set everything in advance so I cannot overrule your wishes," Ilona said with a wicked smile.

"*That* at least will be true," Lara replied and Ilona laughed. Then, before Lara, the shining tunnel opened again and she could see the lamp she had left flickering in her hidden chamber. She arose, as did the queen. Lara kissed her mother's cheeks. "Thank you," she told her. "Sometimes I think of my father keeping us apart when I was a child and I grow angry at him again, but it was meant to be, wasn't it?"

Ilona nodded. "When you are ready to leave, call my name, Daughter. The tunnel will open for you and at its end will be the Great Corridor of Shunnar. I will meet you there." She returned Lara's kisses, then giving her a little push watched her depart, the tunnel closing behind her as she went until no trace of it remained. Then the queen of the Forest Faeries said, "Well, Kaliq, we have no choice. We must return Lara's memories of her time with Kol to her and hope she is strong enough to bear the burden."

The prince stepped forth from the shadows where he had been standing and listening. "Did you know Swiftsword had faerie blood in him?" he asked her.

Ilona shook her head in the negative. "I did not. Now I must look in the Faerie Record to learn how far back it is. It will not appear in any of his sons, for their mother is pure mortal I am certain. She is too dull and Hetarian to be otherwise."

"What, Ilona, is that jealousy I hear in your voice?" Kaliq asked wickedly.

She gave him a scathing look. "I was young, beautiful and eager to couple with a mortal. He was handsome and vigorous. I am still young and beautiful. He is older and dull. You know as well as I do, Kaliq, that that is how it is with a mortal-faerie affair. I had been chosen to have this daughter with a preordained destiny. John had a rustic charm and I knew his fate. He was the right father for Lara. But while I loved him then, I have not loved him in years. Now let me consult the Faerie Record to learn how

Swiftsword gained faerie blood that even he did not know about." The queen of the Forest Faeries called a serving maid to fetch what she required. Then she and Kaliq sat and waited.

The Faerie Record finally arrived, brought into Ilona's chamber by six sturdy faerie serving men. It was an enormous volume bound in gilt-covered leather, hinged in silver gilt, its cover decorated in multicolored gemstones and pearls. It was set upon a golden platform to which four silver and gold wheels were attached. The queen arose, dismissing the servants as she did. Then she walked over to the great book and commanded the platform to lower itself so she might more easily peruse the record.

"How far back does it go?" Kaliq asked her, curious.

"Before time as mortals document it," Ilona answered. "Even the Peris in your family are here." Then she looked at the book and said, "Lara, daughter of Ilona, granddaughter of Maeve. Show me the line of descent through her father, Swiftsword."

Slowly the book opened and the pages began to fly past until finally they stopped. Kaliq came to stand by Ilona's side to view what the Faerie Record revealed. What they saw made Ilona laugh aloud and Kaliq cocked his head questioningly.

"Swiftsword's grandmother was my great-uncle Rufin's lover briefly. She bore a son she believed was her husband's, Swiftsword's father," Ilona said laughing. "That is where Swiftsword got his natural ability with the blade, for my great-uncle was famed among the faerie world for his skills with that weapon. How fascinating that Lara's blood on both her mother and her father's side comes from my family, the royal family of the Forest," the queen remarked. "In a mortal, the blood weakens with each passing generation. But faerie blood strengthens with each new line born. Perhaps one of Swiftsword's sons will have a talent after all. I will have to watch them."

"Then you believe Lara can bear the burden of knowing her time in the Dark Lands as Kol's mate," Kaliq said quietly.

"Close now," Ilona said to the book which quickly shut itself. "She believes she can, but I still fret that perhaps it is her curiosity that drives her on, my prince. You must question her carefully tomorrow when we meet at Shunnar." Ilona sighed. "I wish we could have put a mortal woman into Kol's eye, but no mortal could have created the two from the one."

"I am disturbed that he is able to reach out to her even with her memories hidden away," the prince said thoughtfully. "Without those memories she is better protected."

Ilona reached out and took Kaliq's hand in hers, squeezing it gently. "You cannot always protect her," she told him softly. "She must tread her own path. And she still has more to do before her destiny is completely fulfilled."

His look was anguished. "So much responsibility upon such delicate shoulders," he said. "I do not know how she bears it, Ilona."

"She bears it because she is my daughter," the queen answered. "Because she is faerie. More faerie than even we knew, Kaliq. And we will always be here to aid her when she needs us. *Always!*"

He nodded. "Aye, we will," he agreed. Then he shook himself. "I must return to Shunnar. I will await your coming tomorrow." And turning, he was gone into the shadows of the queen's chamber.

Ilona sat alone for a long time. Lara was strong. But the

memories she demanded were going to pain her deeply. And she would have to keep them secret from her beloved Magnus. That, the queen knew, would be the hardest thing of all for her daughter. But then Ilona suddenly knew that her grandson, Dillon, would be there for his mother as he always was. He would sense her pain and comfort her. And she would be there. They would not allow Lara to suffer from the forbidden knowledge she was about to receive. There was too much more for her to do.

MAGNUS HAUK WAS PLEASED when his wife returned from visiting her mother in a relatively short time. He was not pleased when she told him that evening during their family meal that she would be leaving them again on the morrow.

"I am going to Shunnar and will be away overnight," Lara said.

"Why?" he demanded, his look dark.

"Because the time has come to discuss Dillon's future schooling with Kaliq. My mother wishes to be there and I will not have her making decisions for my son that I should be making. It is important to me, so I do not wish to rush back as I did today. Had I not promised you I would return immediately, my mother and I would have gone to Shunnar from her palace in the Forest, but I always keep my promises to you, Magnus. Do I not?" She gave him a sweet smile.

He glowered at her in return. "Can this not wait until another time? What is the rush? It is another year before Dillon leaves us, Lara."

"Why must you make this so difficult, my lord?" Lara countered cleverly, totally ignoring his questions. "I know how fond you have become of my son, and he of you, but Dillon has magic in him and it must be fostered properly. Kaliq wishes to discuss the program for Dillon's first year because there are things I will have to instruct him in before he goes. It will not only be Master Bashkar teaching my son in his autumn term. I must teach him, as well."

The Dominus sighed irritably. "I cannot forbid you," he groused.

"Oh, you could try," Lara teased him, attempting to help him regain his good humor. She chucked him beneath his chin. "But I know you love me enough that you will not." Leaning forward she kissed him lightly on his lips. "You may never understand me, Magnus, my love, but I know I can be certain of your affection."

"You are wheedling me," he said, but his lips were twitching with their urge to smile. "One night, Lara. And I want you sleeping in the same chamber as your mother."

She laughed aloud at that. "As if I should be unfaithful to you, my dear lord."

"May I come to Shunnar with you, Mother?" Dillon asked eagerly, leaning forward.

"If he gets to go, then I should, too. And Zagiri," Anoush piped up.

"None of you are going," Lara told them. "I go to discuss your brother's future, Anoush. And if I am correct, none of you has a school holiday. I will be gone one night."

Her children looked disappointed, but said nothing further on the matter.

When the next morning came Lara went to her private chamber and called her mother's name thrice. Immediately the shimmering golden tunnel opened before her. At its end she could see the columns and balustrade of the Grand Corridor in Kaliq's palace. She stepped through into the tunnel and walked its length. When she had traversed the passage she stepped out into the wide corridor, and the heat of the desert surrounded her.

"Lara." Her mother stepped forth from another glistening tunnel.

Lara hurried forward to greet her parent and as they embraced, Kaliq appeared in his pure white robes to welcome them.

"Your mother has told me why you have come," he said quietly. "Let us go into my private garden where we may take refreshments and speak together." He led them from the Grand Corridor, through a hallway that was familiar to Lara. The prince's private garden was pleasant, and silent servants brought refreshments, frine and sweet faerie cakes iced in pink sugar icing. Settling themselves, they partook of the sweets but Lara could hardly contain herself. Finally she could no longer make polite conversation.

"My mother has told me of how you and she manipulated the memories of all when you retrieved me from the Dark Lands. But now, Kaliq, I need to have my memories restored. This Twilight Lord is reaching out for me and I cannot fight him without a complete knowledge of what happened. You cannot fully protect me now. My poor mind seeks to reconstruct those months. I need the truth, not whatever this Kol may implant in my brain in order to regain my person."

"Those memories can only make you unhappy, Lara. And you must keep them from your husband. That will not be an easy thing, my love," the prince told her.

"You treat me like a child, Kaliq," Lara told him angrily. "I am not a child. I understand you allowing Kol to take me and to mate me. Your plan to cause chaos in the Dark Lands was clever and no mere mortal could have accomplished it. But you had no right to steal my memories of the time I had to spend with this Twilight Lord."

"I have sealed him up in his castle," Kaliq said. "I have taken away his reflecting bowls. You are safe from him."

"Nay, I am not," Lara replied. "He draws me to the Dream Plain and calls my name. And you cannot make him cease for the Dream Plain heeds the laws of neither the mortal nor the magical world. I cannot fight the Twilight Lord if I do not know what happened while I was in his charge," Lara repeated. "Return my memories to me, Kaliq!"

"The pain may do you irreparable harm," he pleaded with her.

Lara looked at him with a stony-eyed gaze.

"Very well," he said, resigned. "I must call the Munin lord to do this for while I have kept your memories, I need his aid in restoring them to you. You will have to sleep, Lara. It will not hurt you if you are sleeping when it is done."

"But it will hurt when I awaken, won't it?" Lara replied.

He nodded, his deep blue eyes agonized.

"Do it!" she commanded him.

Reaching into his robes Kaliq drew forth a small vial and after uncorking it poured a stream of pale-gold liquid into Lara's half-empty goblet of frine. "Take it across the gardens to the chamber that is always yours," he told her. "When you drink it you will instantly sleep and you will sleep until I awaken you. I will not allow you to rest yourself for too long a time. Your mother and I will need time when you awaken to help you come to terms with what happened to you. I cannot allow you to return to Magnus Hauk until you are at peace with yourself, my love."

Lara nodded. "I understand, Kaliq, and I am grateful for your care of me in this matter." Then picking up the goblet she stood and walked across the gardens into her bedchamber.

Ilona looked at the prince. "I am sorry," she told him.

"Do not be," he answered her. "I have loved her from the moment I first laid eyes upon her but I am not fated to be with her." He arose. "Come, let us summon the Munin lord, and I will have him bring the jar into which I stored Lara's memories. I fashioned it myself, Ilona, of silver and gold, and stopped its opening with a crystal so the light would always keep her memories alive."

"Call the Munin," Ilona said a trifle impatiently. She was always surprised by this Shadow Prince's romantic attachment to her daughter.

"Lord of the Munin, hear my plea. Cease all else, and come to me," Kaliq said.

Satordi, lord of the Munin, appeared almost immediately. "I did not expect to hear from you so soon, my lord prince," he hissed in his whispery voice. Then seeing Ilona he bowed quite low. "I greet you, oh queen of the Forest Faeries."

"I greet you, lord of the Munin," Ilona replied, nodding respectfully.

The Munin reached into his filmy robes and drew out the vessel in which Lara's memories were stored. "You will want this, of course. Does she sleep?"

"She sleeps," Kaliq said. "How did you know?"

"The daughter of Ilona and Swiftsword is strong-willed, oh Prince. You sought to protect her but she must protect herself. And to do so she needs *all* her memories returned intact," Satordi said. He held out the silver-and-gold jar. "Look through the crystal. Her memories are stirring restlessly. Unless they are restored to her they will be corrupted into something that they are not."

"I was not aware such a thing could happen," Kaliq replied.

"It is not usual for stored memories to behave in such a manner," the Munin Lord whispered, "but her memories are still true. There is time, my lord prince."

Kaliq said nothing more but in Ilona's company led Satordi across his garden and directly into the chamber where Lara now slept deeply. "Do it!" he said.

Ilona watched as the Munin lord carefully opened the beautiful jar and slowly poured the glittering threads of Lara's memories back into her head.

When he had finished he held out his hand to Kaliq who handed him the vial he had kept. Satordi added it saying, "It is done, my lord prince. The Domina's memories are complete again." He bowed to both of them. "If I may ever be of service again, you will call." Then the Munin lord quickly disappeared back to his shadowy home.

Kaliq led Ilona from the chamber. "We will let her sleep an hour and then awaken her," he said.

Together they waited, seated on either side of the bed where Lara slumbered. She grew restless, moaning softly, her body twisting. And then before they might awaken her Lara sat up with a start. Her green eyes were confused at first and then, as she focused, she saw her mother and Kaliq looking anxiously at her. Suddenly she burst into fulsome tears, sobbing as if her heart would break. Neither of her companions made any move to comfort her as she cried. Gradually her weeping died away and finally she looked up at them. Kaliq's heart contracted in his chest. Her look was one of utter sorrow.

Reaching out, Lara took his hand in hers. "Thank you for trying to protect me, Kaliq," she said. "You are right. These memories are difficult to bear, but bear them I must, for everyone's sake. What a dark destiny I have been given, yet I sense that it will not all be cruel."

The prince squeezed her hand. "Nay, my love, it will not all be dark," he told her reassuringly. "Your sojourn in the Dark Lands was the worst of it, Lara."

She turned to her mother. "Did you know how carnal a creature Kol is?"

Ilona nodded. "I did."

"And yet you created me for the purpose of being his mate," Lara said slowly. "How cruel you are, Mother! I am your flesh! You planned this before my birth, didn't you? You made me almost entirely in your image so that Kol would want me. Did you also manipulate the Twilight Lord's Book of Rule for your purposes?"

"Do not blame your mother for this," Kaliq told Lara. "Those of us who were privy to Kol's direction a century in advance planned this. You were created from the love between your mother and your father, but when we saw how beautiful you were becoming and that you had magic in you, we realized you were the perfect vessel. The Book of Rule does not warn its Twilight Lord of danger or of enemies. It simply states what is to come. We could not change the book if we wanted to, for its creator built fail-safes into it to protect his descendants. Do you know from whom Kol descends?"

Lara shook her head.

"Usi the Sorcerer. The same foul creature that you defeated when you removed his curse from the men of Terah. Usi got children on two of his women and sent them away into safety to protect his line. One was taken to the Dark Lands for his brother was the Twilight Lord then. The other child was brought to Hetar."

"Do you know who that descendant is?" Lara asked.

"It was a daughter and her line was felt to be of no importance. We can learn that information should we need it. Usi's brother had no son to follow him, so his nephew did. Down through the centuries that line has been kept pure and while each Twilight Lord is the father of many daughters, he fathers only one son a generation."

"Until me," Lara said softly.

Kaliq nodded. "Until you," he said. "Your tactic to divide the child in your womb into two sons was brilliant."

"It seemed only logical when you restored my memories and explained to me why I was there," Lara agreed. She turned to her mother. "I am sorry I railed at you, Mother. It has been a shock to learn all that happened to me."

"I am not angry at you, my daughter. You have a right to be angry. No woman should have to bear children she does not want," Ilona said.

"I was but a vessel like any mortal woman," Lara responded with a small smile. "A means to an end. It is so odd. I feel nothing for those children."

"Thank the Celestial Actuary that your faerie heart has protected you from your human nature in that regard," Ilona replied.

"Yet I love my own children," Lara noted, sounding a little confused.

"You love them because you love their fathers," Ilona said.

"But how could I give those children to Kol when I did not love him?" Lara wanted to know.

"Because he had you believing that you were his mate and you loved one another," Ilona said impatiently. "You must remember everything, Lara, if you are to carry the burden of your knowledge. Magnus can never know for he would never be able to forgive you."

Lara nodded. "I believe I can shoulder this secret," she said. "But I do not know if I should, even if it was a part of my destiny and it was meant to be." She pierced Kaliq with a sharp look. "However, you were very wicked to tempt me so."

The Shadow Prince actually flushed beneath his tanned cheeks. "I but sought to help you," he said, but he could not quite look at her.

Lara laughed. "You sought to help yourself, Kaliq. You are a devious prince."

"What is this?" Ilona looked at the two of them, her head turning this way and that. Then her green eyes narrowed. "Kaliq!" she scolded. "You made love to my daughter when you knew you should not?"

"Her memories of the Dark Lands existed then and were painful. I but made love to her to soothe her cruel memories," he excused himself.

"That is the real burden I will carry," Lara teased him wickedly.

Ilona laughed, then she said, "You really should not have a husband, Lara. Husbands are such a bother. You are more faerie than mortal—your blood runs hot."

"I am as much mortal as faerie," Lara said.

"Nay, you are not. It seems your father has faerie blood in him, too, although he never knew it. Your great-grandfather was half-faerie, although his mother believed him the son of her Midlands farmer husband. She had dallied one Midsummer's eve with Prince Rufin of the Forest Faeries, a member of my own family. So says the Faerie Record which lists all those born with faerie blood. Your faerie blood is weightier than your mortal blood, my daughter. And those with mortal blood who show signs of magic as you did grow stronger if their powers are developed as yours have been. Dillon will be a great sorcerer one day," Ilona said in pleased tones. "Perhaps I shall send your half brother Cirillo to study with him." She turned to the prince. "Do you think you and your brothers could manage two lively boys, Kaliq?"

"I should prefer to have Dillon alone with me his first year," the prince said.

Ilona thought a moment and then agreed. "Aye, that would be best. My grandson is a bit crude yet. A year with you will smooth those rough edges of his."

"Anoush is showing signs of being a healer," Lara said. "It would seem both of Vartan's children have magic in them."

Then she grew pale. "Oh! What if Kol tries to steal my children from me?" she asked. "Magnus would want to know why and what could I tell him?"

"Kol is secured at Kolbyr," Kaliq reassured her.

"But he is reaching out to me on the Dream Plain. What if he reaches out to Magnus and tells him what happened?" Lara fretted. She had grown paler.

"We cannot prevent him from reaching out to the Dominus if he dares, but why would Magnus believe him? Magnus would think he was just having a bad dream," Kaliq said to her. "Your husband does not really understand the ways of magic."

Lara shuddered. "Kol wants me back. It is not enough that I have given him heirs. The Twilight Lord loves me. I can feel him reaching out for me, Kaliq! It frightens me. I know him well enough to know he will do what he must to get me back."

"He is imprisoned at Kolbyr," Kaliq repeated.

"I could not live in that awful place again," Lara said. "There was no color. Everything was gray or black. The mountains, where they were not slate or craggy, were covered in dark green pines and fir trees. No sunlight filtered into the valleys. In fact, I do not believe I saw sunlight at all in my year there except for some rare sunsets. I remember looking out through the mountains at the colors of the sunset and thinking how beautiful they were and wondering why there could be no color in the land about us." She trembled. "I should die if I had to go back there, Kaliq! What if Kol sends the Munin to take my memories again and steals me back? I could not bear it! I could not!"

"I will weave a spell about you, my daughter," Ilona said reassuringly, "that will not allow anyone to ever again steal your memories."

"The Munin will never again aid Kol," Kaliq told her. "They learned his generosity was but an enticement to trap them so they would always be forced to do his bidding. I rescued them and they are safe now, my love. You need have no fears."

"I suppose I am being foolish," Lara replied. "But as the memories of those months in the Dark Lands come to the surface of my consciousness I do become afraid. I suppose it was the helplessness I felt when you made me once more aware of who I was, and I had to face the lies Kol had woven about me while pretending to be his beloved."

"It will take time, my love," he told her, "but those memories will eventually slip into your past and no longer be so painful."

"Ah!" Suddenly her eyes lit up. "I believe I met Og's father in the Dark Lands. His name is Skrymir, and he was the giant lord of the Dark Lands giants. He was on a hunting expedition when the Forest Lords murdered the Forest giants. He and his companions fled to the Dark Lands. Kol gave them sanctuary, and they are loyal to him as are the dwarfs and the Wolfyn. What if Kol sends one of them after me?" Lara wondered aloud and her fears came racing back to overwhelm her as she began to tremble.

"We are going to have to enchant Kol and his castle into sleep," Ilona said. "We cannot allow Lara to fear him. She will alert Magnus that something is wrong and when he learns what it is he will never forgive her, foolish mortal!"

"I will have to discuss that with my brothers," Kaliq said. "I do not know if we can enchant the Twilight Lord into sleep. It would swing the difference between the light and the dark too far one way and unbalance it. Too much good is no better than too much evil, Ilona. Balance is always best."

"You can't enchant Kol into a lengthy sleep," Lara said. "He rules the Dark Lands. Without him chaos would reign and more than likely spill out into the New Outlands."

"Then you must learn to master your fears," Kaliq told her quietly. "Your magic is stronger than his because it is pure. That is one reason he wanted you for himself. Without your pure magic he cannot accomplish all he wishes to complete."

"I can do nothing until I have convinced Kol that I will not return to him," Lara replied. "He is a difficult creature at best. Almost like a child when he doesn't get his way, Kaliq. Have you ever tried reasoning with a child who would have his own way?"

"Surely you are not considering returning to the Dark Lands," Ilona said, horrified.

"Nay. I will have to summon him to the Dream Plain and reveal myself. I must control the situation. I cannot allow him to gain the upper hand," Lara said thoughtfully. "It must all be on my terms. What of Og? Will you tell him?"

"I must think," the prince said slowly. "It is possible that these giants may be convinced to ally themselves with us. I will speak with Og."

"Does Og know the truth of my destiny?" Lara wanted to know.

"He knows little of what has happened so far, my love, but as your mother and I have told you, you have not completely fulfilled your destiny," the prince answered. "Here at Shunnar there was no reason to wipe memories clean of that year. However if Og is to understand how you came by your information then we must tell him of those months. Do you trust him enough to burden him with the truth?"

"I have always trusted Og," Lara replied quietly. "Send for him."

The prince nodded and called for Og to be brought up from the valley where he spent most of his time working with the horses that belonged to the Shadow Princes. The giant had not been born when the Forest Lords had massacred his people, but his mother, Oona, had managed to escape to the deepest part of the forest where she had given birth to her son. They had lived in the forest until he was four and they were discovered. Oona saved her only child by telling the Forest Lords that he had not been born when they had killed her people. Her captors had slain her, taking the child giant back with them to their hall to be their servant. They did not know he possessed the collective memory of his people. While she had been in the custody of the Forest Lords, Lara had met Og, and together they had escaped the forest and come into the desert kingdom of the Shadow Princes. Lara had moved on eventually, but Og had remained with Prince Kaliq caring for the horses.

He strode into the garden where they now sat for, while he was a small giant, he was still over ten feet in height. His pale blue eyes lit up with pleasure seeing Lara. Going to her he knelt, taking her hands in his and kissing them reverently. "My faerie princess, I am overjoyed to see you once again!" he said with a wide smile. Then he sat, his legs crossed, before her.

Ilona raised an eyebrow. Was she invisible to this giant lout?

"Og, I am glad to see you, too," Lara said. "You remember my mother, Queen Ilona, I am sure."

The giant turned his head. "Greetings, oh Queen. You are as always the fairest."

Slightly mollified, Ilona nodded in return. "Greetings, Og."

"We have asked you here, Og, because we need your help," Prince Kaliq began.

"This is burdensome, Og," Lara told him. "I have learned something that may or may not please you, but before I can tell you, I need your word that you will keep my secrets, my old friend."

"I would die for you, Lara," the giant told her and they knew it was true.

Prince Kaliq then began to speak. He explained to Og how Lara's destiny had brought her to the Dark Lands, and for what purpose. Og listened silently, but his countenance grew more and more sorrowful as Kaliq's tale unfolded.

At last, Lara spoke. "As I have previously told you, Og, I met the lord of the giants, who is an ally of the Twilight Lord. His name is Skrymir."

"That indeed was my father's name," Og said.

"Then Skrymir must be your father," Lara told him. "He returned shortly after your people were massacred, and your mother had escaped into the deep forest. He and his party fled the carnage into the Dark Lands. The Twilight Lord gave them sanctuary and they pledged their loyalty to him. They have been there ever since."

Og looked devastated. "Why did he not look for us?" he asked aloud.

"That is a question you must ask him yourself," Lara said. "Og, I need your help."

"Anything!" he exclaimed.

"Nay, wait until you have heard what I want of you, old friend," Lara responded.

"Kaliq has imprisoned the Twilight Lord within his castle for the next hundred years, but alas, Kol seeks to reach out to me through the Dream Plain. Magnus Hauk knows nothing of my adventures, his memory of that year having been taken away. I love my husband, Og, but I also understand his mortal nature well. I doubt he could forgive me that time with Kol or the fact that I gave the Twilight Lord two sons when I have not yet given him the one thing he wants more than anything. His own son. He would see what was meant to happen and did happen as a betrayal of sorts. I cannot allow that to happen for Magnus's sake and for the sake of my children."

"Tell me what you would have me do, my princess," Og replied.

"If Kol cannot be dissuaded to leave Lara in peace," Kaliq said, "and I do not think that he can, then he is apt to send his giants, his Wolfyn or his dwarf allies into Terah to fetch her back to him. That would be disastrous. If you could meet your father upon the Dream Plain, Og, perhaps you would be able to convince him to eschew the Twilight Lord. The Forest Giants were once a gentle race."

"They are no longer gentle," Lara said. "They are hard and fierce men, I fear."

"My father, my mother told me, loved her above all others. He would not even keep another woman after they had mated.

It was the one thing that broke her heart. That she did not dare to seek him out and he would never know what became of her or the child she carried," Og said. "If I can find my father upon the Dream Plain I believe I can convince him to throw in his fortunes with us, for the love he surely still bears Oona. Tell me, Lara, do I look like him?"

"But for your eyes, aye," she told him.

"Then I must have my mother's eyes," Og mused. "Can he see my eyes upon the Dream Plain? Will he see Oona in them? It would be a great advantage to us if he could," the giant said thoughtfully.

"He can see your eyes," Kaliq replied. "But what he will see in them is another thing. Still, I will give you a charm that may help you to reach out to Skrymir."

"I have never attempted to reach the Dream Plain," Og said.

"You have but to lie down to sleep and concentrate upon reaching out to your father," the prince told his horse master. "I will send a message to your wife that you will remain here with me this night and not go home. It is better that you sleep where we may monitor you. That way when you awaken it will all be fresh in your mind."

Og nodded solemnly. "I hope my father likes me," he half whispered.

Lara slipped one of her hands into his huge hand. "How could he not be pleased with a son who has become such a fine and honorable man?" she asked, knowing better than most the pain that losing his parents had cost her giant friend.

Kaliq invited the giant to eat with them in the garden as the evening fell. And afterwards he brought Og to a large room with a great long bed that he had conjured up so the giant could be comfortable. He placed a golden charm shaped like a tree in full leaf about Og's neck. The tree's leaves were enameled in various shades of green. "This will keep you safe upon the Dream Plain."

"What is it like, my lord?" Og asked.

"It is a misty place, but you will feel a firmness beneath your feet, and the mists will clear allowing you to see your father and he you," the prince explained. "If at any time you find yourself threatened or even frightened you may simply picture yourself away from the Dream Plain. When you lie down, concentrate upon your father and call him to you," Kaliq instructed. He handed Og a goblet of frine. "Drink this, my friend. It will aid in your sleep." When Og had drained the large goblet, Kaliq said, "Now I will leave you. Dream well."

Alone, Og looked about the chamber. It was large and simple with a long single window opening onto a garden. The giant sat down upon the bed and pulled off his boots. Then swinging his legs up he lay flat upon his back. The bed was more than comfortable, he was pleased to note. Outside the window he could hear the song of a night bird. Og closed his eyes and thought of the giant who was called Skrymir. Lara said that his father looked like him, but Og had only seen himself a few times in his life. Still, he concentrated and as he did he felt himself relaxing, slipping away into a deep sleep.

Opening his eyes suddenly, the giant found himself surrounded by a pale mist that swirled about him gently. This, he realized after a brief moment of fright, was obviously the Dream

Plain. Could he move? He sat up and stepped forward cautiously. Aye, he could move. But where was his father? Then he realized it might help if he called him. "Skrymir, son of Thrym, son of Eggther, come to me!" his voice boomed out.

"Who calls me to the Dream Plain?" a voice thundered back. "Who dares to speak the hallowed names of my father and my father's father?"

"I am called Og. I am the son of Skrymir and Oona of the Forest Giants," Og replied. "If you are that same Skrymir, son of Thrym, son of Eggther, then you are my father. Show yourself to me."

Og waited in silence wondering if the other giant would reveal himself, but then the mists fell away from the form of a huge man with red hair who did indeed look like him but that his eyes were amber. Skrymir stood at least two feet taller than Og. He was dressed in a green gown with a leather breastplate, but he was unarmed.

"You are small," Skrymir said. "Why are you so small?"

"My growth was stunted by lack of nutrition and the conditions in which I was forced to survive," Og answered. "Why did you not look for my mother?"

"You have Oona's eyes," Skrymir said sadly. "I see her now looking out at me. When we returned from the hunt four days after we had left we found the killing ground the Forest Lords had turned our home into," he began. "The bodies had been mutilated. Some had already fallen prey to the beasts of the wood, and the crows and ravens had taken the eyes from many. We could identify no one. I assumed that your mother had died and our child with her. How did you both survive?"

"My mother was on the hill picking berries when the Forest Lords swept into our village. She could see the slaughter and mayhem from her vantage point and realizing what was happening she fled into the deep wood, where several months later she gave birth to me. When I was four a party of Forest Lords discovered us. She saved my life by telling them that I had been in her belly on that fateful day. She begged for my life knowing her own would soon be taken. The Forest Lords slew her before me, and then thought it would be amusing to have a giant child as a slave. Since I had not been born until after the destruction visited upon our people the Forest Lords believed their secret was safe. They were not aware that our people have a collective memory that is passed to infants in the womb."

Skrymir nodded slowly and then he asked, "Are you still in the forest? If you are we will come and rescue you and slay as many of the Foresters as we can!"

"Nay, Father, I escaped several years ago. I am the horse master of the Shadow Princes. I make my home at Shunnar, in the desert of Hetar. I have a wife and children."

"How have you found me?" Skrymir wanted to know. "If you have a happy existence then why do you seek me out?"

"You serve the Twilight Lord, my father," Og said. "Why do you and those with you who are of the light serve the darkness?"

"Because Lord Kol was the only one willing to shelter us after our families were destroyed," Skrymir said. "We dared not take our complaints and our case to the High Council of Hetar. We dared not even allow the Forest Lords to learn that some of us had survived. Look what they did to your mother. One frail woman with a small child and they still feared exposure enough to murder her because she knew their secret. Do you believe they would have shown you any mercy had they known of our collective memory? We fled from the forest across the desert and, finding a sea at its far edge, we waded across it. But the land upon the other side, even though empty of mortals, was not suited to our way of life so we traveled onward toward the mountains that make up the Dark Lands. It was here we found safety. We owe Lord Kol much for his kindness to us."

"Your master wishes to conquer Hetar and Terah, the land below the mountains," Og said slowly.

"Hetar is a weak kingdom. It needs a strong master, and the Twilight Lord means to be that master. As for Terah, its people are simple folk who will be easily taken," Skrymir said.

"Father, while Hetar is in its decline, Terah is not. And that land you found deserted on the other side of the Obscura when you fled Hetar is now populated with the clan families of the old Outlands of Hetar. They accept the Dominus of Terah as their overlord. He is a strong man and his wife is a powerful faerie woman."

"How do you know this?" Skrymir asked.

"Because the Domina of Terah is my friend, and Prince Kaliq of the Shadows is her mentor. The Twilight Lord is now penned within his castle by Prince Kaliq's magic. He will remain there for a hundred years. He can lead no armies of unjust conquest against Hetar and Terah, Father. The Dark Lands is leaderless right now."

"Lord Kol may be confined, but the rest of us come and go at will," Skrymir said. "We will follow his orders and go forth to conquer."

"To what purpose?" Og countered.

"Because he has asked us to," Skrymir said. "Because he is the only one to shelter our people, my son."

"You never asked others, Father. Your complaint is not fair. Why would you follow after someone who would do to the peoples of Hetar and Terah what the Forest Lords did to our people?" Og wanted to know. He looked up at this father he had never known. "Many will die."

"You are slight of stature," Skrymir noted, "but you are large of intellect, my son. I have not considered the consequences of a war before now."

"At their height the Forest Giants were few in number," Og pointed out. "The City of Hetar has a large population and then there are the provinces outside of The City which now include the Outlands. There are many who will suffer from your master's desire for conquest. And why does he seek Hetar and Terah?"

Now Skrymir looked confused. These were questions to which he had no answer.

"Is there hunger in the Dark Lands? Has the population grown too large for your borders?" Og persisted. "If these things are so then could you not seek aid from your neighbors in Hetar and Terah? Why must you march forth and slay them? What have these innocents ever done to you?"

"You are hurting my head with all your questions," Skrymir complained. "Our people owe the Twilight Lord their allegiance."

"The lord Kol sits in his castle directing his minions to go forth to their destruction," Og said. "Do you believe Hetar and Terah so weak that they will not fight back? They already know of your coming and are preparing to defend themselves," Og lied. "The surviving Forest Giants are few. How many will be killed in this foolish foray? And are the dwarfs and Wolfyn so numerous that they, too, can allow their ranks to be decimated? While you go to war, Kol will sit back and watch. He has not even the courage to lead his armies himself, Father. And this is who you would follow into death?" Og stood tall before his sire, his big hands upon his hips.

"I can listen to you no longer," Skrymir said irritably. "You confuse me, my son. If indeed you *are* my son and not some fabrication of magic."

"I am your son," Og assured his father. "If you doubt me then come down from your mountains. I will meet you on the other side of the sea which you previously crossed in your flight. You will see I am real. Just be careful in your passing that you do not harm any of the Outland clan families or their livestock who now populate the region. I will await your coming." He could feel himself fading from the Dream Plain. It was an amazing sensation. "Come to me!" Og called to Skrymir, then he awakened in his large bed. He lay quietly for some long moments. He could see the day beginning to overcome the night outside of his chamber and all was quiet about him. Finally he arose and pulled on his boots.

It had been a wondrous night, although he felt just the tiniest bit tired. He had to have been sleeping for at least six hours. Had it all be real? Or just a dream? The prince would know. Og departed the chamber and went down into the valley, where the horses he tended were grazing placidly in the early light of dawn. He walked among them, for the beautiful beasts soothed him, and he was yet disturbed by his meeting with his father. Skrymir seemed a hard man. But searching his collective memory, he could not find the words *hard* or *cold* in relation to his race. Forests giants were known to be gentle creatures. The man he had met in the night did not fit that description. He had looked like a hardened warrior. But that the face that had looked at him had been his own, he would have doubted that Skrymir was his sire. Og sighed, turning back to cross the great meadow back to the prince's palace. Kaliq would be awake now and he would want to know exactly what had happened when Og traveled upon the Dream Plain. The giant found his master, Lara and Ilona in the garden eating their morning meal.

The prince waved Og to his side, offering him a cup of fresh-squeezed juice. "You look tired, my friend," Kaliq said. "Can you tell us of your journey?"

Og swallowed down the liquid in his cup. It seemed to restore him. "I met Skrymir," he began and then he told them everything in careful detail. "I did not once mention Lara by name," he said. "I do not believe that Skrymir knew that the mate Kol chose was the Domina of Terah. And he did not ask me how I found him, which was curious."

"His surprise probably outweighed his curiosity," Kaliq noted. "What of his loyalty to the Twilight Lord?"

"I sense he feels more gratitude to Lord Kol for sheltering the surviving Forest giants than any deep loyalty to him," Og said thoughtfully. "The many questions I posed to my father seemed to confuse him, but I believe when he has time to consider them he will think harder on those issues. He told me that while I was small of stature I was big of intellect." Og chuckled. "It is the first time I have ever been accused of being wise."

"But you *are* wise, dear Og," Lara told him.

"My lord prince," the giant said, "I have challenged my father to meet me on the edge of the Sea of Obscura that he may see I am not simply a dream creature but his flesh and blood son. Will you use your magic to transport me there?"

Kaliq nodded. "I will go with you, but I will remain in the shadows unless you need me."

"Why does this giant lord wish to see Og in the flesh?" Ilona asked irritably.

"Because he is a father who has only just learned he has a son, Ilona," the prince dryly answered her. "Surely you understand a parent long separated from a child wanting to see that child, to touch that child, to embrace that child."

The faerie queen flushed. "Aye," she said softly, reaching out to take her daughter's hand. "I understand."

"When is this meeting to take place?" Lara wanted to know.

"I expect he will come in the next day or two," Kaliq said slowly. "He will be curious." He turned to Og. "We will depart today. Go and tell your wife that the prince needs your company for the next few days. You do not want her worrying."

Og arose from the grass. "Very good, my prince," he said and hurried off.

"What good does this face-to-face meeting do when it is Lara we are attempting to protect?" Ilona said impatiently. "I do not care a whit for Hetar or Terah. It is my child I would have protected."

"If Kol cannot leave Kolbyr," Lara said, "but can direct his armies nonetheless, Mother, it is important that we weaken his alliances before he begins this conflagration. Gaius Prospero has no idea what he could be up against. And even with strong magic it will be difficult for Terah to defend itself against Kol's creatures. If Kol took Hetar, it would be difficult for Terah to defend itself on two fronts. We must prevent this war and that means we must destroy the bonds the Twilight Lord has forged with his allies."

"It would be far simpler if we just saw that this dark spirit slept for the next thousand years," Ilona said.

"The balance, my queen," Kaliq reminded her. "The balance."

"Do not lecture me, oh Prince," Ilona said, sniffing irritably. "But tell me, what would be so dreadful if the balance was tilted far to the light and toward the good for the next thousand years? Would it really be that awful?"

"Before a true balance might then be restored," Kaliq said, "we would be forced to live through an equal period of evil and darkness, my queen. Would you visit that upon us all? For now the balance is shifted just slightly to the good and to the light. It is the way it should be for we shall never be able to eradicate the darkness entirely. It will always lurk about the edges of our world. Even the fabled world of Belmair which glows like a great star in our skies struggles to keep perfect order. Light and dark. Good and evil. It is a never-ending battle, Ilona, and I know you know it."

The faerie queen sighed. "This Twilight Lord is just so difficult a conundrum, and I fear for my daughter."

"Your daughter has only begun to fulfill her destiny," Kaliq said quietly.

Og returned at that moment. "I have spoken with my wife.

She will take the time I am away to visit her family in the desert below," he said. "I am ready whenever you are, my prince."

And then to their surprise Prince Kaliq began to grow in height until he was as tall as Og. Flinging his cloak about himself and the giant they disappeared.

"I did not know he could do that," Lara said, amazed.

Ilona laughed. "He can do anything," she said admiringly.

"Why, Mother," Lara teased her parent, "I am surprised. Was Kaliq ever your lover? Do you know how old he is?"

"Whether he was ever one of my lovers," the faerie queen said, "is not a matter for discussion. As for his age, he is just slightly younger than time itself."

"Yet he never changes," Lara murmured softly.

Ilona made no reply.

"I suppose," Lara finally said, "that I should go home now. Magnus will probably already be beginning to fret."

"Not yet," Ilona replied. "There is still the matter of your approaching the Twilight Lord on the Dream Plain. I think it too dangerous, my daughter."

"It is dangerous," Lara agreed, "but he will not stop seeking to bring me back to him unless he can be convinced that I do not love him enough to go with him."

"Do not tell me that you came to love him?" Ilona exclaimed, horrified.

"Kol is a lonely man, Mother. He was never cruel to me. I believe that is what made it easy for me to deceive him once Kaliq regained my memories for me."

"You must harden your heart, Lara," Ilona said. "That bit of humanity within you will cause your downfall if you are not careful. The Twilight Lord stole you away from your husband and your children. He caused them and the clan families much grief. He set Gaius Prospero to making plans to war with Terah. The Twilight Lord is evil, my daughter, and evil sometimes disguises itself so that it appears almost palatable. But it is not! Kol thought only of himself, his desires, his needs. His kindness toward you was for a purpose. To convince you that he was your mate, your lover. To cajole you into depending upon him and him alone. Do not be fooled, Lara. And do not allow him to draw you back into his dark web. His heart is black to its core."

Lara sighed. "I know you are right, Mother," she agreed. "But if I am to protect Magnus and the children, if I am to prevent this war that Gaius Prospero is attempting to foist upon Terah, I must be completely free of the Twilight Lord. I cannot banish him as I did his ancestor, Usi. I must convince him that what we had was false. That I cannot ever love him as he would have me do. I will not venture into the Dark Lands again, but I will summon Kol to the Dream Plain. I am safe there, am I not?"

Ilona nodded reluctantly. "Aye, you are safe there, but be certain before you go that you protect yourself, for Kol will try to trick you."

"I must go now," Lara said, rising from the table where they had been eating. "Let me know when Kaliq is back and what has transpired for Og."

"I will," Ilona replied. And then she opened the golden tunnel for her daughter.

Lara saw at its end the small room in her own home, the

candle on the table almost burned down to a stump. She stepped into the tunnel's entrance. "Farewell, Mother," she said and then she walked through back into her own castle even as the tunnel closed behind her.

13

"I CANNOT FORGET her," the Twilight Lord groaned.

"But you must, my lord," Alfrigg said.

"Never! She is mine and I want her back!" Kol roared angrily.

"My lord, she was naught but the female vessel needed to give the Dark Lands its next lord, but she could not even do that right. She gave you identical twins instead of one son. Thus we are thrown into chaos."

"The Book of Rule said my mate would be a faerie woman and Lara is a faerie woman," Kol said irritably. He longed to strike out at his chancellor, who was becoming very annoying, but he could not relieve the dwarf of his position for Alfrigg had been named specifically in the Book of Rule as his chancellor. Still, the thought of taking his head from his shoulders and pickling it was enticing. Kol ground his teeth.

"I would never gainsay the Book of Rule," Alfrigg said. "I merely question if the female vessel you chose was the correct one."

"Of course she was the correct one, you blithering old fool,"

Kol shouted. "I saw her in the reflecting bowl when I asked to see my mate. Would the bowl have lied?"

"Perhaps you were shown what you were supposed to see," Alfrigg said quietly.

"Of course I was supposed to see her!" Kol's normally pale skin was growing crimson with his outrage and frustration. "Why else would the reflecting bowl have revealed her to me?"

"My lord, we both know the power of the magic world. And we both know that the balance between the light and the dark must be maintained—" Alfrigg began.

"Why?" Kol interrupted. "Why should there be any balance between good and evil? Why cannot one overcome the other? Show me where it is written that there must be balance, you imbecile! It is not in the Book of Rule. *Show me!*"

"I do not know if it is written, my lord, but that is the way of it," Alfrigg replied calmly. "The Shadow Princes know everything there is to know. Their magic reaches even into the Dark Lands, my lord. I believe that they arranged for you to see Lara and want her with all your being. And having engaged your lust they allowed you to take her so you might get your heir on her, for she was a faerie woman and met the requirement in the Book of Rule."

"She loves me. She would not have given me children other-wise. Faerie women will not give children to those they do not love. Now they have stolen her from me." Kol flung himself upon his throne and looked out into the stormy sky outside. "I want her back, Alfrigg. *I want her back, and I shall have her back!*" His severe, handsome face bore a look of determination.

"My lord, you must face reality. You robbed this faerie woman of her memories of who she was, of her husband, of her children. Then you convinced her that she was your wife and you loved her. She was frightened and confused. You gained her trust. She did not know she was faerie, therefore you were able to impregnate her. Once her memories were restored she schemed against you, deceived you and with the help of her mentor, the Shadow Prince, she fled the Dark Lands to return to her husband, her children and their home. She does not love you, my lord. *She does not love you!*"

Kol leapt from his throne, picked up the dwarf and flung him down the length of the long chamber. Alfrigg landed with a loud thunk and for a moment Kol believed he had killed his chancellor. He was torn between a feeling of deep satisfaction and panic, but finally Alfrigg arose from the floor, shaking himself and running his hands over himself as if he were checking for broken bones. Satisfied he was still in one piece he reached up to inspect his head and discovered a trickle of blood. The dwarf turned and bowed stiffly to his angry master.

"I will leave you to yourself, my lord, while I attend to my wounds."

"Krell damn you to Limbo!" Kol cursed Alfrigg as the doors to his throne room closed. His chancellor was wrong. Lara loved him. He would regain her even if he had to unleash all the powers of the Dark Lands into Terah. The Shadow Prince had enchanted him so he could not leave his castle for a hundred years, but he did not have to leave Kolbyr to get her back. He could send his giants or the Wolfyn after her, after the Dominus of Terah who claimed her as his wife, after her children. But first he had to contact her upon the Dream Plain. Unless she returned to him he would destroy Terah and all that was in it. Her loyalty to the Dominus was only based upon the children they shared. Well she had given him children, too, and his sons needed their mother. He needed her *and he would have her.*

The Twilight Lord strode from his throne room to his bed-chamber, a small, narrow, dark room, its walls and ceiling painted black. He flung himself down upon the bed, and his dark eyes closed as he reached out to her, commanded her to come to the Dream Plain. He had done this for many nights, and while he had sensed Lara's presence he had never been able to get close enough to her to treat with her. But tonight she appeared to him in a sudden burst of golden light, and he stepped back, surprised, for it hurt his eyes.

"Enough, my lord Kol! I will speak with you this night but after this night *nevermore.* Why do you call me to the Dream Plain?" Lara demanded but she knew the words he would utter.

"You are shining. Your brightness is making me ill," Kol complained.

"I am more faerie than you can imagine," she told him. "I am more faerie than even I knew. I am not a creature of the half light and the darkness like you, Kol. When you had the Munin steal my memories from me you took away the knowledge of who I was and thus dimmed my light. You will not do it again."

"Come back to me," he said.

"No," Lara answered him quietly. "I will never come back to you. To live in the Dark Lands would kill me. I need the light, the flowers and the birds about me."

The brightness about her had lessened now and he could see her clearly. She was, it seemed to him, even more beautiful than he remembered. He felt his lust rising as he gazed upon her. "I need you," he said softly. "I love you and our sons need you."

"If you indeed love me, my lord, then take that love and shower it upon the sons you forced me to give you," Lara said coldly, her faerie heart hardening. He *was* a monster! And she could never forgive this creature for what he had done to her. And using his sons, Kolbein and Kolgrim, to attempt to reach out to her was unspeakable.

"You love me," he told her, his eyes changing from gray to black, glittering as he encompassed her with his burning glance. "You love me!" he repeated.

"I despise you," Lara answered him.

Her icy tone discomfited him. Was it possible? Was it just possible that she was speaking the truth? If it was then it would be unbearable. "Tell me that you love me, Lara." His voice was almost pleading. His lust for her, painful.

His love for her was weakening him, Lara realized in surprise. She had not considered that Kol could be weakened by anything. This was interesting. "I find the very sight of you repellent," Lara told him. "I do not love you, although perhaps the poor creature you created of me loved you a little. But *I* do not."

Black anger rose up to fill Kol's soul with fury. "Do you believe that because I am sealed within Kolbyr that you can escape me, escape my vengeance? Consider Magnus Hauk and how he would feel if he learned you have given me what you will not give him," Kol sneered. "And what of your daughters?

Perhaps I shall use my magic to bring them to my House of Women, and take them for concubines. Your eldest female child is already half-grown. And then there is your son by the Outlander." He smiled wickedly at her, but his smile faded as he jumped back to avoid the small ball of fire she threw down at his feet. It singed his robe.

"I would not consider coming after me or mine if I were you," Lara warned him. "I am capable of killing you, Kol, even as I vanquished your ancestor, Usi. Perhaps I shall just take your sons and drown them instead. I would make you beg for their lives, but in the end I would slay them without mercy," she told him.

"There is darkness in you yet, my jewel," he murmured, pleased.

"There is darkness in all of us, Kol, both mortal and faerie, but most of us learn to overcome that darkness and let the light shine within our souls. There can be no wickedness in protecting those you love, my lord."

"Do you not love our sons?" he asked her.

Lara shook her head. "They are nothing to me, Kol. Only by stealing my memories were you able to convince me that I was who you said I was. Because I did not know I was faerie—nor knew their customs, I gave you the children that you wanted. Be satisfied, Kol, with that, for there is nothing more I can or will give you."

"If you do not return to Kolbyr to sit by my side I will create havoc in both Hetar and Terah, my gem," he told her. "That, I can do, even imprisoned as I am."

"For each blow you strike out at me, I will return two blows," Lara warned him. "Do not be confused by my beauty, Kol, or your memories of the creature you made me. I am a warrior born and I will destroy you. My sword, Andraste, longs to sip your blood, my lord."

"You cannot slay me here on the Dream Plain," Kol told her. "You must come into the Dark Lands to do that, my jewel. If you come, my creatures will capture you and bring you to me. When they do I will never let you go again." And suddenly he was by her side. Reaching out, his arm went about her waist. His hot breath touched the fair skin of her neck and he kissed it. "You belong to me, Lara," he said as he fondled her plump breasts. "Consider what we could do together, my precious one. We could conquer our worlds." He turned her about, his thumb rubbing across her lips. Then he kissed her in a deep, demanding kiss, his forked tongue snaking into her mouth to hotly caress her tongue while his fingers pinched the nipple of a breast with which he had been playing.

Lara sagged against him, shocked by the sudden weakness that overcame her. She struggled feebly against him as he pulled her gown up and lifting her up impaled her upon his dominant rod. She tried to scream but her throat seemed to be constricted and she could utter no sound. She felt his great dominant rod pumping and pumping within her tight sheath. She tried to awaken, but he would not permit her to do so.

"Feel my strength and my lust for you, my jewel," he murmured against her ear. "My desire and need for you is every bit as strong as your hate for me. You are yourself now, Lara, not the weak creature I made you. Yet you are about to know pleasure with me again as you did before."

"Noooo!" Lara insisted, her voice now restored. Desperately she attempted to push him away, to get free of his dark hunger. She could feel him within her. Thick and long and probing deeply. He stretched the walls of her sheath with his fierce burning and throbbing rod. *"Noooo!"* she cried again. *"Noooo!"*

His dark laughter echoed, surrounding her, imprisoning her with its evil. *"Yes! You will yield yourself to me because you have no choice, Lara. You are mine. Mine alone to command. I am your lord and master, not Magnus Hauk of Terah."*

Lara screamed as she felt his boiling juices scalding her—and *worse* her own satisfaction as she reached her pleasure peak. And then she heard Magnus's voice calling to her and the sound of it gave her the courage to shove the Twilight Lord from her and flee the Dream Plain.

"Lara, my love, wake up!" the Dominus said to his wife. "You are having a very bad dream. Wake up, sweetheart!" He shook her gently. "Wake up."

Lara's green eyes flew open and she almost wept with her relief. Clinging to Magnus, she wept wildly.

"What is the matter, my love?" the Dominus asked his wife. "What did you dream that has frightened you so greatly? I do not believe I have ever seen you really fearful, Lara. Tell me, my darling. What is it?"

The sound of his voice soothed and comforted her. She drew a deep breath and cleared her mind. She could hardly tell Magnus what had happened, that the Twilight Lord had raped her upon the Dream Plain. How had he wielded such power over her? The Dream Plain was supposed to be a neutral place. She needed to speak with Kaliq, but she could hardly return to Shunnar having just been there. But she must summon him to her as quickly as she could. "I cannot recall what I dreamed," she lied to her husband. "But suddenly I was very frightened, Magnus, and that as you know is unlike me. Just hold me, my darling, and I will be all right," she said, horrified further by the stickiness between her thighs.

He stroked her disheveled hair quietly, curious. How could she not remember a dream that had had such a powerful effect upon her? He had awakened with the sound of her voice crying *no*. And she had appeared to be thrashing and struggling against someone, but of course there was no one there. Strange, he considered, but then Lara never lied to him. If she said she could not recall her nightmare then she could not. But he wondered why. Lara lay against him and wondered what time it was and how long she had been dreaming. She could swear she could scent the muskiness of Kol's skin on hers. Could her husband smell it? She shuddered and Magnus's arms closed tighter about her.

"It's all right, my love," he told her reassuringly.

She nodded her head silently. She needed to get up. She needed to think. She needed to speak with Kaliq. Pulling away from Magnus she said, "I think I will get up and walk about a bit, husband. I would rid myself of these night terrors more easily, I believe. Go back to sleep. I am sorry to have awakened you." She arose from the bed.

"If you are certain you are all right," he said slowly.

"Whatever I dreamed," she told him, "I sense I need to move

about a bit to calm my nerves." She forced a small laugh. "It really must have been quite dreadful to put me into such a state, Magnus." Bending she kissed his lips lightly. "I'll be fine, my love. Perhaps a warm bath and a stroll in our gardens."

"If you are certain," he repeated, lying back, his eyes already heavy.

"I will be fine shortly," Lara replied and then making a great effort not to hurry, she walked from their bedchamber through the passage that led to her private bath. She was already naked, for sleeping garments were but an impediment to the frequent lovemaking she and her husband shared. No attendant was about for it was obviously still the middle of the night. Lara washed herself in the small sunken shell, rinsed and took a large thick towel from the shelf nearby. She did feel better, but she was still seriously concerned by what had happened. She wafted herself to her private room so as not to disturb Magnus or be seen by the guardsmen. *"Prince Kaliq, heed my call,"* she said. *"Come to me from out yon wall."*

Immediately the Shadow Prince appeared within the little chamber. He raised an eyebrow seeing her garbed in but a towel and he grinned. "My love, your attire is quite fetching, but I do not think the Dominus would approve of our meeting under these circumstances." Then seeing her face, he quickly amended his tone. "What is it, Lara?"

"I met Kol upon the Dream Plain tonight, Kaliq. We talked and I told him in no uncertain terms I would not return to the Dark Lands. He threatened Magnus and the children. I told him I would kill him if he touched them. But then suddenly he was by my side, touching me, kissing me. And…" She hesitated, going very pale. "He…he…"

"Say no more, my love, I understand," the Shadow Prince said. "You do not have to kill him, for I will. I have done something extremely foolish and underestimated his powers, even bottled up in Kolbyr as he is."

"Kaliq, how could this have happened upon the Dream Plain? He should not have been able to touch me at all, yet he did," Lara said.

"He took the power of an incubus into him," the prince said. "They are creatures of the darkness who can make reality of dreams. Your encounter would have killed it once Kol awoke, but he will undoubtedly have another he can use."

"Kaliq, he is so determined to regain my person," Lara told the Shadow Prince. "I am actually afraid of him, which I never was before."

"You are wise to fear evil. Did you tell Magnus of your dream?" the prince asked.

"I told him I could not remember it," Lara answered. "I do not know if he believed me. I have never really lied to him. I wish I had had Andraste with me. I think I would have sliced Kol's head from his shoulders but I could not have, could I?"

"If you treat with him again," Kaliq advised, "you must purge yourself of all emotions, Lara, my love. He and his incubus grew stronger because they fed off of your anger and then your fear," the prince explained. "The Dream Plain is neutral, but even it can be set awry by intense feelings."

"I will never deal with him upon the Dream Plain again," Lara

said firmly. "He is too dangerous there, especially if I am prevented from fighting back. Kaliq, he made me feel pleasures!
He is evil incarnate. He must die so that the Dark Lands can be
set into even greater confusion than the birth of his sons caused.
No one will dare to kill either of the twins, so they will have to
wait until the Book of Rule dictates which of them is to be the
next Twilight Lord. Alfrigg will see to it, for he is a stickler
about the rules, and his dwarfs will follow his lead. The giants
may be swayed to relinquish their loyalty to the Dark Lands if
Kol is dead and we can offer them another home. It is the Wolfyn
that I am most concerned about, for I suspect their fealty is to
themselves first."

Kaliq nodded in agreement. "Aye," he said, "the Wolfyn will
either challenge the Twilight twins for supremacy of the Dark
Lands or they will run rampant out of that land to cause havoc
among Terah or Hetar. They have no true civilization. They
exist solely to feed their various appetites." He grew thoughtful for several long moments. "The clan families have not
expanded their territories from those which Magnus Hauk gave
them, have they?" Kaliq asked Lara.

"Nay, they have not, for each of them received double the
lands that they had held in the old Outlands. Why?"

"If the last of the Forest Giants would relinquish their loyalty
to Kol, then we could settle them in the forests beneath the
mountains of the Dark Lands. It is part of Terah's New
Outlands. The clan families do not stray from their own territories. They are not explorers by nature. And Terah is so large
in land mass that even your husband does not know all he pos-

sesses, or what or who exists in those far places. We could resettle the giants in those far woods and as they are a solitary people, who would even know?"

"From the little Og has told us I do not believe that Skrymir and his giants will slough off their loyalty to Kol, but once he is gone from the picture it could be a different matter altogether," Lara responded. "These giants are not warlike by nature. I do not believe they will want to involve themselves in the quarrel that will erupt between the factions supporting Kolbein and Kolgrim. It will be many years before either is old enough to take up their father's mantle."

"Then we are agreed," Kaliq said quietly. "Kol must, like a poisonous viper, be defanged if we are to preserve peace in our world."

Lara nodded but then she said, "Kaliq, you know far more than you tell. Is it meant that Magnus Hauk remain my husband? If Kol can indeed reach out to him, the union I treasure can be destroyed. I do not want my family torn apart because of this damned destiny with which I have been saddled. It isn't fair, Kaliq, and while I know that life is not always fair, does not my sacrifice earn me a small bit of happiness?"

The prince sighed. "There is something your mother has not told you, Lara, but you should know. Now that we have learned that you are more faerie than mortal it is a surety that you will live far beyond a mortal's lifespan. You will be forced to stand by and watch those about you grow old, and eventually die. But the faerie race does not really grow old as mortals do. When you met your grandmother before she faded away you found her beautiful, yet she was hundreds of years old. You may not live as long as Maeve or your mother, Ilona, for you are not pure faerie, but you will live far longer than any mortal and you will have other loves in your life, Lara. For now, however, be certain that Magnus Hauk will love you until his death."

Lara was thoughtful for a moment and then she smiled at him. "I cannot believe you have given me a straight answer, Kaliq. Usually when I ask questions like that you speak to me in riddles," she gently teased him.

He chuckled but then grew serious. "This was not a time for being cryptic," he said. "There is going to be a war, Lara. We cannot escape it for Kol will not allow it. His plans are twofold. He desires conquest to spread his darkness and evil. And he wants you back and thinks that he can make you believe that if you will come back, he will cease warring. He will not, however. I believe he will attack Hetar first as a warning to you. He hopes if he does, you will bargain with him to save Terah, but of course he means to have Terah, too. We cannot stop him, but we can keep it brief, my love."

"I want to destroy his power," Lara said, her voice gone hard.

"I do not see how that is possible," Kaliq replied. "We cannot allow you to return to the Dark Lands. It is far too dangerous."

"Then give me the power to do it upon the Dream Plain!" Lara begged him.

"That will take time," Kaliq told her. "The Keepers of the Dream Plain must be consulted and give permission." She would not destroy Kol. *He would!*

"If they gave Kol permission to assault me on their territory then surely they will give me permission to slay him," Lara responded angrily.

"It is not likely the Dream Plain Keepers gave him any such permission," the prince told her. "Do you really believe Kol would even ask such a thing?"

"I would slay Kol myself," Lara said grimly. "Please, Kaliq, you must speak to the Keepers of the Dream Plain. I cannot go into the Dark Lands again while Kol lives and I am terrified of Magnus learning what has happened to me. If I am indeed to have a long faerie life then I would remain with the man I love for as long as he remains alive."

"I will speak with the Keepers of the Dream Plain, but I do not believe they will give you permission to kill another, even one as evil as Kol, within their territory," he told her.

"Then you must allow Kol to come forth from the Dark Lands," Lara said. "You know as well as I do that he will continue to call to me until he gets his way or until I kill him. I will not go to him willingly again, but after what happened tonight I do not know what he will do and neither do you. If I sleep I cannot escape him now. And I must sleep sometime, Kaliq."

"I will not persuade the Keepers to allow you permission to slay him there, but I will see if there is some way in which they can prevent him from entering there and disturbing your rest," the Shadow Prince promised.

Lara nodded. "Very well," she said quietly. "If I cannot have one, I must be satisfied with the other. Thank you, my dearest friend. Without you as my mentor I do not know what would happen to me."

"I should go," he said softly, running a finger across the top of her towel, a small smile tugging at the corners of his mouth.

"Aye," Lara agreed, then she suddenly grinned at him. "I do not believe I have ever consulted with anyone attired thusly."

"It is a most fetching garment, but I suspect Magnus would not approve. And how is it that you are more concerned he learn about Kol than you standing here in your towel discoursing upon weighty matters with me?"

"Good night, Kaliq," Lara said, and she wafted herself back to her bedchamber where her husband lay sleeping. As she did, she could hear the echo of Kaliq's laughter and she smiled. *What would she do without him?* she wondered. From the moment he had taken her from the desert, under his tutelage her life had been amazing. Once, he had warned her not to fall in love with him, but it was he who loved her and Lara knew it. He would have liked nothing better than for her to live by his side at Shunnar, but Lara could never have been content without children nor without the constant adventure her life had become. Tossing her towel aside she crept into bed next to Magnus Hauk.

He stirred and rolled over, his arms enclosing her. "Did you speak with Kaliq garbed only in your towel?" he surprised her by asking.

"How do you know I was speaking with Kaliq?" she countered, snuggling against him. "Have you developed the gift of second sight?"

"I do not sleep soundly if you are not by my side," he said. "I awoke and you were not here. I arose and you were not in your bath although I could see you had been. I assumed that you had retreated to your private chamber and called the prince to you. Am I wrong, Lara?"

"Nay, you are not," she answered.

"What was the nightmare that upset you so much?" he asked her softly, his kiss brushing her brow.

She could continue to lie to him, Lara thought, but Magnus would not believe her; or she could tell him a truth. Not *the truth*, but *a truth*. "I dreamed I was attacked upon the Dream Plain. It was very frightening because the Dream Plain is a neutral place and such things are not allowed to happen there. I needed to consult with Kaliq. He will speak with the Keepers of the Dream Plain for he believes an incubus managed to slip onto the Plain. It must be caught, of course, and punished or disposed of quickly. That, of course, is the province of the Keepers to decide. Forgive me for not telling you immediately, but I was so startled by what had happened I knew I must calm myself first and then go and speak with Kaliq." Lara kissed her husband's shoulder.

"What is this incubus?" the Dominus wanted to know.

"A small demon who likes to enter your dreams, change them and then feed off the emotions they create within their victims," Lara told him.

"Oh," was all he said, then, "But what were you dreaming about before this incubus crept into your dreams?"

"I honestly don't remember," Lara said casually. "Oh, Magnus, let us not discuss this any further. It was a most disturbing incident. I do not want to relive it."

"I am sorry, my darling," he apologized and kissed her lips as she raised her face to him. The kiss deepened, tongues entwined and he groaned, rolling her onto her back.

Lara took his face between her two hands. "I want to take pleasures with you, my husband," she told him. Not *want,* she thought. She *needed* him. Remembering how Kaliq had wiped away the horrors of her time in the Dark Lands, Lara now sought to wipe away Kol's earlier assault on her. Kol sought to possess and control her. But Magnus sought to give and take pleasures with her because he truly loved his wife. She kissed his mouth, his nose, his cheeks, his eyelids. *She loved him!* And she would not allow the Twilight Lord to destroy what was between them.

Magnus let his hands roam over her lithe body. He caressed every inch of her, his fingertips moving seemingly from memory. And then his lips began to follow the trail of delicate shivers left behind by his fingers. They slid down the curve of her slender throat, lingering in the faintly shadowed hollow to feel the thrumming of the blood coursing through her veins. His dark golden head lay for several long moments upon her chest, while he inhaled the familiar fragrance of her body. He felt her fingers tangling in his thick hair, lightly massaging his scalp.

Her beautiful breasts beckoned him onward and his mouth closed over a nipple. He suckled hungrily, grazing the tender flesh lightly with his teeth. She murmured low.

He moved one hand down to slip between her legs, stroking the soft flesh of her inner thighs, trailing down the narrow slit dividing her nether lips, pushing past them. Locating the sensitive little nub of her he teased it, and all the while he sucked on her nipple.

Lara sighed. She would not forget the nightmare in which Kol attacked her but lying now in her husband's arms as he made tender love to her, it receded into the dimness of her mind as he pushed two fingers into her love sheath. His hand was quickly drenched with her juices as he swirled them about within her tight, hot sheath. He moved his head from one breast to the other now and his fingers moved in rhythm with his lips as he pleasured her slowly, gently until she was writhing with her building hunger and he could no longer keep from joining himself with her.

"Oh yes, my darling!" Lara cried as he withdrew his fingers and mounted her. She reached for his love rod, guiding it eagerly into her sheath, sighing as he thrust deep.

Her slender limbs wrapped themselves about him as he drove deeper and deeper and deeper until Lara was almost mindless with the joy his passion engendered within her. She shuddered with her pleasure, her hands caressing his long lean body.

Magnus Hauk slowed his pace, drawing himself almost all the way out of her sheath and then slowly, slowly, pushing himself back inside her heated body. His mouth took hers in a lingering kiss that left them both breathless. "I love you, my faerie wife, and I will allow no one to harm you, awake or dreaming," he told her.

She almost wept at his declaration. If only he knew how helpless he really was among those who possessed magic. But this declaration of his love was wonderful. She tightened the muscles of her sheath about him and he groaned with delight as his juices spilled forth. What a pity, Lara thought, as she allowed herself to drift away surrounded by his arms and his love, that this was not the night to create a son for him. But that time would come, she vowed, and then she cried his name aloud as the final pleasure washed over her, leaving her weak and content.

They slept the few hours remaining of the night. It was to be their last peaceful moment for some time, for in the morning the Dominus's brother-in-law Corrado brought word that the Hetarian fleet was preparing to set sail for Terah.

CORRADO, MARRIED to the Dominus's youngest and favorite sister, Sirvat, had been lurking off the coast of Hetar, something Terahns never did. They always met their trading partners at the midpoint of the Sea of Sagitta which separated the two kingdoms. But recently with the talk of war Corrado had taken it upon himself to spy on Hetar and Lara had aided him by making the small vessel he was sailing invisible. He had gone into the harbor where the Hetarian ships were being assembled and seen the men, the supplies and the weapons being loaded upon the waiting vessels. Then he had beached his own small craft in a hidden cove and walked into the village of the Coastal Kings where he sat in a tavern and listened to the talk about him.

"And what is the talk?" Lara asked him as they sat in the Domina's private dayroom. "Is their emperor still propagating his lies about Terah?"

"Aye, but then you would have expected it, Domina," Corrado replied. "But I learned a great deal more as I ate a rather tasty fish stew. The women of Hetar are in rebellion over Gaius Prospero's latest campaign. They will do nothing to help their men. The Pleasure Houses in The City have opened their doors to the women who would come to shelter there and have refused service to all men. The new headmistress of the Pleasure Guilds is being made to look useless, for Lady Gillian is one of the leaders of this movement and she is greatly respected due to her many years in power, as well as her reputation for kindness and fairness. The women say that the emperor instigates wars, claiming that Hetar is in danger when it is not, and promises riches to everyone, yet the common folk of Hetar grow poorer with each of these misadventures. What is worse, they claim, is that their men are being killed off and the women and children are being left to fend for themselves. What kind of a world is Hetar that families do not care for one another when they lose members? Profit and acquisition seem to be their only values.

"The poor are being swept up to serve in many capacities. The men, all but the truly old, are being sent to the ships; the women and children go to the factories and to the farms in the Outlands. They are no better than slaves now. Hetar, not being a sea-faring nation but for the Coastal Kings who traded with us, is attempting to set to sea with a group of inexperienced men. If any storms should hit while they are afloat, I fear many lives will be lost," Corrado concluded. "This emperor of theirs must be totally mad to even attempt such folly."

"It was very brave of you to go into the tavern and listen, Corrado," Lara told him. "Did you learn the date they have scheduled to sail forth?"

"They were to sail in three days' time, Domina."

"So with any luck, they are three days behind you," Magnus Hauk said.

Corrado laughed. "They would need a great deal of good

fortune, my lord. More than likely they are still struggling out of the harbor of the Coastal Kings who have refused to partake in this venture. They have trained the more intelligent among the Hetarians to manage the ships, but will not sail with them. New ships had to be built to transport men and weapons. They found the merchant ships would not do, and besides, the captains of those merchant ships would not put them in the hands of strangers, especially as those ships are alive, and house sea spirits."

"I will contact my mother and have her raise the fog bank off our coastline," Lara said to her husband. "They will get no closer than a hundred miles." She hurried off to her private chamber, and pouring water from a stone pitcher into her golden reflecting bowl Lara looked into the crystal liquid and called to her mother to come to her.

"Good morning, darling!" Ilona's voice echoed about the chamber.

"Hetar has set sail or is attempting to, Mother," Lara told her parent. "The emperor could not be deterred in his foolishness. Will you set the fog you promised Magnus a hundred miles off the coast, please?"

"Oh, I can do much better than that," Ilona chuckled. "Within the hour all of Hetar's little fleet will be thoroughly encased in a fog as thick as a mutton stew. The only way they will be able to escape it will be if they become turned about and are sailing toward Hetar." She laughed merrily. "And I believe I shall even conjure up a few fearsome sea monsters to frighten them even further."

"Don't hurt them, Mother," Lara said. "Their ships are peopled by fools, incompetents and innocents."

"I shall let them sail about in the fog until their water and foodstuffs are almost gone," Ilona said. "Then perhaps one fierce storm to buffet them the night long and they will be ready to return home, for they will be well terrified at that point. With their water and food gone they will be glad to see Hetarian shores again. I doubt Gaius Prospero can get them back to sea for another year, if then," Ilona chortled.

"And it will certainly prove a costly venture that yields absolutely no return," Lara noted. "Thank you, Mother."

The queen of the Forest Faeries flashed her daughter a brilliant smile and then was gone from the surface of the reflecting bowl, and when Lara waved her hand over the vessel the water itself vanished from the bowl leaving it completely dry. Lara placed it back on its shelf and went to find her husband, so she might relate to him her mother's plans for the Hetarian fleet.

Both Magnus Hauk and Corrado laughed heartily when Lara told them her mother would send several sea monsters to be clearly seen by the Hetarian ships.

"They are sure to wet themselves," Corrado chuckled. "There won't be a dry pair of breeches to be had and their ships will stink of piss."

Within the hour as Ilona had promised, the Hetarian fleet found itself encased in a thick fog. The watchtowers along the Terahn coast reported that they could see a thick wall of gray sitting atop the horizon. Aboard the Hetarian ships there was consternation. There should be no fog upon the sea at this time of year, yet the mist was so thick they could not see a hand before their faces, let alone another vessel. Several ships hit one another over the next few hours. And then night came.

The sea surrounding them was flat. They could hear nothing but murmuring sounds of confusion coming from the ships around them. The sky was not visible at all, so there were no stars by which they might plot their course. And all about them an eerie silence prevailed. Fifteen ships had set sail, each carrying a full crew of five hundred Mercenaries, and eighty Crusader Knights. Once they reached Terah and sent back word, another fifteen ships would follow them. Over the next ten days three of the Hetarian ships escaped the fog only to find themselves back where they had started. Their inexperienced captains drew straws and two of the ships returned into the fog to seek the rest of the fleet while the third ship remained skirting the edges of the mist.

Aboard the fog-bound ships, panic began to ensue as the rations grew smaller and the water barrels began to empty. Reaching Terah was no longer an option for the Hetarians. Escaping the fog that encased them was. The air about them remained still and hot. There was not the faintest hint of a breeze and even breathing became difficult. Over the last few days the inhabitants of the ships had been badly frightened at various times by great sea dragons, some with blue and green scales, others with red and green scales, and all with long graceful necks and heads with small horns, rising from the sea around them to peer curiously down upon the vessels bobbing in the calm waters. Several of these monsters nibbled upon the ships' masts. And one mercenary leaning over the side of his ship puking his supper suddenly found himself face-to-face with a beast who swallowed him whole and then regurgitated the man back onto the deck with a disgusted snort. Both the mercenary and the sailor who had been next to him died of their terror, to the consternation of those about them.

And then early one evening, lightning began to blaze in the foggy skies. Thunder rolled across the sea as it began to rise and roil. Darkness fell and the storm became ferocious. The Hetarian fleet was tossed upon the waters, up one side and down another. Enormous waves crashed over the ships. The men were unable to control their vessels, and one by one they sank beneath the waves, carrying all who had embarked with the fleet to their deaths.

The only ship to survive was the single one that had remained outside the fog. It had seen the lightning and heard the thunder within the thick gray mist, but the sea surrounding that one ship had remained calm. When the morning came, the sunrise splashing across the blue waters of the now peaceful Sagitta and tinting the gentle waves golden, the sailors upon the surviving vessel saw to their horror that the waters were strewn with the wreckage of the fourteen other ships and the bodies of all those who had sailed upon them. The wind in its favor, the remaining ship returned to its port in the harbor of the Coastal Kings to report what had happened.

WHEN KING ARCHERON, the emperor's governor of the former Coastal Kingdom, now the Coastal Province, heard the tale told him by the captain of the surviving vessel, he smiled grimly. He had warned Gaius Prospero not to embark upon this ridiculous venture. Terah was no danger to Hetar and with Lara as wife to its ruler, it was certain to be protected by strong magic. Archeron grew angry.

"Eight thousand four hundred men lost to the sea, dead because of this ridiculous venture! Seven thousand mercenaries! Eleven hundred and twenty Crusader Knights, and two hundred and eighty incompetent men forced to sail ships they did not know how to sail!" the Coastal King raged.

"You must send a faerie post to the emperor," one of his fellow kings said cautiously. "He must be advised not to allow the second half of the fleet to sail."

"Will he listen?" another king asked nervously.

"Probably not," Archeron answered, "but I will not give the order sending them to their certain deaths. We all know Terah is no danger to us. Now we also know that strong magic is protecting it from any attack by Hetar. That fog bank that arose and surrounded those ships was no natural occurrence. And the storm that destroyed the fleet? Who among us has ever faced a fierce storm at sea amid a thick fog? I will write to the emperor in the strongest terms that his attempt to conquer Terah must be abandoned."

"If the women in The City learned of what has happened it might save the other half of the fleet," the king named Balasi ventured softly. He was not known as a brave man, so they were all surprised to hear his suggestion. "They say this movement against the war is very strong and that the emperor hoped a quick and easy victory against Terah would silence it for good. But when word of this disaster is made known, who knows what the women will do, Brother Archeron?"

The other kings nodded in agreement.

"I would protect the remaining men of the fleet," Archeron said. "Are the rest of you brave enough to support me in this matter? Or do I stand alone?"

"We will support you," Balasi replied, and the other kings murmured, "Aye!"

"Can your son, Arcas, help us at all?" King Pelias asked Archeron.

"I will not ask him," Archeron responded. "You all know I have disowned him. I have no son. And besides, I have it on the best authority that he spies for Lord Jonah, the emperor's right hand. Given the opportunity, Arcas would betray us all once again as he has betrayed us in the past. Where is my secretary?"

A hovering servant hurried to fetch Archeron's secretary. When the man had come, Archeron dictated a terse letter to Gaius Prospero informing him of the disaster visited upon the Hetarian fleet. He told the emperor in no uncertain terms that he would not give the order to the remaining fleet to embark to their own doom, for Terah was obviously protected by great magic. And all of the Coastal Kings were in agreement with him. If Gaius Prospero wanted to conquer Terah he would have to find another way. When the letter had been written and signed by all the Coastal Kings, it was dispatched by faerie post to The City.

Upon reading Archeron's missive, Gaius Prospero flung the parchment from him, and began to rant. "He dares to say he and his fellow kings will not obey my orders? It is treason! Perhaps it is time I kicked his dignified ass from his throne and replaced him with Arcas. I did after all promise the weasel that he would serve me as governor of the province one day. At least I can control Arcas."

"My good lord," Jonah murmured, "I know how upset you must surely be by this betrayal of your governor, but Arcas is indeed a fool, as you have so often said. If you sent him to the Coastal Province the kings would not obey him and I am quite certain Archeron himself would cut his son's throat. I regret to tell you that word of this disaster is already spreading throughout The City. We will have to do all we can to put down Lady Gillian and her women. This is a terrible loss for Hetar. This is not seven wagons of dead driven into The City. This is over eight thousand men, mostly Mercenaries and Crusader Knights. This is the cream of our defense and now it has been halved."

"It is that damned faerie woman again!" the emperor snapped. "If I had known what troubles that exquisite girl I once sold was going to create for me, I would have taken my pleasure of her and seen her strangled afterwards!"

"Alas, my lord, hindsight is no real gift," Jonah said dryly.

Gaius Prospero looked sharply at his good right hand, but Jonah's face was its usual emotionless mask. The emperor wondered if Vilia took pleasures with her new husband. He somehow could not see Jonah sweaty with passion.

There was a soft knock upon the door and Jonah's servant, Lionel, entered. "Forgive me, my lord emperor, my lord, for interrupting, but an urgent message has just been brought from Squire Darah of the Midlands."

"What is it?" Gaius Prospero demanded to know.

Lionel beckoned to a shadowed figure in the door and a man entered into the chamber. "My lord, the messenger," Lionel said.

"Well, what have you to say?" Gaius Prospero shouted impatiently.

"My master, Squire Darah, sends me to tell you that creatures he believes to be Wolfyn are streaming forth from the forest and laying waste to our Midlands. Fields are being fired, livestock slaughtered, women and children carried off. Squire Darah requests your aid, my lord emperor. We are doing our best to hold them off, but our men are few, and most are old. They cannot fight these creatures."

Gaius Prospero looked surprised. "I thought the Wolfyn were but a legend meant to frighten naughty children," he said to Jonah.

"All legend is rooted in fact, my lord," Jonah answered. This was not good. He had hoped to use the disaster in the Coastal Province to help him unseat Gaius Prospero.

"I cannot help your master," Gaius Prospero finally said. "All of our mercenaries are in the Coastal Kingdom, for the invasion has begun. There are less than a thousand Crusader Knights here in The City and they are mostly elderly. Besides, we will need them to defend us should these Wolfyn come here."

Squire Darah's messenger look both outraged and devastated.

"What the emperor means," Jonah quickly put in, "is that we must prepare The City for any attack by these Wolfyn, but we could spare you one hundred Crusader Knights to help you mount your own defenses and train your few men. Is that not so, my lord?" Jonah looked encouragingly at the emperor.

And to his credit Gaius Prospero understood his good right

hand. "Yes! Yes! Of course I will send you a small force to help out," he said.

The Squire's messenger knelt and kissed the emperor's hand fervently. "Thank you, my lord! Thank you!"

"Lionel," Jonah said sharply. "Make the arrangements."

"Yes, my lord," came the answer. Lionel escorted the messenger out.

"Well, now," Gaius Prospero said, "what mischief is this and why did the Forest Lords not warn us of this new peril? We must quickly recall our forces from the coast. And send to Lord Enda, the Head Forester, for an explanation."

"At once, my lord," Jonah said. He bowed to his master and then hurried out. He had to apprise Vilia of this new and sudden danger that faced them all. They would have to decide how to use it to their own best advantage. Gaius Prospero's time was fast coming to an end. Jonah smiled one of his rare smiles. He could almost taste the power that would soon be his.

14

"HOW COULD YOU allow all those men to die?" Lara demanded of her mother. She had just learned the depth of the tragedy that had afflicted the Hetarian fleet.

"You have one weakness, my daughter," Ilona replied. "You yet have mortal compassion in your heart, even for your enemies. Destroying that fleet was necessary to protect Terah. And only half the fleet had put to sea. The second half was meant to follow after Hetar reached Terah."

"Was my father among those you slew?" Lara asked.

"Nay. He was on the vessel that was spared," Ilona said. "I suppose some part of me still cares for him or perhaps my love for you caused me to keep him safe."

"Well, some good has come of it all," Magnus Hauk said.

"What possible good could come from the deaths of over eight thousand men?" Lara wanted to know.

"Hetar is now very afraid of us," the Dominus replied. "They have recalled their armies. It is not likely they will consider attacking us again until the memory of what has happened fades from their history."

"You have a greater problem now," Ilona said. "The reason Hetar recalled their troops is that they cannot fight a war on two fronts. The Twilight Lord has sent the Wolfyn into Hetar. He put them by means of his magic into the forest and from there they spread out into the Midlands. The City is already scrambling to protect itself."

Lara grew pale, and feeling faint, clutched at a chair to steady herself.

Seeing this the Dominus asked, "What is it, my darling? What is distressing you so?" He reached out to put an arm about her, but Lara pulled away.

Mother! She spoke silently to her parent. *My secret cannot be kept any longer. Kol is following through on his threat, and eventually he and Magnus will meet. He will tell the Dominus of our time together, of the sons I bore him, and even if I deny it Magnus will always have some doubts. It is the nature of mortal man, and my husband may never trust me again. I must tell him of that lost time, for if I do not he will always believe me untruthful.*

Do not tell him quite yet, Ilona said. *Not until you are carrying his son. That way what will at first seem to him a betrayal will be softened.*

We are about to be forced into a terrible war. Is this really the time to give Magnus his son? Lara asked her mother.

Under the circumstances, it is the best time, Ilona told her daughter. *And Kaliq and I will explain to Magnus why this part of your destiny was necessary, not so much for you, but for our worlds. He may not be happy with what has happened, but it will seem a less treacherous act.*

Last night we had a most passionate encounter, and I thought it was a perfect moment to conceive a son were it not for this threat of war, Lara admitted to her mother.

Ilona looked closely at her daughter, and then she smiled. *It was a perfect moment,* she said with a small emphatic smile. *If we love, sometimes the moment is chosen for us.*

Do you mean... Oh, Mother, thank you!

"Are you all right, my darling?" the Dominus asked his wife.

Lara nodded in the affirmative. "I just grew dizzy for a moment," she said.

Immediately Magnus Hauk became alert. "Do you think... Is it possible?" He didn't dare to finish the sentence. But his face was hopeful.

Lara blushed. "Perhaps," she said. "My mother seems to think so."

"It would certainly account for your overreaction to the sinking of Hetar's fleet," Ilona remarked. "I mean, really Lara, these people were out to violate Terah's sovereignty and attack your people. Surely you remember what happened the last time Hetar annexed territory that was not their own. The Tormod and the Piaras clan families suffered greatly."

"It is a son?" he asked.

"It will be a son," Lara promised her husband. "Mother, we need Kaliq now."

"Now?" Ilona questioned her daughter sharply.

"Now," Lara replied.

Kaliq! Come to us! the queen called and when the prince appeared, his white robes swirling about him, Ilona silently explained the discussion that had taken place earlier between her and Lara.

And she would tell him now of Kol? the prince said.

She has no choice, Ilona responded. *Terah will need to help Hetar and to do that both Lara and Magnus must stand together. My daughter cannot do that if she is living in fear of Kol revealing his relationship with her. He hopes by doing so to separate Lara from Magnus. To give her no choice but to return to him.*

Even if Lara lost Magnus, the prince said, *she would never return to Kol.*

I know that and you know that, Ilona answered, *but Kol, for all his evil, is in love.*

Lara greeted the prince with a kiss upon the cheek, then she invited them all to sit down. "My lord," she addressed her husband, "there is something that you must know. I have not wanted to tell you this, for I fear your love for me will die once you have learned it. But I have never intentionally lied to you, Magnus. And I cannot now, no matter the consequences." She reached out and took his big hand between her two small ones. "You know of the Dark Lands beyond the New Outlands. That placed is ruled by pure evil in the person of a creature known as the Twilight Lord."

Magnus Hauk remained silent, listening carefully, absorbing her words.

"I was lost to you for a year, Magnus, although your memory of that time has been taken from you to protect me, to protect you, to protect us all. Taken from everyone in both Hetar and Terah. Taken even from myself, for a time. When I was returned to the New Outlands from whence I was stolen, it appeared to you, to everyone, that you had come to bring me and the children home as you always did. But the year before that the Munin lords came in the night and stole my memories from me and then when I awakened I was in the bed of Kol, the Twilight Lord."

"How can this be?" Magnus Hauk wanted to know.

"In time I will do my best to explain it," Lara said. "For now just let me tell the tale. Without my memories I knew not who I was. Kol told me I was his mate and wove a pretty story about how that had come about. The Twilight Lords are guided by something known as the Book of Rule. Kol was told by the Book of Rule that his mate—she who would give him a son— was a faerie woman. Twilight Lords only sire a single son a generation. He had looked into the reflecting bowl and seen me many times. He interpreted that to mean that I was the faerie woman meant to be his mate."

"Did you give him his son?" the Dominus asked her in a tight voice.

"It was part of my destiny to do so," Lara said, aching at the hurt and anger she saw in his turquoise eyes. "But before my time came, Kaliq came, and had the Munin restore all of my memories. I was horrified by where I was. More horrified at my growing belly. And most horrified by the fact that this bit of my destiny would hurt you should you ever learn. I never wanted you to know."

Magnus Hauk looked at the prince and at his mother-in-law. "Tell me what purpose was served by whoring my wife to another?" he asked them coldly.

Ilona looked infuriated by his words, but wisely held her tongue.

Kaliq, however, spoke calmly to the Dominus. "At intervals of several hundred years," he began, "the balance between the light and the dark begins to shift to the darkness. And when that happens something must be done to restore that balance. The last time this happened, Terah was almost rent asunder by the sorcerer Usi. Only the bravery of Geltruda saved your land and your people. And it was five hundred years before Lara came to you and removed the curse of Usi completely. This Twilight Lord is Usi's direct descendant, Magnus. The Book of Rule was written by Usi. He could look into the future, which he did, and see what was necessary."

"But why my wife? Are there not others like Lara who might have served this purpose?" the Dominus asked.

"There are indeed others, but none as pure of heart and as strong of will as Lara. None who could do what needed to be done," Kaliq said.

"What needed to be done that only Lara might do?" Magnus demanded.

"When I came and restored her memories," Kaliq responded, "and explained to her that only a single son was born each generation to the Twilight Lord and why, Lara cast a spell that separated the infant in her womb and created of it twin boys. When they were born, their births created chaos in the Dark Lands, which we hoped would prevent Kol's plans to dominate our worlds. You see, no one at the birth could recall which of the twins was born first. They were identical, of course. Their father has now marked them so he may tell them apart, but with each birthday they celebrate those marks shall be faded entirely in order to keep the confusion. No prince of the Twilight may be harmed in any way by their own, and so Kol is forced to raise both of his sons."

"But why was it necessary that Lara bear these children? And how could she conceive if she did not love him?" Magnus wanted to know. He was trying to understand for although he could barely look at his wife now a quick glance revealed her pain.

"That was one of the many reasons her memories were stolen from her. She did not know she was faerie or remember faerie ways," Ilona quickly put in. "She became like any mortal female and Kol was fated to impregnate her."

"And remember, Magnus," Kaliq said, "that the Book of Rule directed this." *Fool!* Kaliq thought. *You do not deserve her, but she loves you, and so I will do whatever I have to do to make this right between you.*

The Dominus turned to his wife, his face a mask of anguish. "Why do you tell me this now, Lara?" he asked her. "You have kept your secret since your return. Why now?"

She reached out to touch him, but he drew away and it was like a knife to her heart. Curse Kol of the Twilight! If only he had accepted that she was not his, nor would she ever return. But instead he was behaving like a spoiled child; if he could not have Lara then no other man would. "Kaliq felt the memories of my time in the Dark Lands would be too painful for me to bear. He arranged to have those memories taken by the Munin lords and stored away in their vault beneath the Obscura. But Kol's memories were intact and he began to invade my dreams, attempting to reach me upon the Dream Plain. I did not know who was haunting me, or why, but I realized something was wrong. That is why I went to Kaliq. He explained he had taken certain memories from me that would pain me and make our life together difficult. But I insisted those memories be returned, for I could not fight whoever was trying to get to me upon the Dream Plain without full knowledge of what had happened to me in the first place.

"The knowing has been painful to me because I knew how hurtful it would be to you, Magnus. Know that the creature I am did not betray you. I love you and I always will love you, my dear lord. I never knew that this terrible trial that was visited upon me would be a part of my destiny. I could not have imagined such a thing. Kaliq has said that the worst of it is now over. I should have never shared this with you but that the Twilight Lord has refused to accept that I do not love him, nor want him, nor will I return to the Dark Lands by his side. He has begun a war with Hetar who would have begun a war with us. And now we must go to Hetar's aid, Magnus."

"But why," he demanded again, "did you choose this time to share your misadventure with me, Lara?"

"Kol threatened to seek you out upon the Dream Plain and tell you of that lost year," Lara explained. "I thought it better you learned of it from me than from that evil creature. My destiny has not been an easy one, Magnus, and it is not yet totally fulfilled. Ask me what you will about that year. Satisfy your curiosity."

"You do not ask my forgiveness," he said softly and he heard Ilona gasp, shocked.

"Do I need your forgiveness, my lord?" Lara answered him in equally soft tones. "I did not know what was planned to happen to me. I should have never gone willingly into the Dark Lands to be the Twilight Lord's mate. I did not even have the memories of that terrible year until Kol began to haunt me and I needed to have them back so I might do battle with him. Why do I need your forgiveness?"

"Could you not have protected her better?" Magnus Hauk demanded angrily of the prince. "You love her, too. I know that, and yet you let that damned evil reach out to Lara. Why did you not take better care of her? Now we must both contend with the memories of that year and I don't know if it can ever be the same between us."

"Ohh, arrogant mortal!" Ilona exploded with her anger. "How dare you whine over your wounded pride when my daughter has done our worlds such a great and terrible service? Though Kaliq penned the Twilight Lord in his castle for a hundred years and took away his reflecting bowls, Kol is yet managing to give orders to his minions from his castle. Regretfully we cannot put evil to sleep for that century. The balance would be destroyed entirely, but you do not understand that, do you?" Her green eyes were icy with her disdain. "If my daughter did not love you so deeply I should turn you to stone, Magnus Hauk! Beware if you should make my daughter unhappy!" And then in a clap of thunder and a flash of light, Ilona, queen of the Forest Faeries, was gone in a burst of deep purple smoke which indicated her anger at her son-in-law.

"Magnus," Kaliq said gently, "none of what has happened is

Lara's fault nor is it of her making. Your pride is hurt as any man's would be, but you cannot hold this against her, my friend. She loves you."

"Your sons," the Dominus said to his wife. "How were you able to leave them so easily? You make a habit of leaving your children, I note."

If he had struck her he could not have hurt her more. "I was only the means by which Kol's sons were birthed," Lara told him, her voice shaking. "They were not mine." Her eyes were filled with tears. "And I did not want them."

Magnus Hauk closed his eyes briefly. Her honesty touched him. Kaliq was correct. His pride had been hurt but it was not Lara's fault. Opening his eyes he reached out and pulled her into his arms. "Forgive me, Lara! I am a fool, but I love you so greatly that the thought of any other man possessing you is like a knife to my heart."

Feeling his strong arms about her Lara began to cry, her tears wetting his tunic front. "I am pained to have hurt you so, my husband," she sobbed. "Even though I didn't know what was to happen or what I was destined to do. You are my life, Magnus! And now I carry a new life, *our son,* within my womb. I do not want you angry at me and I do not wish to be angry at you." She clung to him and his arms tightened about her.

Knowing that they would now settle their differences Prince Kaliq stepped quietly into the shadows and disappeared. They never realized that he was gone, so wrapped up in each other were the Dominus and Domina of Terah. Lara caressed her husband's strong face with gentle fingers, her eyes devouring him. Magnus

Hauk stroked her golden hair tenderly, whispering small endearments into her ears as he did so. It was a hard truth for them to swallow, but they both realized that their love for one another was greater than the hurt each had suffered when Kol of the Twilight had involved himself in their lives. Their love would always be stronger than anything meant to harm them.

And having faced the hard truth of the lost year, Lara and Magnus decided together to tell no one else. They had Hetar to consider. Lara insisted on using her magic to go to Lady Gillian and learn what was really happening. The Dominus was concerned but his wife assured him that she would be safe. She was surprised that Gillian had not called to her for she had given her that privilege.

She found the retired headmistress of the Pleasure Guilds in her privy chamber. Gillian looked up surprised as Lara appeared in a burst of mauve smoke. "Tell me what is happening," Lara said by way of greeting. "If Terah is to help Hetar at this time I must have accurate information. Have the Wolfyn invaded The City yet or are they still rampaging about the Midlands?"

"Did you work your magic to destroy our fleet?" Gillian responded.

"No," Lara said. "And I did not know it would be done. My mother was simply to create a thick fog bank in which your ships would sail about until they ran out of water and supplies. They would then have been forced to return home. But then she created a great storm. I think she did it more to frighten your people," Lara lied to defend her mother for as appalled as she was by what Ilona had done, she still loved her. There was no need for Gillian or anyone else in Hetar to know the truth of the queen of the Forest Faeries' cruelty. "I am sorry, Gillian, but sadly in war lives are lost no matter our good intentions. This is why we must prevent war if it is at all possible."

Lady Gillian sighed. "The Wolfyn have not yet attempted to breach The City's walls and gates," she said. "The Celestial Actuary help the Midland folk, for no one else can. Most of our army is caught in the Coastal Province. The Crusader Knights remaining in The City are older men who have seen better days."

"And the emperor?" Lara asked.

"Holed up in the Golden District, reinforcing its defenses, of course. He is frantic, especially now that word of the fleet's demise has reached The City," Gillian replied. "I thought the Wolfyn were mythological creatures, Lara."

"Nay, they are all too real," Lara answered. "They made their home in the Dark Lands, which is ruled over by the Twilight Lord. His name is Kol and he means to begin a war that will eventually yield him both Hetar and Terah. He himself is penned by magic in his castle right now but he is capable of giving orders from there. He believes that Hetar is weak and easily taken, while Terah is stronger."

"Alas, Hetar *is* weak," Gillian said. "The Mercenaries and the Crusader Knights have become useless and exist only because of tradition."

"As long as The City remains locked and barred the Wolfyn should not be able to enter it. The Shadow Princes have cast a spell making it impregnable, but that knowledge is ours alone. We do not want Gaius Prospero feeling safe, for that would be foolish. Besides, without supplies from the Midlands the food will eventually run out and being safe behind these walls will not matter then," Lara said.

"But without aid from the Coastal Province and with no food, how can we prevail over these creatures? Over this Twilight Lord?"

"Your only hope is Terah," Lara told her. "The rightness of the Women's Movement that you have begun is now proving to be truth. Gaius Prospero must be removed from his imperial seat. What Hetar does about a new government is their decision, but the emperor cannot be allowed to rule any longer.

"You cannot hope to beat back the Wolfyn or any other of the Twilight Lord's minions. His armies are great, and are comprised of dwarfs and giants. The Wolfyn are the most frightening of his creatures, so he has sent them first to burn and loot and do rapine in order to terrify you. But when he finds The City is blocked to him he will destroy the forest and the Midlands, then move on to the coast. The desert is useless to him, and he is afraid of the Shadow Princes. They will be left in peace. In the end The City will be isolated. Terah will be his next objective after he has destroyed Hetar and brought it under his heel," Lara said.

"But how," Gillian asked, "can we stop him?"

"Here is where our women can help," Lara told her companion. "We have among our group several wives and daughters of Crusader Knights. Many will have been widowed when the fleet was destroyed. There are women among the Mercenaries now without husbands, fathers and sons. These women must convince those remaining of their men to work with Terah.

When the Wolfyn have gathered before The City, as they eventually will, we can catch them in a pincer movement. The remaining fighters in The City will march out to do battle with the Wolfyn while the Terahn forces come at them from the other side. Caught between us the Wolfyn will be crushed and defeated. The Twilight Lord's remaining armies will reconsider their position at that point."

"The emperor will never agree to work with Terah," Gillian said.

"Of course he won't, for he is a fool," Lara agreed. "This is where the women come in. They must force Gaius Prospero to do their bidding—and they can, Lady Gillian. The emperor would like to dismiss the women as he previously has done but too many of your men have died in pursuit of his dreams. We all need peace."

Lady Gillian considered Lara's words in silence for several long minutes. Finally she spoke. "Aye, we need peace and the prosperity that comes with it. Would your husband really aid Hetar even after we attempted to war with you? Why would he do that? What advantage does it give Terah over Hetar?"

"Aye, Magnus would aid you, for it is to all our benefit, not just Terah. We wish to live in peace, trading with you for our handcrafted and luxury goods as we always have, but other than that Terah wishes no communion with Hetar at this time."

Lady Gillian nodded and then she said, "What happened in the Outlands before Hetar invaded? The common folk do not question, Domina, but I know you were first wed to an Outland clan chief who was murdered by his brother."

"The plot to murder Vartan was instigated by Gaius Prospero,

who believed by killing him he would set the Outlands into confusion, making it easier to conquer them."

"But the Outlands were empty of people, of livestock, of
villages when Hetar pushed into it. Even the mines in the mountains were gone. What happened?"

"The Shadow Princes were not pleased with what Gaius
Prospero wanted to do. They took the clan families under their
protection, and as a final punishment for the emperor they
sealed the mines and raised up growth over them. It will be many
years before they are discovered again," Lara said. She didn't
really think it was necessary for Lady Gillian to know the entire
truth of the matter.

"The Shadow Princes are really the most powerful among us,
aren't they?" the older woman said softly.

"I believe they are," Lara agreed.

"You have great powers, too. Oh, you need not answer. I
remember the exquisite innocent you were the night Gaius
Prospero displayed you for sale," Lady Gillian reminisced. "Your
aura was light and beautiful. Now it shimmers with incredible
force. To have survived all you have survived, that strength had
to be already within you."

"You have the sight?" Lara asked, surprised.

Lady Gillian nodded. "That is how I knew you must not be
sold within The City," she answered. She paused and then said,
"I almost forgot! Kigva, a trusted servant of Lady Vilia, has been
attending our meetings. Since she is not a woman who makes
decisions on her own, I must assume she had been coming as
Vilia's spy, but to what purpose I am not entirely certain. I sense

that Lord Jonah is preparing to attempt to unseat Gaius Prospero and will use his failures against him with the magnates and the High Council. But why does Vilia's woman bother with us?"

"Perhaps Lord Jonah will use the Women's Movement against the emperor or perhaps he wants their support if they appear to be gaining momentum," Lara suggested.

"Lord Jonah's mother is my successor," Lady Gillian said. "Farah is no fool. Whatever she does will be to protect herself and her position. But so will Lady Vilia. She is a patient woman and willing to bide her time to gain her objective."

"If she is like many women," Lara considered, "she will be in silent competition with her mother-in-law to be her husband's chief advisor. It is just possible that we might win her over to our side if she believes it is to her own benefit. She may be Gaius Prospero's former wife but I will wager she yet has influence with him. She would be more of an advantage to us than Lady Farah. Can you arrange a meeting between us?"

"I can," Lady Gillian said. "When?"

"This time tomorrow night," Lara replied. "Now I must go, for Magnus worries when I am gone too long."

"I will try," the older woman said. "Do we have time though?"

"Not a great deal, but enough," Lara told her. And then with a nod she disappeared in a puff of mauve smoke.

When Lara told her husband of her meeting with Lady Gillian and the plan she had devised, he was well pleased. "I will go with you tomorrow night," he said.

"Why?" Lara wanted to know.

"Lady Vilia is a proud woman. While I believe she will respect you and listen to what you have to say, I think we would get quicker action from her if the Dominus of Terah were to ask for her aid. You must remember that this lady has been raised in a society where they are taught to revere their men. Time is of the essence for us, and if the Mercenaries and Crusader Knights remaining in The City are to be brought back up to their strength, then we must begin training them sooner than later."

"You are right!" Lara agreed. "I had not thought of that. I have been so busy strategizing I did not consider Lady Vilia's sensibilities. I am certain that your charm will win her over. But the question is, who will she win over? Gaius Prospero, her former husband, or Lord Jonah, her power-hungry new husband?"

"It doesn't matter as long as Hetar will ally with us to defeat the Twilight Lord," Magnus Hauk said. "And if Og can win over the giants, Kol will be truly weakened."

"I will ask him to meet with his sire upon the Dream Plain again," Lara answered. "But we must have something to offer Skrymir and his people. We cannot just ask for their aid and give nothing in return. The hilly lands that abut the Dark Lands are uninhabited and the clan families do not need them and are far from them anyway. Can I tell Og that you will offer those lands to Skrymir in exchange for his aid?"

"He must pledge me fealty yearly, the price to be at his discretion," the Dominus answered his wife.

"It is generous," Lara said and then kissing her husband upon his cheek she wafted herself to Kaliq's palace of Shunnar, sought out her mentor and told him of their plan to lure the giants to their side.

"I think you may win Skrymir over," Kaliq answered. "His people were never really hard or brutal. They only became so to protect themselves after the Forest Lords betrayed their long friendship and the survivors were forced to flee. In all the years they have sheltered in the Dark Lands, Kol has never before asked of them what he will soon request. I believe they will welcome an opportunity to leave his realm and settle on the far edge of the New Outlands. Yes, find Og, and speak with him. When he is ready to sleep, tell him to come to me as he did before."

Lara sought out Og in his green valley among the horses, and explained to him what she wished of him. "Your father was not hostile to you when you last met," she said. "Do you think he can be turned from the dark back to the light?"

Og sighed. "Oddly, Lara, the impression I got was that he was afraid of what might happen to his people if left to Kol's tender mercies, but that he did not know what else he might do. I can but make the offer and attempt to convince him. I will seek him out tonight with the prince's help," Og agreed. He absently rubbed the muzzle of a small bay mare. "Aye, the sooner the better."

"Thank you, my dearest friend," Lara said and then she wafted herself back to her own castle in Terah.

Og chuckled at the puff of mauve mist that she left behind. Then giving the little mare a swat on her rump he sent her off as he walked across the great green meadow to the palace, where he knew the prince his master would be awaiting him. Again, as the first time, Prince Kaliq set the green enameled gold amulet in the shape of a tree about Og's thick neck. Then he conducted him to the great chamber with its long bed. Og drank down the cup of frine that had been mixed with herbs to help him sleep. Then he lay down while Prince Kaliq sat in a chair by his side. Soon the giant was snoring.

As he was falling asleep Og had concentrated on his father, silently calling out his name as he drifted into unconsciousness. Then he found himself standing surrounded by a gauzy mist and knew he had once again attained the Dream Plain. "Father," he called out. "I need you to come and speak with me."

All remained silent about him and then Og realized that his sire was probably not used to be addressed thusly.

"Skrymir of the Forest Giants, I need you to come and speak with me," he said.

"Who calls me?" his father's deep strong voice answered.

"Your son, Og, horse master to the Shadow Princes," Og replied and then he saw Skrymir striding through the mist toward him.

"What is it you want of me, Og?" his father asked as they now stood face-to-face.

"I bring you an offer from Magnus Hauk, Dominus of Terah," Og began.

"Who is this Dominus of Terah?"

"He is the ruler of the vast territory beneath the mountains of the Dark Lands. His wife was my savior and is my dearest friend to this day. My lord father, you know that the greatest of the Shadow Princes, Kaliq by name, is my master and patron. He knows that the nature of our race is a gentle and kind one. He believes the harshness that you must now exhibit is what has kept you alive since the treachery of the Forest Lords changed our way of life. But my master also believes that given the chance, you would return to your former selves. And it is through him that the Dominus makes this offer. It is a good offer, my lord father.

"Leave the Dark Lands. Eschew the Twilight Lord's influence and again become the race we once were. The Dominus will give to you and our people all the lands beneath the Black Mountains from the Obscura to beyond infinity if you will reject Kol and his plans for conquest. The land is not harsh like the mountains you now inhabit. The land is rolling, forested hills with broad fertile valleys. It is a good place," Og said.

Skrymir's amber eyes grew almost misty at the thought of such a land, but then he said, "When my liege lord conquers Terah, those lands can be ours if we ask him."

"The Twilight Lord will never conquer Terah," Og replied. "Without a faerie woman he has not the power to do so. And he must watch his back more carefully than ever before, for there are those who would seek to place one or the other of his sons on his throne. The Dark Lands borders on civil war, my lord father."

"My lord Kol's faerie mate gives him all the power he needs for his conquest," Skrymir boasted.

"She is no longer by his side, my lord father," Og told his sire. "Lord Kol stole the faerie wife of the Dominus of Terah, but only after stealing her memories so she would not know who she was." Then Og went on to tell Lara's tale to Skrymir. He told him that Kaliq had restored her memories and that the beautiful faerie used her magic to create two sons from the one. "It was all planned in advance," Og said. "The Domina Lara was sent deliberately by the Council of the Magic Kingdoms to bring this chaos to the Dark Lands. It was a part of the great destiny she has. Without her, your master cannot accomplish all he desires. Lord Kol attempts to wreck the perfect balance between the light and the dark. But he will not be allowed to do it.

"Now he seeks out the lady Lara on the Dream Plain for Prince Kaliq has penned him within his castle for the next hundred years. He cannot leave it to lead his armies. He cannot leave it to even visit his House of Women or teach his sons how to ride one day when they are old enough. So he makes his feeble attempts to draw the Domina back into the darkness so he may use her powers, but he will never succeed. The lady Lara is the very essence of light, my lord father. Tell me, how do you communicate with him?"

Skrymir's large but slow brain absorbed all that he heard from Og. The last time they had spoken he had fled his son with a terrible headache, but this time he swallowed down the pain of so much information and considered Og's words. Finally he said, "The Chancellor Alfrigg has built a new reception hall. The end where he stands is an original part of the castle. The new end is where petitioners and liegemen go, yet they are connected and appear to be one chamber. It is here we listen to the Twilight Lord's directives and receive our orders from him."

"And no one goes to the foot of the throne of Lord Kol?" Og queried gently.

"There is a filigreed silver railing across the room and none may move past it," Skrymir said slowly. "Is that because we *cannot* get past it, my son?"

"Indeed, my lord father, I believe it is," Og replied. "This chamber has been fashioned to make it appear as if all is well, but it is not. Still, 'tis cleverly done."

"So we may have no fear that the Twilight Lord will punish us if we desert him?" Skrymir wanted to know.

"My master, Prince Kaliq, will weave a protection spell about each of the Forest Giants and about your new lands," Og said.

"If we take this chance and go against Lord Kol, we must leave everything we have behind," Skrymir noted. "We will have no goods nor homes to call our own. We will be little better off than when we fled the Forest Lords all those years ago."

"I am certain the Domina Lara would use her magic to see that everything you lost was replaced," Og promised.

"I had a large hall in the old forest," Skrymir murmured slyly.

There was a tinkle of laughter that startled them both and then Lara appeared through the mists of the Dream Plain. "Greetings, Skrymir, lord of the Forest Giants," she said smiling at him. "Darling Og, take me up in your hand so your father and I may speak face-to-face." When the giant had done so and Lara was settled comfortably in his palm she continued. "A large hall with a great stone fireplace and sleeping spaces for your retainers would suit you, I am certain. And a fine chamber behind the hall with its own fireplace for you to sleep in. It should have a good-sized bed for I am certain that once you have been safely resettled you will want to take pleasures with a new wife. The giant woman, Thrym, pleases you but you have never felt safe enough in the Dark Lands to offer her your protection."

"How can you know these things, my lady?" Skrymir wanted

to learn. He looked at her closely. Aye! It was the same beautiful woman Kol had told them all was his mate. But she was not. Kol had used this beautiful creature for his own ends. If she were not powerful, with powerful friends, he could have destroyed her, for Skrymir could see that Lara was no part of the darkness. Indeed, even here upon the Dream Plain where much was muted, she glowed with a radiance that could only come of good.

"I am Lara, daughter of Swiftsword and Ilona, queen of the Forest Faeries," Lara said gently. "I know much, my lord."

"You are Maeve's granddaughter?" Skrymir suddenly knelt. "She was a great lady and I can see that you take after her. Will you follow your mother one day, my lady Lara?" he asked her.

"Nay, my half brother Cirillo will follow our mother. I cannot, for I am not all faerie," Lara explained. She reached out and touched Skrymir's russet head. "Help us defeat Kol of the Twilight, my lord. You will not suffer for it."

Skrymir looked up into Lara's beautiful green eyes as he knelt. "I know that I can trust Maeve's granddaughter," he said. "The Forest Giants, those of us who remain, are yours to command, my lady Lara."

"When you awaken, my lord, gather your people and depart the Dark Lands as quickly as you can. Once you have crossed its borders into Terah, my mother's people, with whom you are familiar, will meet you and guide you to your new home. Og did not finish what needed to be said, however. You must acknowledge the Dominus of Terah as your overlord. Once a year he will visit you and you will offer your fealty to him by whatever means you choose among yourselves. It is the only thing he will require for the lands he cedes to the Forest Giants," Lara explained.

"The Dominus is your husband," Skrymir said.

"He is, and a finer mortal you have never met. Nor are you likely to meet a better man," Lara told him with a little smile.

"It is little enough to ask of us," Skrymir said. "I will swear fealty for us all. And the land is ours and our descendants' to do with as we please, my lady Domina?"

"The land is yours but you cannot destroy it," Lara said.

"We did not destroy the old forests in which our kind lived for so many centuries. We tended that forest. We will cherish and tend this new forest that your lord husband gives us."

"Rise then, Skrymir, and take my faerie blessing with you when you awaken. The Forest Faeries will await you," Lara told him. "Be cautious, however, that you are not caught as you make your escape," she warned him. "Remember, take nothing with you but the clothing on your back. You do not wish any part of the darkness intruding upon your new life. This will be difficult for some of your people, but make certain they leave all behind them lest you bring discord into your new life."

"What of our weapons?" he asked her.

"Take only those you brought with you, my lord. And now I will leave you to bid your son farewell," Lara said. "Please put me down now, Og."

Og set Lara gently back upon the ground of the Dream Plain, bending as he did so to murmur, "Thank you, my lady."

Lara smiled up at him. "Forgive me for intruding, but our time is short, dearest Og. I like your father." Then she kissed his ruddy cheek and turned back into the mist of the Dream Plain to disappear from his sight.

"I like Maeve's granddaughter," Skrymir said.

Og straightened up and nodded at his father. "She is a good faerie, my lord."

"I will keep my promise to her," Skrymir nodded. "Come and visit your kin in our new home, Og. You will be welcome." Then the giant lord turned and walked away, the tendrils of the gauzy gray mist obscuring him quickly from his son's view.

Og turned to go and then he heard a deep hypnotic voice calling from somewhere in the haze. The sound sent a shiver down his back.

"Lara! Come to me, my only one. You are mine! I will let no one else have you! Lara! Answer me! Come to me!"

The Twilight Lord! Og realized. It had to be the Twilight Lord. He backed away from the sound, forcing himself to waken. He gasped and sat straight up in his bed. He was drenched in his own sweat and his great heart was hammering wildly.

"What is it?" the Shadow Prince sitting by his bedside asked.

Og told him all that had happened upon the Dream Plain. "And then, my prince, I heard a voice calling out for Lara. The very sound of it frightened me," Og said. "And I have rarely if ever been frightened. Was it the Twilight Lord or was it my imagination playing upon my fears?"

"Nay, it was undoubtedly Kol," Prince Kaliq said. "I have no doubt he lurks upon the Dream Plain waiting to sense Lara. The Keepers will not forbid him the Dream Plain."

"Could he have heard our plans, my prince?" Og wondered.

"It is unlikely," came the reply. "Kol's only passion is for Lara, but he did not sense her until she had gone. And your amulet kept you safe from his detection."

"If Lara had not come I might not have been able to convince my father to take our people and leave the Dark Land," Og said. "I was relieved when she arrived. I am not a clever fellow, my lord. I am happier with my horses."

The prince chuckled. "Whether you realize it or not, Og, you have the makings of a diplomat," Kaliq told his horse master.

Og roared with laughter. "My prince, you cheer my soul but I know what I am. I am the finest horse master the Shadow Princes have ever had or ever will."

"Indeed, Og, I am inclined to agree with you," Kaliq responded with a grin. "I thank you for your efforts tonight. Now go back to your beloved creatures."

Og bowed and hurried off.

THE SHADOW PRINCE SAT amid the beauty of his personal garden, musing. A third of the Twilight Lord's allies had been removed. Reaching for his reflecting bowl he gazed into the water at the castle of Kolbyr. It was night and a storm raged with great flashes of lightning crossing the black skies above it. *"Sleep. Deep."* Kaliq murmured the small incantation. All in Kol's castle would sleep until the Forest Giants had made their escape. Only when Kol wanted the giants would he discover that they were missing. It would be too late then for the giants would be gone and if Kol found them, the prince's spell would be set in place. But now, Kaliq thought, they must turn their attention to the Wolfyn attacking The City. There had to be a way to destroy them. The prince put his mind to it.

The Wolfyn had all the worst characteristics of both man and wolf. But if they could choose between one species or the other, which would it be? Kaliq wondered. Some, of course, would prefer to remain as they were. Yet in any group of creatures there were always those who were dissatisfied with themselves. *It could be a way to weaken the Wolfyn,* Kaliq thought. And for now that was the best they might do.

He would have to walk among the Wolfyn himself to learn who was discontent. The prince set a cloak of invisibility about his shoulders and stepped into the shadows. When he stepped forth from the shadows he found himself in the Wolfyn encampment which was now set up in the home of Squire Darah, the governor of the Midlands, who had wisely fled the onslaught of savage invaders. Unfortunately, the squire had not informed his servants of his departure. Nor had he bothered to mention his plans to his pretty young wife who was now seated in the lap of the Wolfyn lord's commander, a young Wolfyn named Ulf. The woman did not look happy as her captor vigorously kneaded one of her plump breasts, for his nails were long and they marked her skin.

"You are hurting me," the woman complained as the nails drew blood.

"You have wonderful tits," Ulf told her. "Our females do not."

"Do not hoard the wench all to yourself," another young Wolfyn complained.

"Would Hrolleif share such a prize?" Ulf demanded of his men who sat about Squire Darah's hall. "There are plenty of women for you among the servants."

"Just because the lord is your uncle," grumbled another Wolfyn, "you think you are entitled to the cream because he made you commander of the invasion force. Why did not he lead us himself? I've never know Hrolleif to run from a battle."

"He'll be here when it is time to take The City," Ulf replied. He pushed the woman from his lap. "I dislike it when you sulk, Fernir. Here, amuse yourself. You may all have her to play with if it pleases you."

The group of young Wolfyn stripped the garments from the squire's wife.

"She is very smooth," one said running a furry hand down the woman's back.

They pulled her down on the floor of the hall and began to sniff and lick at her.

The woman screamed as a cold snout pushed between her legs and a long hot tongue began to lick at her most private parts.

"Ummm, she tastes good," the Wolfyn said, looking up with a grin and ignoring the woman's distress. He rolled her onto her stomach and growled into her ear, "On your hands and knees, my pretty bitch, and see how Wolfyn take their females." And in fear of her life now she scrambled to obey him. He mounted her and took his pleasure of her. He was followed by several, but not all, of his companions who enjoyed the squire's wife and then, satisfied, left her in a moaning heap upon the hall floor.

"Don't you want her?" Fernir asked Ulf. "Her sheath is hot and tight."

"I do not like sharing my females," Ulf said softly. "It is too animalistic."

"We are animals," Fernir said.

"Nay, we are half-animal, half-human," Ulf responded. "If I had my choice I should prefer to be one or the other."

Ahh, Kaliq thought, *that is interesting. Hrolleif's nephew is discontent.*

"If I could be one," Fernir said, "I would choose to be all wolf."

"You have not the balls to be the Alpha wolf," Ulf remarked insultingly.

"I wouldn't want to be the Alpha wolf," Fernir surprised them all by saying. "I don't want responsibility for the pack. I want to run free with it, fighting over and mounting the females, taking my share of the kill. This human body I am encumbered with is too difficult to control and maintain. In my heart of hearts I am more wolf than Wolfyn. And I know that some of the others feel the same way, too. Would you choose if you could to be one or the other of our interbred species, Ulf?"

Ulf thought for a long moment and then he nodded. "Aye, I should rather be mortal—as long as my face were as handsome as it is now," he opined.

The other young Wolfyn laughed at that remark.

"I'd stay as I am," another said. "Wolfyn have bigger rods than mortals."

"Not necessarily," Ulf said. "Their rods are all of various sizes. Some bigger than others. They are no different than we are."

"I'd like to have two rods like the Twilight Lord," chuckled a

Wolfyn named Hrote. "Imagine the pleasure you could give with two rods to a woman."

Prince Kaliq, clutching his cloak about him, stepped back into the shadows once again and removing the garment, was back in his own chambers. He was not interested in the young Wolfyn's fantasies, but he had learned all that he needed to know. The Wolfyn, like any other species, could be tempted by something that they dearly desired. Now he must devise a way to reach each of them. And when he did, he would make the Wolfyn an offer that some of them would be unable to refuse. Hrolleif, the Wolfyn lord, had just so many fighters. If even a quarter of them preferred being all wolf or all mortal, and were willing to accept the prince's offer to make that dream come true, then the Wolfyn horde would be weakened.

Lara had struggled to stop any bloodshed. He and his brothers had made equal attempts. But the Twilight Lord would not be denied. He wanted more power than he had any right to have. He wanted Lara. He would have neither in the end, but he would cause a great deal of carnage in the effort. Prince Kaliq sighed. Mortals were bad enough when they were at odds with one another. But when the magic kingdoms fought it was far worse because magic folk really did know better. And Kol knew that the balance between the light and the dark must be kept. Neither Hetar or Terah could be allowed to fall into darkness lest the balance be tipped.

LORD JONAH'S WIFE, Vilia, looked directly at Lara. "You are more beautiful than ever, if such a thing is possible," she said.

"Thank you," Lara replied politely, "but we are not here to discuss my beauty."

"Then why have you asked for this meeting?" Vilia wanted to know.

"You love Hetar, do you not?"

Vilia nodded. She sat with Lara in Lady Gillian's privy chamber.

"And you know that Gaius Prospero is a fool." It was a statement, not a query.

Vilia burst out laughing and nodded. Then growing more serious she said, "Aye, he is a fool but a powerful fool. One who has managed to gain the support of the magnates and can manipulate the High Council to his ends."

"True," Lara agreed. "But he cannot win against the forces of the Twilight Lord without the aid of Terah. You are not silly enough to believe that Terah has ever been a threat to Hetar, Lady Vilia. If Terah was the threat that Gaius Prospero claims, then why would we have insisted on our trading vessels meeting in midsea, and forbidden Hetar from even coming in sight of our shores for all the centuries these two nations have been involved? Until the past few years, neither Hetar's government nor its people, save for the Coastal Kings, even knew of Terah's existence. Terah wishes to remain as it always has, untainted by foreign influence and at peace."

Vilia sighed. "What is it you want of me, Domina?" she asked.

"You yet have influence with your former husband," Lara began. "We need you to convince the emperor that without Terah, Hetar will fall. And when it falls it will enter into the darkness that surrounds the Twilight Lord. Gaius Prospero, so adept at escaping the consequences of his actions for all these years, will not escape Lord Kol. The Twilight Lord will execute him, for he knows the kind of man that the emperor is, and not one of his allies will step forward to speak for Gaius Prospero. And then Kol will put one of his own in the emperor's place to rule Hetar for him. His laws will be harsh and he is not a creature given over to merciful behavior."

"How is it that you know so much about the Twilight Lord?" Vilia asked.

Lara took a deep breath and began to speak. When she had finished telling her tale, Vilia's beautiful face was a mixture of both shock and admiration.

Finally she spoke. "I think you are far more powerful than you have ever been to have survived so terrible an adventure. I think your husband is a brave and compassionate man that he can live with the knowledge of what you had to do and yet still loves you. But why does he care what happens to Hetar?"

"Kol's plans were always to dominate our worlds," Lara replied. "But he also wants me back. He has come to me upon the Dream Plain and threatened Magnus Hauk and our children if I will not return to him. He attacks Hetar first to show me that he will not deviate from his plans. He wants me to see the destruction he will wreak upon Hetar, and then he will attempt to convince me that if I return to him he will show mercy to Terah. But he will not. He will destroy it even as he does Hetar. The Twilight Lord represents the darkness, but there must always be a balance between the darkness and the light. If Kol is allowed to conquer our worlds that balance will be lost. We cannot permit that to happen. Hetar's forces are split right now, and those who survived its misadventure in the Coastal Kingdom will have to fight their way across the Midlands in order to reach The City. The Wolfyn are fierce adversaries. You will lose more men before they get here, and those fighting men remaining in the Quarter and the Garden District are old and no longer the soldiers they once were. With the Wolfyn guarding The City's gates from without, how will those who return be able to even get into The City?"

"Then how can you possibly help?" Vilia wanted to know. This was terrible. She and Jonah had to find a way to escape The City as soon as possible or they would die. Dying was not a part of their plans.

"Convince Gaius Prospero for his own sake, for the sake of the thousands in The City, to ally with Terah. My magic can bring enough soldiers into The City to help with its defense. And then our other legions can join with the Hetarian troops making their way back from the coast. With the aid of the Shadow Princes we can quickly place our combined armies both before and behind the Wolfyn, catching them in a pincer movement that will allow us to destroy them."

"You would save Gaius Prospero's little empire then," Vilia said. "'Tis most generous considering his treatment of you, Domina."

"Everything comes with a price, Lady Vilia," Lara replied. "And even an emperor must pay. You will be aided in your attempt to convince Gaius Prospero to ally with Terah. The young empress, Shifra, will agree with you and you know that the emperor can deny her naught. Between you he can be convinced. But you must work quickly."

"What is the price he will pay?" Vilia wanted to know.

"You have never forgiven him for not crowning you empress, have you?" Lara said. "And you mean to have your revenge on him by taking his throne from him."

Vilia gasped, but then she realized that she shouldn't be surprised. The faerie woman was all-powerful. Her hard heart hardened more. "Aye," she answered. "To both of your questions, Domina, for to lie to you would be useless, wouldn't it?"

Lara smiled. "It would," she agreed. "Now trust me that you will have your revenge, Vilia of the House of Ahasferus. But before you can, we need to defeat the Twilight Lord."

"Surely Kol has more allies than just the Wolfyn," Vilia said.

"Aye, he does, but one group of his allies have already left him and will not partake in this war or help him ever again. And between us, Hetar and Terah will destroy the Wolfyn. His remaining forces will then refuse to leave the Dark Lands for Kol's heirs—the twin sons I gave him—must be protected so that one of them can one day take his father's place as Twilight Lord. But unless we can destroy the Wolfyn, Kol will prevail over Hetar, and the plans that you and Lord Jonah have made will come to nothing," Lara murmured softly. "I understand your desire for power, Vilia. It is good to be a queen, an empress, or a Domina." She smiled knowingly at her companion.

Vilia shivered. Lara frightened her, for she seemed to see right into one's very heart. Still, Vilia believed that the faerie woman was to be trusted if only because her own interests were threatened. "You still have not told me how Gaius Prospero will be punished," she said softly. "I need to know."

Lara smiled a small smile. "His heart will be broken, as for the first time in his life, he is truly in love," she said. "Now ask no more of me, Vilia. But make certain when that event occurs that your husband is prepared and his own allies are in place."

Vilia wanted to know more of just how Gaius Prospero's punishment would be accomplished but instead she said, "I expect your husband has sent you to treat with me on this mission. However, I wish I might look into his eyes to see if it is truth you bring me. You are faerie and I cannot be certain of you although my instincts tell me to trust you. But he is a mortal like me, and I have always been good at reading another's thoughts and heart. Especially those of men."

"Magnus thought you might want to meet him again," Lara said. Then the handsome Dominus of Terah stepped forth from the dark corner where he had been listening to the two women in their discourse. He bowed to Vilia, kissing her hand and then drawing her to him. "My heart is true, Lady Vilia. What Lara has told you are not just her words, but *our* words. I wish no harm to befall Hetar, land of my beloved's birth. Terah wishes to remain as it has always been. We need no conquests to feed our people or keep them content. Let us help Hetar in our mutual defense and then we will be gone again. If you are wise, you will forget us."

Vilia felt her legs go weak as she gazed into Magnus Hauk's beautiful turquoise eyes. Never had she seen eyes like that. The color was so clear, and as she looked at him she saw the incredible strength and nobility of the man before her. Had not his grip upon her hand been so firm she might have collapsed at his feet, Vilia thought. She managed to nod to him, then said in an almost trembling voice, "I must speak with my husband first. I agree with what the Domina has said, but Jonah is a proud man, and should I act without his approval he would not be happy."

"I understand," Magnus Hauk said. "You are quite obviously a good wife to Lord Jonah, but then so were you a good wife to Gaius Prospero. That he deceived you so and then cast you off tells me that he was not worthy of you, Lady Vilia. Time, however, is most precious to us, so I would beg you to go quickly to him." He kissed her hand again, and then certain she could now remain upright on her own he released her.

"Let me transport you," Lara said and without waiting for an answer she waved her hand over Vilia, who then disappeared.

"What do you think?" the Dominus asked his wife.

"I believe we have instilled in her just the right amount of fear and awe," Lara said with a little grin. "She is truly a most intelligent woman. And easy to read. It is Jonah with whom we must be concerned. He is ambitious beyond all and an extremely wily man. He cannot be trusted. To have seduced Vilia under Gaius Prospero's nose was very daring. And to not get caught in all the years he was taking pleasures with her was more than good luck. It was cleverness. His daring intrigues her." Lara chuckled.

"Will he be emperor of Hetar?" Magnus Hauk asked his wife.

"I do not know if Hetar will want another emperor after the debacle of Gaius Prospero's reign," Lara answered him. "Jonah is master of the Merchants' Guild, as well as the emperor's right hand. He fills both positions well, but it will not be enough for him once Gaius Prospero is finished. Still, he is cautious and will not make any move until he is certain of his own success. I do not believe he has enough support right now to make his grab for complete power. He has his mother in a high place—the Mistress of the Pleasure Guilds wields a great influence. And perhaps some of the magnates are looking to Jonah since Aubin Prospero has refused to pursue his father's throne and the empress has not borne a child. But I believe that the powers that be will be wary about choosing just one man to lead them again, at least for a while. But 'tis only my opinion. As my faerie blood grows stronger, my mortal advantages seem to fade a bit."

"What did you mean when you told Vilia that Gaius Prospero would die of a broken heart?" Magnus Hauk asked his wife.

"The young empress is but an illusion created by the Shadow Princes," Lara explained. "She does not really exist. And when this war is settled, hopefully for the good, they will retrieve her. Since Shifra is the first thing Gaius Prospero has really ever loved, her loss will send him into a fatal decline. 'Tis better that way for no one will have to shed his blood or cause civil war. Hetar will be free to rebuild itself."

A light knock sounded upon the chamber door, which opened to reveal Lady Gillian. "Could I have some refreshments sent to you?" Looking about, she asked, "Where is Lady Vilia?"

"I sent her home to speak with her husband," Lara answered. "And yes, some refreshments would be lovely. Thank you."

"Do you think she will help us?" Lady Gillian wanted to know.

"I believe she will, because it is in her own best interests to do so. I have told her and I will tell you that when this is over, before Gaius Prospero can claim victory in his name, he will die. When that happens Hetar will be faced with a power vacuum. A very few will want another supreme head of the government. Others will want to return to the old ways but the women must not allow it. The High Council must be enlarged—at least half of its members should be women. You will face resistance over this but you must prevail, Lady Gillian. Only if women can be a part of the government can reason prevail. Women are not invisible nor are we mindless. We did not cause this disaster, but we must be a part of the solution," Lara told her.

Lady Gillian nodded. "I agree, but many women who now support us are apt to fall away once peace comes. They will be too busy trying to help their families survive."

"I know," Lara responded, "but you must convince them that

only if they will take their share of the responsibility for Hetar will peace prevail and prosperity return."

"Is it that way in Terah?" Lady Gillian asked.

"It is becoming more so with each day," Magnus Hauk said with a smile. "My Domina is very insistent upon it. And the truth is that while Terah believed its women devoid of speech and we were unable to seek their council, we were frozen in time. But both sexes must participate in life if it is to be successful. Decisions will not always be equally shared. Sometimes the males will prevail, at other times the females. Or both will agree. But both must maintain a voice in the governance of their peoples."

Gillian nodded. "I will see refreshments are brought," she said and left them.

"You have done well," the Dominus told his wife.

"We have not yet succeeded," Lara reminded him. "We must deal with Lord Jonah before we can deal with Gaius Prospero. I think Jonah the more dangerous."

"How sad that Shifra will be taken from him. It is said he loves her above all else," Magnus Hauk said quietly. "His end will be a sad and lonely one."

"He has caused much misery to others in his lifetime," Lara replied. "His death will be an easy one considering all the wickedness he has done. My faerie heart is hardened against him."

"And yet," the Dominus said, "if he had not set you on the path to your destiny…"

"I suppose that might have been part of his destiny," Lara allowed, "but I cannot forget his greed and lust, both for me and for Hetar."

Magnus Hauk reached out and took his wife's hand in his. His turquoise eyes met her green ones. "But he can never have you, and I do," he said. "And he has never loved you, and I do. More than my own life, Lara."

She turned his hand in hers and lifting it up kissed it fervently. "And I love you, my lord Dominus. I will always love you."

"You make it sound as if you are leaving me," he told her.

"Nay, I will not leave you while you remain in your mortal body, Magnus, but there is something Kaliq and my mother have spoken about with me that I must share with you. Because my faerie blood is stronger than my mortal blood, I will live far longer than any mortal and for most of that time I will remain as you see me now," Lara told him. Her beautiful eyes filled with tears as she spoke. "I may even outlive our children."

"But I will grow old as mortals do," he said softly. "I have wondered for some time about that, my love. Do not fret yourself over it. I am a mortal man who has had the supreme good fortune to fall in love and be loved in return by a beautiful faerie woman." He leaned forward and kissed her lips most tenderly. "I regret none of it nor will I in the years to come. How can I as long as you remain by my side?" He gently brushed the tears away that had begun to slip down her cheeks. "Now put this unhappy truth from you, my love. I am content by your side and will always be. You must think of the days ahead for they will be very important for us all."

Lara nodded and swallowed back her bout of sadness.

Lady Gillian returned, carrying a tray with a carafe of light wine that she informed them was from her vineyards in the

Outlands. There was also a plate containing delicate rectangles of dark bread and a board of buttery cheese. "I did not think this was a time for sweet treats," she said with a small smile as she set the tray down on a table.

"Remain with us," Lara invited their hostess. "You must be a part of the negotiation with Lord Jonah, for you are an important part of Hetar's society."

"I was," Lady Gillian amended modestly. "Now it is Lady Farah's place."

"Nay," Lara corrected her. "Lady Farah will never have the respect that you have earned over your tenure as headmistress of the Pleasure Guilds. You were, if memory serves me correctly, the youngest woman ever elected to that position. Even now in your retirement you are looked to, especially by the women of Hetar. And you are one of few Pleasure Women to ever own her own establishment."

"You flatter me," Lady Gillian said with a small smile. "I have simply worked hard."

They sat drinking the lovely fragrant wine and nibbling upon the bread and cheese. A knock came upon the door, then a serving woman stuck her head into the room.

"Your guests are even now arriving," she said tersely. "Shall I show them directly in, my lady Gillian?"

"Aye, and be sure no one sees them who should not," Lady Gillian said.

The serving woman nodded briefly, and her head disappeared. Several minutes later the door opened and two cloaked figures entered quickly as the portal closed quickly behind them.

Lady Gillian herself took their garments and carefully put them aside on a small bench. Silently she bowed to her two guests.

Jonah turned and stared at Lara and her husband. "Why should I help you?" he said without any preamble.

"Because without our help you will never rule Hetar," Lara said candidly.

"You do not believe I can make an arrangement with the Twilight Lord?" Jonah replied. He looked straight at her.

"Kol of the Twilight would immediately see the darkness about you and the deceit in your heart, my lord," Lara answered him. "He would slay you himself. If he can take Hetar he will put one of his puppets upon the throne here and you will not be alive to enjoy the fruits of your many years of scheming."

Jonah barked a brief laugh. "You mince no words with me, Domina, do you? Will you help me if I help you?"

"If Terah comes to Hetar's aid, my lord, it will save your skin. That is all the help we will give you. As for your ambitions, they are yours to fulfill," Lara told him.

"Terah wants no part of Hetar, my lord," Magnus Hauk now spoke. "We will trade with you as we always have, but no more. How you govern, how you come to the manner of your government is not our concern. We do not wish to conquer Hetar. We offer only to aid you so that you may save yourselves from Kol and his darkness. So that the balance between the light and the dark may be maintained."

"And you are certain that between us we can defeat the Twilight Lord? What if we fail and he wreaks an even harsher vengeance against us?"

"United, we cannot fail," Lara said in positive tones.

"And the emperor?" Jonah demanded of her.

"Your hands will be free of his blood," Lara told him. "His punishment has already been decided in the magic kingdoms. He will be no impediment to your own climb to power, my lord. And his demise will not be laid at your door, which should only enhance your reputation as a good and loyal servant."

Jonah's dark eyes narrowed speculatively, then he looked sharply at Lara. "Will the magic kingdoms help me?" he asked her.

"Your ambitions and your fate are in your own hands and those who would support you, my lord. We do not make it a regular habit to interfere in the ways of mortals," Lara said. "You will plot your own course."

"But will you hinder me?" he wanted to know.

Lara laughed softly and shook her head. "Those of the magic realms will return to their own places and I will be back in Terah. What happens in Hetar after we defeat Kol and his minions is not our business."

"I must be certain I understand you," Jonah responded. "Terah, along with its magic allies, will help Hetar stave off the Twilight Lord and the forces of darkness in exchange for *nothing?* This is neither reasonable nor possible. There must be something that you want from Hetar in exchange for your aid."

"Are you so stupid," Magnus Hauk burst out, "that you cannot understand the terrible danger we all face from the Twilight Lord? He must be defeated! And as he has begun his hoped-for conquest of us all here in Hetar, it is here we have rallied to destroy his aspirations! This creature and his minions threaten

us all, my lord. There is naught the magic kingdoms desire of
Hetar in return. What do you have that you could possibly give
them? You are a mortal land peopled by mortal folk. As for
Terah, you already know our price. You will leave us to ourselves, for if you do not my ships, with sailors who know how
to sail, will sweep across the Sagitta carrying my armies, who
know how to conquer—and they will conquer Hetar. If I am
forced to do that I swear to you that I will set my wife and her
sword, Andraste, upon you, my lord. Now do you understand?
And now will you let the gracious lady Vilia go to that pompous
fool, Gaius Prospero, before it is too late? There is no time left
to any of us to bargain, Hetarian."

Jonah looked astounded by the Dominus's words and stance.
Magnus Hauk had always seems a quiet and reasonable man. But
standing before him now, the Dominus of Terah, his turquoise
eyes flashing anger, appeared every bit a strong and fierce ruler.
I have misjudged him, Jonah thought, irritated with himself. *I have
looked only to the faerie woman. Why did I ever consider that she would
have wed a weak man?* "My lord Dominus," Jonah replied, "I apologize for my hesitation but it is, as you well know, our way to
negotiate. You are correct when you say there is no time left to
such civilities. My wife must go at once to the emperor if Hetar,
if all of us, are to be saved."

"I can transport you immediately to the young empress's
quarters," Lara told Vilia. "Go to her first and then together you
must go to Gaius Prospero."

Vilia nodded.

"Do not fail us," Jonah warned his wife.

Vilia glared at him, her look almost scornful. "Have I ever failed you?" Then she turned to Lara. "I am ready."

Lara smiled, and then she silently made a little incantation. *Prepare, oh Shifra, for your guest. Then do what you know is best.* Waving her hand over Vilia she sent her to the emperor's palace and into the privy chamber of the young empress.

"I have been awaiting your arrival," Shifra said by way of greeting.

"You knew I was coming?" Vilia didn't know whether to be surprised or not. She felt a tiny stab of jealousy. The girl was as beautiful as ever with her red-gold hair, no longer loose, but dressed in a number of bejeweled braids and heavy curls. *Even in my prime I was not so beautiful,* she thought.

"Of course," Shifra said in her soft sweet voice. "Now we must hurry for the hour draws near when the emperor retires into his own privy chamber to drink Razi and forget his troubles. Even I cannot console him in these terrible times. If we do not catch him now he will be too drunk and filled with dreams to make sense. Come quickly!" She led Vilia from her own rooms and down a connecting corridor to the emperor's quarters. The guards at the door stepped aside to let them pass, surprised to see the empress with the emperor's former wife.

Gaius Prospero was signing some papers at his large desk. His eyes lit up seeing Shifra, but his look turned to one of shock at seeing her companion. "My love, what is it?" he asked Shifra. "Vilia," he acknowledged the other woman curtly.

Shifra went immediately to Gaius Prospero and settled herself in his lap. Instinctively he put his arms about her and kissed her lips. "My dearest lord and husband, Lord Jonah's wife has come to speak with me this day. Her words are wise and in the best interests of Hetar, I am absolutely convinced. You must hear her out, for my sake. For the sake of any children I may be fortunate enough to bear you," Shifra said.

"You know I will do whatever pleases you, my dove," the emperor murmured, kissing her ripe lips again. Then reluctantly he turned his gaze to Vilia. "You have my ear," he told her. "Say what you need to say."

Vilia spoke in quiet but urgent tones, telling Gaius Prospero of Terah's offer; explaining the great dangers that Hetar faced, for until now the emperor had refused to believe the Wolfyn were anything more than just raiders. Even the frantic Squire Darah had been unable to convince him of the peril that they all faced. Besotted by his wife and drunk much of the time now with Razi, Gaius Prospero had almost lost his grip upon reality. The loss of his ships, of half of his armies and now the prospect of a terrible future had turned the once powerful, ambitious ruler into a weak and frightened man.

But this day he had not yet begun to drink and Shifra was imploring him to heed Vilia's words. Like Jonah, he was astounded that Terah would offer their help, that the magic folk would aid him. The news encouraged him and the old Gaius Prospero suddenly reappeared from the wreckage. "Do you trust them?" he asked Vilia.

"I do trust them, my lord emperor," Vilia told him.

"The faerie woman hates me," Gaius Prospero said. "Why would she help us?"

"Oh, indeed, my lord, the lady Lara thinks you are no better than the sickly green-black scum that coats a backwater pond, but while she is Domina of Terah, she retains a fondness for her native land. If Hetar falls, Terah will be the Twilight Lord's next target," Vilia explained. "This Lord Kol means to have us all under his thumb. He means to spread his darkness all throughout our worlds. As he has chosen Hetar to attack first, it is only logical that our combined forces stop him here."

"But to want nothing in return," Gaius Prospero mused.

"They want to be left in peace by Hetar," Shifra said quietly to her husband. "Does that not mean you have successfully ended their threat toward us? The people will be very pleased by this knowledge, my darling Gaius, but it can only happen if you give the order that will combine our Hetarian forces with those of the Terahns and the magic kingdoms, my dearest lord. Those dreadful Wolfyn are at our gates, and it is said they ravish all females—old and young, high and low—that they encounter when they conquer a place. The most beautiful are passed about so all might partake of them," Shifra told him with a visible shudder. "We have not much time in which to act."

Gaius Prospero had viewed the Wolfyn from the heights of The City's walls. Their fierce wolf heads set upon the bodies of mortal men frightened him just looking at them. The thought of them mounting and ravaging his perfect young empress terrified him. "I will agree," he said. "Tell the Dominus Magnus Hauk and his allies that I agree to their proposals. Lord Jonah will act as my intermediary." He waved his hand at Vilia. "Go quickly, woman! Go!"

"I must have something written in your hand," Vilia told him. "You know Jonah is a stickler for protocol."

Shifra leaned from her husband's lap and drew a thin sheet of vellum from a basket on the emperor's desk. Then taking up the quill she inked it and wrote, *Hetar's glorious emperor, Gaius Prospero I, gives permission to his right hand, Lord Jonah, to join Hetar's forces with those of the Dominus of Terah, Magnus Hauk, for the sole purpose of defeating the forces of Kol, the Twilight Lord. This is done in the name of the people of Terah, and with the blessing of the Celestial Actuary.* She then handed the quill to her husband, who reaching around her signed, *Gaius Prospero I, Emperor of Hetar.* Then he dripped a bit of sealing wax from a pot onto the document and pressed his seal of office into the wax, making a clear impression.

Vilia reached out and dusted the parchment with sand. Then she rolled it tightly and bowed low to the imperial couple. "Thank you, my lord emperor, my lady empress. Long live Hetar!" Then although she had not been given any instructions her own instinct told her to call out, "My lady Lara, I am ready to return." And sure enough she found herself suddenly in the chamber at Lady Gillian's house where her husband and the others were awaiting her. She handed Jonah the rolled document. "His permission in writing!" she said triumphantly.

Jonah unrolled the parchment and read it quickly before handing it to Magnus Hauk. "Now, my lord," he said, "what do we do?"

The Dominus read the emperor's permission, then handed it to Lara.

She nodded. "Now," she said, "we begin to even the odds that have been against us. I will go to King Archeron and the remaining commanders of the Crusader Knights in the Coastal Kingdom to prepare for the transfer and division of our forces."

"And I will return to Terah to marshal our army," the Dominus said.

"What are we to do?" Jonah demanded to know.

"You will come with me," Lara told him, "so the commanders know what is being done is not a trick but on the emperor's orders."

He looked askance. "I am safe with you?" he demanded rudely.

"My lord, my powers over the years have grown greatly, and if I wanted to turn you into dust I should have done it long since. You are not worth my time. Aye, you are safe with me. It is my mother you have to fear. Her patience with mortals is not great." And Lara laughed as Lord Jonah paled briefly. She turned to her husband. "Are you ready, my lord?" And when he nodded with a small smile at her she waved her hand over him and he was gone.

"Will we be safe while you are gone?" Lady Gillian asked Lara.

"Remember that Prince Kaliq has put a spell about The City walls that will keep the Wolfyn out until we are prepared to act," Lara assured her. She looked to Jonah. "Now if you are ready, my lord," she said and before he might answer Lara swirled a mauve mist about them and when it evaporated they were gone.

"Stay with me at least for the night," Lady Gillian invited Lady Vilia. "The streets are dangerous in the best of times now and it is growing dark. You will be safe here. The Domina has said we are safe."

"Perhaps I will," Vilia returned. "I am alone in my own home but for the servants and many of them have gone into hiding. Servants are not as loyal as they once were, I fear," she complained with a sigh.

"Nothing is as it was," Lady Gillian replied. "Once everyone had a place here in Hetar, and everyone knew their place. We had prosperity and order. I am still trying to figure out what happened to bring us to such a pass as we now face."

"Greed for more and more," Vilia replied. "Too much prosperity being shared by fewer and fewer of our people. If a person's belly is full and they are useful, they are content. But when the people grow hungry and are idle, that is when trouble ensues. That is why the emperor shipped so many of our poor to the Outlands so they might be useful again."

Gillian laughed dryly. "The poor in the Outland province may have been put to labor, Vilia, but they are still hungry and unhappy. The magnates work them to death because there are always more of them to be used. But one day it will not be so. Then what shall we do? Whoever seeks to rule Hetar will have to solve all the problems that these past years have caused."

"And what do you favor?" Vilia asked slyly. "Shall we return to the old days of the High Council and no single head? Or shall we retain the imperial rule begun by my former husband?"

"I have not yet decided," Gillian replied. "But I do believe Lara is correct when she says that it is time women made up at least half the ruling body, whatever it is. Our population is now more women than men because of all the turmoil Gaius Prospero has caused us. We should have a say in those things affecting our lives. Our voices should be heard and our wishes should count for something, Vilia. Present whatever face you wish to present to your husband and to others, but speak the truth to me."

Vilia was silent for a long few minutes, and then she said,

"What if a woman ruled Hetar, Gillian? Not from behind the throne, but *on* the throne?"

"It is an interesting concept," Lady Gillian said slowly. "But I think it too soon, Vilia. First we must make our voices heard within the High Council. That will shock enough people as it is, but once they are used to it, then aye!" She chuckled. "I wonder what your mother-in-law would think of these thoughts you harbor."

"Farah? Pah!" Vilia said scornfully. "She gave no real thought to Jonah until she saw him rising to power. When his father's widow sold him into slavery as a boy she might have bought him herself and rescued him. But she did not. Her only concern is for her own prestige. I personally question whether she will be a good headmistress of the Pleasure Guilds, but then of course time will tell. Why did you retire? You are yet young enough to manage the responsibilities."

"No headmistress may serve more than three ten-year terms. I had served my time and under the law I had to retire," Gillian said. "Besides, I am not unhappy to be free of the burden of management."

Vilia nodded and then she said, "I hope Jonah is all right. He has never been comfortable with magic. And I think the Domina frightens him although he would never say it. She is not the girl she once was, is she?"

"Your husband will be fine with Lara," Gillian assured Vilia. "They will even now be speaking with the surviving commanders of the Crusader Knights."

And Gillian was correct. Lara and Lord Jonah had appeared

in King Archeron's hall in a swirl of smoke. Everyone had been startled but Archeron had stood up smiling.

"Greetings, Lara, Domina of Terah," he said, coming from his high board to take up her hands and kiss them. His curious glance went to her companion. "Lord Jonah, I bid you welcome, too," he said.

The Crusader Knights and their commanders in Archeron's hall looked uncomfortable. John Swiftsword stared at his daughter as if she were a total stranger.

"Greetings, my lord king," Lara said. "Greetings, my lord commanders of the Crusader Knights. Greetings to all the knights gathered in this chamber tonight." She did not single out her father. "I have brought Lord Jonah to attest to what is true." Her gaze swept the hall, commanding their attention. "The Dominus of Terah and the magic kingdoms have offered to aid Hetar in its battle against Kol, the Twilight Lord, whose forces even now assail The City."

A babble of surprise erupted among those gathered in the hall, but King Archeron signaled for silence so Lara might explain to them.

"While you attempted to invade a peaceful land, a land that has done you no harm, the Twilight Lord has sought to spread his evil and his darkness into Hetar. The Midlands have been ravaged," she concluded.

"We must return you quickly to Hetar," Lord Jonah said. "I bring the emperor's written command. We will join with the forces of Terah to defeat the Twilight Lord."

"Let me see the document," the head commander of the

Crusader Knights said. When Jonah handed it to him he scanned it carefully.

"It could be a forgery," an under-commander suggested.

"Nay, it is Gaius Prospero's signature," the head commander replied. "I have seen it often enough to know his scrawl." He turned back to Jonah. "Just what are we facing?" he asked the emperor's right hand.

To their surprise, Lord Jonah deferred to Lara.

"The Twilight Lord has three groups of allies. We have already convinced the giants who have been serving him to eschew his rule. They will not turn against Hetar. The fiercest of Kol's warriors are those he has sent to Hetar—the Wolfyn."

"Wolfyn are naught but a myth to frighten children," a Crusader Knight said.

"Wolfyn are very real," Lara told them. "They are creatures with the heads of wolves and the bodies of men. They are savages who kill for the pure joy of it and who enjoy violating mortal women for no other reason than just to hear them scream with terror as they force them to yield pleasures. There is no kindness or pity in them. Kol sends these minions of his darkness to take The City, the heart of Hetar. Take The City and the rest will fall or be taken as the Midlands have been taken. And then Kol will turn his eyes to Terah.

"The emperor realizes that we must stop the Twilight Lord now before he takes The City, before Hetar is lost to Kol. To do that, all of us must band together. Hetar, Terah and the magic kingdoms," Lara explained. "The Shadow Princes will transport you along with Terahn forces to a position just behind the

Wolfyn. They will bring a small number of Terahns into The City to join with those remaining Crusader Knights and Mercenaries who remained in order to protect The City. When all is in readiness, we will have the enemy caught in a pincer movement and together we will crush them."

"And the emperor is truly in accordance with this?" the head commander asked. "For once he appears to show some foresight."

"You know well what he is like," Jonah quickly put in, seeing an opportunity for himself, "but I worked hard to convince him that this was the wisest course."

"To treat with our enemy?" a voice among the Crusader Knights called out.

"We have only recently come into new information," Jonah said smoothly, "that convinces us that the Terahn threat was nonexistent."

"What a pity you did not have that information before you lost your men and your ships," King Archeron murmured dryly.

"The Terahns are not our enemies," Lord Jonah continued. "They are, it would seem, our friends, as their offer to help ward off the Twilight Lord has proven, my lords."

Lara almost burst into laughter at this and struggled to maintain a serious face.

"And what will Terah's help cost us, Lord Jonah?" the head commander asked. "How high a price must Hetar pay to escape the clutches of this Twilight Lord?"

"We seek nothing from Hetar except that you keep to your own borders," Lara told them all. "Terah has avoided Hetar for centuries. We would continue that policy, my lords. There is nothing that we want or desire from you."

They looked at her, astounded. Hetar was the pinnacle of the known world. There was no place like it. Yet Terah wanted naught from them? How could that be? The faerie woman had to be lying. But before they might explore this further, Lord Jonah spoke.

"My lords, we have little time to debate this issue. The emperor has given you his orders. You must obey them or be held accountable for treason. In wartime especially, such a thing cannot be tolerated." He looked to Lara.

She was impressed in spite of herself. Jonah was obviously not a man to dither over a decision. "I will return to Terah," she told them, "and then the Shadow Princes will come to you. Have your men ready immediately for transport, my lords. I will see you in the Midlands shortly." And then she was gone in a puff of her signature mauve smoke.

"I do not like this," the head commander said. "Have you actually seen these creatures, my lord? Or is this all faerie smoke to frighten us?"

"I have seen them. Squire Darah has seen them. He was so terrified he fled to The City, leaving behind his latest young wife to the tender mercies of the Wolfyn," Jonah told them with a sneer.

"Coward!" a voice among the Crusader Knights called out.

"The threat is real and not something imagined by Gaius Prospero?" the head commander persisted.

"The threat is horribly real. The emperor hides in his palace with the empress, drinking Razi and dreaming his dreams, my lords," Jonah told them. "When the Domina of Terah came to us and offered her husband's aid, I was suspicious, but then I saw the Wolfyn with my own eyes and I heard Squire Darah's terrified tale. The danger is real, my lords, and without the Terahns we should be at a terrible disadvantage."

"Why should we trust the magic kingdoms?" a Crusader Knight asked. "That storm that destroyed all the fleet but for one ship was nothing natural nor was the fog that preceded it. John Swiftsword can tell you. He was on the single ship that survived."

Lord Jonah looked to Lara's father. "Tell me," he said shortly.

"We were not far from the shore when this thick mist began to form. We spent days lost in it, never knowing where we were. Three of us managed to escape it, and at first we were not certain if it was the coast of the province, or if we had reached Terah. Finally, we realized it was our own shores in the distance. The other two vessels returned into the fog to tell them what we had found. And shortly thereafter, the storm began. But it raged only within the mist, my lord Jonah. While the sea around our ship was rough, the skies above were clear and sunny. And when the storm finally ceased and the fog bank was lifted we saw the destruction of our fleet and the dead floating in the waters of the Sagitta. It was no ordinary storm. It could only have been created by the magic kingdoms. Now these creatures offer to help us?"

"Would your daughter lie, John Swiftsword?" he was asked.

"The daughter I raised was a truthful girl, but this woman she had grown into is more her mother's child now than mine. Faeries can be deceitful," he said.

"There is no deceit about the danger we all face," Lord Jonah told them.

"And perhaps the magic kingdoms did not approve of your attempt to attack Terah," King Archeron said quietly. "Terah has always been peaceful."

"They are so undoubtedly to hide their great riches," a Crusader Knight said.

"I have been to Terah," Jonah told them. "I saw nothing but a vast green land."

"But the beautiful and costly goods they send us—" another Knight said.

"Produced in their own villages by their own hands," Jonah told them. "There are no large manufactories, my lords. It is all craft work."

"And you have seen this?" a Crusader Knight asked.

"Although I was kept to the castle of the Dominus most of my time in Terah, I was permitted several visits to the various fjords where the Terahn villages are located and the craftsmen and women live," Jonah said.

"What of their city?" came the query.

"There are no cities of any size. Not even a small one. Terah is ruled by the Dominus from his castle."

"It sounds quite primitive," someone said.

"Indeed, I consider it so," Jonah replied.

"Then how could such a primeval folk be considered a danger to Hetar?" a Knight Crusader commander demanded to know.

"We were told that the faerie woman who is its Domina had gained greater powers. You all know of her antipathy toward our emperor. It was believed that she was planning a new revenge upon Gaius Prospero that involved harming Hetar and The City itself. Rumors abounded, brief whispers heard in the main market square of The City by our spies. The emperor grew paranoid and became convinced that Terah presented a grave danger to Hetar. Nothing any of us said—myself, the young empress, my own wife, the lady Vilia—could dissuade him," Jonah told them. "A reasonable man would see that Terah in all its centuries of trading secretly with the Coastal Kings wanted nothing to do with Hetar. Why would they suddenly decide to attack us? As for the faerie woman, while she may not like Gaius Prospero she is Hetarian-born and has never shown any animosity toward her native land that I know of." He turned again to John Swiftsword. "You would know better than any, Swiftsword. Does your daughter have an enmity toward Hetar? I have never seen that she does."

"Nay," John Swiftsword replied. "Lara does not dislike Hetar. While her faerie destiny called her elsewhere, I have never known her to show disloyalty."

"Yet she speaks of Terah as her home," the Crusader Knight standing next to Swiftsword said suspiciously.

"She is wife to Terah's ruler," Jonah answered for Swiftsword. "Like any well-born and mannerly Hetarian woman, she has cleaved to her husband's house."

"Have you not talked enough?" King Archeron demanded. He knew the Hetarians' propensity for debating an issue until it was ragged. "Terah and the Shadow Princes have agreed to help Hetar. Gather your forces for transport, Knight Commanders.

Day will soon be breaking in the Midlands and you must have your people in place before the first light. Surprise will be your greatest advantage."

There was agreement around the high board, and as the Knight Commanders moved from the great table to gather their troops into the proper formations, a bevy of Shadow Princes appeared from the darkness in the back of the great hall of King Archeron. Their garments almost blinding in their whiteness, each of the princes attached themselves to a Knight Commander and soon the hall began to empty. Eventually only the Coastal King and Lord Jonah remained. It was then a prince came to the emperor's right hand and with a bow to King Archeron, transported Lord Jonah back to The City.

Alone for the first time in months the Coastal King sighed audibly. He did not need to be told that Gaius Prospero was through. Lord Jonah's careful and reasonable speech had already begun rallying the Crusader Knights away from the emperor. But he would lobby with others to prevent Jonah from becoming the next emperor. Hetar needed to return to its old way: a new High Council was needed. That was an idea he would most certainly get behind and so would his brother kings.

But now while the rest of Hetar was busy fending off the forces of the Twilight Lord, the Coastal Kings would meet together and begin ridding their territory of those Hetarians who had usurped their lands. The manufactories attempting to replicate cheap luxury goods in a bad imitation of Terahn products would be torn down. Greenery would be planted again and the sand dunes would protect them once more from the winter seas. The beaches would grow wide as they had once been. It was time to slough off the invaders and return to what they had once been. The new government would be so busy repairing the damage done to the Midlands and to The City itself that little thought would be given to the faraway Coastal Kingdom.

King Archeron smiled to himself. It would soon be time to bring their living vessels from the sea caves where they had been hidden from Gaius Prospero and his minions. Had they possessed such vessels they would not have lost half of their army. It would soon be time to set to sea again and meet the Terahn traders at the midpoint of the Sagitta. Aye, in just a little while life would be back to normal once again.

16

THE FOUR WOLFYN MOVED carefully through the tunnel beneath The City. It had been carved from rock and was dry. How long it had been in existence they did not know. They had found its entrance only by chance when digging a foundation for one of their fire machines for their master, the Twilight Lord. The four Wolfyn were curious to see where the tunnel ended and if there was an exit into The City. If such an entry could be found it would save a great deal of damage and they might present The City intact to Kol.

At last the winding tunnel came to its end and before them was a narrow stone staircase. Cautiously the four made their way up the steps and there at its top was a door. It was locked, of course. There was no key but one of the Wolfyn took his knife and thrust it into the lock, wiggling it this way and that until they heard a distinct *click*. The Wolfyn placed a hand on the door and it opened, its hinges creaking noisily.

Quickly they stepped through the door to find themselves in a cellar filled with wine barrels. They could see on the other side of the chamber another set of stairs.

"Where are we?" one of the Wolfyn asked softly.

Their leader, Ulf, signaled for silence for his sharp ears had picked up the sound of feet coming toward the cellar's door. He stepped back into the dimness with his three companions. The door at the top of the stairs opened and a pretty female carrying a silver pitcher hurried down and went directly to one of the barrels. Turning the spigot in the barrel's head to one side she thrust her pitcher beneath it. When it was obviously full the girl closed the spigot, turned and went back up the stairs. Before she closed the door sounds of merriment could be heard coming from above them.

"It is a Pleasure House," Ulf said. "We must wait for a bit, then we will venture above to see what we can see. Hrolf, go back and tell Lord Hrolleif that we have found a way into The City that has not been enchanted against us. When we know a little bit more of where we are we will come back and tell him."

The Wolfyn known as Hrolf detached himself from their party and made his way back down the tunnel staircase. The three remaining Wolfyn waited patiently. Several times in the hours that passed a servant girl carrying a pitcher or two would come into the wine cellar to fill her vessels and then hurry out again. And as the cellar door opened and closed the Wolfyn listened to the sounds coming from above them.

Eventually some time passed without anyone coming for more wine. Ulf climbed the stairs, then slowly opened the door into a hallway. It was deserted and the sounds of revelry were now silent. He signaled to the two Wolfyn below to join him.

Cautiously the trio made their way through the corridor until they entered a kitchen. There they found a single servant woman taking loaves of bread from a warming oven and placing them in the baking oven. Coming up behind her they caught her, muffling her cries and forcing her into a chair. Her eyes widened in shock and terror as she recognized what they were and almost instantly she fainted. They roused her with a bucket of water.

"Whose house is this?" Ulf asked low. "And if you make any attempt to rouse help you will be killed. Cooperate and we will spare you." He nodded and the Wolfyn whose hand covered the serving woman's mouth removed it.

The servant's mouth opened and closed several times with her fright.

"Speak up, woman! I grow impatient," Ulf growled.

"Lady Gillian!" the woman finally managed to gasp. "You are in Lady Gillian's house. Ohh, do not kill me!"

"It is a Pleasure House?"

"Yes! Yes!" the servant said.

Ulf nodded curtly and the Wolfyn behind the woman quickly strangled her. She slumped forward in the chair. "The Pleasure District is near to the center of The City," Ulf said. "If we can secure this house then the tunnel may be used freely by our soldiers. With enough of us inside The City we can fight our way to the main gates and open them. First we must take all here prisoner. We will go floor by floor."

"What will we do with those we find?" one Wolfyn asked.

"Kill any men. Put the women in the cellar. Pleasure Women are valuable," Ulf said and led his men upstairs. But to their surprise they found no one in the house until they reached the top floor. There, in a spacious suite with a large terrace that offered a magnificent view of The City, they discovered two women whom they roused. Both recognized them for what they were, yet neither screamed.

"Who is the lady of the house, and if this is a Pleasure House why are there no other women here but you two?" Ulf demanded. "We heard sounds of merriment last night as we waited."

"I am Gillian and this is my sister, Vilia. We have just been retired by the Guild. Last night we were feted by our women and clients. The house is empty because it will be given to another Pleasure Mistress to run and she will want to choose her own women. Now I have answered your question, you answer mine. How did you get in here?"

"I do not have to answer your questions, Pleasure Woman," Ulf told her. Then he reached out and drew Gillian to him. His hand fondled her large breast. "I have always wanted to take pleasures with a Pleasure Woman," he said. "And if you were the mistress of this house then you must be skilled beyond an ordinary female." He ripped away the sleep garment she had been wearing and, pushing her away, looked at her admiringly. "You have a fine body, woman." He grinned, showing his sharp teeth. "What think you, Fernir? Rolf? Shall we have a little taste of one of The City's Pleasure Women for ourselves before the rest of our Wolfyn arrive to enjoy them?" He fumbled with his garments and drew out his male organ. "What think you of this, Pleasure Mistress Gillian? Is this not a fine sight to set a woman's heart aflutter?"

Gillian reached out and stroked him. "Indeed it is, but of

course I have seen bigger," she smiled as she moved next to him and stroked his face with a silken hand. "Vilia, go and fetch us some wine and bring some restoratives for I expect we are in for a long session, are we not, my lord Wolfyn?"

"Rolf must go with her," Ulf said.

"Of course," Gillian purred, turning to face him, her large breasts rubbing against his leather breastplate. "Ohhhh, I love the hard feel of leather on my nipples." She cast Vilia a look that told her companion she was going to have to save herself and if possible go for help.

"Do not use them all up," Vilia responded provocatively. "I want my share, too, Sister."

Ulf growled his laughter and, twisting Gillian about, bent her over the arm of the salon's couch, kicked her legs apart and thrust into her. "You won't miss a thing, Pleasure Woman. I have plenty for you both." And then with a grunt he began to move himself upon his helpless victim.

Her heart pounding with a fright she managed to conceal, Vilia walked from the apartment in the company of the Wolfyn called Rolf. She almost ran the three flights down the stairs, her companion right behind her. When they reached the bottom of the staircase he grabbed at her, ripping the front of her night garment away, and pawed at her breasts as she struggled. "We must get the wine, you wicked beastie," she protested.

"Let me have a little taste," he growled. His fingers pinched at her nipples.

"Oh, you are so fierce," she flattered him as she attempted to squirm out of his grasp. "But we must fetch the wine and the restoratives if we are to spend time enjoying ourselves. Pleasures are best enjoyed over a long period of time, Rolf."

His hand pushed between her legs and two fingers dove into her love sheath. "You're wet!" he growled low. "Take my member in your hand, woman!"

Vilia saw a slender brass vase on the table near where they now stood. If she could just get her hands on it. But until then the Wolfyn had to be distracted. She reached down and drew his male organ from his leather trousers. "Ohhh, you're so big," she cooed at him. "I am so little and you are so big. Oh, I do not think I can take such a big rod in my tight little sheath."

"Aye," the Wolfyn snarled. "Aye, woman, you can!" And before she realized it Vilia found herself impaled on the Wolfyn's long thick member. Surprised, she almost swooned with the pleasure it was offering her. Well, she thought, I might as well enjoy the ride this creature is going to give me. The Wolfyn groaned and whined with his lust as he pistoned the female in his grasp. He realized she was obtaining pleasures from him from her little cries and he lifted his head, howling as his crisis approached.

And it was at that exact moment that Vilia reached out, her slender fingers wrapping themselves about the brass vase, smashing it down as hard as she could upon her assailant's head. Then she hit him a second and a third time before the Wolfyn slid away from her, a large gash in his head bleeding profusely. Vilia didn't stop to see if she had killed him. She headed immediately for the door of the Pleasure House, stopping only to open the trunk in the entry that held outerwear and snatch up a cloak to cover her ripped garment. Then she fled the house.

Upstairs as Ulf continued to labor over the now almost unconscious Gillian his companion grinned hearing Rolf's howl. "Looks like Rolf couldn't wait for his pleasures," Fernir said. "It will be a while before we see that wine."

Ulf grunted in agreement.

Vilia ran as fast as she could to the gates of the Pleasure District, and roused the guard there. Recognizing her, they snapped to attention. She quickly explained that three Wolfyn had somehow managed to enter Lady Gillian's house and that the lady was keeping them entertained while she had allowed Vilia to escape to warn the authorities.

"You've been injured, my lady," one of the guards said.

"It doesn't matter. I'm fine," Vilia said impatiently. "You must go to Lady Gillian's and learn how these creatures entered The City. They cannot have come over the walls or through the gates, for they have been enchanted to protect us. You will find the one I injured, killed perhaps, in the front hallway. The other two are in Lady Gillian's apartment atop the house."

"I have heard stories about old tunnels beneath The City," said one of the older guardsmen, a retired mercenary.

"There is a wine cellar in the house!" Vilia cried. "Perhaps this tunnel is there."

"More than likely," the old guardsman said.

"If the Wolfyn can enter through those tunnels they can circumvent the walls and take The City. We must stop them. Oil! We need several vats of cooking oil. We can pour it into the tunnel and set it afire! It's the only way until we can destroy that tunnel. And you must kill the two Wolfyn in Lady Gillian's house. They cannot be allowed to live," Vilia said angrily.

Guardsmen were dispatched to fetch the barrels of cooking oil, and others returned to Lady Gillian's house accompanied by Vilia. Rolf was not dead but before he might get his bearings again the old guardsman slit his throat. Vilia remained in the hallway while the cellar was inspected and the entrance to the tunnel confirmed. The barrels of oil were carefully brought in and taken down into the tunnel to be emptied onto the hard dirt floor. The empty barrels were left at the foot of the staircase. It was then that the old guardsman, a wily fellow, discovered that the steps from the tunnel were not stone at all, but ancient hardened wood. The steps would be drenched in oil and set aflame once the tunnel was fired. It would stop any immediate invading force. They had but to wait until they heard the Wolfyn approaching.

A second party of guardsmen crept up the stairs to the top of the house. Bursting into Lady Gillian's apartments they slew Ulf, who was sprawled exhausted in a chair, having satisfied his initial lust, while Fernir vigorously rode Lady Gillian, seeking his own glory. Fernir's throat was slit before he might howl with either his surprise or his emotions and his lifeless body was dragged from Gillian.

"My lady! My lady!" A guardsman sought to rouse the obviously abused woman, but then to his surprise she arose, naked and so beautiful that his eyes bugged from his head. Never had he seen a Pleasure Woman of this rank! He would always remember this if he lived to be a hundred.

Gillian walked slowly across the chamber and opening a wardrobe, drew out a garment that she quickly wrapped about herself before turning a brilliant smile upon the party of guardsmen now crowding into her apartment. "Thank you," she said simply.

"Are you all right, my lady?" the guardsman who had dared to touch her asked.

"I have in my day entertained far more vigorous lovers," Gillian said. "Is Lady Vilia safe? She was keeping me company when those creatures burst into the house. Do you know how they got in, guardsman?"

"I believe one of the old tunnels beneath The City was used," he said.

"Of course," Gillian murmured. "That is how they would have circumvented the enchantment of the gates and walls." She moved quickly past the guardsmen and down the stairs into the cellar where Vilia stood with a second part of guardsmen. The two women embraced. "You are all right?" Gillian asked. "How did you escape your guard?"

Vilia's voice was soft and low. "I let him have his way with me and when he was fully involved I hit him several times with that lovely heavy, brass vase in the hallway. Let that be our little secret, however."

"Was he as lusty and satisfactory as my Wolfyn were?" Gillian murmured and Vilia laughed softly. "You are obviously a very bad girl, my lady Vilia."

"I used to help Anora whip Gaius and I must admit to quite enjoying it," Vilia answered. "What a pity there are no Pleasure

Houses for women to visit. While I love Jonah and will be ever loyal to him, I do enjoy a bit of variety now and again. I expect that most women do if they would but admit it. Why should we be censured for it? Men are never censured for desiring change."

"Now there is something we might consider in the new Hetar," Gillian replied low. "And it would certainly solve some of the employment problem, wouldn't it?"

"I hear something," the old guardsman said softly. He crept down the steps into the tunnel, looked back at them and nodded. Then he tossed the lighted torch as far down the tunnel as he could and scrambled back up the stairs just a moment before the oil in the tunnel blazed fiercely up. Suddenly frantic screams were heard from the tunnel as it filled with flames. One enormous guardsman hacked with a great ax at the wooden landing, leaping back through the door just as it gave way and the stairs to the tunnel collapsed partly, catching fire. The flames, however, were not high enough to reach the door of the cellar, so the house was safe.

"I will leave a contingent of men here, my lady Gillian," the old guardsman said. "We must report this incident to the authorities. A search must begin immediately for any other tunnel entries beneath the houses of The City."

"Thank you for all your help," Lady Gillian said. "Be certain that the emperor will learn of your devotion to duty. And Lord Jonah, too."

The old guardsman bowed gallantly and left them.

"Come back to my house," Vilia said.

Gillian shook her head. "It is here we have hatched our plots and here that Lara will come back to us, Vilia," she said.

"Then I will remain with you," Vilia answered. "We should try to get word to Lara of what has happened. Perhaps if we just call to her she will come to us."

"We can try," Gillian responded. Together the two women walked back upstairs to Gillian's apartments.

Both women bathed themselves in Gillian's private bath and then donned fresh garments. They discussed quite frankly their encounter with the Wolfyn males, noting that indeed below the neck they were quite human if perhaps a bit larger. And both admitted to have obtained pleasures with their partners but then swore each other to secrecy with a smile. When they had settled themselves again they decided to call out to Lara and see if she would come to them. She had told them that she would.

"My lady Domina, Lara of Terah, please come to us," Gillian said. "We need you." They waited.

And then after a short time Lara appeared in her colored haze. "Why have you called to me?" she asked them.

"The Wolfyn found another way into The City," Gillian began.

"We believe we have stopped them for now," Vilia added.

"Tell me," Lara said, her face suddenly grave. When would this all end?

They explained what had happened and Lara nodded finally.

"There could be more tunnels," Vilia said. "And we cannot be certain if our oily flames have stopped the Wolfyn from the tunnel beneath this house."

Prince Kaliq, heed my call. Come to me from out yon wall, Lara intoned.

At once the handsome Shadow Prince was with them and Lara explained her need for him. Kaliq nodded. "We shall seal all the tunnels," he told them. "I had forgotten about them as they have not been used in centuries." Then he turned to both Gillian and Vilia. "You were very brave, my ladies. Hetar can be proud of you both. You are heroines."

"Hetar must never know," Vilia said quietly and Gillian nodded in agreement.

"You fear what people would say?" the prince asked.

"I am wife to the emperor's right hand," Vilia replied. "That Gillian and I saved The City by yielding our bodies to these Wolfyn would not be considered an honorable act. My husband would be embarrassed and it could harm his ambitions. Whatever I may be, my lord prince, I love Jonah. I did not seduce him and cuckold Gaius Prospero on a whim. There is no need for Hetar to know what happened."

The prince bowed again and nodded to her. "It will be as you wish, my lady." He bowed to Lara and Gillian, then faded into the shadows of the room.

"What of the guardsmen who helped us?" Gillian wondered aloud.

"They will remember nothing more than that Vilia sought their aid when a trio of Wolfyn invaded Lady Gillian's home. And that Lady Gillian kept the Wolfyn entertained and at bay with wine and promises until the guard arrived. Then the tunnel was discovered, oil poured into it, and fired. The Wolfyn were killed or beaten back and the tunnels now sealed by Prince Kaliq," Lara said. "It is all anyone need know about this matter. You will both be commended for your bravery before it is forgotten."

"Thank you," Lady Gillian said quietly.

"Can you tell us what is happening?" Vilia asked.

"The combined forces of Hetar and Terah are even now being transported into position," Lara told them. "Some have been placed behind the Wolfyn encamped outside of the city waiting to attack. Within The City Terahn forces have joined with the remaining Crusader Knights and the Mercenaries. They are now massing before the main gates of The City. Your husband has been returned, my lady Vilia, but he is with the troops. Even now the guardsmen are going through The City warning the folk to remain indoors this day. Those without homes are being shel-tered by whomever will take them in."

"Send me women and children," Lady Gillian said. "I have more than enough room. Vilia, will you remain and help me?"

To Lara's surprise Lord Jonah's wife nodded. "I'll stay," she said.

"Where are your servants?" Lara asked Gillian.

"I let them go to their families if they chose," the older woman answered. "All but old Rona, my baker, who has no family." Then Gillian paled. "The Wolfyn came from the cellars. If they passed by the kitchens…" Her voice trailed off.

"I smell baking bread," Vilia noted.

"I will go and see for you," Lara said. The two mortal women had had more than enough this day, she thought. She knew what *entertaining* the Wolfyn would have involved. Gillian's bravery hardly surprised her but Vilia's certainly did. She left them and went down to the kitchen where she found the poor baker dead in a chair. With a wave of her hand Lara sent the body to its grave and then removed the loaves of bread from the ovens. Return-ing to Gillian and Vilia she told them the baker had been killed by the Wolfyn and that old Rona had been disposed of with honor. "Now I must leave you," she said.

"Where will you go?" Vilia asked her.

"First home to tuck my children into their beds, for it is night now in Terah. Then I shall return to fight in the battle that is to come. Remember, Hetar is the land of my birth. With the blessing of the Celestial Actuary we may defeat the forces of the Twilight Lord this day." And then she was gone from them.

"What an unusual creature she is," Vilia noted. "In the midst of all this chaos she thinks of her children. I would not have thought her a good mother given her life."

"I suspect when she does not have the weight of our worlds upon her slender shoulders, she is happiest being nothing more than a wife and a mother," Gillian remarked.

"Do you think her children have magic?" Vilia wondered.

"Mayhap, although their fathers have been mortal," was the reply. Then Gillian said briskly, "We had best prepare for the women and children we are to shelter," as a knock sounded upon her front door downstairs.

Throughout The City the doors and windows of every available building were being shut and barred. The morning was breaking, but the skies above were gray and dark clouds loomed on the horizon. Those on the walls could see the fires of the Wolfyn encampment and the shadowed figures of the enemy hurrying back and forth. They saw the fire machines anchored in their pits, kettles of pitch burning next to them. Tightly woven balls of oily wool stacked in piles next to the kettles were to be dipped into the pitch and flung from catapults. The fire machines would be used to destroy enough of The City to bring its inhabitants to their knees in abject surrender. Many could die.

Hrolleif, the high commander of the Wolfyn, paced back and forth within his tent. He had lost his favorite nephew, Ulf, whose head had been thrown from the battlements of The City along with Rolf and Fernir's. Hrolf and at least a dozen other Wolfyn had been roasted within the tunnel when it had been set afire. He had been mad to even consider using the tunnel. Battling face-to-face with an enemy was far preferable to sneaking up on him. Hrolleif looked into the reflecting bowl on his camp table.

"My lord, we are almost ready," he said.

The Twilight Lord's face appeared upon the surface of the water. "Try not to destroy everything or kill everyone," he cautioned his general. "And remember that the faerie woman is mine. She is not to be harmed. As for the rest of them I care not what you do. Slay her husband if you can."

"And the Hetarian hierarchy, my lord?"

"Kill its pompous emperor. You may have the empress for yourselves. I do not want her but I believe she will scream quite nicely for you, Hrolleif," Kol said.

The Wolfyn commander smiled toothily. "What of the rest of them?"

"Leave them be for now. I believe I may have kin among them and I should never kill my kin," Kol murmured. "Family is so important, is it not?"

"Indeed, my lord. Will Skrymir and his giants be joining us?"

"The traitor has deserted us, but one day we will repay him for his perfidy," Kol said darkly.

"Do not fret yourself, my lord," Hrolleif said. "My Wolfyn and I can take The City easily and then will Terah fall to us," he boasted.

"Be certain that you do," Kol said, his dark voice heavy with menace. And then his image disappeared from the watery surface of the reflecting bowl.

"We are ready to attack, Commander Hrolleif," his second's voice announced.

"Then let us begin," Hrolleif said. "I want to spend my evening in one of those Pleasure Houses for which Hetar is so famed," he growled as he walked outside to view his troops. They were a fine-looking bunch, he thought. He raised his hand in signal. At once those on the great horned battering ram began to pound upon the main gates of The City, but try as they might, and despite Hrolleif's roars of encouragement, the gates did not give way in the slightest.

Up on the walls the Hetarian soldiers looked down and laughed until the tears rolled down their faces. They knew their gates were secure thanks to the Shadow Princes. There would be no battle until they were ready. The Wolfyn howled with their anger and frustration.

Hrolleif had not planned on using the fire machines until the last, but now he signaled to the soldiers standing by them to begin hurling some of their pitch-covered balls into The City just to teach these arrogant Hetarians a lesson. The first three fireballs soared toward the roofs of The City, but then as Hrolleif watched in amazement the fireballs seemed to hit some barrier and they bounced back to his encampment, setting several tents afire. He roared with his fury as his attack on The City came to a halt while the Wolfyn scurried to put out the fires before the entire camp was ablaze. The Hetarians on the wall roared with their laughter.

And then suddenly the gates to The City opened wide, revealing a great army which marched out to meet his own men. And when they had all exited, Hrolleif saw a great platform set up in the open gates. On it sat the fat and foolish emperor of Hetar and his beautiful wife, along with other dignitaries including the faerie woman, Lara, his master Kol's mate. But the faerie was not garbed as befit a woman. Instead, she wore tight-fitting doeskin breeches that clung to her supple form, a white shirt, and over it a small golden breastplate. The long golden gilt hair he remembered was hidden beneath a golden helmet and upon her back was a sword the like of which he had never seen. Even from here he could see there was something special about the weapon. Why would a beautiful woman carry such a weapon? Women did not own weapons.

Hrolleif suddenly realized that men and Wolfyn were fighting all around him, and he swung his sword, engaging the enemy in battle as he had been taught so long ago. He battled his way through the mass of fighting men, something seeming to lead him onward toward the platform in the gate. And then suddenly he found himself standing before the faerie woman, Lara. "Woman!" he shouted. "Step aside!" But she did not. Instead she drew her weapon from its scabbard and raised it aloft. Hrolleif was astounded.

Her green eyes were like ice and he felt the cold as if he had been encased in it. Her great sword met his, metal clanging noisily against metal. He drew back. He didn't want to fight her. She was Kol's mate. It was his duty to return her to the Dark Lands so his master would be happy again and would reward him. But then he saw the glowing eyes of a face in her sword's hilt. And he heard a deep dark voice begin to sing.

"I am Andraste, companion to the mighty swordswoman, Lara. I have come to drink the blood of the evil ones."

"Come, Hrolleif," Lara's voice mocked him. "Surely you are not afraid of a mere woman? If I allow you to live, how will you explain it to Kol?"

"I would rather die with my own sword in my hand than face the Twilight Lord with my failure," Hrolleif said.

"So be it," Lara told him. They began to battle in earnest.

He was a good opponent. He was strong but Lara was quicker and, Hrolleif soon realized, far more skilled than he was. He was astounded by her expertise. For every blow he offered, she blocked him. Twice she blooded him. Her sword sang as it tasted his flesh. He had never imagined that any woman could be so fine a warrior. But he fought on, for to yield to a woman was simply unthinkable. About them the fighting slowly stopped as both sides watched the two battle. The other Wolfyn were shocked that their commander would even engage a woman in battle, but they could see Lara was no ordinary warrior. The sound of metal on metal resounded loudly about the battlefield. Hrolleif was visibly tiring. He stumbled over his own feet and Lara stepped back to allow him to regain them. If it had been her, Hrolleif thought, I would have killed her. He struggled to his feet. He could feel his heart laboring hard in his chest cavity. He was near his end—he sensed it. Then an icy chill went down the backs of both friend and foe as the mighty sword Andraste began to sing once again.

"I am Andraste. Yield to the swordswoman, Lara of Terah, Hrolleif of the Dark Land. Yield or die! I am Andraste, and I am prepared to drink your blood, oh servant of the evil one! Yield or die!"

Lara fought the high commander of the Wolfyn fiercely, driving him to his knees. Then their eyes met in complete understanding and she quickly thrust Andraste into Hrolleif's heart and as quickly withdrew it. He fell forward and his second raced to his side to seek a pulse. There was none. Suddenly all the Wolfyn raised their heads to the dark skies and howled. A moment later, however, the full battle was renewed. None would dare fight the faerie woman, so she withdrew to the platform within the open gates of The City and watched as the ground was flooded in blood, until every Wolfyn lay dead, caught between the army before them and the one behind, which had advanced from the Coastal Province.

When the last of the enemy had been slain the skies opened and a heavy rain came down on the battlefield. The downpour was so thick that they could see nothing of what had been. When it ended, the clouds fled northward and the skies became a clear bright blue and the sun shone down on them so that they saw all signs of the carnage were gone. There were no bodies to be seen. The tremulous voice of Gaius Prospero was heard as he came down from his throne to peer about. "Where are the bodies?"

"The magic kingdoms have taken them," Lara said. "You will find those slain Hetarians in a newly created graveyard to the west of The City where their kin may come and pay their respects."

"And the Terahns?" the emperor quavered.

"Our casualties were as bad as yours, Gaius Prospero, perhaps worse. Our people are not martial by nature. A great deal of Terahn blood has been shared to save Hetar and keep it safe. Remember that, for Hetar now owes Terah a debt. We will want to collect on that debt one day."

Gaius Prospero nodded slowly in reply. Then he turned to address a slender young boy who had run up to where they stood. "What is it?" the emperor asked impatiently.

"I must speak with the lady Lara," the boy said. To Lara's eye there was something familiar about him.

"What is it, lad?" she asked him gently.

The boy's face suddenly crumpled and he began to weep. "S...Sister," he sobbed. "Our father is dead. Our father has been slain in the battle." Then he flung himself at her and Lara's arms closed automatically about him.

"Mikhail?" Her arms tightened around the boy.

His tear-stained face looked up at her and he nodded.

"You were an infant when I left Hetar," Lara said. "And I know that your mother told you nothing about me. How did you know I was your sister?"

"Father told me," the boy said low. "He was proud of you, but my mother is a jealous woman."

"How came you here on the battlefield, Little Brother? And how do you know our father was killed?"

"He was beginning my training in warfare," Mikhail said, his voice trembling as he spoke. "I awaited him on the edge of the battlefield with an extra sword and a mace. I saw him fall from his horse. When he tried to rise, a Wolfyn leapt upon him and slew him. Then his body disappeared as the battle ended. John Swiftsword, Hetar's greatest swordsman, is dead, Sister."

Lara stroked his nut-brown hair. "You must be the man of the family now, Mikhail. Susanna will need you. Be good to her. You will find our father's grave, marked with his name, in the new graveyard west of The City. He rests upon the highest point there." Then she tipped his face up so she might look into his eyes. "If you should ever need me, Mikhail, son of Swiftsword, you have but to call my name and I will come to you, for we share blood between us." She kissed his cheek. "Go."

The boy gave her a tremulous smile, then turned and walked away. Lara looked again at the emperor. "We will take our dead and be gone."

"Now my people and I will bid you farewell, Gaius Prospero. Do not attempt to venture into Terah again. Let things return to the way they were between us, emperor of Hetar," Magnus Hauk said in a stern voice.

A mighty clap of thunder shook the entire city and the Dominus of Terah, his wife, his soldiers and the Terahn dead disappeared. A gasp arose from those still present, then it was silent.

Finally Lord Jonah spoke. "My lord emperor, I believe the entertainment is now over. You will want to return to your palace." He helped Gaius Prospero up.

"Yes, yes," the emperor said. "Where is Shifra?"

"I am here, my dear lord," the young empress said as she escorted her husband to their elegant gold litter. "I will see he is made comfortable, Lord Jonah." Then at her signal the imperial litter was quickly borne off.

Vilia came to her husband's side. "It has been a full day, my lord, has it not?"

"Why were you at Lady Gillian's?" he surprised her by asking.

"She was alone and I was alone. She asked me to remain. I was glad to do so as you were gone, our servants had scattered into hiding and the streets are not safe at night," Vilia said quietly. "Would you have preferred I walk home to an empty house in the dark, Jonah, my love?"

"How did you and Gillian hold off the Wolfyn?" he demanded to know. "I have heard naught but how brave you were, my wife, in seeking out the guard."

"Then you know that three Wolfyn gained entry into Gillian's home through one of the old tunnels beneath The City," Vilia told him. *Be careful,* her instinct warned her. "There was no one in the house but Gillian's baker. They killed her and then found us in Gillian's apartment. Stupid creatures! They had heard of Pleasure Women, and were impressed by Gillian's manners and elegance. She pretended I was her sister and sent me for wine and restoratives."

"And they let you go alone?" Jonah asked. "Then they were indeed stupid."

"Nay, they sent one of their number as my escort. He came behind me. As we reached the bottom of the staircase in the main hall I spied a thin brass vase. I grabbed it, swung about and hit the beast with it several times. Then I fled from the house and found the guards."

"Did you kill it, Vilia?" Jonah asked softly.

"Nay, he was still alive when the guards returned. They delivered the death blow, my lord," Vilia told him.

He took her face between his thumb and his forefinger. "Were you ravished, Vilia? Do not lie to me, for I will know if you do," he said in even softer tones.

"My lord! Nay! How can you even ask such a thing of me?" Vilia protested, shuddering with open distaste. She stared directly into his dark eyes as she denied it.

His strong thin fingers pressed hard against her cheeks. "I would have to kill you, Vilia, if I knew another had had you, my love."

"You are jealous, my lord," she taunted him. "But without reason. If I had been ravished I should have killed myself rather than bear the dishonor. Remember the noble house from which I spring, Jonah. Is it possible, just possible, that what began between us as an alliance of ambition has turned to love?"

A ripple of something passed so quickly across his face that she wasn't even certain she had seen it. "Love," he said coldly, "is for fools."

Vilia laughed. "You were always a bad liar where I was concerned, Jonah, but I will leave it at that. The danger from the Twilight Lord has passed. The Terahns have left us to our own devices. Now, my lord, what are we to do next?"

"We will build our alliances, my love, while we wait for Gaius Prospero's promised demise. It should not be long, Vilia."

She smiled at him. "I agree. So let us go home. You could

probably use a nice bath, some food, some wine from our vine-yards. And then perhaps we may spend the night taking pleasures with one another. I have missed you while all of this has been going on, my lord. I long to have your manhood within me making me weep with delight. Are you not eager, my lord, for our reunion?" she purred, her tongue running provocatively over her lips.

"Aye," he said. "I am hungry for you, my love."

Thank the Celestial Actuary, Vilia thought. His suspicions were allayed. The thought that he would have killed her had he known of her encounter with the Wolfyn angered her. How in the name of holy Hetar did he think a woman escaped a situation like that in one piece? Were all men fools? Gillian was right. It was time for the women of Hetar to take over.

Life slowly returned to normal, but the poor were poorer and the economy did not improve. Small grumblings were beginning to be heard in the public squares of The City. There was even some talk of removing the emperor, but no one dared move further. One morning the news flew through The City that the young empress had disappeared in the night. The emperor had fallen asleep in her arms and when he had awakened she was gone. A search of the palace was made, but no trace of Shifra was found. It was as if she had simply evaporated into thin air.

Gaius Prospero was convinced that his wife had been kid-napped. He offered a great reward for any information leading to her safe return but no one came forward to claim the bounty. And then to everyone's surprise the emperor began to have nightmares that Shifra was calling to him from the Dream Plain.

He would awaken covered in sweat and shouting her name. The physicians were called and they dosed the emperor with sleeping medication so he would have no dreams. Drugged at night and drunk on Razi most of the day, Gaius Prospero began to sink deeper and deeper into depression. He wept for his lost wife during his conscious moments. His children came to see him. His daughters brought his grandchildren but the emperor did not care. He kissed them absently and then sent them away. The most beautiful of The City's Pleasure Women were brought to him yet he was not in the least interested, which amazed everyone, for Gaius Prospero had always been noted for his appreciation of a beautiful woman.

His other appetites declined, as well. He was no longer interested in the rich foods he had always loved. The palace cooks did their best, but other than a forkful or two his meals were returned untouched. His desire for fine wine was gone. Gaius Prospero, always a man of grand proportions, grew thin and wan. His hair fell out. He suffered great pains in his joints. And now even his need for Razi left him, for when he drank it he no longer dreamed of glory but suffered from terrible head pains. And he continued to weep for his lovely young empress who had been the only creature in all his life that the emperor had loved. Then one stormy, moonless night, as his faithful slave woman Tania sat weeping softly by his side, Gaius Prospero died, his lost love's name on his parched blue lips.

Lord Jonah knew first, for Tania, though heartbroken, was wise in the ways of her late master. She left her master's dead body and hurried to find the emperor's right hand. There were new alliances to be made now even for a slave. She was amazed when Lord Jonah told her that as the keeper of the emperor's will, he knew its contents. Tania would now be free and given a small pension for her years of devoted and loyal service to Gaius Prospero.

Tania immediately knelt before Jonah. "Then it is as a free woman, my lord, that I offer your house my small services," she said.

Jonah nodded. "And I accept them, Tania," he told her. "You will watch over my wife for me, will you not?"

"Does Kigva not watch over the lady Vilia?" Tania said slowly.

"Indeed, Kigva is Vilia's most loyal servant. But you, Tania, will be mine," Jonah said meaningfully.

Tania arose from her subservient position before him and bowed from the waist. "As I loyally served my late master, Gaius Prospero, so will I loyally serve you, my lord Jonah," she promised him, her face serious with her intent.

He gave her a nod of acknowledgment. "Go back and sit with the body so that no one else knows yet that he is dead. I will put my plans into motion."

"Yes, my lord," Tania said and hurried from his presence.

Kigva was crossing the far end of the broad hallway when she saw Tania coming from Lord Jonah's library. She ran quickly to tell her mistress.

"The emperor must be dead," Vilia said softly. "It is the only reason that Tania would go to my husband in the middle of the night. The clever creature is currying his favor. Quickly! I must send a faerie post to Lady Gillian. My husband must not be allowed to seize power. At least not until the women of Hetar have entrenched themselves in the ruling body. We will have no more of the men taking us into war and impoverishing our people. There must be change."

Kigva brought her mistress her writing box and Vilia scrawled a message to Lady Gillian. The faerie post messenger, given the rolled parchment, dashed off to deliver the message. It had no sooner gone than Lord Jonah entered his wife's apartments.

"Gaius Prospero is dead," he told her without any preamble. "I am gathering my allies so that I may be given charge over Hetar before the High Council can meet to debate the issue to death and in the end do nothing."

"You would be emperor then?" Vilia asked him.

"Nay, Gaius Prospero has given the title emperor a bad reputation. I would be called the Lord High Ruler of Hetar," Jonah said.

"And I will be?" she pressed him.

"You are my wife," he said to her. "You are the wife of the Lord High Ruler."

"It is a great honor you do me," Vilia murmured, but he did not, to her surprise, pick up on her sarcasm.

"Aye," he muttered, his mind obviously somewhere else. "You have always been a perfect wife, Vilia. It is your forte." Then he kissed her absently. "I must go, my love, there is much to do to cement my position. Of course, my first act once I am declared Lord High Ruler will be to plan a glorious funeral for my predecessor and beloved friend, Gaius Prospero. His contributions to the welfare of Hetar have been many." He hurried off without another word to her.

For several long minutes Vilia stood silent and still. Once again she had been cut off from the power. Jonah had many times promised her that when he became emperor that she would be his empress. But now he would arrange a different title, Lord High Ruler, and she was again thwarted in her quest to rule. She would be relegated to nothing more than wife. Then Vilia laughed. Jonah was right. Love was for fools and she had been a fool for falling in love with him. He thought of her as all Hetarian men thought of all women. They were good for pleasures, for bearing children, but little else. Why had she believed he was different? Because until now he had treated her as his equal, but that had only been a ruse to help him climb the ladder of success.

Finally Kigva spoke. "What will you do now, my lady?" she asked softly.

Vilia laughed and then she turned to Kigva with a brilliant smile. "Let him be made Lord High Ruler if he can indeed manage it," she told her serving woman. "Becoming it and remaining it are two different things, my girl. I have said it is time for the women of Hetar to speak up and indeed it is. Thanks to Gaius Prospero's wars we are now the majority. We must now speak up for our rights and the rights of the generation of women to come."

"Not all women will support you, my lady," Kigva replied.

"More will than won't," Vilia answered. "I will not be pushed aside any longer because of my sex. Besides, women are wiser than men. It is not simply Lady Lara's magic that makes the Domina of Terah respected by her husband and her people. It is her wisdom."

"Would you rule Hetar, mistress?" Kigva queried.

"I *will* rule Hetar one day," Vilia responded. "It is my fate as the twelfth generation of the descendants of Ulla, the favored concubine of a great sorcerer. It is said that before she died she said that the twelfth generation of her descendants would rule Hetar. I am the only descendant in the twelfth generation. I once believed that it was my lot to be Gaius Prospero's empress, but it was not. And then Jonah promised me that I would be his empress, but now he makes himself Lord High Ruler and tries to relegate me to a subservient position. Is it not obvious to you, Kigva, that if I am to rule Hetar that I will do it in my name and not a man's?"

Kigva nodded.

"Then you will help me to work toward that goal," Vilia told her serving woman. "And you will continue to keep my secrets, will you not?" She smiled at the younger woman. "I am quite certain that Tania, the late emperor's slave woman, will offer her services to my lord Jonah. She probably already has. She is a clever woman, and quick to watch for every advantage. Do not trust her, Kigva. She will attempt to worm her way into your confidence, but beware of her no matter what she says."

"If she is a slave, can she not be sold away?" Kigva asked.

Vilia shook her head. "The emperor will have freed her with his death. He was always most fond of her and she was totally loyal to him."

"I will be careful of her," Kigva promised. "I will not reveal your secrets, my lady, and one day you will fulfill your ancestress's prophecy. I know that you will!"

Vilia smiled again. "Yes, I will," she said.

17

"THE EMPEROR IS dead," Lara told her husband.

"It is as you said it would be," Magnus Hauk replied. He was no longer interested in Hetar. The danger had been nipped in the bud, and everything was back to normal. The Twilight Lord was penned in his castle in the Dark Lands. The giants were now allies of Terah. The Wolfyn had been decimated. And as Lara had predicted, the dwarf nation was not about to go to war for Kol. Their task was to protect the two heirs to the Dark Lands.

"Jonah has managed to get himself elected something called Lord High Ruler," she continued. "How quickly he has distanced himself from everything having to do with Gaius Prospero," Lara said. "He has even managed to relegate Vilia to a place of unimportance. I doubt she is pleased with that. Once again, a husband has betrayed her."

"We need not be concerned with Hetar or its convoluted politics," Magnus Hauk said. "It has naught to do with us, my love." He lavished a warm and loving smile on her. On her swelling belly where his son now resided. *His son!* He could hardly wait to hold the boy in his arms. He loved Lara's children and he loved their daughter, Zagiri, but a man needed a son to carry on his name. This child would be his heir. This child would be the father of generations of Terahn rulers to come.

"There is no escaping Hetar, my lord," Lara told him. She had felt his thoughts, and frankly found herself irritated. This child in her belly had come from her love for Magnus Hauk, but suddenly he was behaving like a typical man and not the man she loved. "There can be no pretending that everything will return to what it was before our lands knew one another. Everything has changed, Magnus."

"Aye, we know one another, but praise the Great Creator that an ocean separates us. The rules for trade between our nations have not changed. To all intents and purposes Hetar does not exist for us," the Dominus said.

Lara sighed deeply. "Magnus," she said, "Hetar very much exists for Terah. Do you think that Jonah will be content to leave things as they are, knowing that we are here? We will gain some respite from him while he rebuilds his power base, but then we will have no choice but to deal with him and with Hetar."

"But for now they are out of our lives, and we don't have to," he replied. "You must not distress yourself, my love." His hand reached out to touch her growing belly.

Angered by his refusal to see or understand, and furious that he was treating her like some prized breeding animal, Lara abruptly got up and left him. Going to the stables she saddled Dasras and rode out from the castle. "Fly," she told the great stallion. "I need to get away from my husband, who is behaving like a perfect fool. If I remain I may say something I should not."

Dasras unfolded his great white wings and took to the skies above. "Where should we go?" he asked her. "And if he is concerned by your condition I must tell you that I agree with him. A mare in foal should be treated carefully."

Lara sniffed irritably at him. "Just fly up the fjord," she instructed him. "No! Take me to the Temple of the Daughters of the Great Creator. I shall visit with Kemina."

"Perhaps the high priestess can talk some sense into you," Dasras muttered.

"You are becoming a worse old woman than Magnus," Lara snapped at him.

The great golden stallion said nothing more. When they were within a few miles of the temple Dasras touched down as was his custom and galloped the remainder of the way, finally trotting into the courtyard where a young priestess came forward to take his bridle as he came to a stop. The bell announcing visitors was already being rung to herald her arrival. Recognizing the horse and its rider, the priestess bowed as Lara slid from Dasras's back.

"Where is Lady Kemina?" she asked.

"You will find her in the small garden of her house, my lady Domina," the young priestess said to Lara.

With a nod of thanks Lara hurried off to find the high priestess while Dasras was led off to be fed and watered.

Kemina had heard the visitor's bell and was already coming from her garden to greet Lara. Her deep blue eyes were welcoming as the two women embraced. Setting Lara back, she looked at her sharply. "You are with child," she said.

"I am giving Magnus his son," Lara told her.

"How lovely of you to come and tell me yourself," Kemina replied. "I suppose the Dominus is behaving like a perfect fool, attempting to keep you encased in cotton wool," she chuckled. "I know how you dislike it when he treats you like a child."

Lara laughed. "I had to get away from him or this babe would have been fatherless," she admitted. "May I remain with you for a few days?"

"Does he know where you are?" Kemina asked softly.

"Nay," Lara answered. "I simply went to the stables, saddled Dasras myself and came. It is not like this is my first child, Kemina, yet he persists in behaving like I am some fragile creature who will shatter if breathed upon."

"But it is more than that," Kemina noted wisely.

"Is it that obvious?" Lara said.

Kemina smiled. "Aye, it is. What else has he done?"

"He thinks because the forces of the Twilight Lord have been beaten back that all is well. He thinks that everything is now back to the way it was, but of course it isn't! He actually believes that we will never have to be bothered with Hetar again because an ocean separates us. He has said nothing about my slaying the Wolfyn commander, Hrolleif. You would think the battle between us had never happened, Kemina."

"Come and sit with me in my garden," Kemina said and she took Lara by the hand to lead her to a comfortable chair. "The lavender and the camomile are very soothing today as their fragrances are being released in the warmth. Soon it will be autumn again. I do love the autumn." She sat in a chair opposite Lara. "My child, have you considered that this battle you fought with the Wolfyn commander frightened Magnus? He is Terahn in his heart and soul, and until you came into his life neither he nor any male born in Terahn had ever heard the sound of a woman's voice. Women were thought to be helpless and so in need of protection that few ever even left their own homes. But you lifted Usi's curse and now women are once again beginning to regain the place they once held in our society. But Terahn women were never warriors. I can but imagine his fear when you took on the Wolfyn, Lara."

"But I am a warrior without peer," she said. "The Shadow Princes taught me to fight, Kemina. And with Andraste in my hands I fear no one and certainly not death. The Wolfyn commander was more bluster than skill."

Kemina laughed. "You are a beautiful creature, and although I know the Dominus understands your power on one level, seeing his delicate wife battling a great vicious creature with a wolf's head must have frightened him to death. He does not discuss it because he can't without wanting to shout at you for taking such a chance, especially when you are carrying his son," Kemina explained. "Please do not be angry with him over it, Lara. He loves you so deeply."

"He loves the delicate golden creature," Lara replied. "I am more than that and I cannot be what I am not. I will never be content to sit quietly at my loom while my children play about my feet, Kemina. I yet have a destiny unfulfilled."

"What more can you do, my child, that you have not already done?" the high priestess wondered. "You have lifted a terrible curse from us, vanquished the shade of an evil sorcerer, saved the people of the Outland nation from annihilation and found them a new home. You have prevented a terrible war from destroying Hetar and kept it from our shores entirely. I am certain the Great Creator is more than satisfied with you, Lara."

"There is more to do," Lara told her. "What, I do not yet know. But I know I have not completed all that it is meant that I do."

Kemina shook her snow-white head in wonderment. "It seems to me that a great deal of responsibility has been loaded upon your shoulders," she said. "Let me suggest that you forget about your destiny until it calls to you once again, Lara. Just enjoy the good life you have been given. Your husband. Your children. Your home and the child that is to come in a few months. You have done this before. You need not stand guard awaiting your destiny's next call."

Lara sighed. "You are right," she said. "These last months have been so frenzied I have forgotten how to enjoy my life."

The high priestess took Lara's slim hand in her own. "I understand how the responsibility that we bear for others can do that, my child."

Lara laughed now. "Aye, I imagine that you can, Kemina. Now I know I was right in coming to the temple. A few days of prayer and meditation with you and your priestesses will soothe and calm my frantic spirit."

"We will send a faerie post to Magnus so he knows where you are," Kemina said.

The Dominus was not happy that his wife had taken Dasras and gone off without telling him. But as he read the high priestess's message his irritation eased. He remembered his faerie wife's independent spirit. He could never confine it and he had to remember that she was not a frail creature who needed his protection. She was a strong woman, and while he wasn't certain that he would ever get used to having such a wife he knew he loved her beyond all else. And so he would learn to be content.

When Lara returned from the temple several days later, her restless spirit seemed to have quieted. When he saw her coming from the stables he held out his arms to her and without any hesitation she walked straight into them. "I missed you, my lord," she told him.

"I missed you more," he told her softly, kissing her brow.

"Then perhaps, Magnus," she murmured low, "we should find a quiet place and there you can show me just how much you missed me." Her fingers brushed his groin.

"Can we..." he began. But he was already hard for her.

"I would not say it if we couldn't," Lara told him as her tongue traced the shape of his ear both inside and out. "I have a great longing for you, my lord. Surely you would not deny the woman who will give you your son." Her hand slipped beneath his long gown and she cupped him in her warm palm a brief moment before stroking his manhood. Her slender fingers slid the length of him, once, twice, a third time.

The Dominus let a hiss of excitement escape him. "You are a shameless faerie woman," he told her. His lust for her was boiling. His heart beat rapidly.

"I am joyously shameless with you, my lord," she whispered hotly in the ear she had been teasing so delicately. "And you are eager for me, I can see. Let us find our bed, for it is past time we indulged our senses in each other."

In the great bedchamber they now shared they quickly shed their garments and tumbled into the bed. She smelled of flowers and fresh air and horse. He told her so, and laughed when she said she would bathe if it offended him. "Nay, sweeting," he told her. "I am not going to let you go until I have explored every delicious inch of you." And he proceeded to do just that. His hands, his tongue, his lips touched and tasted and kissed her until Lara was dizzy with sensation. His mouth closed over one breast, his teeth gently scoring her nipple as he licked and tenderly suckled. Lara screamed softly with the pleasure-pain his lips gave her tender breasts.

She pushed him onto his back and straddled him so she might taste and tease his nipples. She bit them gently and then licked away any pain she might have given him. Her kisses covered his long torso. How many times had she made love to him, and yet she never grew tired of his body. She slid down him, taking his manhood into her hand, and forcing a groan from him. Slowly, slowly she licked up one side of him and slowly, slowly she licked down the other side. The taste of him was unique and she loved it. She licked provocatively at his seed sac, taking it into her mouth, swirling her tongue about it. Then her lips closed over his length and she sucked strongly, drawing it deeply into her mouth.

Magnus Hauk groaned as he felt her tongue swirling about his manhood. He was near to bursting but he forced his hunger down. "Let me go now, my love. The pleasures between us will be greater if I am buried deep within you, feeling the walls of your hot sheath enclosing me." And when she released him, kissing the tip of his manhood, he pulled her so that she sat upon his trunk. From his own half-seated position he kissed her slowly as his hand pushed between her nether lips so he might push two fingers into her heated wetness. He moved those fingers slowly, withdrawing and thrusting, until she gave a little cry of pleasure. His mouth never left hers as he played between her nether lips, but then he realized that they both needed more. His hands gently fastening about her waist, he lifted her up and set her down upon his manhood.

Lara sighed deeply as she felt him filling her with his hard heat. "Oh, Magnus!" she purred and then she leaned back and rode him until neither could bear another moment and the pleasure burst over them as his big hands fondled her breasts, gently caressed her belly. She fell forward onto his broad chest.

He was still buried deep within her and was not yet ready to withdraw, but he did roll them over, one of his long legs swinging over her hip. "Why is it," he asked her, "that no matter how much you give me it is never enough, my beautiful faerie wife?"

"I feel the same way," Lara murmured. "You give me pleasures in excess and yet I want more, and more and even more, my darling husband."

"Then I suppose I must see that you are content," he told her as he began to move upon her once more. She was so hot. So wet. He could feel his member throbbing fiercely within her tightness as he thrust and withdrew until they were both half sobbing with the delight that they brought to each other. His juices flowed a second time and her sigh of happiness brought a smile to his face as he groaned with the pleasure of his release. "I love you," he said into the tangled golden hair that surrounded them. "I will never stop loving you, Lara, my wife."

Relaxed and content, filled with happiness beyond measure, Lara curled against him with a sigh. "He is going to be the most beautiful boy," she said, her hands enclosing her faintly swelling belly. "He will look just like you."

Kissing the top of her head he replied, "I should rather he look like you, my darling. You are far prettier than I am."

"Oh, no," Lara told him. "He must look like you so our people will accept him as a Terahn. We want no one claiming he is too faerie to rule Terah. Have you decided what you will call our son?"

"I will decide when I see him," the Dominus told her. "He will tell me his name."

THE SUMMER WANED, and the autumn came. Magnus Hauk was content that Terah had returned to what he considered normal. In Hetar, however, the women of The City had been insisting on a greater voice in the government and they would not cease their demands to the surprise of the magnates, the High Council and the new Lord High Ruler.

Jonah suspected that Vilia was involved with the agitating females but thought it better not to confront her on the matter. He would rather learn from his wife just what it was the women of The City wanted. "You hear things," he said to her one evening as they lay together.

"What can you mean, my lord?" Vilia asked him coyly. She had a great surprise for him, but she was not yet ready to share it.

"The women around you surely talk," he replied. "And you go out into The City to shop. Lady Gillian says that the women are not yet ready to speak with the High Council. If these women want something, why do they not tell us? Why do they delay?"

"They delay because they have not yet finished deciding how to word their manifesto, my darling," Vilia told him.

"*A manifesto?* Vilia, my love, surely you are jesting with me? What could the women of Hetar possibly want that they do not already have?"

"They want the freedom to decide for themselves, my lord. They don't want their husbands and their fathers telling them what to do," she told him quietly.

"But women are frail and need to be protected," Jonah told his wife. "They do not have the wisdom to make decisions for themselves. It is the way the Celestial Actuary created them. Surely you agree with me, Vilia."

"Nay, my lord, I do not agree with you. Women are strong both in body and in mind. Men may own the Pleasure Houses, but it is the women who manage them.

"Shopkeepers' wives and merchants' wives can all tell you the inner workings of their husbands' trades and businesses. Women in the lower orders all manage to keep their homes running and all women, no matter their class distinction, bear children. We have women who are healers, but dare not practice too openly lest they offend the physicians who are all men.

"Yet, my dear husband, the women of Hetar have no say in

how it is governed. But now, having suffered through the late emperor's ridiculous and bumbling reign—a reign that has cost us at least half of our able-bodied male population—the women of Hetar have decided that it is time for us to take part in the government of the land," Vilia concluded.

"Ridiculous!" Jonah exclaimed. *She was involved.* The wife of Hetar's ruler was involved in what was going to become an insurrection unless it was stopped now. If it were discovered by his enemies—and he was not foolish enough to believe he was beloved by all—they would have a merry romp making a fool out of him. And Hetar had had enough fools ruling it.

"Nay, my lord, it is not," Vilia told him firmly. "You are in danger of becoming Gaius Prospero, Jonah. You cling to the old ways which are no longer viable for Hetar. Make a different road for yourself and take it, my lord," Vilia encouraged him.

She was right in many ways. He was becoming his predecessor except that he was not as big a fool. Terah was blocked to them for now. Hetar had to rebuild itself and regain its prosperity, yet the council was full of the same old faces. They were dull and their ideas were stale. He needed fresh ideas to help Hetar. "If I were to set my spies to learning about the Women's Movement," Jonah said, "I would find you were implicated, my love, wouldn't I? Tell me exactly what it is these women want, and I will tell you whether I can help them."

"Wait for the manifesto, my lord," she told him. "I will see that you have an early copy of it before it is made public. That will give you time to consider what is possible right now and what isn't." She did not directly answer his question, he noted.

"You are an ambitious woman, Vilia," he said to her, and he took up her hand and kissed it, nibbling on her small knuckles. *And a clever bitch,* he thought silently.

"Surely you always knew that," Vilia replied coolly.

He laughed. "I knew. Very well, I will be patient and allow you to orchestrate your scheme, my darling, because I know whatever you do it will be best for me. Now tell me this other thing you would tell me."

"I am with child," Vilia said quietly.

He was speechless. He had not known if she could bear him a child and he would need an heir eventually. His mother had only recently pointed that out to him, suggesting he divorce Vilia and marry a young girl of good family who would serve him as a breeder of his progeny. Or, she had said, if he preferred he might take a second wife. Vilia at her age would surely not want to bear another child, and yet here she was telling him that she was going to do just that.

"Say something, Jonah," Vilia murmured at him. "I cannot believe I have rendered you speechless, my lord."

"I did not think you wanted any more children," he finally managed to say.

"I could have hardly given you a child while I was yet married to Gaius Prospero," Vilia replied dryly. "And a child while Gaius Prospero lived would have made you vulnerable, my lord. Now, however, your position is secure. Now is the time for you to have an heir. I am still young enough to give you two or three children. Or did your dear mother suggest otherwise? Such a troublesome woman, Husband, and one who until it appeared you were climbing the ladder of success barely acknowledged you. Yet I have always had faith in you. Faith enough to betray Gaius Prospero for you," she reminded him. "What has Farah ever done for you but use your power to gain her election as the new headmistress of the Pleasure Guild?"

"She gave me life," he said softly.

"Because she knew that your father loved her. Had he not, she would have rid herself of you, Jonah, but by keeping you she bound your wealthy father to her. Do not become sentimental about Farah at this point in your history, my love. When Rupert Bloodaxe died and his wife sold you into slavery, your mother did not protest. She let it happen because it was easier for her than having to pay for the schooling that your father had begun. Farah did not care what happened to you, my husband. She cared only about herself. Only when it appeared that you were, indeed, despite everything, becoming a person of importance did she acknowledge your existence."

"You are hard," he said to her.

"*I love you, Jonah,*" Vilia answered him. "I took you to my bed when you were still a slave. Your status mattered to me not at all. I will never desert you or this child of ours that I now carry. Your mother drops her poison into your ear because she sees the love I have for you. She does not know how to love, has never loved. But she understands power. And she wants no one influencing you but her."

"Aye, you are hard," he repeated, "but you are also astute, my love." He turned on his side so he might look down into her face. "If this child you carry is a son, Vilia, you will never have to fear being replaced in either my affections or my council. I know what my mother is, but having gotten her elected headmistress of the Pleasure Guild, I now need her influence. Now tell me, is she involved in this group of women? Are any of the Pleasure Mistresses?"

"Nay," Vilia said. *We did not believe she could be trusted.* She did not completely answer his question which told him exactly what he wanted to know and she knew it. But at least he would not know who, or how many women from the Pleasure Guild were implicated.

Jonah nodded. "It is possible," he said, "that these women can be of help to me. You accuse me of falling back into the old ways and not moving forward. But if I could aid Hetar's female population in obtaining a modicum of power I should be their hero. And while I prefer the order and civility Hetar has lost in recent years, it is entirely possible that with the best and most intelligent of our women helping to manage the government we could once again rebuild the finest of what was once Hetar." He leaned forward, and kissed her lips. "You have given me much to think about, Vilia." He bent lower, pulling aside her garment and licking at her nipples.

Vilia enclosed his head in her hands and smiled to herself. Jonah was hers and no one, not even his mother, was going to take him from her. While the magnates who owned the Pleasure Houses had chosen Farah to succeed Lady Gillian, the new headmistress was not particularly well liked. It would not be difficult to arrange an accident. She stretched her body, squirming out of her night garment, further arousing Jonah. She teased him with kisses, licks and wicked touches until he was almost whimpering with his need to be inside her and then she spread herself wide for him, crying out as he entered her lush body. "Be gentle, my love," she purred in his ear. "Remember the child." Her nails raked lightly down his narrow back as he pistoned her. Yes, Jonah was hers to command. Pulling his head to her, Vilia kissed him passionately.

When the headmistress of the Pleasure Guild learned that her son's wife was with child she shrieked with her outrage and frustration. "The bitch has done it deliberately!"

"Do not refer to my wife as a bitch," Jonah said softly. "You should be happy for me. I will have an heir at last."

"If it is indeed your child," Lady Farah snapped.

"What can you possibly mean, madam?" he asked in a low, dangerous voice.

"She cuckolded Gaius Prospero with you while she was his wife. Who is to say she has not taken another lover now that she is your wife?"

"Anything is possible, but I am no fool. From the day Vilia became my wife she has been followed wherever she went. There is no one else. The child is mine," he told his mother. "The love slave I bought her is not fertile. I am not a fool."

"Unless, of course, when she goes to Gillian's her lover is awaiting her," Lady Farah murmured. "She was never before particular friends with my predecessor. But suddenly they are as thick as thieves. I find that most curious."

"I imagine that you would," he said, amused. "However I know why she meets with Gillian and it has nothing to do with a lover, madam. I do believe that Vilia is correct when she says that your renewed interest in me is because of my power."

Lady Farah hissed her annoyance. She was not pleased to learn that her daughter-in-law was far cleverer than she had previously thought. "You should have a second, younger wife," she finally said. "There is no guarantee that Vilia will be able to carry this child to term. She is, after all, in her late thirties. And what if it is not a son? She only gave Gaius Prospero one living son, but several daughters."

"She has promised me a son," he said implacably, "and I do not need a second wife. One wife is more than enough for me."

"I am so glad that Vilia has the gift of sight and can guarantee you a son," Lady Farah said sarcastically. "When did she gain this gift?"

"If she says it will be a son, then it will be a son. It is not like Vilia to disappointment me," Jonah told his mother. But truth be known, he, too, had wondered at his wife's conviction that the child she carried was a son. How did she know? And what if the child was indeed a female?

But Vilia insisted the child in her belly was a son. And, she told her husband, his name would be Egon. "It means *formidable*," she said.

"But if you should birth a daughter—"

"I will not," Vilia told him. There was no female in her belly. She knew. Oh yes, she knew. Just before she had realized that she was with child she had found herself upon the Dream Plain one night as she slept. She had heard a voice calling her name and then she had come face-to-face with a tall and slender man with dark eyes, and black hair. He was the most handsome man she had ever laid eyes upon.

"I have been waiting for you, Cousin," he told her.

"I do not know you," Vilia said. "You are not my cousin."

"Are you Vilia, the descendant of Ulla?" the man asked her.

"I am the twelfth generation from Ulla, aye," Vilia answered him. "Who are you?" He really was lovely and there was something both intriguing and frightening about him, as well, yet she found herself fascinated by him.

"I am Kol, the twelfth generation descendant from Jorunn. Both of our ancestresses were impregnated by the great sorcerer, Usi. Before he was foully slain, Usi sent his concubines away so none would know of the seeds he had planted in their bellies. Ulla went to Hetar with her father. Jorunn was sent to Usi's brother, the lord of the Dark Lands. So as you can see we are related by blood, my beautiful cousin."

"Why did you attempt to invade Hetar?" she asked him.

"Because I wanted your lands," he told her with a charming smile. "And as your emperor was a weak fool, I thought to take advantage of him. If Terah had not aided you Hetar would now belong to me. I still want it but I shall gain it in another way," Kol told her. He reached out and drew her into his arms. His hand caressed her face. "You are a beautiful woman, Cousin," he told her, "and I would take pleasures with you."

Suddenly there was a wide black silken couch with a single broad rolled arm before her, and her night garments seemed to have dissolved, leaving her naked. Kol was naked, too, and Vilia's eyes widened as she viewed his massive organ. She gasped. He had two manhoods! A prominent long and thick one and a thin silvery one with a pointed tip much like an arrow. She had never seen anything like it and she was fascinated in spite of herself. But it was nothing more than a dream, she reasoned, and you could do whatever you wanted in a dream. And she wanted to take pleasures with this man who called himself her cousin.

And yet she demurred. "I do not know," she told him.

"It is but a dream, *Cousin*," he murmured in her ear, one arm slipping about her waist while his other hand began to play with one of her breasts.

Vilia felt as if every ounce of resistance had drained from her body. She didn't want to repel this man. She wanted to lay with him and make love. She would never in her reality be unfaithful to Jonah for she loved him. But this was naught but a dream. Oddly, she already felt wet and her love bud was throbbing with its need. She moaned as he dipped his dark head and began to suckle upon the breast he had been toying with but seconds before. "Aye, I want to take pleasures with you," she whispered as he lay her on her back and straddled her as she spread herself wide for him. Her breath was coming in short hard bursts. She wanted him! *"Hurry!"* she begged him.

Kol laughed, and without another word drove himself deep into her eager body with his dominant rod while his lesser rod pushed between her buttock cheeks and buried itself in her fundament.

Vilia attempted to shriek with her surprise but Kol put his hand firmly over her mouth and shook his head at her.

"Nay, Cousin, you must take both. Cease being afraid and realize that you like it," he whispered. "Note the lesser rod will remain still while I am able to thrust myself back and forth within your delicious hot sheath." He pumped her vigorously until Vilia was weak with exhaustion.

She had reached her pleasure point several times now but he seemed not to be satisfied. She could feel both of his rods quite distinctly. They were swollen and throbbing within her lusty ripe body. Her lips felt raw with the kisses he was pressing upon her, yet she still wanted more of him. Vilia wrapped her legs about the man riding her and felt him slip even deeper into her body. "Yes!" she hissed at him, and Kol smiled down at her as he worked her harder and her nails raked his back ferociously.

She is a juicy piece of lust, he thought, as he used her lush body to satisfy himself. Penned within his castle he had been unable to visit his women except upon the Dream Plain, but none had satisfied him. Until now. The carnal creature now gasping and moaning beneath his attentions pleased him well. She was newly with child by her husband, but his juices when he released them would bathe the tiny creature growing inside her with his essence. It would be almost as if he had created the child himself. And he planned for that child to one day accomplish what he had been unable to do. Conquer! His sons, he knew, would spend more time fighting each other than spreading darkness across the face of the land. But this child his cousin carried would be a perfect combination of both Vilia and Jonah—a man after his own heart, Kol thought. Perhaps one day he would visit him upon the Dream Plain.

The woman under him was about to faint away. "You are going to have a son, Vilia," he whispered in her ear. "Trust me, *my cousin,* that you will bear Jonah a son. You will name him Egon for it means formidable and he will be a great conqueror." Then Kol let his lust burst forth and Vilia swooned with the power she felt filling her.

When she awakened she was in her bed, amid a tangle of bed-clothes. It was almost dawn and Jonah, as was his custom, was already in his library with his secretary, Lionel. Vilia reached down and touched herself between her legs. She was wet, sticky and naked. She knew she had gone to sleep in a light night garment, but even after she had gotten up and looked around her chamber, she could find no trace of it. Her lips felt raw, as if they had been kissed over and over again. Her nipples were tingling and sore as if they had been sucked and sucked upon. Of course it had been a dream. A terribly real dream, but a dream nonetheless. And yet it had seemed so real....

When word finally reached Terah that the Lord High Ruler's wife was expecting a child, Lara was not pleased. "I had hoped that if Jonah remained childless Hetar would continue to flounder. This child, especially if it is a son, will be a rallying point."

"They are an ocean away from us, my lady," Magnus Hauk reminded his wife. "Hetar does not exist for us any longer."

"I wish that were true," Lara murmured. Magnus Hauk, by virtue of the time in which he lived, was an insular man. It did no good to argue with him. Instead she waited until her husband slept, then she transported herself from the privacy of her little magic chamber into Lady Gillian's house where she was warmly greeted.

"You have heard our news then," Gillian said.

"It is certain?" Lara wanted to know.

"Aye. She proclaims it is a son and that she will call him Egon," Gillian replied. "I see you are with child also."

"It was time that the Dominus had a son," Lara answered. "Tell me, how goes the attempt to get women into the government? Have you made any progress?"

"Indeed we have," Gillian responded. "I believe that the Lord High Ruler is going to support us to a certain extent. Lady Vilia has said he is interested and agrees it is past time that the women of Hetar had at least some voice in what happens to them."

"Interesting," Lara remarked. "He obviously is not entirely certain of his position and seeks your influence and help."

"What does it matter, my lady Domina," Gillian remarked, "as long as we get our slipper into the door?"

Lara laughed a short laugh. "I am amazed to find Hetar ahead of Terah in this matter. Perhaps it is time I put my efforts to helping my own people. You obviously have everything well in hand here in Hetar. You have my permission to call me should you ever need me or my help." She began to fade away.

"Wait!" Gillian cried and when Lara had rematerialized she said, "Will you not continue to aid us, my lady Lara?"

"I do not believe that you need my help now, my lady Gillian. You have a strong group that still remains passionate. Lord Jonah knows what you want and appears willing to help you. There is naught more I can do for you."

"But what if Jonah is simply placating his wife who carries his child?" she wondered. "What if he is trying to learn more about us so he can arrest us?"

"You do not need me to tell you what to do if that should

prove the case," Lara said. "You are capable of making your own decisions. You must accept the consequences of taking responsibility." She leaned forward and kissed Gillian's cheek. "Farewell, my friend," she said. And then Lara was gone in her mauve mist. And Lady Gillian had to admit that the faerie woman was right.

THE SUMMER HAD gone, and now autumn was almost over. Lara was slipping slowly back into the contentment she had once known with her first husband, Vartan. Kemina had been right in her advice. Reaching up she touched the crystal star that hung from its gold chain about her neck. *You have been silent of late, Ethne. Have you nought to say to me any longer?*

For the moment you do not need me, Lara, her faerie guide said. *To be honest with you, I have welcomed the respite from the tumult that usually surrounds you.*

Lara laughed softly. *It is almost like it was in Vartan's time, isn't it? I grow fat with child and am content with my life and my family.*

Ethne chuckled, sounding like water running over a bed of little rocks in a forest stream. *You've done much, my child. Rest is not a bad thing. How grows the child, this son you will give the Dominus?*

He seems more restless in my womb than the others.

It is the sign of a brilliant creature. One who will lead his people, Ethne answered.

Will he have magic like the others? Lara wondered.

I do not know, my child. But given your bloodlines I would expect that he will have some magic about him.

Poor Magnus. Lara giggled softly, and Ethne chuckled again.

As her belly swelled Lara drew closer to her children. Dillon was shooting up into a giant of a boy. He was his father's image and gave evidence that he would one day be as tall as Vartan had been. He longed to leave Terah and attend the school of the Shadow Princes. Even without training his powers were growing. Lara found him in her private chamber one evening playing Herder with her half brother, the faerie prince, Cirillo.

"How did he get here?" she demanded to know.

Both boys looked nervously at her.

"Do you want me to speak to Mother?" she asked Cirillo who paled.

"I brought him," Dillon said quickly. "It's an easy spell, Mother."

"You are not to cast it again," Lara said sternly. "If you want to visit with your uncle I will bring him to you, Dillon. I am astounded that both of you would be so cavalier as to use magic when neither of you has been properly trained. Magic is not just words, and you, Cirillo, should know that better than Dillon, for you are faerie. Go home!" She waved her hand strongly at him and Cirillo tumbled over himself as he disappeared. Lara put an arm about her son. "I understand, Dillon, I truly do, but you must be patient."

"It seems so long until next autumn," he sighed.

"Patience is something you should learn to cultivate, Dillon," Lara told her son. She ruffled his dark hair. "You are not to come in here again without my permission," and he sighed again, causing Lara to smile over his head.

Anoush seemed to grow up a little bit that icy season. She was tall like her brother and slender. She had Vartan's dark hair and blue eyes but her profile was delicate. While she didn't look quite like Lara, it was obvious she was going to be beautiful one day. She kept the magic beginning to grow within her well masked for she was not yet certain that she even wanted it, and of course the choice would be hers.

As for Lara's littlest daughter, Zagiri, she was a mischievous and adventurous child who seemed to need far more watching over than her siblings. With her dark blond hair and her turquoise eyes she was her father's child in every way. Lara worried that when Magnus Hauk's son was finally born Zagiri would find herself relegated to second place. She was not a child who liked being put aside and she adored her father. Zagiri was quick and like her siblings excelled at her lessons. She was plainly Master Bashkar's favorite student for she had the habit of rhyming and making up stories, and her tutor, being Devyn-born, appreciated her talent, especially when she composed music to accompany her tales.

The Icy Season set in. Terah's trading ships were all in port, for the Sagitta was not a hospitable place at this time of year. The vessels would be refitted and repaired over the coming months in preparation for the next trading season. In the villages the Terahn folk crafted the goods that would go to Hetar. In the warm weather they would tend to their livestock and gardens.

When the Icy Season was half over, the time came for Lara's child to be born. The Dominus's mother, Lady Persis, had traveled from her own home up the fjord and through the snows to be there when her grandson arrived. She arrived wearing the beautiful fur cloak that Lara had given her when

Lara had wed the Dominus. Because it had been fashioned through magic, the fur cloak always appeared as if brand new. The Dominus's mother loved it dearly. Lady Persis was not a woman to mince words but she was in awe of her faerie daughter-in-law.

"So, at last you are giving Terah an heir," she said as she settled herself into a comfortable chair in the great hall of the castle, accepting a goblet of rich wine.

"I have already given Magnus one child," Lara replied, amused.

"Zagiri is a female and cannot rule Terah one day," Lady Persis said. "This is not Hetar, where I hear the women of the land are suddenly involving themselves in how it is governed. Ridiculous! We all know what we are good for and governing is not it."

"Why not?" Lara asked. "Government affects women. Why should we not have a say in how it is run?"

Lady Persis sniffed. "Ridiculous!" she repeated.

"I agree with my lady wife," Magnus Hauk said, surprising his parent.

"What? You would have women telling us all what to do?" his mother cried, shocked. "I cannot believe that you said that, my son. This is the influence of your faerie wife, I fear. The Great Creator help us all!"

"Some changes must come to Terah if we are to survive successfully," Magnus Hauk said. Lara's eyes were bright as she listened to him. "Our family has always produced benevolent rulers, but we have ruled without any council from our people. I would create a ruling council to advise me and I will want women's voices in it, Mother."

Lady Persis shook her head. "Terah will not stand for such a thing," she said.

"I think they will. Every village has its leader and I know, though it is not spoken of aloud, that the women of the villages advise their men. It is time for the women to speak for themselves. After our son is born I intend implementing my plans to do just that," the Dominus said. "In the New Outlands the women sometimes lead."

Lady Persis said no more but she did send a fierce glare in Lara's direction.

And it was at that very moment that an odd look crossed the Domina's face.

"Are you all right?" Lady Persis asked Lara.

"Aye, but I believe the child has decided it wishes to be born," the Domina announced. "Mila," she called to her body servant. "I think the time has come now for me to go to the birthing chamber. Someone send for the midwife." And arising slowly from her chair, Lara left the great hall, her hand on her great belly.

The birthing chamber had large windows that ran all around the room, and the view of Terah's green mountains and the fjord below was spectacular. It was believed that, be it day or night, the newborn should greet the world into which it had come. The room had a small fireplace to bring warmth into it should it be needed and this night it blazed with a rosy fire. There was a large wide comfortable birthing chair of sturdy ashwood with a padded back. The seat was also padded with soft material so that the infant slipping from its mother's body through the hole in its center into the hands of the midwife would not be harmed in any way. There was water, swaddling clothes and a woven willow basket with comfortable bedding for the newly born child set upon a table. There was a decanter of sweet frine and goblets. Everything was in perfect readiness for Terah's heir.

Lara was already naked and seated upon the chair when the royal midwife, Aminta, arrived. She smiled broadly at her patient. "Greetings, Domina!" she said. "So the time has come, has it, for our next Dominus to make his entrance into our world? Let us see how far along you are. Mila, elevate the chair, please."

The seat of the birthing chair was cranked up by the serving woman with a strong arm, and Aminta stepped under to inspect Lara. Her small size was her greatest advantage to her chosen profession. Most of the midwives had to crawl beneath an elevated birthing chair. Aminta just had to bend slightly.

"Ah, my lady, you are well along, but then this is your fourth child, isn't it?" she remarked as she withdrew. "The pains are regular now?"

Lara nodded. She wished it were her fourth child—and not her sixth—but few knew that, of course. She pushed away the thoughts of her last delivery and labor, and concentrated upon this child. The pains grew stronger. She kept Aminta informed, and finally the midwife knelt beneath the chair and told her when she might push.

"I see the boy's head," she said excitedly. "His hair glistens like gold, my lady!"

Lara gazed out at the night sky that was now, after several hours, beginning to glow faintly with the coming dawn.

"Push, my lady! Ah, yes, that is it! His head and shoulders are now free. Oh, he is beautiful!" Aminta said excitedly.

Her son! *Their son!* Lara could barely wait now to hold him. What would Magnus name him? she wondered.

"Push, my lady! He is coming! He is coming!" Aminta said, her voice trembling with her delight. "Mila! Have the warm oil ready to cleanse him! One more push, my lady!"

"Welcome my son to Terah!" Lara cried with a loud voice as she pushed the infant entirely from her body and heard his strong cry. "Oh, let me see him, Aminta!"

The midwife held the squalling child up, beaming with pleasure. "He looks just like the Dominus, my lady! The nose! The high cheekbones and forehead!" She handed him to Mila. "The Dominus will be so pleased, my lady," Aminta said. "But now we must attend to the rest of this business."

Suddenly Lara cried out in genuine pain. Distressed by the sound of it the midwife bent once again beneath the birthing chair. "The pain! The pain!" the Domina cried.

"There is another child," Aminta gasped, "and it wishes to be born now. Push, my lady! You must push!"

"Nay, there cannot be another!" Lara said angrily.

"My lady, there is, and the child will not wait. It comes!" Aminta said.

Pain such as she had never before known racked Lara. In spite of herself she screamed, her cries of agony mingled with her cries of fury. There could be but one heir to Terah! *Ethne!* she called out silently to her faerie protector.

Be calm, Lara, Ethne's soft voice counseled her.

I do not understand! I wished a son for Magnus. One son, not two!
Then it will be one son, Ethne assured her.

A female? This child is a daughter? I did not ask for a daughter! Only
a son! Tears began to roll down Lara's face. *Find Kaliq for me,*
Ethne! He will know what has happened. Find Kaliq! Find Mother! I
must speak with them!

I will bring them to you, my child. Now let this infant be born,
Ethne said.

"Push!" Aminta instructed her. "Push!"

Lara bore down with every ounce of her strength and the
child slid forth in a rush from her straining body. Her shriek of
final pain echoed about the room mingling with the furious
cries of the child.

"A daughter!" Aminta cried out. And then she grew silent.

"What is the matter?" Lara wanted to know. "Show me the girl."

Aminta held up the baby for its mother to see.

Lara stared. The infant had a head full of black curls and pale
skin.

"Why, she favors my great-aunt," Ilona, queen of the Forest
Faeries said as she appeared in her usual haze of mauve smoke.
"She will be a great beauty one day. My son-in-law should be
well pleased, daughter." And she bent to kiss Lara's moist brow.

18

"WHAT GREAT-AUNT?" Lara demanded to know as Aminta handed the female child to Mila and began attending to her patient.

"My grandfather's sister," Ilona said calmly. "She was the off-spring of his mother and a mortal who was as pale as the moon, and had hair as black as night and deep violet eyes. She became a Nix, a guardian of a beautiful pond and had many lovers both mortal and faerie. Her name was Marzina."

Lara's heart was beating furiously. Her mother was lying. Why was her mother lying? But she could hardly accuse her before Aminta and Mila.

"And she was not the first dark-haired faerie in our midst," Ilona prattled on. "There must have been others, for now and again one will be birthed. And of course, your father's mother had dark hair as a girl, too. I shall now go and fetch Magnus, Daughter."

"Lady Persis is here," Lara said.

Ilona smiled sweetly. "She will be quite jealous that I have seen our new grandchildren first." And with a wicked laugh she exited the birthing chamber.

"One more push, my lady Domina, and the afterbirths will be expelled," Aminta said briskly. "Then we must prepare you and your children for visitors."

The windows beyond revealed a glorious dawn breaking. It tinted the snows on the far peaks of the mountains a rosy golden peach. It would be a beautiful day and all of Terah would rejoice with the news that the Domina had birthed a strong son. Lara was exhausted with her long night's labors. And she was distressed by the dark-haired female child who had followed her son. Something was wrong. She had planned a son. She had not planned another daughter, nor had she planned twins. And her mother knew something. And where was Kaliq? Why had he not answered her cry of distress?

Aminta had finished with her. The midwife lowered the birthing chair so Lara might stand up, which she did. Her children had been placed in the willow basket. Mila quickly sponged her mistress with perfumed water and dressed her in a purple silk robe trimmed with gold and sparkling crystals. Lara was then settled in the birthing chamber's large bed where she would remain for the next several days, recovering. A knock sounded upon the door. Aminta hurried to answer it as Mila brought the babies to their mother, fitting one in each of her arms.

Ilona, having taken complete charge, tripped into the room with the Dominus, Lady Persis, Dillon, Anoush and Zagiri. "Ah," she trilled, "here we are to see the newest members of our cojoined families."

Magnus Hauk stepped forward and took his son from the curve of Lara's right arm. "I name this child, my first-born son,

Taj, which means *exalted*." He smiled down into the baby's smooth little face. The boy's eyes were tightly closed, his thick sandy lashes touching his cheek. The Dominus touched that smooth rosy cheek. "He is beautiful, Lara, thank you."

"And he looks just like you!" Lady Persis approved. "I am not so old that I do not remember the day that you were born in this very room, Magnus. I am well-pleased."

The Dominus handed Taj back to his mother with a smile. "And what have we here?" He took the infant girl from her mother's left arm. "I name this child, my second-born daughter, Marzina, which was the name of her faerie ancestress whom she strongly resembles, Ilona tells me." He turned to Lara. "You did not tell me you would give me both a son and a daughter, my love."

"We needed a son," Lara said, "but I thought Zagiri would enjoy having a little sister to play with and I was not of a mind to wait, Magnus. I hope you are not too distressed with me. I wanted it to be a surprise for you."

Well done, my daughter, Ilona murmured silently.

Where is Kaliq? I want an explanation! Lara snapped irritably.

Patience, Ilona replied.

The children now crowded about the bed so they might better see their new siblings. Anoush observed that Marzina looked more like her and Dillon with her tuft of dark hair while Taj was more like Zagiri and their mother and the Dominus. Dillon stared hard at his new sister and Lara knew he suspected something. Zagiri, however, was delighted to now be the big sister of not one, but two babies.

"I shall compose a song for them," she said. "Master Bashkar will help me."

"We must leave your mother to rest now," Magnus Hauk said quietly. "She has had a busy time bearing your new brother and sister. Mila, take the twins to the nursery and arrange for another nursemaid to join the one chosen for Taj. Aminta, I thank you for your services. You will be well rewarded for this fine night's work." He turned to his mother and mother-in-law. "Leave me with my wife now, ladies."

Mila took each twin, placing them carefully in the willow basket, and hurried out in the company of the midwife. They were followed by the two grandmothers and the three children. Lara could not refrain from a giggle as she heard her mother-in-law say, "I don't understand why you should have been in the birthing chamber, madam."

"Do not be silly," Ilona replied tartly. "I am Lara's mother. Where else would I be but at my beloved daughter's side in her labors, Persis? Were you not with your daughters when they birthed your grandchildren?"

The door closed behind them before Lara could hear Persis's pithy answer.

Magnus Hauk smiled, as amused by the two older women as his wife was. "They will always squabble for precedence," he said. Then he bent and kissed Lara's lips. "You looked tired, my love, as you well should be. But before I leave you to your rest I wanted you to know how delighted I am with your surprise. Taj will not be so babied growing up now that he has a sister by his side. You were clever to consider it."

"I did not realize she would look quite so different," Lara answered him.

He shook his head at her words. "She will indeed be a great beauty one day," he noted. "And she is not really all that different from Anoush. Three beautiful daughters." He smiled at her. "I am a happy man, my love."

Anoush's *father* was dark-haired, Lara wanted to say, but she did not. This baby was nothing like Anoush, whose dark brown hair was lit with red and gold highlights. Marzina had hair that was blue-black. And skin that was too pale by far. She was clearly not a mortal child, while the boy that had shared Lara's womb with her did possess mortal blood. Still, thanks to her mother's words, no one thought it odd that this infant was so very different. And Magnus had easily accepted her and given Marzina her name.

"I am glad you are happy, my lord," Lara told her husband. Then she yawned and he jumped from the bed where he had been seated at her side.

"I have been thoughtless," he said, then he bent and kissed her again. "You need your rest, my love." With a loving smile at her he left the room.

Lara lay in the great bed looking out at the beautiful day. The sky was a clear, bright blue. The sun beamed down and it was obvious that spring was nearer today than it had been the day before. She needed to sleep but she could not. Not until she had some answers to the myriad questions troubling her.

And then Kaliq stepped from the far shadows of the chamber and walked across the floor to sit by her side. "You will want to know what has happened, of course," he said to her and he took her hand in his.

"The female is not Magnus's child," Lara spoke. It was a statement, not a query.

"Nay, she is not."

"How could this have happened?" Lara demanded of him. "And why?"

"The why I do not know," he said. "The how I can but surmise."

"Tell me," Lara replied.

"Do you remember when you met Kol upon the Dream Plain and he forced you? You wanted to know how such a thing could have happened when the Dream Plain is a neutral place. Do you recall what I told you then?"

"You said he had taken the power of an incubus to be able to do what he did to me," Lara said.

"Precisely," Kaliq said. "And when he assaulted you he left his seed within you. It waited until you were fertile with the Dominus's son to reveal itself and grow along with the boy into the daughter you birthed this day, for Kol could not create another son."

"You are telling me that Marzina is Kol's offspring?" Lara's voice was shaking.

The Shadow Prince nodded silently.

"And is this, too, a part of my vaunted destiny, Kaliq?" she asked him bitterly.

"Nay," he said, wanting to reach out and enfold her in his arms. Wanting to comfort her, but knowing that if he did she would shatter. The past few years would have destroyed a mere mortal and they were now close to destroying Lara. He had to force her to be strong in the face of this news.

"Then this is Kol's revenge upon me," Lara said softly. "I sent his kingdom into chaos by giving him twin sons. I would not mother those children. So he has forced another of his children upon me to be born with my husband's son so I will have no other choice but to mother it." Silent tears began to slip down her face.

"No one will ever know," Kaliq said quietly.

"I will know," Lara told him bleakly. "How can I love this child, my dear lord and friend? How? Yet I will have to pretend so as not to raise questions over what would surely be considered my odd behavior in rejecting one child while adoring the other."

"Listen to me, Lara," the Shadow Prince said sternly to her. "Marzina is innocent of her creation. And thanks to Ilona there will never be any questions about her strange beauty. Everyone believes, will believe, that she is Magnus's daughter. The twin sister of the heir to Terah. Part of her is your creation and you will raise her as you have raised your other children. With love and with caring. With tradition and with manners. With a strong morality and the knowledge that in the end the light always outweighs the darkness. Kol has sought to revenge himself on you. You can turn the tables upon him by raising Marzina to be so filled with light that she will blind him should he ever come near her. And you are the only one who can do this, my love."

"Can I?" Lara wondered in bleak tones.

"Yes," the Shadow Prince said. "You can. You have always trusted me, Lara. Trust me now. You will not be harmed by loving this unexpected daughter of yours. And she is yours. Not

Kol's. *Yours!* I promise you as much as I can that he will never again harm you or anyone whom you love. I see now by simply confining him to his castle I gave him far too much freedom. I will correct that error in judgment. And the Keepers of the Dream Plain will forbid him entry from now on. With this evidence of his abuse, I have convinced them to do so."

"What do you intend to do?" Lara asked.

"I will place him in the deepest, darkest part of Kolbyr. No one will know where he is, not even his faithful Alfrigg. He will be blinded and chained, without food or drink, for the next thousand years. No one will hear his cries for his vocal cords will be frozen so he will not be able to make any sounds at all. As for his offspring, Kolbein and Kolgrim, I will put it in Alfrigg's mind once the Twilight Lord has disappeared that in order to protect Kol's sons he must hide them in separate places until they are grown. At that point the factions shall once again rear up behind them and it will be a fight to the death to determine the next Twilight Lord. Unfortunately, even I have not the power to erase the darkness forever, my love."

"Who does?" Lara asked him.

He laughed almost ruefully. "That task belongs to the mortal race," he told her.

"The Celestial Actuary has a sense of humor then," Lara replied. Knowing that Kol would no longer be able to reach out to her, she was beginning to feel a little bit better about her situation. Kaliq was right. It wasn't her newborn daughter's fault how she had been created. Kol wasn't Marzina's father. Magnus was. And she was Marzina's mother and she would love her child as she had not loved Kol's sons. "Will Kol be able to dream?" she asked the Shadow Prince.

"Nay. Each day and each night will be an eternal monotony for him though he will not know one from the other."

"Let him dream of me now and again," Lara said. "And let the dreams be painful beyond measure for him. Let his two rods burn with a fire that cannot be quenched. Let the pain continue until he can get me out of his mind, my lord prince. I need to know that I have had my revenge on the Twilight Lord not for the destiny that was foretold for me, but for his assault upon me on the Dream Plain."

A slow smile lit Kaliq's handsome face. "Thus speaks an icy faerie heart," he said. "It will be done, my love. It is most worthy of you. When I tell Ilona she will be proud. And you will love the little princess? Your mother's tale was quite clever."

"I will love her," Lara promised. "And Ilona is nothing if not creative."

"I must go now," Prince Kaliq said. "I would be in Hetar when Vilia births her son. Jonah will shortly have an heir."

"Will Vilia survive? She is not a young woman," Lara remarked.

"Vilia will more than survive," Kaliq told her. "She will thrive." He bent and kissed her forehead. "Sleep now, my love," he said, smiling as her eyes closed and she slumbered. Then stepping into the shadows from whence he had come, he was gone from her. Now he stood in the darkness of a corner in the house of Hetar's Lord High Ruler as the lady Vilia gave birth to her son. Kaliq muttered a soft incantation so that the lady who had just begun her labor would birth the child quickly. To everyone's surprise Vilia did just that. Her labor was swift and virtually painless.

"It is a boy!" the midwife screamed joyfully, catching the baby as it was expelled from its mother and holding it high for all to see. The infant screamed loudly.

The room was crowded with Jonah, Lady Gillian, Lady Farah and several of his most devoted supporters from the magnate class along with several of the magnates who up to now had not supported Jonah. Jonah's half sisters were present, as was Vilia's family led by her uncle, Cubert Ahasferus, along with Aubin Prospero and his two sisters and their husbands. The Lord High Ruler of Hetar had made certain that there would be no doubt about his son's birth. As the child howled, the audience to his birth clapped their congratulations.

Jonah took the baby, still covered with blood and birthing fluids, into his hands, and holding him up again declared, "I accept this child as my son. He shall be called Egon, the formidable one. None shall stand successfully against him."

The audience again clapped wildly.

The infant was taken back by the midwife, cleaned and then put with his mother.

The guests to his birth then departed the chamber, leaving Jonah alone with his wife. When the infant cried, Vilia put him to her breast, and when he tugged upon it a great rush of maternal love overwhelmed her and tears filled her eyes.

"You may nurse him for one month until you have regained your strength again," Jonah told his wife. "I have already chosen a wet nurse, my dear one." Seeing the protest in her eyes he continued, "I need you to return to your work with the women of Hetar. Remember that in three months we shall hold our first elections. I want at least half of those elected to be of the fair sex."

"*You* chose a wet nurse? I think you mean your mother chose one," Vilia said sharply. "I will choose my own wet nurse for Egon. One I can trust not to poison our child through her milk." She gazed down adoringly at the infant. "Is he not beautiful, Jonah? And look at that midnight-black hair of his. It is like silk to the touch."

"He is very pale," Jonah noted. "You are certain he is healthy?"

"He suckles strongly, my dear lord," Vilia assured her husband.

"I like watching you nurse him," Jonah said. "I am jealous, however. One month, Vilia, and no more. I mean it."

"You want to suck upon my nipples yourself," she taunted him.

"And stuff you with my manhood," he replied bluntly.

"You have my permission to visit the Pleasure Houses," Vilia said sweetly.

"Nay! I have not these last months and I will not. I will lust for you until we couple again, my wife. There is no weakness in me as there is in other men," he told her.

Vilia smiled archly at him. "Nay, there is not. Nor was there ever. That is why I fell in love with you all those years ago, Jonah. You are strong. You do not give in to your baser nature as Gaius Prospero did. You know what you want and you take it and you hold it. In one month I shall turn Egon over to a wet nurse of my own choosing. And I will give you pleasures beyond measure as we work together to rebuild Hetar."

He smiled one of his rare smiles at her. "You are indeed the most perfect woman for me, my love," he told her. Then kissing her brow, he arose, saying, "You will want to take your rest now. I will send the child's nursemaid to take him. Sleep well, my lovely Vilia. I am well pleased with you."

She watched him go, and then handed over her new son to his nursemaid with the instruction, "Bring him to me when he hungers again."

"Yes, my lady," the woman said and hurried out with the now sleeping infant.

From his place in the shadows Prince Kaliq had seen and heard all that he needed to, so he slipped silently away back to Shunnar.

Vilia lay back in her bed and considered the road that lay ahead of her. The creature who had called himself her cousin had not lied to her. She had birthed a son, an heir for Hetar. She wondered if she would ever see Kol again. She had never known that her ancestress, Ulla, had shared the sorcerer's affections with another. Another who had given a son. That part of Ulla's history had never come down to her female descendants but then Ulla would not have wanted it known that she shared a husband with another woman. Was Kol's line a male one as her line had been a female one?

Vilia remembered the time just before her marriage to Gaius Prospero. She had always known the history of Ulla as handed down to all the females in her family. What she had not known and was then told was that in each generation a single female was said to carry the sorcerer's blood more strongly than her female siblings and cousins. That female was identified by a small black birthmark in the shape of a star on her left shoulder. Vilia had that mark. And her mother had whispered to her, it had been foretold that the twelfth generation would rule Hetar. Of course her mother, being a properly raised Hetarian woman, believed that Vilia would rule through her husband and so had Vilia. Only the women in her family knew these secrets. Not even her uncle Cubert, the current patriarch, was aware of it.

For now, however, Vilia mused as she lay in her comfortable bed, she would allow Jonah to rule for her. She sensed that her time had not quite come. She wondered if the Domina of Terah had birthed her son yet. Tomorrow she would advise Jonah to send a message to Lara and Magnus Hauk that Hetar had a strong young heir. They should cultivate closer ties with Terah. By the time Egon was grown Hetar would be restored to its glory, and if he and the Dominus's heir were friends, might it not be easier to betray and conquer? With those happy thoughts in her head Vilia fell into a deep sleep.

ACROSS THE SEA in Terah, Lara began to recover from the shock of the births she had just experienced. For several months she nursed both of her children before turning them over to wet nurses. By the time Taj and Marzina were six months of age each had distinctly different personalities. Marzina constantly wanted her mother's love and attention. She could be a charming child but she had a decided temper when crossed. Taj, like his father, was quiet and determined. And he was the only one who could cajole his twin from her anger, or her doldrums when Marzina became depressed. Lara considered it an amazing connection, considering the only blood the twins shared was hers. She was not unhappy to release both children into the care of others for if she were honest with herself she had to admit that while she loved all of her children, she preferred her husband's company and the governing of Terah to all else.

It was late summer, and the royal family had been paying a brief visit to the New Outlands. In late autumn she would return for the Gathering with her husband so he might accept his yearly tribute from the clan families. In midautumn Dillon would go to Kaliq to begin his training. Lara could not believe that her son was old enough. But his powers were obviously growing; she had no choice. Without a complete understanding of the responsibility his powers carried, Dillon could easily allow his mortal nature to abuse them.

Her oldest son came to her side now as she sat upon the hillside staring out over the land before her. "I will miss you, too," he said sitting down next to her.

Lara smiled. "I should find it disconcerting that you can so easily read my thoughts," she said and took his hand up and kissed it.

"I know all that happened to you, Mother," he answered.

"What on earth do you mean?" Lara replied.

"The Dark Lands. *All of it.* Kolbein and Kolgrim, my half brothers. Marzina. All," Dillon responded. "When Prince Kaliq erased everyone's memories, mine did not disappear. I remember that year you were gone from us. When you walked upon the Dream Plain that night, Mother, I was there. I saw what the Twilight Lord did. It was then I spoke to the prince. He said it was obviously meant that I know, but for what reason he could not yet divine."

"Why did you wait until now to tell me?" Lara asked her son. She was very shaken by his revelation. And like Kaliq she was curious to know why he had been made privy to this part of her life she wanted to keep hidden.

"I do not want to have secrets from you, Mother, and soon I will go to Shunnar. I wanted you to know that I share your pain and your sorrow." Dillon moved now to sit facing his mother. He took her hands in his. "I am young, I know, but the love that you shared with my father, Vartan of the Fiacre, has made me stronger than most boys my age. And I seem to have inherited your talent for magic." He gave her a small smile. "I am proud of what you did, Mother. You walked into the darkness, created chaos to protect both the magic and the mortal worlds, and then returned filled with more light than ever before. But I know all of it weighs upon you. And I know it is not easy to carry both mortal and faerie blood in your veins. I wanted to tell you that I am here for you to lean on, Mother. No matter my youth, I am here for you."

Lara pressed her lips together hard to stifle the cry that wanted to erupt. That this beautiful son of Vartan's should offer to bear some of her sorrow upon his own shoulders almost broke her heart. He should not have known. *He should not have!* It was a hard burden for her, but he was still a child. And yet sitting there looking at Dillon, Lara could see he was not quite that child she thought him. She could see the man he was one day going to be. "I am not easy that you should know of Kol and what happened, my son, but there must be a reason that you of them all retained that knowledge. Because Kol was taunting me, I had Kaliq restore your stepfather's memories of that time and told him of Kol's sons. I could not keep secrets from him." She reached out and ruffled her son's dark hair. "You have not shared your knowledge with anyone, of course."

"Nay," he said.

She nodded. "I am glad you are here for me, Dillon." She would not offend him by suggesting he was too young to help share her burdens.

"I will miss you when I am gone," he said. "Yet I am eager to go to Shunnar. The prince says Amir is trained and ready for me to ride. He says we will ride out into the desert and he will take me to the Oasis of Zeroun where he first saw you." Dillon's young voice was filled with excitement. "And I will finally come to know Og better."

Lara smiled at her son's enthusiasm. "You understand that for your own sake it will be many months before we see one another again," she told him.

"I know, but if I grow lonely for you, Mother, I shall view your beautiful face in my reflecting bowl."

"You do not have a reflecting bowl," Lara replied.

"The prince says I am to have one," Dillon answered excitedly. "I have tried to bring images up in the garden birdbaths, but I cannot hold them long enough to enjoy."

"Of course you can't," Lara remarked. "Birdbaths are not magical." She was amazed that he had tried and impressed that he had managed to gain any image at all, even if it had dissolved. Yes, as much as she regretted losing him, it was definitely time that Dillon went to Prince Kaliq.

Before the Domina's return to the castle the Fiacre held an end-of-summer feast for Lara and her family. A field of flowers outside of New Camdene was the setting, with trestles and benches set up, the tables groaning with food. Representatives from the other Fiacre villages had come to join them. Lara delightedly greeted Vartan's favorite cousin, Sholeh. "Before we speak on pleasantries, tell me of Cam?"

"Though he does all he is asked and studies hard, I see the darkness growing in him," Sholeh answered. "I do not know what we can do for him."

Lara nodded. "I should have strangled him when I slew his parents. But now time and the Celestial Actuary protect him, for no one else will."

Sholeh shrugged. "I suppose you are right," she said. Then, "So you have twins! Did you bring them?"

"We left them at the castle with their nurses. They are yet too young to travel," Lara said. "But the others are with us. Dillon goes to Prince Kaliq in a few weeks for training. His magic is growing of itself."

"You were wise to take Dillon and Anoush to Terah when you did," Sholeh said. "Our folk are not used to magic, and find it difficult to accept."

Lara knew that Sholeh was right. After all she had done for the clan families she had hoped they would be less suspicious of her. But many, despite their kind words, were not. It was their nature, she supposed, and it could not be helped.

Dillon and Liam's sons were playing with a ball in the meadow. Anoush was helping Noss add more food to the feast tables and Zagiri was helping with little Mildri, who was now walking and chattering away. Zagiri seemed to love the New Outlands even as her older siblings did. It was the freedom to run and play in the sunlight, Lara realized. At the castle the children were mostly confined to a small garden except when they rode.

The whole day long the Fiacre ate, drank and played games in the meadow. There was music and dancing as the day began to come to a close. Shy at first of the Dominus, the women grew less so as he insisted on dancing with as many of them as he could. Lara laughed watching him, but then joined the circle herself to dance with the men of the clan family. Soon the children were emulating their elders in their own dance. Then as the darkness fell the sky was filled with flying stars and everyone stopped to watch the beautiful display as the fires grew dim. And then it was over and they gratefully found their beds.

In the morning, Lara and the Dominus returned to the castle. The children were still tired and Lara was anxious to see her twins. Since their birth she had come to honestly love them both. Taj was a sturdy infant with a serious demeanor. He was, Lady Persis insisted, very much like his father at that age.

"As I cannot remember," Magnus said with a wry grin, "I cannot dispute it."

Marzina for all her hot temper adored her mother with an almost slavish devotion. Taj was the only other person with whom she would willingly share Lara. When any of her three older siblings came into proximity with their mother Marzina would begin to whine softly, sometimes so low that it could almost not be heard. But the look on her baby face was one of jealousy, plain and simple.

When Lara saw it she would scold the little one. "Mama has other children, too, Marzina," she would say. Having gained her mother's attention Marzina would break into a smile and then laugh.

As for the Dominus, Magnus Hauk loved all his daughters devotedly, Anoush among them, which pleased Lara.

The time was drawing near for Dillon's departure. Lara had thought to take her son to Shunnar herself, but Prince Kaliq himself arrived on the appointed day to escort his new pupil.

"I thought it better that Dillon bid you all farewell here," he told them.

"Will Cirillo be there when we arrive, my lord?" Dillon asked excitedly.

"Your uncle will not come for several months," Kaliq explained. "He has magic, and has lived with it his whole life, Dillon. You will need to get use to living with magic. When you have then Prince Cirillo will join us. But you will have Og as a friend and Amir is waiting for you. And we will have many adventures as I teach you all about the world of magic, my son."

"Will you teach me about magic one day?" Anoush asked the prince.

"Perhaps," Kaliq answered her with a smile. "Now before we go I must tell you of Hetar and what has happened in the last months."

"Yes," Lara said. "I would know. They are not planning any more invasions, are they? I shall be most put out with them if they are."

The prince laughed. "Nay, my love, they have far too much to do right now in Hetar to consider entering another land without an invitation. As you know Vilia delivered a son for Jonah. Egon is the light of his mother's life right now. The elections for a more representative High Council have been put off until next spring. The magnates believe that they can stop the women if they hold them off long enough but of course all they are doing is making Gillian and her party stronger. They have, however, bribed Lady Farah lavishly and she is attempting to work her influence upon the women of the Pleasure Guilds. Sadly, she has not the respect of her constituents. The magnates have yet to learn that. They believe because their influence got her elected to her position that she will be able to wield her power as did Lady Gillian. Of course, she cannot. The Pleasure Mistresses and the Pleasure Women will give her lip service and then do as they please. Lady Gillian is not about to back down. They will get a number of their women elected to this new council but it will not be called High. It will be called the Hetarian Council. The High Council will remain as it has always been with two representatives from each of the provinces. With the Outlands added to Hetar that will mean a total of ten. And the Hetarian Council will also have ten members."

"What happens if their votes cancel each other out?" the Dominus wanted to know. "How will they break a tie?"

"The head of the High Council will toss a coin and they will leave it to chance," the prince told them. "Since the High Council head rotates with each term it simply becomes a matter of bringing hard matters up for a vote when you know you can get them passed. With women on both of the councils, common sense should prevail." He looked to Magnus Hauk. "And what of Terah and your own High Council?" he asked quietly. "You cannot allow Hetar to get ahead of you."

"We will be moving ahead in the Icy Season, when the children are well settled into their schooling with Master Bashkar. Lara and I will visit the villages along each of the fjords to explain to them our concept for a governing body. By the time Taj is grown it will have long been in place and will not seem as strange to him as it does to me. We will ask for four representatives from each fjord for a total of twenty-eight members. As Dominus I will vote to break any ties should they arise."

The prince nodded. "Then I will leave you. Bid your mother farewell, Dillon."

The boy flew into his mother's arms and she wrapped him tightly in her embrace. "Remember who you are," she said. "You are Dillon, son of Vartan, lord of the Fiacre, and Lara, Domina of Terah. Your blood is noble and brave and faerie. Listen to the prince and his brothers. You will learn so very much from them. More than I, my son. But most of all, remember that I love you. That your stepfather and your family love you. Love is so important, Dillon. Without it we wither, both mortal and faerie. Without it the darkness creeps into our souls. But that will not happen to you for you are so dearly loved, my son, and you are filled with the light." She kissed him on both his rosy cheeks and quickly on his lips. Then she said, "Before you go I have a gift for you, my son." And she brought her walking staff forward. "Verica is now your companion as he was once mine. He wishes to accompany you, for my life has become too dull for him."

"Indeed it has," Verica's ancient voice agreed. "I spend more time in a corner now than on fine long walks, and 'tis no way for a creature like me to live. At least with you, young Dillon, I shall be able to go adventuring once again and escape all this domesticity."

They all laughed at Verica's comments, then Lara said, "Make us proud, Dillon."

Dillon looked up at Lara, his father's blue eyes shining with happiness. He took Verica from her. "I will make you all proud, Mother," he promised her. Then gently extracting himself from her arms he went to his stepfather. "Will you give me your blessing, Magnus Hauk?" he asked and he knelt before the Dominus.

Magnus placed both of his hands upon his stepson's dark head. "You have my blessing, *my son,*" he told Dillon. "Go with it and return to us when you can. We will all miss you, but like your mother you have a destiny to follow." He raised the boy up and kissed him on both cheeks.

Dillon then stopped before Anoush. "Be patient with our parents," he told her softly and Anoush smiled.

"Indeed, young mistress," Verica put in. "Do not try them too greatly. Your mother is a very wise faerie. Listen to her, I pray you."

"I think I have gotten better," Anoush said. "But then you have always been here to remind me of my faults, Big Brother. And Verica, as well." She patted the staff's head.

"But now you are the big sister and you must set the example for Zagiri and the little ones. I will think of you often, Anoush," he told her. And then Vartan's children embraced tenderly, tears in their eyes, for they had never before been separated.

Dillon knelt before little Zagiri.

"I do not want you to go," Zagiri said, pouting.

"But I want to go," Dillon told her.

"Don't you like us?" Zagiri asked.

"I love you with all my heart," the boy said. "But I have inherited magic and magic must be taught and nurtured by magic, Zagiri. It is a great honor to be taught by the Shadow Princes. When you are older, you will understand that."

"Will you come back to us, Dillon?" Zagiri wanted to know.

"I will come back," he said.

"When?" she demanded.

"One day," he told her and kissing her gently he stood up. He stopped before the nursemaids to hold his youngest siblings. He kissed them each, smiling at Taj. "Be strong, my brother," he said. Then he kissed Marzina, chucking her beneath her fat chin. "Be good, my little sister," he said and she favored him with a smile. Dillon turned now and walked over to the prince. He bowed formally. "I am ready now, my lord." His fist clutched Verica tightly.

Kaliq swung his great shining white cape about the boy by his side and in an instant they were gone.

Zagiri began to cry, but Anoush picked her sister up and said, "It is his destiny, Little Sister, and destiny plays a strong part in this family."

"Do you have a destiny?" Zagiri asked her older sister and Anoush nodded. "And do I have one?" Zagiri pursued. Anoush nodded again. "And Taj and Marzina?"

"Aye," Anoush said. "All of us possess a destiny. Some for good, some for great, but we all have one."

"Papa?" Zagiri persisted.

"Aye, Papa's destiny is to be Terah's greatest Dominus." She brushed the tears from Zagiri's little face.

"And Mama?" Zagiri queried.

"Ah, Mama," Anoush replied and suddenly her blue eyes grew so bright they seemed to be silver. "Mama's destiny is the greatest of all, Zagiri, for she will one day unite us as one." Anoush's eyes returned to their own beautiful blue, then they closed and she grew pale, slipping toward the floor.

Lara quickly snatched Zagiri from her older sibling's arms before she could be hurt even as Magnus Hauk caught his step-daughter before she crumpled to the floor. With a nod to the nursemaids holding the twins he sent them from the room.

"Is Anoush all right?" Zagiri asked, her little face frightened.

"Your sister is fine," Lara assured her little daughter. "She possesses what we call *the sight,* which means she can sometimes see into the future."

Anoush moaned. Seeing that she was returning to herself the Dominus set the girl upon her feet. "What happened?" she asked them, looking a bit confused.

"You had a small vision, my darling, that is all," Lara said. "How do you feel now, Anoush?" Dillon had told her that Anoush had this gift, but Lara had paid it very little mind until this moment. "Have you done this before, my daughter?"

"Not often, but now and again I see things," Anoush admitted. "I've never fainted from it, however."

"I think the excitement of Dillon's departure, followed by your vision, probably made you weak," Lara soothed her. "Take Zagiri, go and lie down. I will come to you shortly."

Anoush nodded and taking her little sister by her hand she led her from her parent's dayroom where they had been bidding Dillon farewell.

There was a long silence. Lara sat down. Her legs suddenly felt weak.

"What did Anoush mean, you would unite us all?" Magnus Hauk asked his wife quietly. His eyes searched her face.

"I don't know," Lara told him honestly. "Kaliq has said that my destiny is not yet fulfilled, but he will not tell me what remains to be done or even if he knows. Nor will my mother. All I can tell you is that for now I will be by your side with our children even as I was in my time with Vartan. I feel no pull to go anywhere else or do anything else. What remains of my destiny will reveal itself to me when it is time and not a moment before, Magnus. Let us be content with what we have."

She will unite us all. The Dominus could hear his stepdaughter's voice in his head. What could it mean? But then he sighed, realizing that Lara was right. Whatever remained for Lara to accomplish would reveal itself in its own time, and rarely did magic time conform with mortal time. He sat down next to his wife, putting an arm about her. From the moment that Lara had entered his life it had been one adventure after another. He wondered what would have happened had he married one of those sweet Terahn girls his mother had always attempted to foist on him. But he knew—his life would have been one long, dull monotony.

He would never be bored with his faerie woman. His life would continue to be filled with adventure. And why not? He was married to Lara, daughter of Swiftsword and Ilona, queen of the Forest Faeries. He had a mother-in-law who arrived and departed in a cloud of mauve mist. A prince who stepped in and out of their lives from the shadows. A stepson who would be a great sorcerer. A stepdaughter who had visions. The Great Creator only knew what Zagiri, Taj and Marzina would turn out to be one day. He could not even begin to imagine. The reality would probably be something that no one, especially a mere mortal as himself, could conceive.

Magnus Hauk began to laugh and he shook with his amusement.

"What is so funny?" Lara asked, turning to her husband who was doubled up with his mirth. What could have caused his hilarity? she wondered.

"I love our life together," the Dominus of Terah told her. "I love you! I love the children! I love everything! I can't wait for tomorrow to see what is around that corner."

"Hopefully not a dragon," Lara said with a smile.

"Why not?" Magnus Hauk wanted to know. "*Why not a dragon?* We have had faeries, and dwarfs and giants, and the powers of darkness running through our lives from the moment we met, my darling. What could be next but a dragon?"

"What indeed?" Lara answered and then she joined in his laughter. For now, she realized, she was happy. And she deserved this happiness, didn't she? She was going to enjoy what she had. And she had so much. *And,* Lara decided, she would not think about her destiny until it called out to her again. Whatever destiny held in store for her next, she could wait for it.

Two unforgettable classics from
New York Times bestselling author

DIANA PALMER

Get swept away once again by these vintage tales
celebrating two Diana Palmer heroes we dare
you to forget...

Rediscover HUNTER and MAN IN CONTROL
in HARD TO HANDLE.

"The ever-popular and prolific Palmer has penned
another sure hit."
—*Booklist* on *Before Sunrise*

*Available wherever
trade paperbacks are sold.*

HQN™

We *are* romance™

HQNDP77261TR

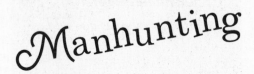

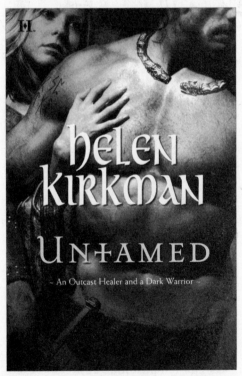

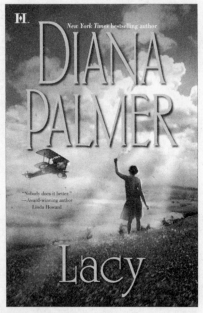

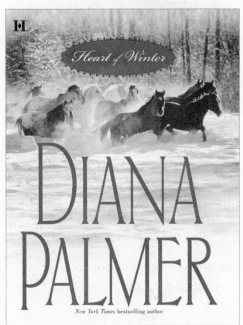